Dovetails in Tall Grass

Dovetails in Tall Grass

A Novel

SAMANTHA SPECKS

Published by SparkPress, a BookSparks imprint, a division of SparkPoint Studio, LLC
Phoenix, Arizona, USA, 85007
www.gosparkpress.com

Published 2021
Printed in the United States of America
Print ISBN: 978-1-68463-093-6
E-ISBN: 978-1-68463-094-3
Library of Congress Control Number: 2021904336

Formatting by Kiran Spees

To those who planted the seeds and inspired them to grow.

Dale and Dolores Lundgren & Gary and Suzanne Zimmerman
and
The Dakota 38 + 2 Memorial Riders

A Note to the Reader:

Dovetails in Tall Grass is a fictional story; it is an act of imagination and story-telling. This book is based on the U.S.–Dakota War of 1862, and some dialogue follows very closely to transcripts of historical record. However, this storyline departs in many (some minor and some significant) ways from the facts. Actual events are depicted in several scenes, but in a fictitious manner meant to develop the emotional journey of the protagonists.

A Note on Language:

This novel refers to the tribal peoples in this book as Dakota; while commonly called the Dakota, this fraction of the Great Sioux Nation is sometimes referred to as the Sioux or Dakota-Sioux. The name Sioux originated from the Ojibwe people and means "little snakes," an Ojibwe name for their enemy. In this story, most Dakota names and words are anglicized. As the author, I worked to reflect the history of this time as depicted by Dakota historians.

This war is also referred to as the Sioux Uprising, Sioux Outbreak, Dakota Conflict, or Little Crow's War but I chose to use "U.S.–Dakota War" for the reason that it identifies both parties involved. While writing, I hesitated to include some of the racial and ethnic terms used during the 1860s or include the violence that occurred during wartime. However, I selectively incorporated pieces of both for a more accurate representation of the world and events at that time.

A Note from the Author:

While I have familial connections to residents of New Ulm and the surrounding countryside, I do not speak for my family or the residents of this area. Furthermore, I am non-Native. I do not and cannot speak for anyone in the Dakota Nation. The very concept of this story is non-Native—as I can't erase my inherent white lens and the influence of the colonialist culture in which I live and participate.

I am grateful to the Native and non-Native Minnesota and Dakota-Sioux history keepers and storytellers who have come before me. I wrote this book because I was seeking a greater understanding of a complex and difficult past. While I still have much to learn, my creative interpretation here is meant to acknowledge the wrongs— moral, social, political, legal—that occurred before, during, and after the U.S.–Dakota War. I encourage readers to reflect and further educate themselves on this part of history and how it influences our world today. I hope an increased understanding of the past will promote both personal reflection and an interpersonal dialogue that builds a future based on justice and respect for all people who share or identify with this history.

A writing scholarship for a Native American woman writer has been created with the hope that more stories dovetail from here. Visit samanthaspecks.com for more information.

PROLOGUE

On December 26, 1862, at 10:00 in the morning, thirty-eight Dakota men were hung by the U.S. Army in Mankato, Minnesota. To this day, this is the largest mass execution in United States history.

Emma Heard

December 26, 1862 12:00 p.m.

The wagon rocked along the frozen trail as the horses pulled our family towards home. I felt myself swaying back and forth, as the hanged men had just hours ago. My stomach convulsed with the memory. Bent with shame. Repulsion. Not at the dead men . . . they had their dignity. My repulsion was from *our* acts. At what I had done. All the words my own hand had written, documenting the events forever. I had sealed 38 fates. Ida sat across from me, beautifully bundled in her finest winter coat, silent. I couldn't read my sister's face like I usually could so easily . . . what was she feeling today? After what was done to her, Ida more than anyone in our family, could claim today's horror as some kind of justice. *Justice*. Would I ever understand that word? My own pen was the one to record the war trials. What they did to us . . . what we did to them. I'd tried to do the right thing . . . yet, it seemed that I was feeling more disgrace than anyone. My family surrounded me, but I was lonely as the empty sky on this winter prairie. I shifted in my seat and the length of my scarf caught between the slats of the wagon bench, pulling up into my mouth, gagging me. I loosened its choke and wondered if this was perhaps God's way of telling me—I should have just kept my mouth shut.

Oenikika

December 26, 1862 12:00 p.m.

My mare's steps were exhausted as my spirit. I hopped from her back, in search of firewood to keep my lonely tipi warm enough to survive another night. But this part of the windswept prairie was wide open to the sky . . . not a single tree as far as my eyes could see. I walked out in the swirling snow; my moccasin bumped against a hard-frozen pile. Buffalo dung. I stared at it, my breath fogging in clouds of desperation. It would have to suffice as fuel for my fire. I fell to my knees and tried to pry the rigid buffalo chip from the tundra. It wouldn't budge. I pulled my husband's axe from my belt and battled to keep his memory from flooding my mind. I started chopping at the edges of the pile, but the more I swung, the more my body loosened the feelings I fought so hard to keep in. I hit the earth with my fury and pain, the loss I could hardly bear. I'd had many moons of mourning. I couldn't cry again and let the tears freeze to my eyelashes. Frostbite would be quick to my cheekbones.

Finally, I pried up the chip . . . I would need to find more to keep me warm through the night. Wearied, I looked out upon the open plains. Forlorn snowdrifts pushed by the relentless wind surrounded me. An empty blur. Had the Great Spirit left me? Just a memory ago I'd been in the summer sun with my family. But the tides of war shifted the seasons, and winter swallowed me alone. My entire tribe was now gone or dead. Everyone I knew. Everyone I loved. Every person who had ever loved me—taken. Disappeared. I was once a wife. I was once a daughter. I should have known this would be my fate; my first breath killed the most precious person in my world. Why was I still left on this earth?

I wanted to take off my father's buffalo hide cloak, walk out into the cold, let the earth take me back. Had I taken a wrong path somewhere? I'd clung so tightly to my healing plants, tried so frantically to save the ones I loved. I was still alive, but all I could think of was everyone who was gone. A gust of freezing wind blasted my face, the stinging cold brought tears to my eyes as it howled in my ears. And for a split second, his memory was so real I could see him in the blur. Hear him calling out in the howl.

He told me, "Oenikika, hold on."

PART ONE

ONE

Oenikika

May 5, 1861

In the late days of spring season, when the earth began to breathe again, and the creek beds filled with snowmelt, we moved our village to this sheltering group of ancient pine trees. The Great Woods of the north ended here, and the vast openness of unceasing plains began, continuing farther than the sky could stretch, or a horse could ride. Like the earth, my spirit began to breathe again when we returned to the edge of the pines. It meant we had outlasted another winter and the promise of springtime had returned. And it meant returning to the place that reminded me of my mother.

I emerged from our tipi as the dark veil of evening fell above. The centerfire of camp circle leapt brilliantly towards the sky; people were gathering. I looked back, beyond my home, to the deepening of twilight across the prairie. Gentle wind swayed the tall grass; long green stalks bowed and lifted in the breeze. Energy buzzed in the spring sundown. My soul was listening as much as my ears. I was sensing it again—their pull. The plants of healing whispered through the rustling grasses. The fragrance of blooming life rode the breeze, telling me the plants were ready. Calling me. *Oenikika* . . . I smiled at the beckoning of the medicinal plants. I've lived 16 winters, old enough to know—I was meant to be a healer. The earth guided my purpose. *I hear you! I'm coming for you!* I thought as I looked into the beyond with hope. I turned and walked to join the evening gathering of my people.

My grandmother, Owl Woman, caught my eyes; she motioned with her curled knobby hands for me to come to sit. Tucking my legs under me, I leaned back against her shins. She pulled my hair behind my ears and started braiding as she had thousands of times before.

"There was no one as special as your mother. She'll always be with you."

My wise grandmother could always tell when I was thinking of the mother I never knew. Though she died when I was born, I knew she was with me. My mother became Mother Earth. Her body was placed in the grass, and her bones sunk into the soil, and the rain washed her heart into the earth. Her soul now danced in the changing clouds above me. My whole being was connected to this place and to my mother, who created me and spoke to me still. I felt her in every spring season. In every raindrop. Every breeze. She was as strong as the towering pine and no season could shake her eternal presence.

We had been in our camp for many moons already. On arrival, tipis were rapidly assembled, drying racks laid out, and the centerfire started. There was ample grass for the horses, deer were plentiful, and the men had caught many fish in the large lake nearby. With such bounty, there was much work of butchering, tanning, and cooking for us women. In years past, after the busy days, Aunt Mika and I always found time to search for medicines in this sweep of prairie. This was the place she first taught me the ways of healing she'd learned from my mother—which roots, herbs, and trees are filled with an extraordinary healing spirit. When I was very small, we'd share the same horse. I'd sit in front, and she'd let me hold the reins, pointing out the particular plants. Five summers ago, we discovered an exceptional licorice bay, the medicine that heals stomach aches, sore throats, and coughs; every year we return to that bay.

Tonight, cousin Brown Wing minded the fire; his were always splendid, the burning logs roaring with passion in their final glorious moments. Brown Wing and I were the same age; his taking over evening fires was a sign that our generation's leadership in the tribe was beginning. While I sat watching flames ripple the darkness, my grandmother and aunt shared a seat behind me, chatting agreeably with Dina and Scarlet Woman. Men congregated on the opposite side of the fire. Cousin Brown Wing's friends, *immature* friends, Red Otter and Breaking Up, suddenly tossed a pebble towards me, seeking my attention. The rock skittered past; I brushed the bits of dirt off my legs as I looked over to the two young men.

"Oenikika, ask Red Otter who caught the most fish today," Breaking Up said with a grin.

I gave an exasperated half-smile and shook my head, unwilling to participate in Breaking Up's attempt to boast.

Not to be made to look weak, Red Otter pulled up his bow and drew back an arrow. With a slight squint of his eye, he traced an invisible trail in the night sky. In a silent and swift second, Red Otter's fingers released the bow. From the darkness above, a tiny bat with an arrow through its middle fell to the ground between us. Breaking Up jumped atop Red Otter, and they began wrestling like boys that were four-winters-old, not men about to be eighteen. Their attention was becoming an increasing part of life—we would soon be partnering. Young men would make offers to fathers for a daughter to be taken as a wife. *Please, not one of these fools,* I thought.

I ignored their antics and returned to watching the blaze. I thought back to the baskets of licorice I gathered last year. That plant was shared with many families; I even passed some out to other camps when we visited after the Sun Ceremony. Chief Red Iron told my father he was grateful for our generosity; Father said I brought him honor at that moment—and honoring a father was the highest praise for a daughter. But with the bounty of fish and deer this year, Mika has been too busy to gather medicine. When I was young and had not learned all our ways, I would have waited for Mika to take me. But I was older now; my hair was long, midway down my back, and I knew the ways of my people. What if I was soon bound to a husband who didn't value my calling? A restless determination settled inside of me; I had to return to the licorice bay. I'd never been permitted to go alone, but this year—I could hear my calling, my purpose, that it was finally time for the spirit to guide my own medicine ride.

My determined thoughts were interrupted when little Wolfchaser and Bonko ran past, yelling, "The chief is back!" Bonko, exhausted from his brief sprint, announced to the group, "I saw him first."

The chief was back. My father was back.

While others murmured in excitement, a mix of feelings stirred inside of me. Hearing of Father's return immediately sent a wave of relief for his safety, but a flood of nervous eagerness also filled me. A father who is chief has made it hard for me to occupy much of his attention. And even harder to win his approval. I'd silently struggled—feeling simultaneously special as the only daughter of the greatest chief of the Eastern Dakota but unnoticed by the one I wanted to see me most . . . him.

While chubby Bonko was still catching his breath from his proud announcement, families who had been in their tipis now circled in anticipation around the fire. The arrival was certainly news as we had been missing our chief for almost three full moon cycles. This was my father's second trip to meet the Great White Father in Washington, which was quite a distance. After the first trip, Father told stories of riding on a white man machine that spilled clouds of smoke into the sky as it traveled faster than even the wildest stallion at full gallop.

I'd been afraid knowing my father was immersed in the white man's world, their unfamiliar ways and speeding things.

Without a word, he emerged from the darkness beyond the fire. He sat tall atop his dark horse Mato. The gathering quieted in awe as his angular face shone in the firelight. Warm tears filled my eyes, and I felt heart-quenching gladness at the sight of him. My father was home.

The celebration of our chief's safe return lasted until the moon was high overhead and children were asleep across their parents' laps. Father spent the night standing in close conversation with the other men. Eventually, he told Brown Wing to let the fire die. Owl Woman and I returned to our family's tipi at the edge of the tall grass. We'd adjusted to it being just her and me; my father's bed across from us on the floor had been empty for so many nights. I tucked myself in under the heavy buffalo hide blankets and laid my head on the soft pillow. My thoughts returned to the licorice bay. Now that my father was back, he alone could grant me permission to venture there by myself. I wished I'd just ridden off today before his return. What if he wouldn't let me go? I rolled over impatiently and sighed.

The flap to the tipi opened, and father stepped inside. Although his presence was grand, he was not chief when he was in our tipi. He was my grandmother's son and my father. He let out a long exhalation as he sat down in his familiar bed for the first time in many moons. In the Dakota ways of kinship, women do not speak first in the tipi, so I waited for Father to engage us.

"This is how a bird must feel when returning to its nest," he said warmly.

"Few birds have journeyed as far as you have, Taoyateduta," Owl Woman replied, calling him by the name she gave him at birth.

"We're thankful to the Great Spirit for returning you to us," I said.

His eyes surveyed the tipi walls, painted with stars and shapes, each carrying the meaning of a different event in our lives. He looked as if he were contemplating something. I've always been keenly aware of my father's moods, his reactions, his posture. Perhaps having my father as chief made him larger than life to me. Maybe every daughter was especially attuned to these things. Or possibly, it was his connection I craved especially since I didn't have a mother. Owl Woman, Aunt Mika, Uncle Chaska, and my whole tribe surround me in safety, but I've always felt the most protected in the shadow of my father.

"You have grown, Oenikika," he said as if the change was equally undeniable and displeasing to him. "When I left, you were running around in the woods with the other children. I return, and you're sitting amongst the women at the fire. How has life changed us so quickly?" He glanced at Owl Woman. I *had* grown since he left; I felt quietly glad that he noticed.

Owl Woman lifted her eyebrows. "How do you think I feel looking at my son who has survived forty-two winters? Oenikika hasn't played in the woods for some time. But fathers are the last to accept when their daughters are turning into women. You're no different." She laughed her hearty laugh. "Oenikika is very beautiful. Red Otter and Breaking Up watch her as if their eyes are stuck. I think you should expect many offers for her soon. We knew this day would come."

I looked up, anxious to see my father's reaction. I desired a husband who was steady and strong, of a smart, independent mind but dedicated to his people. Someone who saw me for who I was. I felt a careful unwillingness to give any attention to foolish Red Otter or Breaking Up. Still . . . I did feel the quiver of excitement knowing I was on the cusp of offers and even a marriage ceremony someday.

"Bah. Enough." He reacted to his mother as sons do no matter how old they are. "Many offers . . ." he said as if he were already evaluating what could be negotiated.

I hoped if Father recognized how I'd grown, he'd grant me permission to venture to the licorice bay on my own. We'd been at this camp for many moons—now that he was back, I presumed we would be leaving soon, and I'd need to ride tomorrow for the licorice.

I took a breath of bravery as I questioned my father. "How long will our camp be here?"

"Why do you ask me such a thing?" he asked with surprising defensiveness. The mood in the tipi quickly darkened as I had clearly upset him with my simple question. My heartbeat thumped with anxiety in my chest. "Has my daughter ever asked me such a question before?" he continued with an unusual suspicion. "Explain. Why do you ask me this?" I averted my eyes and shook my head, ashamed to have offended him. Confusion swam through my body. Why had the visit with the white men caused my father to be on edge?

I took a deep breath. "This is where Mika and I gather licorice for the year. It's the only place we've ever found it. I know the trail; it is less than a half moon's ride from this camp. Mika is busy tanning hides . . . but I *know* I can find it by myself."

"By yourself? I just returned. My daughter will stay near our camp. You will help with the hides. It is decided," he said definitively. I was dismissed. Frustration and insecurity simmered together inside of me. How could he see that I have undeniably grown but then reject my hopes like they were a foolish child's? I turned over in my bed with my back to Father, hiding the feelings bubbling up inside of me. For the second time tonight, tears came to my eyes. But these were not the warm tears of relief I felt earlier. These were hot tears of resentment. Father's intense reaction to my question about moving camp seemed out of character. He was usually steady, wise, unshakable. His daughter asking a simple question upsetting him? I couldn't understand it. I couldn't understand him. As was expected of any daughter, especially the chief's daughter, I'd obey his wishes. But bitter tears fell down my face. I was overcome with longing for the precious licorice. It would be devastating to have no licorice root remedy. I would bring no honor if there were no plants to share. The tears soaked my pillow. Maybe I was just a child after all.

The next morning, Father motioned me out of the tipi and without explanation said. "You may go. Be back before the ceremony fire tonight. I have important news to announce." Just as unanticipated as his reaction had been, so too was his reversal. I didn't take a second to think about announcements; I snatched three baskets, and as quickly as my moccasins would carry me, I ran down to the pasture of horses and climbed onto Ahone's back.

My breath caught with excitement as I used pressure from my calf to cue Ahone, my paint mare, forward underneath me. Her canter pulled us onward over the grassland. I was buzzing with energy; as if my mighty wings were open for the first time. Lifting me high. No watchful eyes overseeing me . . . No following the lead of my aunt or my father. I was free with the Great Spirit guiding. After a quarter day's ride, I scanned the horizon optimistically, looking for the group of three maples. I swelled with satisfaction and certainty as I saw the familiar cluster of trees. With slight pressure on the reins, Ahone's head turned, and we moved downhill towards the shallow creek. The river was stony here but upstream the bed widened with sandy banks. I remembered summers past, Mika's short arms pointing ahead to this sheltered sandy pocket, teaching me where the plant hides.

But as I rounded the final bend in the creek, my eyes spotted something new. I pulled Ahone to an abrupt halt as I took in the sight. On top of the riverbank sat a white man's house—it was square and tall. Panic flooded my instincts; my hands tightened on the reins. Whites had never been this far west. I'd never encountered a white man by myself. What should I do? What would Aunt Mika do if she were here? I stared at the house. Seeing the white man's permanent building made me feel unsettled; it was so starkly different from the sleek, decorated tipi I called home. Father warned me; there was much to worry about with new people festering on the prairie. They lie and swindle. They kill more buffalo than they can use. Rotting buffalo carcasses told me all I needed to know.

I listened and observed my surroundings carefully. There did not appear to be any activity around the structure. The creek looked unchanged. The licorice plants—just as I remembered. Winds passed along the top of the water, and hundreds of stalks of licorice danced along the shoreline. The leaves rustled against one another . . . calling to me. I glanced up at the house once more but plunged ahead, sending Ahone splashing forward in the creek.

I dismounted and stood in ankle-deep water. I brushed my hands over the top of the licorice and smiled. They were stunning, perfectly made, from their deep green stems to the bunches of white at the top. Running my hand down the long stalk, I reached under the cold water for the submerged bottom of the plant. Gently wiggling it loose, I pulled it up and examined the thick fibrous roots—feeling pleased.

I gave Ahone's neck a pat and untied the baskets. I got to work, tenderly removing each stalk and lying them at the shoreline to dry. My feet and hands were chilled from the creek water, but my arms and top of my head were heated by the midday sun. The work was satisfying; the plants plentiful. But my mind wandered back to my father; I hated upsetting him as I had last night. We changed camp location so frequently; I couldn't understand why asking about moving had offended him. Perhaps he was preoccupied with the news he would be announcing tonight. As chief, everyone in the village respected his influence. He shared his thoughts slowly and deliberately. His voice was captivating. I prayed the chief would feel proud of his daughter when he saw the overflowing baskets of medicine I'd bring to the village tonight. That he'd see how important these plants were to my purpose on this earth.

Suddenly, a movement streaked across the top of the riverbank.

Ahone sensed it too, perking her ears in the same direction. I stood tall and still, watching with a hawk's intent eyes, but the hillside was still. I waited, and finally from behind the maple bobbed the brown hair and big eyes of a white woman. My eyes caught hers. I was standing, completely exposed in the creek.

There was no use in running or defending myself, especially from what appeared to be an inquisitive settler woman hiding unwisely behind a lone tree. Ahone snorted, unimpressed, and folded her long neck down to return to eating grass.

"Hello," I called out. *Hello* was one of the few white men words I knew.

I waited. The first moments of interaction between our people and theirs involved a few hesitating seconds, as both parties determined the intentions of the other. I'd seen this before, between my father and the white Indian Missionary at our camp and once when a wagon with a white man rolled by our village and Uncle Chaska traded a deer hide for a skillet. If it were up to me, we'd always avoid the palefaced. But our worlds continued to overlap. It seemed inevitable as they spread farther into the land of our ancestors; as unavoidable as the woman standing in front of me now.

"Hello," I called again in her language.

She poked her head out from beyond the tree. She pointed down at me and shook her apron at me. I quickly realized the woman did not know what these plants were or understand that she was living above one of the most precious wild licorice beds on the whole prairie. She was shooing me away.

I picked up a plant from the ground and said in my language: "Pejouta." Showing her the wonders of the earth she lived near. She shook her head. I held the white flowery top of the plant and held it against my throat—a cure for sore throat.

"Pejouta," I repeated. My mind searched for the white man word. Father mandated I learn some of the white language from Riggs, the

Indian Missionary who frequented our camp. I hadn't believed it would be useful, but I was now grateful for my learning.

Unexpectedly the word reemerged in my mind: "Medicine," I called out, hopeful.

At that moment a white man came running from the side of the house. The barrel of a gun in his hands glinted in the late afternoon sun. My heart panicked, and immediately I scrambled, grabbing my baskets and leaping to Ahone. Water splashed down from the baskets and up from the river as Ahone broke into a slippery gallop away from the riverbank.

Ahone ran strong below me, and before long, the white house was long out of sight and the vast plains looked as they had for hundreds of generations before me. The sun had begun its final crawl towards tomorrow and hidden crickets chirped to welcome the cool of evening, I remembered Father wanted me back to camp for an announcement. I leaned forward as Ahone moved faster across the grassland. Frustration squeezed my insides; why had the white people settled near the licorice if they didn't even understand its power? I'd warn Father as soon as I got back to camp . . . but, I glanced down at my medicine baskets as the green grasses blurred below, if he knew the white men were spreading would he ever let me go on a ride by myself again?

Looking up, the oranges of sunset burst on the horizon. Had that white woman understood me? Had she heard me call out *"Medicine!"*? Or had the glinting barrel of a gun separated our worlds in one quick flash?

TWO

Emma Heard

August 18, 1861

A piece of paper had never felt so heavy. But this letter with my secret hope for my future carried much weight. I held the letter close—writing out the words, I could literally see my own potential on the page. It was scary, thrilling, to allow myself to take a chance. Though the sweeping prairie around me was quiet and still in the bright bluebird morning, I could hear something . . . a voice inside urging me on. As if a future, wiser, braver me was whispering courage to my ear. My boots quickened as I trotted hopefully down the long final hill into town.

I've walked this well-worn trail through the tall grass countless times before, but it looked different to me today. Every time I walked this path previously had been at the instruction of someone else. They sent me for simple chores: "Emma, walk into town and trade Mr. Richter pork for his maple syrup," or "Emma, go buy two blue buttons for your father's church coat." The worst was the dreaded instruction: "Go help Mrs. Ulrich with her laundry." Buckets of hot water and lye, the grated washboards, my hands raw and burning, and Mrs. Ulrich's chronically displeased oversight made laundry day the worst. But today I walked with a secret purpose. My heart beat with resolution, and my spine shivered at the risk I was taking. I was on the trail in front of me for myself.

A strong gust of summer wind tousled my golden hair around my face. I tucked it behind my ears and took in the familiar view of New Ulm just a half-mile away. Our little town had grown since we settled here; the crisscrossed grid of streets was now six bustling blocks long. A wave of nerves flipped in my stomach as I tucked the letter up the edge of my dress's sleeve—hiding it before I got into town. Though my mother had made it abundantly clear that the farm comes before anything else, I'd written this secret letter to my former teacher to inquire about becoming a teacher myself. Somehow, I'd managed to conceal this envelope from Ma, Ida, Otto, and Uncle Allen when I left the farm this morning. Although, it doesn't take much to sneak by Uncle Allen. If anyone knew they'd call me foolish, or worse, forbid me from mailing the letter at all. My family wouldn't understand my hope to do anything other than being a good daughter now—or a good wife someday. The address on the outside of the envelope was handwritten in my penmanship that Miss Knudsen herself called "lovely and well-practiced" just a few months ago in class. I missed my former teacher; she'd inspired me and taught me so much in the year she ran our schoolhouse.

I was seven when our country school opened. Mr. Albrecht, an unenthusiastic man, was our first teacher. Despite his dispassionate lessons in the dusty schoolhouse, I loved learning. I raced through my exercises to hear his monotone, "Correct." Although my older brother Otto complained that the school day dragged, I never tired of sitting at that iron desk. After five years, Mr. Albrecht announced his departure for Chicago, but the school board was unable to find a replacement; our deserted schoolhouse sat empty for the next year. I longed for my little chalkboard, my well-worn niblets of chalk. In the classroom, my mind had felt like it was powerful. Reading books was the ultimate adventure; imagination was my first taste of freedom. That long following year without school, the chores at home felt all the drearier and more burdensome.

Last October, a new teacher was announced. A *woman*. The sky was covered with gloomy clouds but reentering the small schoolhouse on the first day of class was like returning to the most delightful dream. The fireplace had been lit hours beforehand, so by the time we walked in the room was warm and glowing. The desks sat neatly in line; at each desktop was a brand-new slate and piece of chalk. And in the front of the room, stood a young Swedish woman with rosy cheeks and a welcoming smile. That year in the schoolhouse passed in a pleasant blur. I loved every moment. Miss Knudsen, a diametric of Mr. Albrecht, repeated her encouraging motto, "We continue to learn in all we do." Because I finished my schoolwork so quickly, Miss Knudson allowed me to help the primary students in their lessons. I felt like I was blooming in the warmth of that classroom and wanted to stay there forever.

At the end of the school year, we received the devastating news that Miss Knudsen would not be returning in the fall.

The last day of class was such an unusually warm and optimistic May morning, it was decided we would spend the day outdoors. My older brother Otto played a game of tag with the boys; my sister Ida and the other girls sat in the sunshine. But I stayed inside at my desk, anxiously reading more pages of Miss Knudson's favorite Walt Whitman book she lent me to read during breaks. A heavy sadness settled in my stomach as I knew my moments in the classroom were preciously few. Each turn of a treasured page was a fleeting comfort.

The door creaked as Miss Knudsen hollered inside, "Emma, why don't you join in the fun in the schoolyard?"

My throat tightened as I turned to her and explained. "I'd rather read as much of *Leaves of Grass* as I can before you leave."

"Ah, of course, you would," she said with a kindness in her eyes. She walked inside and instructed, "Please, hand me that text." She took the book to her desk and opened the cover, writing something on the inside. Walking back, she set it on my desk, patting the cover as she said, "This is my goodbye gift to you, Emma. I've read this Whitman countless times, and I hope you do, as well."

"I cannot accept such a lovely gift," I stammered, overwhelmed at the generosity that I had done nothing to earn. But I stared at the beautiful hardcover—I'd never owned a book before, and the thought of such a possession just my own—not Ida's, nor little Catherine's, nor Otto's, nor Ma's, nor Pa's, but my very own—was overwhelmingly wonderful.

Miss Knudsen nodded. "I'd like for you to have it."

I whispered an inadequate, "Thank you." Bringing the book home would be like taking a delightful piece of the classroom with me into the long hours of summer work ahead. I felt a small sliver of relief to think of coming in from the field and reading this in the final twilight hours of a July night.

"I have written the mailing address of my next placement—Iowa City—inside," Miss Knudsen explained, "Please, write to me. Let me know how things continue here in New Ulm. And certainly, let me know if you become a teacher someday."

Teachers came from the eastern states and were bright and independent. I was a sixteen-year-old girl on the prairie. Ma said I still couldn't even fold a quilt properly. Surely, I wasn't capable of being a teacher. "If I become a teacher?" I asked.

"You worked through every primary and secondary lesson I created, helped with younger students, and you read the same books as your teacher . . ." She smiled and motioned to the book on the desk. "If I were returning, we would work together on your teacher application next year."

Just then, hollers came from the schoolyard and interrupted our discussion. Miss Knudsen hurried to the door to investigate the commotion in the yard. On her way out the door, she pointed back at me and said, "Emma, like I said, let me know."

Though the school doors closed for good that afternoon, the seeds of what Miss Knudsen had planted continued to grow in my mind. I always presumed I would stay near my family not only because my mother depended on me but also because I felt responsible for my older sister, Ida, who couldn't speak. We moved from Germany to the United States when she was three years old; she stopped talking during the journey and hadn't spoken since. Upon our arrival a country doctor examined her, prodding an impolite forefinger wildly about Ida's mouth, announcing with a shrug, "Ain't tongue-tied, must be mute." At the time, I was a babbling two-year-old, and for my family, Ida's infirmity was just another part of adjusting to the frontier. A slight flicker of her brow or twist of her lip told me precisely what Ida felt. I read her like the sky; a dark cloud doesn't say a word and I know it's about to rain. Though, she was a sky no one else lived under like I did. At church, in town, and while doing chores, I spoke for Ida as naturally as if she were an extension of me. As if I were an extension of her. But Ida would never be able to lead a classroom as a teacher . . . speaking was a necessary part of the instruction to students. Could I really separate from my sister? Leave her? Still, I felt an interest to explore what becoming a teacher might entail.

The memories of that schoolhouse replayed in my mind on my walk today. Earlier this week, the school board announced that due to the war going on between the North and South, there was a shortage of teachers; there'd be no school held this year. Being sixteen years old, this had likely been my last chance to attend classes; I was crushed with disappointment. Ma said we children had already learned plenty more than we'd ever need for the farm and with a bumper crop of corn expected this summer, there'd be more than enough work to go around at home. Nevertheless, Miss Knudsen's words were stuck in my mind. I needed to know how to become a teacher. Finding out was worth the risk of my mother's disapproval and my father's lectures.

The trail in front of me widened and joined with others, eventually forming the main dusty road into New Ulm. I headed towards my father's law office which was attached to the country courthouse. Nervousness nipped up my spine and exhilaration bit at my bootheels as I approached Father's office. *I'm Emma, the agreeable and helpful middle child.* But I'd already written the letter and addressed the envelope; the only thing left to do was get it to the mail stagecoach. The postage cost a penny, which I did not have. I planned to deceive my father and sneak my letter into his outgoing mail.

I turned the handle on the heavy door. The familiar musty smell of the law office greeted me. The room was chronically dim regardless of time of day thanks to the heavy velvet curtains hanging over the tall windows.

"Emma? Well hello . . . what're you journeying in here for? I actually didn't forget my lunch today." My father greeted me with a clever smile as he held up the biscuit tin I sometimes brought him. I worried for a split second that I had not thought of a reason for my visit—how hadn't I planned an excuse for the trip? But my distractible father was already looking back down at the papers on his desk.

"Just running an errand," I replied and quickly redirected. "Pa, your office is looking . . . busy," I said as I took in the sight of the room. Two oversized mahogany desks at opposite ends of the space were heaping with open books, scattered papers, steel point pens and inkwells. The table in the center of the room was similarly swamped. Bookshelves along the wall sat half bare as most of the enormous law texts were scattered and stacked about. The smaller table along the wall contained a tray of overflowing mail. The outgoing mail—full. Just as I suspected. My heart skipped a beat. I was eager to sneak my letter into the stack. With my back turned to my father, I walked quickly toward the table and curled my fingers under the edge of my sleeve, pulling out the hidden letter. In one swift motion I slid my letter in between the other envelopes in the middle of the brimming pile. I pushed my hand against the edge of the mail to align the stack.

"Tidying up, Emma girl?" my father asked.

"Oh, yes!" I startled, then replied more confidently than I felt, "Your mail was overflowing, and I just wanted to make sure nothing fell out." Lying to my father. I closed my eyes and my toes curled with my sharp wave of conscience. Nothing in my being had ever done anything so selfish before. My entire life I earned my father's love with my helpful nature; I helped Ma with the babies, helped Ida communicate, helped Otto with his school lessons, helped, helped, and helped some more. To do something for myself risked losing the one thing I knew he loved about me. My natural tendencies overwhelmed me, and I felt anxious to find a way to please my father and rid myself of this uncomfortable feeling.

"Ah I can't keep up with it. I can barely keep up with anything in this office anymore. Mail goes out tomorrow . . ." he explained. The mail stagecoach reliably came through town twice a week. But looking around the disorganized workplace, I feared Father would likely forget to bring the mail tomorrow too. Pa had been first drawn to New Ulm for the fact that the town was growing and would likely benefit from the occasional services of a country lawyer. He'd studied law books late at night in Germany; but there was no opportunity for him in crowded Munich. It took little convincing for his brother to join him, and two months later our heavy-set wagon rolled onto the 100 acres in Minnesota Territory for the first time. Initially, Pa was thrilled with the sporadic requests for him to draw a contract deeding land. But in the last year, as town had rapidly grown, father had gone from the occasional lawyer to an in-demand fixture of New Ulm. Pa's void on our farm has been filled mostly by my older brother

Otto who teased Pa that he could thrash a field and milk the cows in the time it took Pa to dip his pen in an inkwell.

"Maybe I could help you," I said. "Tomorrow, do you want me to bring the mail to Myrick's General Store for you?"

"Well, sure." My father looked up, surprised. "That would be helpful. Yes. Certainly. And you may return tomorrow and tidy."

"Certainly," I said. A smile of hope tugged at the edges of my mouth at the thought of my letter's safe delivery. That letter reaching Iowa City was my chance to earn my way back into a classroom. And if I could be the teacher, I would never have to worry about school going away ever again.

"Very well. You'll help your mother in the morning and father in the afternoon. A daughter who puts her family first. Very good, Emma." My father's approval was what I yearned for in every choice I made. But instead of pride at his compliment, I felt another wave of self-reproach swell in my throat. Putting my family first . . . when, in fact, sending that letter was the first time I took a chance to be someone *I* wanted to be. Putting myself first. But my family was all I truly knew in this world. Who was I, if I was not the pleasing and helpful Emma in the Heard family? If I was Miss Heard, a teacher? Shame wrestled the budding dream inside of me.

"I will be back tomorrow," I said, and as quickly as I'd arrived, I headed for the door and departed. I had new purpose in my steps but confusion in my heart. I hadn't realized what a selfish feeling hope could be.

THREE

Oenikika

May 5, 1861

In the Moon When the Ponies Shed, the darkness of evening didn't quickly swallow you as it did in the dead of winter. Instead, the late spring night came on like a slow yawn. This was my favorite time of year and my favorite time of day. Plants were springing back to life, and so was I. My moccasins moved quickly over pine needles on the soft soil. I felt so quietly proud walking up to camp circle with my heavy overflowing baskets; I couldn't wait for Aunt Mika to see my bounty. I almost hoped someone would complain of a sore throat . . . I'd immediately pull out a stalk of licorice and offer remedy.

Small fires inside each glowing tipi lit the way under the pines. I walked past my cousin Wenona's place and saw she was inside with her children, Wolfchaser and Kimimela.

"Auntie O!" Kimimela's little voice called out. I ducked myself inside, setting my heavy baskets down with a dramatic huff. Kimimela pulled herself away from Wenona and snuggled close. I was like a second mother to Kimimela and Wolfchaser. Wenona, older than me by four winters, was my sister as much my cousin.

"I was on a *special* mission," I said into Kimi's ear, though I was the one who felt like a little girl in my childish excitement for my own adventure.

"Your Auntie learned from your Grandmother," Wenona explained to her daughter. Kimimela's big eyes looked curiously at me and the baskets. I relished my niece's interest and showed her my licorice plants, explaining their abilities. As children who are four winters-old do, Kimimela grew distracted, and soon went back to playing with the dolls Aunt Mika had sewn.

Wenona flashed her eyes at me, a familiar look of when she was at the edge of gossip. "You *did* miss out while you were off on your medicine quest," she said.

"What this time, cousin?"

"I believe Red Otter was lingering near your tipi," she whispered. "Hoping Oenikika would want company while gathering firewood."

"I hope you told him that I was busy," I replied, annoyed my cousin was talking about a foolish boy instead of my medicine baskets.

"Red Otter has the very best shot of the young men in our village," my cousin explained to me, as if I hadn't seen him shoot a bat out of the night sky last evening. "Your father should certainly consider an offer from such a marksman."

Before I could respond, a new voice chimed in from the tipi opening, "Oh, *certainly!*" Mika mocked her daughter's feisty attitude. "There's far more for a father to consider a marriage offer than the shot of a bow and arrow or a rifle."

Wenona replied to her mother with a playful laugh, "I suppose."

"The chief is out smoking a pipe, preparing for an announcement," Aunt Mika said. She turned to her grandson. "Time to help your Uncle Brown Wing with the fire." Wolfchaser jumped from his seat and ran outside. She spotted my baskets. "Oenikika, these could last us through winter." She said with awe as she tenderly took the plants, admiring them in her hands.

I was warm with satisfaction at my aunt's praise. I wondered if my mother—if she were alive—would be as proud of me as my aunt.

Aunt Mika once, and only once, told me the story of my birth. I arrived quickly and unexpectedly, under the willow tree by Circle Lake. My mother, Woman of the Winter Sun, stopped crying out when they placed me on her chest. I nuzzled under Mother's chin, and she kissed me while long tears ran off her sloping cheeks and fell tenderly onto my newborn head. Her adoring tears rolled down my body with each new breath I took, but as I came to be, she slowly slipped away. Sometimes, in the nights when I couldn't sleep, and there were no more cedar logs to throw on the fire to calm me, I wished I hadn't taken her place on this earth. I looked back to the baskets of licorice. These plants were the closest I could come to knowing her.

Owl Woman hobbled into the tipi and passed me a bowl of turtle soup. "Thank you, Grandmother." I was hungry, but before I took a bite, I checked, as was proper: "Has my father eaten?"

"Yes, he had *two* bowls. You're always such a dutiful daughter," Grandmother said, her wrinkles deepening as she smiled.

"I was surprised he let me gather today." I was grateful he allowed me to ride alone; his approval was usually just beyond my grasp. I watched the rest of my family—how my Uncle Chaska waits to walk alongside Wenona. How Little Rapids playfully put Kimimela on his shoulders. Their relaxed relationship. With my father, trying to catch his attention was like a dog chasing its tail. It was a constant struggle to reach, and if I ever did catch it, it seemed to fall out of my hands with my next step.

"I believe he's preoccupied with some matter with the white men," my grandmother said.

I'd thought the same thing when he snapped at me last night. Maybe I should tell him about the white people at the creekside.

"I agree." Mika added, "Something's on my brother's mind." We nodded together in unison. The tipi was so pleasantly cozy between my grandmother, aunt, cousin, and niece. All the generations connected by blood and memories. I watched Wenona braid Kimimela's hair. They certainly appeared to be mother and daughter. I had not yet shifted into this stage of life as a woman. I was not with child. I was not with a husband. I didn't yearn for these things, as I yearned for my plants. But I did know my fullness as a woman was not yet realized. There was a missing piece.

Before I had time to contemplate further, five booms sounded. Drumbeats. Signaling it was time to congregate.

Sparks curled into the air, up into the pines that towered above us. As usual, I sat near Grandmother at the gathering. Brown Wing stood proudly, arms crossed while admiring his blaze roaring in the center. Little Wolfchaser stood next to him, copying his uncle and crossing his arms as he stared seriously at the flames. Other young men the same age as Brown Wing and I sat close to the fire and beat the drums. Breaking Up, Killing Ghost, and Runs Against Something When Crawling raised and lowered their hands; their rhythm was like a heartbeat.

The final group of men who'd been smoking the pipe together made their way to the gathering. Cut Nose, his face mangled with a long scar, strode in from the darkness carrying the pipe. He bent and placed it on a painted buffalo skull sitting near the drummers. Cut Nose was followed by Wenona's husband Little Rapids, then Uncle Chaska and finally, my father, Chief Little Crow. He was the head of our family, so all my daily activities were meant to be of service to him. When I thought of firewood, it was to keep him warm. When I thought of cooking, it was of meals to make him strong. When I thought of sewing, it was to decorate his regalia. But he was also head of this tribe. He was the lead chief of all the Eastern Dakota. Chiefs of the other bands of Dakota in our area—Wabasha, Traveling Hail, Red Iron, Sleepy Eyes—all looked to our Chief Little Crow. Father was the best story-teller and speaker; he knew how to draw in a crowd, and I wondered what he would announce this evening.

Father's voice sang out with the drums. Men's singing echoed him. He stretched out his arms, exposing his crooked wrists. When he was a young man, Little Crow had been challenged by his brothers for the position of chief. One of his brothers shot him, directly through both wrists. Father miraculously survived, and his permanent deformity was a sign from the Great Spirit of his destiny—to be our chief. With his arms and wrists out, everyone was reminded of his power. The men's voices rang out back and forth to each other. I felt comforted hearing their mingling voices. The chief stepped forward closer to the fire, lowered his arms, and the drumming quieted.

"I've returned from a journey with Chief Wabasha and Chief Sleepy Eyes," Father announced. "In the land of the white man . . . their buildings are so many you cannot see the sky." I couldn't imagine this faraway land. Not seeing the sky? How would one follow the constellations without the sky? The bright stars were our guide. I shuddered and scooted myself even nearer to Owl Woman.

"We now see the white men making their buildings all around us. So many of them, like rabbits in the late summer. In my meeting with their leader, the Great White Father, many matters were discussed. We have come to an agreement. Our tribe, the great Dakota of the Seven Council Fires, will journey to an expansive land by the Long River. A reservation. It will be ours to eternity. The Great White Father will bring us carts of goods and gold. These payments will come every year through seven generations."

Moving to the Long River? We all sat in an extended moment of silence. Then grumbling started. Questioning. I too questioned. A reservation? What did that even mean?

I turned to my grandmother and asked, "What is a reservation?"

"Shh, shh child," Owl Woman said lovingly, patting my hands

in my lap—she too was trying to understand. My eyes searched the other faces gathered around the fire.

"But what about in the winter?" Wenona's husband Little Rapids asked. "We follow the buffalo."

"With every white you see, there are a thousand fewer buffalo. Like the buffalo, we won't roam as we used to. We'll stay in one place along the Long River. That protects us," my father said. He looked serious, but I could see deeper—there was a bit of emptiness in his dark eyes.

"And what about the Ojibwe?" Killing Ghost asked from the drum circle. "How easy for the enemy to attack us living in one spot for so long?"

Cut Nose, always ready for a fight, nodded his head in agreement.

"Ojibwe. Pah!" My father gave a haughty laugh to the young man's worry. "We are Dakota—Warriors of the Plains. We only have one other tribe to worry about from now on: the white man."

Father's voice sounded proud. But moving us onto a reservation? That seemed a loss of power . . . How could we stay in one area? It was such an unbelievable idea. My mind couldn't make sense of it. Plants didn't grow in one place—I couldn't be bound to one place. All my favorite medicines—pumpkin, chamomile, mint, licorice, coneflower. They grow in different areas, at different times of the year. If we were constrained to the Long River, I would not be able to go on medicine runs. I pushed my heels into the soft soil under my feet, pressed out my frustration. *Why! Why?* My spirit was agitated . . . living in one place was not our way.

My father was wise. Known for his strategic nature. What did he know that would make him give away our way of life? Shipments of gold and goods—he must see a need for those. More trading with the whites, perhaps. If it's Father's word, I'd obey, but obedience couldn't stop my mind from churning with worry over the unknown.

Father walked closer to the fire. His long body glowed in the firelight as he took command of his audience once again. "At sunrise, we begin the journey to our land, where we will stay, for eternity."

The crowd murmured with the news. Father gave a satisfied nod, his leadership clear, but still . . . I studied his face. The edges of his eyes were different. What was he thinking? How could he choose this? Suddenly, my mind flashed back to last night when I asked Father when camp circle would move again. *This* was why my question was so upsetting to him; he knew our days of moving freely were done. He'd already promised away our fate. I watched my father's serious expression illuminated in the firelight. And I realized, he probably let me gather medicine today because I'll never get to go to that licorice bay again. My heart stung and behind it an anger swelled. The memory of the white man's gun suddenly laughed in my face. I'd let them chase me away from those plants. Looking back at my father, a bitter thought stained my mind, maybe he let me ride for our medicines *because he knows no amount of gold can heal us.*

FOUR

Emma Heard

August 19, 1861

The first thing I needed to do was let in some air. It was August, and the humid summer day improved slightly with the occasional breeze. I had returned to my father's office to clean and tidy. I pushed aside the curtain and heaved open the window, propping it up with a stick. Looking out, I could see Mrs. Schein and Mrs. Richter fanning themselves in the shaded front porch across the street. In New Ulm, every time I looked out a window, I could see activity. If I looked out the window at home, all I'd see were straight rows of blonde tasseled corn and two hogs staring blank-eyed back at me. I felt an agreeable optimism about being in town and an energizing purpose working in my father's office today.

A balmy gust of wind pushed its way in, and I turned back to look at the space. My eyes locked on the stack of outgoing mail. Hidden somewhere in the middle was my letter. Miss Knudsen's response could be the path to my future as a teacher. I wondered where this letter would find her. I imagined her in the middle of thriving Iowa City, gathering supplies to welcome another class to the school year.

As a teacher, I could experience the life Miss Knudsen enjoyed: traveling, exploring, learning. Memories of the classroom filled me with hope; I so wanted to look out a classroom window of my own someday.

"It's hot enough to scald a duck," my father said, patting his forehead with a handkerchief. Despite many hours in the office over the past months, his rolled-up sleeves revealed tanned arms from the prairie sun. His eyes met mine. Ma says all of us children got our big blue eyes from Pa. "Get to work putting away the books first, then organize the papers, careful not to throw any of those out, and next you can . . ."

"Wipe things down," I jumped in, "and bring the mail to Myrick's." I nodded dutifully as I seamlessly integrated my secret plan for mailing my letter. I worried what Pa would say if he knew what I was up to. And if my *mother* knew what I wanted? That would be worst of all. She had often expressed her dislike for 'misguided' women like my former teacher. Ma laughed at Miss Knudsen's address on the inside of *Leaves of Grass*. Said the woman was so odd to wander the prairie alone, working, without a husband. I'd never told Ma I wanted that life Miss Knudsen showed me existed. It's not that I wanted to be misguided or oppositional. I was raised to have manners, be cooperative, and yield to the world around me. Yet I could feel that deep down I was different than my mother's ideal of who I should be; a truth about myself that felt shameful yet undeniable. Otto and Ida didn't ever appear to have this struggle. Otto was dazzlingly confident, strong, and charming. His potential was endless; he'd inherit the farm as if it were both his birthright and his throne. Ida, though unable to say a word, was turning into a perfect lady: unendingly obliging, and hardworking and strikingly beautiful. But these very same expectations for me felt suffocating. I could feel myself slowly growing away from the accommodating child my parents always thought I would be. I didn't want to be a misguided woman; I needed my mind to feel alive again.

"Ah yes . . . the mail. I would've forgotten. You can find rags and a bucket in the hallway closet. Now, I must focus on finishing this contract before the end of the day." Pa was hardworking to the point of complete distraction to the world around him, which was ideal for my mission today. Although mailing the letter was my primary intention, I also relished the feeling of being in his office and missing the day's farming chores.

In the center of the long windowless wall was a door that linked the law office to the courthouse. The door opened to a short musty hallway that connected the courthouse foyer. I walked into the entrance to look for the cleaning supplies. The courtroom was infrequently used for any kind of trial. Most often, the men gathered in the space to talk about town goings-on. Gerald Schein, who started the local brewery, would roll a keg of his beer in and they'd get to discussions. It was considered an official meeting if "Gerald brought the beer." I peeked inside the courtroom. I'd never been inside, and my curiosity drove me in. It reminded me of church; pews in the back half of the room, an authoritative judicial altar sat in the front. I stood in awe, tilting my head upward to take in the grand space. Unexpectedly the door to the front of the courthouse opened with a creaking groan. A big-bellied man stood in the doorway. It was the recognizable shape of one of my favorite townspeople: Bruno.

"Emma Heard!" He recognized me with delight. Though Bruno was as old as my father, he still had a childlike wonder to him. He couldn't read or write and still lived with his parents, who still doted on him as if he were a five-year-old. In most ways, he still was. Bruno wore the same pair of frayed overalls every day, aside from the day each month his mother forced him to allow her to wash them, in which case he'd wear his nightshirt and share his disappointment with everyone he encountered: "Mother made me wash my overalls today."

"Hello, Bruno. It's lovely to see you. Where's Captain?" I asked.

"Captain's my best friend. Captain's right there." With an endearing innocence Bruno pointed out the front door, and sure enough, his faithful collie was sitting on the courthouse steps.

"Of course, Captain's your best friend. It seems you're his best friend too." Bruno smiled a big gap-toothed grin. "Do you know where I can find cleaning supplies? I'm helping my father tidy."

He nodded and showed me to a small closet within the courthouse. Over the years, Bruno had helped clean, tear down, or build up every edifice in town. He aided Mrs. Ulrich with her garden, helped the pastor pass the offering plate, and volunteered to help at any farm harvest from sun up to sundown. Though he couldn't add or subtract, the man had a heart the size of New Ulm itself.

"Thank you," I said as I grabbed my supplies.

"You're welcome, Emma Heard."

I walked back through the hallway with a tub, a brush, and rags. My father barely glanced up when I came in. I began working immediately stacking the dense volumes of law books: *Articles of War, The Principles and Morals of Legislation, A Fragment on Government, The Spirit of Laws, The Art of Cross-Examination.* I was lost in my admiration of the titles. A few books were written in Latin, and some in German, but most were in English. There were bindings of different colors: creamy yellow, olive green, cranberry red. I ran my hands down their marvelous spines. Throughout my childhood, my father read by candlelight in the evenings. It'd been his all-consuming preoccupation to educate himself about law through these pages. I would watch him reading and was always curious what special information these pages held to spellbind my Pa. I heaved the similar volumes into stacks, organizing them according to their bindings. Now I knew that I shared more than just my father's eyes; I was thirsty for the information these pages held. I felt an ache to immerse myself in them; organizing was not enough.

We were interrupted from our work when two women entered the office; Mrs. Kuhn and Mrs. Schein, two of the wealthier women in New Ulm. I didn't care for Mrs. Kuhn. Her hair was always pulled back severely, making her bulging eyes appear even more dramatic with their judgmental glances. Mrs. Schein, on the other hand, was a rotund, flushed face woman whose curly hair took on a life of its own in the humidity.

Mrs. Kuhn cleared her throat and launched into what appeared to be a well-practiced announcement, "The Ladies of Ulm are excited to formally proclaim the date of the annual harvest dance." There was a pause. Mrs. Kuhn nodded with an official seriousness at her counterpart.

With a deep breath, Mrs. Schein spoke, "The annual harvest dance will be held on October 5."

The dance was always a much-anticipated celebration. Though we were thousands of miles from Germany, most of our celebrations looked like they could be set in Bohemia: steins of beer, accordions, dancing, sauerkraut, and schnitzel. Last year I hadn't attended; Otto and my father went while Ida and I stayed home with Ma caretaking the little baby Peter and Catherine. Thinking of the event, a *dance*, excited me in a new way. Besides church, I hadn't seen many of our friends since school let out in spring.

My father looked at the pair, and with an amused twinkle in his eyes, replied, "Noted. Thank you, *Ladies of Ulm*."

Mrs. Kuhn made an odd curtsey as she departed, and Mrs. Schein sing-songed a final reminder as she closed the door behind her.

I turned in my seat on the floor between stacks of books and looked up at Pa. He looked back at me with a quizzical raise of his eyebrows. I laughed aloud. This was the most enjoyable day I'd had in some time. The satisfaction of being surrounded by stacks of books, working beside my father, the amusing encounters that could happen at a moment's notice—all of this was starkly different from the farm. And now the anticipation of the harvest dance. The sound of my laughter was overtaken by the loud GONG of the striking grandfather clock ringing the time on the wall. It was 3:00. I hopped to my feet. The mail stagecoach would be through in just an hour!

"Mail. I'm off," I announced.

"Have Myrick put the postage on my business account. He should know that but be careful with him. Don't let him cheat you. Once you return, we'll walk back home together," Pa replied.

I gathered the brimming pile of outgoing mail and moved towards the door.

"The office needs work, Emma," my father said, "I believe you should return and continue to help me here. I'll discuss the matter with your mother."

"I'd quite like that," I replied. I left feeling delighted at how perfectly things had been aligning. Tidying and cleaning wasn't bad work. Looking through the books was a treat. And here I walked, carrying my secret letter. Just as my pride was swelling, I felt a small tapping of my conscience. As I thought of putting the postage on the business account, I cringed with guilt. Mailing this letter with my father's business letters meant he would unknowingly pay my postage. It was only a penny but still—stealing was stealing. Many things in the Bible confused me, but "thou shall not steal" was as straightforward as could be. I'd never stolen a thing in my life; I felt awful to consciously choose such a transgression. I comforted myself by seeking a way to atone for the sin. I'd find a way to pay my father back one day. I'd pay him back double. If I actually became a teacher, I'd send my family part of my salary to reckon the guilt.

I walked three blocks down Main Street to Myrick's general store. Andrew Myrick also owned the Indian Trading Post at Fort Ridgely. While the store was a mainstay, the man himself was an unlikeable fixture in town. Pa described him as having all the weasel of a traveling salesman. But we were stuck with Myrick and depended on him for many of our needs. The store was located at the absolute center of town, the heart of commerce beating life into what was once an empty stretch of prairie. The building was framed in large logs. A porch with inviting benches wrapped around the front and hitching posts stood out front for the horses.

I quietly entered the store and made my way through the maze of dry goods, groceries, lamps, hoes, umbrellas, and castor oil. Midway through the aisles, I heard men arguing. Andrew Myrick was pointing to his oversized register. "I'm logging your debt of sale, additional trade tax, and my good-faith fee for issuing you these goods prior to receipt of your annuity payment." Myrick was condescendingly and somewhat confusingly rattling off additional fees to the three Indian men standing at the counter. I stood still a moment. Otto'd told me, "You won't see an Indian unless they want you to see 'em," which made me nervous to any encounter with our unfamiliar neighbors. He was right, though. Every so often, on the farm, we'd be in the middle of washing laundry and out of nowhere a Dakota Indian would appear next to us, asking to trade. It always startled me.

These men were bare-chested, wearing buckskin breechcloths and leggings. Their brows were wrinkled, and one man stood arms akimbo, shaking his head back and forth. It was the recognizable look of total frustration. I cast my gaze downward at the bundle of mail in my hands; I worried my attention might make the situation worse. I didn't know much about dealings with the Indians, but my father had reviewed some of the legal treaties made with the Dakota. He said the natives had been paid a million dollars in annuities for their land. The land used to create the state of Minnesota. It was an extraordinary amount. How did Myrick say they didn't have enough funds now?

"We pay fair from our annuity," one Dakota said, adamant, pointing at Myrick's register.

"This matter has nothing to do with fair price!" Myrick rebutted. "I have the best prices up and down the river. Don't insult me."

I couldn't help but watch the scene. I understood the Dakota were explaining their payment, not arguing about prices. And Myrick was the *only* trading post for the Natives within 50 miles.

"Take your missing annuity payment up with your Indian Agent. Or Abraham Lincoln himself. I'm running a business. And *you* want ten pounds of pork and flour. I'll issue goods at whatever price I see fit." Myrick stood with an arrogant power. I was perplexed. The government payments to the Dakota were plenty to keep Myrick's pockets full. I couldn't imagine the men who knew little English could follow any of his runaround. Myrick motioned that he wanted the furs they had brought with them in addition to the payment structure he'd outlined.

"Give me these furs, and I'll let you have the pork and flour. Including the aforementioned extra taxation." Myrick made his final offer. He was imposing his own fees on top of demanding the furs. My stomach turned; the fees Myrick was tacking on seemed unnecessary and unfair.

The men stood, appearing uncertain about whether they should give in for the sake of getting the food they needed or leave the store with their pride intact. I'd be nervous about challenging Myrick if he did anything unfair with me, but I knew my well-respected father would have no qualms to addressing any issues on my behalf. I wondered what the Indians would do. They didn't have anyone backing them.

When the natives began to talk among themselves, Myrick turned towards me. His beady eyes glinted as he looked me over. I felt an immediate embarrassing discomfort in my own skin. Ida had indicated to me in the past that she felt "disgusting" from the store clerk, but this was the first time I fully understood what she had meant. I crossed my arms in front of my chest, which had become fuller in the last year.

"Come forward, my lady." Myrick swept his arms out dramatically.

"These Injuns have no manners; excuse their unsightly presence." His tone was obnoxiously dramatic. "Now, what can I interest a delightful thing like you in purchasing?"

The Indians moved aside for me. I politely nodded in appreciation of their courtesy to give me space at the counter. I looked at the men's tanned arms and chests, covered in some kind of grease. Painted axes were tied to their sides; the sharpened edge of the blades shone with warning. The men looked strong and their dislike for the trader was palpable in the air. My instincts pulsed, telling me that this crooked trader should mind himself carefully. These were powerful men he was dealing with; not mindless less-thans who didn't know they were being swindled.

I walked forward, squirming from Myrick's intrusive eyes. My manners, and my mission, overruled my discomfort. "Thank you kindly, Mr. Myrick. I'm just delivering mail on behalf of my father." I set the stack of mail on the glass countertop, looking at him with as much confidence as I could muster. The man was a rat in appearance as much as conduct. Wiry sparse hairs covered his upper lip in an attempt at a mustache. Myrick picked up the stack, wetted his fingers and flipped through, counting each envelope. A wave of nervous heat pounded through me. What if he somehow knew I was mailing a personal letter? Emma Heard, deceiving her attorney father, what a disgrace. And what if, of all people, Andrew Myrick was the one to discover my dishonesty. I breathed deeply as the summer heat pooled tiny droplets of anxiety at my brow. The seconds dragged, his counting painfully slow. My knees weakened. I could barely stand in the heat, pondering so many crooked intentions, including my own.

"Eighteen," Myrick said, carelessly tossing the stack in the mail basket on the counter behind him. I let out my breath. He scanned his register and murmured, "Attorney Heard" as he carefully recorded a bold "Outgoing 18" next to the name. "Perhaps I can interest you in something for a sinner?" He grinned greasily.

A sinner? Was my guilt obvious?

"Excuse me?" I stammered. My stomach dropped. Were my sins so noticeable? How could my dream be right if I had to commit wrongs to make it happen?

"I saw you eyeing my sinful goods. After all, we're all sinners, aren't we?" Under the glass countertop, sat heaping bowls of tobacco. Atop were oversized jars containing sticks of rock candy and maple sugar taffy. Behind that were brooding bottles of brandy, rum, and whiskey. The indulgences were undoubtedly sinful, but I wasn't interested in any of them. I shook my head vigorously to indicate no, and perhaps to convince myself that my deceitful act at the counter wasn't sinful in itself.

"An angelic creature like yourself cannot be corrupted easily. Not like some of these heathens," he said with disdain as his eyes darted contemptuously to the men standing beside us. Myrick's attempts at charm felt like pond slime. I couldn't understand what was so bothersome about the Indian men. They had been reasonable and polite in request and conduct, unlike Myrick. I wanted to glance at the Indians again, but I didn't want to be impolite. I shifted my weight awkwardly. I needed to get out of the stuffy store as quickly as possible.

"Many thanks for your assistance, sir," I said, excusing myself. Myrick immediately turned back to the native men.

"Pelts now, or no deal!" he shouted. I moved quickly. Walking out the double doors to the wall of afternoon heat had never felt like such a relief. A sudden swell of tears blurred my eyes—secret excitement, hope, and nervousness bubbling to the surface. I let out a long breath of relief at accomplishing my goal: my letter was sent.

FIVE

Oenikika

May 25, 1861

The morning sun spilled on the eastern sky as horses and dogs were saddled with drag sleds full of our supplies. We rose early and quickly broke camp, so we could begin our migration to our reservation. It would take us at least a handful of days to make the journey from the edge of the Northwoods to the Long River. With the light of dawn at their backs, a group of scouts rode out ahead of the procession. Father was at the front of the next group, followed by our men on horseback. I watched as he and his horse took the first steps toward our new life. Father's stallion, Mato, was tall and black as a raven and had been with him since I was a little girl. Mato's dark mane bounced in step with the eagle feathers on the large staff my father held in his right hand. I watched with nervousness, but my father sat tall and confident, leading us to a new future. And us women and children followed, some on horses, some on foot. Dogs trotted beside the horses. In mass we moved across the earth as we'd done countless times before, moving where the season and buffalo took us. But we'd never traveled to a reservation before—the land we were "allowed" upon and whites were not.

As we traveled south, we passed settlers' houses at a distance. I rocked with the rhythm of Ahone's steps. My aunt and cousin chatted from horseback in front of me. Kimimela and Wolfchaser slept in the travois sleigh pulled behind Wenona's horse. But I didn't join the conversation. I looked at the hillsides beyond us. From one home, a handful of light-haired children emerged. They watched us moving by. I looked away as if I didn't see them but inside, I puckered with an irritated jealousy. They were probably like the white people I'd encountered at the creekside—they had just moved to this land, yet *we* were made to leave? Maybe they should be the ones kept to a reservation on the Long River. At midday I couldn't take it any longer. I was near the very back of the group. I softly pulled Ahone's reins and let my seat bones sit heavy into her back. My mare knew to slow. We fell behind . . . intentionally. If this were the last we'd be passing through this area, I had to gather while I could. My choice to separate didn't go unnoticed, Wenona's head twisted over her shoulder, her eyes snappy and questioning, watching me slowly edge away from the group.

"What are you doing?" she mouthed. Only the scouts, like Runs Against Something When Crawling and Little Rapids, were allowed to ride out from the migration. It was dangerous to get scattered and separated. Women especially were expected to stay on course. We were slow; we carried the supplies and the babies.

"I'll be back," I replied, praying my loud-mouthed cousin wouldn't yell at me and cause heads to turn. Once the pack started to move downhill, I pulled Ahone sharply to the side. I wanted to check the ravine we passed for rose hips. We galloped back to the ravine's edge, and I filled with a quiet thrill. I hopped off and made my way to the rosehip bushes. It was only the time of the Strawberry Moon, and as I had feared . . . none were ripe enough yet. But I kissed the green buds, still grateful for their existence. Hopeful for their growth, though I'd never get to see them in their full glory. Beyond the rosehip, some lively mint was growing green at the edge of the rocky ravine drop off. I pulled off the leaves quickly as I was able, their refreshing scent clinging to my fingers. I tucked the leaves in a satchel tied to my waist, and as I finished my gathering, I tucked in a pinch of tobacco at the roots of the mint plant as my hurried offering. "Thank you, kind Earth."

I knew I needed to hurry to keep up with the processional. I ran and jumped up to Ahone's back, nudging her with my heels. We returned down the hill and covered the next rise. It wasn't long before I could see the mass of my slow-moving people. Owl Woman and Mika were midway up the group. They hadn't noticed my absence. I rode to Wenona who was still at the back of the pack. Wolfchaser and Kimimela sitting in the backward facing sled waved their little hands at me. I slowed to a trot and waved back, trying to catch my breath and act naturally, as if I had never left Wenona's side.

"What were you thinking, cousin? Riding off by yourself? You put yourself in danger, put the whole *tribe* in danger!" Wenona told me, cuttingly. "Think how upset Little Crow would be to find out his own daughter rode off during migration."

Part of me thought my father had betrayed *me*, making us move to a reservation, moving us away from my healing plants. But I flinched to think that I'd betrayed my father; the worst thing a daughter could do. I avoided my cousin's harsh look as my heart beat with shame. I put my fingers in Ahone's mane, tried to distract myself with the feeling of her thick hair.

"If we are staying on a reservation, I need to collect every plant I can along the way." I said. My cousin shrugged. She didn't seem to feel the same urgency I did. "What if we can't come back here? Ever?"

"Don't speak so dramatically in front of the children. My husband is not scared. I'm a good wife; I'm not afraid if he says there's nothing to fear." Wenona made the decision sound so simple. A husband. I didn't know what it felt like to have the reassurance of a husband's thoughts and protection. So, I kept quiet. I looked about and took in the fleeting world. We passed many wonderful places—the land of the Sugar Maples. The Lake of the Long Fish. I smiled when I thought of the winter that I turned twelve and the men brought in fish, day after day. That winter didn't feel difficult at all. I looked ahead and watched our people move slowly west across the plain. Something inside of me felt caution. Though the land was flat it seemed to me we were going over an invisible brink—a threshold, something that we could never come back from.

As the sun set lower in the sky, we passed through a valley blooming with coneflower. The flowers were captivating. Magnificent. Bending as if their brilliant purple color made them too heavy to stand. I wanted to steer Ahone out to the middle of the field and stand among the flowers, revel in their power. But we moved like a steady stream, and after what happened earlier, I needed to remain on our current. I could not be a child wandering into every place that called my name. I tried to reassure myself . . . this earth was not something that could be taken away. Yet with every step we took forward, it seemed as if that was what was happening. The darkness of the day deepened, and Ahone's strides didn't stop as they carried us out of the valley of coneflowers. This land was no longer for us—it was where the white man would live. And we, my father had agreed, would never live here again. Anxiety pulled at me, I twisted to look backwards and catch one more glimpse of the purples, but the flowers were already out of sight. The black of night seemed the only thing left behind me.

I whispered goodbye.

June 1, 1861

It was getting late in the day when we finally spotted the Long River; we'd arrived at our "reservation." A lowland of grasses grew along the brown flowing water. The boundaries of the reservation ran along the Long River, one day's ride north of the river, one day's ride south was our perimeter. And the river flowed all the way from the west, past where Chief Sleepy Eyes makes his winter camp. This would be our Dakota land for eternity.

As the masses moved downward into the valley grasses; my father rode to Owl Woman and me and said, "We continue this way." He trotted west, away from everyone else heading southeast to the riverside. Ride away from our people? A weight dropped in my stomach. This was not normal. I looked to my grandmother. Why were we separating from everyone? We always set up our tipi and arranged camp. First thing! I knew better than to question my father, so I kept my mouth shut and instead pulled the reins tight to twist and follow him towards a bluff. Even Ahone hesitated to walk away from the other horses all heading towards the riverside, but I leaned in and reassured her. *We have to follow him, even when we question.*

It didn't take long to make it up the bluff, and as soon as we did, I saw it: A white man's square house. A small building, with a narrow front covered area. My father walked Mato up and dismounted. Why would he walk up to a stranger's house so confidently?

I stared at the structure in front of us. "I thought you said there would be no white men on 'our' land."

"There aren't. This was part of my agreement with the Great White Father—he built a house for us. And supplies for farming are in the shed."

The shed? I looked back at the small building just beyond this one. Shed. I hated hearing my father use white man's words so casually. I

didn't see why my father would need to show off this building when
Owl Woman and I could be setting up camp after our journey.

"I see." I was anxious to get back with everyone else. "Should
Grandmother and I go set up the tipi at camp circle?"

"Oenikika," my father said my name with seriousness, "I am telling you. This—" his crooked hand pointed to the house "—is where
we will live."

I stared at the dark building, bewildered. This was where *they*
lived. Not us. But my father walked ahead, opened a creaking door
and disappeared inside. My grandmother let herself down from her
horse with a groan. I hopped off Ahone. I shook my head in silent
noncooperation at the thought of living in this building. I wanted
Owl Woman to agree with me; this made no sense. But she said, "You
heard your father, Oenikika."

Begrudgingly, I walked up the two hard steps to the heavy entry,
which was covered by a square wood door—like the tipi door but not
nimble and soft. I'd never been in a white man's building before. It
was so different from our home. The hefty door opened to a square
interior. There was a fireplace in the middle of the wall; a small stack
of firewood next to it. Long plank floors creaked as we walked about.
How do people live atop groaning floors? The corners of the house
seemed harsh compared to our tipi. We live in a circle, as life is a
circle. It felt peculiar to be in a room with four corners, each one
like a sharp insult. My father made long, careful strides through the
room. My grandmother slowly walked the perimeter. I was cautious.
It was just a square empty space, but it was foreign and alerted all my
senses.

"The Great White Father will provide a white man's home, eighty
acres, and farming supplies to any Dakota man who converts to a life
of farming," my father explained.

I paused as the meaning of his words sunk in. "Is that what we are
doing? Converting?" Why would we ever *convert* our life? Our life is

guided by Wankan Tanka—the Great Spirit. Why would we farm? We were hunters; following animals where they roam. My heart stopped . . . the bison, the deer, the ducks, geese. They wouldn't be constrained to a reservation, as we would be. How would we hunt now?

"I want options for our people," my father said. I couldn't discern his tone. It seemed forlorn but decided. What did he know that I didn't? What was his mind contemplating?

"We'll set up," my grandmother stated. She and I went out to the travois on the back of her horse, and began unpacking, bringing our life into the empty space. My thoughts swarmed as I attempted the routine task of unpacking in a new environment. What to do with the sacred tipi poles? Who built this home? Who gathered the wood? I could remember the day my father gathered the trees for our tipi poles. The firs were tall and almost perfectly straight. He cut the branches from the trunks, then smoothed them to tipi poles with Uncle Chaska. Grandmother and I have set them up and taken them down hundreds of times since then. We could do it with our eyes closed. This was life. This was who we are. But tonight, I carried the tipi poles inside the house. Laid them down at the back wall. They stretched the length of the house. They looked collapsed and powerless here. Exactly how I was feeling.

I moved to the side of the room and looked out the clear openings in the wall. What a peculiar feeling: looking out from the inside. The house traps you, so you make these windows, to feel like you can escape. From the far window, I could see down the bluff. Camp circle was forming. A fire going. A worry hooked into my heart—would any man make an offer for me now? The girl living in the white man's house. Would I be ruined if we stayed here? A waxing moon rose in the sky. It looked so lonely. I churned with frustration staring at it all by itself; I knew I wasn't meant to be the moon, separate and secluded. I wasn't meant to be lonely. We weren't meant to live eighty acres apart from one another, to be a separated people. I was the daughter of the Woman of the Winter Sun and Chief Little Crow. I had to return to the village.

I stared out, lost in my sad thoughts, but grandmother clucked at me to help unpack cooking supplies. After setting out the final items, I realized my father was still outside. Perhaps he had the same reaction I did to being in the house. Unease. As if we were setting up in the white man's snare. Maybe he'd want us to put up the tipi after all. I walked out to check on him. Even though I was angry, I still felt my duty, and a sense of loyalty to care for him, no matter the circumstance. I walked through the doorway; stepping into the outdoors felt darker than it ever had when we were in our tipi. The long plank floors and wood walls muted my senses in a way that I'd never felt before.

Father sat on the front step, looking out into the night beyond us. I stood behind him, wondering what he was watching in the darkness. "When you were a little girl, what did I tell you about animals?" he asked. "The squirrels? Moose? Hawks?"

My heart loosened and warmed with memories. When I was small, my father always told me to use my senses. My ears. My nose. Feel the wind. Watch the birds. Listen closely to the earth; observe its animals. I remembered his deep voice. "The animals know more about this world than we do," I said. My eyes finally adjusted to the night, and I saw a wolf dart by. My father had been on the front step, watching wolves. He nodded his head as his eyes followed the animals across the open prairie.

"Animals know everything about survival." He looked at me, with seriousness, adamant as he repeated, "We look to them to learn how we keep surviving."

We sat on the white man's steps together, watching the great predators running beyond us. Every few seconds, shapes moved atop the black of the prairie at the deep blue edge of the horizon. A cold howl came from a wolf I couldn't see. A shiver of fear caught the nape of my neck but my father said confidently, "We'll find ways to survive."

We stayed next to each other in the quiet, looking out at the dark horizon line. I thought of the routine of an evening in camp circle. Wenona putting the twins Wolfchaser and Kimimela to sleep. Little Rapids's laugh echoing between the tipis. I longed to be simmering a cup of tea and sitting in the circle of the tipi floor with Owl Woman, hearing the familiar sounds around me. My elbow rubbed against my satchel full of mint leaves. I was glad I'd gathered today. That's what *I* needed to do to survive, I thought. Listen to my heart. To the plants. That's how I'd find my way. I'd begin searching for them tomorrow.

SIX

Emma Heard
September 25, 1861

During the day our farmhouse was a bustling hub of clanking plates, bellowing cows, clucking chickens, and boots stomping off muddy soles. But by evenings the farm drowsied and slowed with the darkening sky above. Pa's hat hung on its familiar hook next to the door and Ma rested her head back on her wooden rocking chair as she rocked baby Peter. Tonight, I sat cross-legged on the bench at the dining table, with the thick book, *An Abridgment of Burn's Justice of the Peace Officer*, open in front of me. Pa let me bring it home; I'd carried the heavy text all the way from the office. Soft candlelight lit the aged pages. It wasn't good as my Whitman, but I'd read anything.

"Well, it's about that time," Uncle Allen said. He excused himself and stood up. He lived in a separate cottage past the barn and behind the garden. Otto stuck his head over the side of the upstairs railing, his mop of golden hair falling in front of his face.

"Unkey, in the morning we mend the north fence?" he asked.

"Better do it before cows go to pasture, I suppose," our quiet uncle replied with a sensible shrug as he headed out the front door. Uncle

Allen, bearing no resemblance to my father, had dull mousy hair interrupted by noticeably large ears.

Otto dangled himself out farther over the rail, balancing at his waist. "Ida, you'll chop firewood for me?" Ida, sitting on the floor, looked up from her needlework, and rolled her eyes at her trickster twin brother.

"Set yourself back off that ledge, Otto. You'll fall straight on your head. Why must you always make me worry?" My mother corrected her seventeen-year-old son as if he were still a child. She turned to Pa, seated at his desk against the wall near my parents' bed. "August, two Indians came by today wanting to trade for eggs, again. They've been here more frequently lately." My mother puckered with discomfort when the Indians appeared, especially when Pa was gone.

My father turned to her. "Again, really?"

Remembering my encounter with the Dakota men a few weeks ago, I interjected. "They're having trouble trading for food. Remember, Pa? I told you Myrick was arguing with them at the store." I'd told my father about my suspicions of Myrick's swindling the Indians, but he had dismissed my concerns without asking any questions and implored me not to worry myself over the matter. I was confused why my father, the town attorney, didn't want to know about fraud, even if it was against the Indians.

My mother's delicate face looked aghast. "Why on earth would my daughter be present for an argument between Myrick and a pack of angry Indians?" Her question was pointed more at my father than me. She hadn't understood my interest in helping in my father's office and fretted that he'd be too busy to make sure I was safe in town on my own.

"Ahh, she was simply bringing the mail for me. I had no idea this trouble occurred. Emma mentioned Myrick was upset about something but that's nothing unusual." My father had disregarded my concerns at the time, but now I realized he hadn't even been listening to me. I felt a wave of irritation that no one understood Myrick's swindling.

"The Indians weren't angry; they were hungry. Their annuity payment hasn't come in from the government. That's what Myrick was twisting against them, as if the delay in payment was their fault. Remember?" I hoped my father would appreciate the difference.

Pa shook his head. "Those annuity payments were the thing I was worried about with this most recent treaty. How's a government start a war with the South then plan to send millions in gold to Indians in the West?" His attorney instincts brought him back to the stipulations in the contracts. Washington was failing to meet the parameters of the treaty. I still felt like he was missing that Myrick had been cheating the men too.

"A young girl doesn't need to know about these things. You mustn't get involved in such matters, Emma. That's their trouble," my mother stated adamantly. I felt smothered under her anxiety.

"I would never get involved. I just noticed it was happening, is all." I was a sixteen-year-old girl; what could I do? But I remembered that day and the repulsive clerk. "I do think Myrick was acting immorally," I said with an edge in my voice, but as soon as the words left my mouth, I remembered my letter. My own sneaky behavior that day. Guilt swept over me as I thought of the teaching "let thou who has not sinned be first to cast a stone."

"I'd say that does sound like Myrick," Pa replied as Catherine toddled towards him. Pa scooped her up and tossed her overhead in the air. "Myrick would even charge sweet little Catherine here double for a piece of taffy." He kissed her chubby cheeks, and she giggled.

My brother barreled down the staircase into the middle of the room. He opened the center fireplace's iron door and added a log. It would keep our large farmhouse cozy through the autumn night. "Pa, I told Mr. Schein we would bring a few chickens for the harvest dance."

"That's reasonable," my father confirmed. "Anna, we're attending this year, correct?"

I looked up from my reading, hopeful for Ma to agree. The dance had been the talk of the town and I was eager to go.

"I do suppose we could make it a family affair," she said with a glimmer in her eyes, "Our little Oktoberfest on the prairie." She looked at my father. "Will there be a place for Catherine and Peter to sleep?"

"We'll need the little ones looked after . . ." He glanced over at me and my heart sank. I knew what was coming. "Emma, you could help with the children of town. Other families will need assistance, as well."

So, we were going to the dance . . . but I wouldn't be joining in on the fun. Mute Ida wouldn't be expected to caretake the little ones. My throat choked back the unexpected disappointment. Unfairness tore through me. Sometimes, I wished I was the one who couldn't speak; Ida avoided so many unpleasantries with her disability. My longing to be part of the festivities raced desperately. Ma didn't wait for me to confirm my participation. As always, these things were assumed and decided for me. My one act of silent rebellion, my letter to Miss Knudsen, was somewhere far away on this darkened prairie. Too distant to bring comfort in this moment.

"Lovely. We'll go and get back in time to rest for church on Sunday morning," Ma said as I turned my eyes downward back to the pages of my book. I buried myself in the words, vowing that I would continue to teach myself with any text I could get my hands on. Adamantly, I flipped forward another page.

SEVEN

Oenikika

September 20, 1861

Everything moved in the Changing Season Moon. Dry leaves fell in swirls from the thinning treetops. Deer traveled at the edge of the woodlands. Geese flew high in the sky. The squirrels, busiest of all, buried their treasures. This year, squirrels were frantic and determined, stashing away acorns, a sure sign that a hard winter was coming. We must prepare as they do. Even though we lived in the white man's house, I was resolute to continue in the tradition and routines with everyone in the village. Every morning at sunrise, I carried my rolled-up buffalo skin tote and met Wenona to gather firewood. We walked the forest on the north side of the Long River. This morning, the autumn air was chilly, but the rising sun encouraged our work. I loved each day beginning with a pattern of reaching toward the earth. Bending, gathering, bending, gathering. Living in the four walls was breaking my spirit, and I needed this rhythm inside of me. Needed to feel the texture of the bark and branches. Needed to feel the familiar comfort of working in tandem with my cousin.

My tote filled more quickly than Wenona's; she kept getting distracted in her storytelling, updating me on every single happening of camp. She stood with one hand on her back, one on her growing belly, rambling on. "This new missionary, Riggs, isn't like the others. He seems a boy on an adventure in the woods. But he has talked about the Great White God," she said with an eyeroll.

"Why is he even here?" I asked, annoyed. It angered me. My father had promised, no white man on our reservation . . . yet the presence of the new Missionary Riggs seemed to be another white-man exception to the rules. In the time of Owl Woman's great grandfather, the very first whites arrived through the Northwoods, coming to our territory to harvest muskrat and beaver pelts. They'd traded us fairly—beads, cups, and pots for our plentiful furs. It was actually helpful to exchange for sharp knives, booming guns, and iron kettles. Those items fit well into life and made some tasks more efficient. But not long after, missionaries followed the fur-traders' trail. The missionaries didn't come and go. Each lingered, living at the edges of our village, offering occasional goods and constant lectures if you were unlucky enough to be seated by one. I've observed two kinds of these missionaries. Some were chubby men with women's bellies and awkward laughs. Those never lasted long. Most were the other type, missionaries talking loud and angry like their God, trying to convince us to feel afraid to die; these ones persisted like an illness in a long winter. They wanted to change us. And now we were supposed to convert to farming. It seemed the white man wouldn't be satisfied until we were invisible among them. Why come here to try to make us invisible? Why come here and tell us *not* to pray to our plants, to our rain, to our buffalo? It was contrary to every part of my spirit. A missionary was like a fly buzzing. I wished I had a tail like Ahone, could flick them away.

"Little Rapids actually likes him. Missionary Riggs learns our ways and isn't quick to speak. He's out helping men with the hunting now." Wenona sighed and looked up towards the sky. "I am worried it'll be a hard winter. The geese aren't stopping to rest . . ."

My cousin was getting distracted from our chore, both hands cupped under the small bump of a baby in her womb. I tossed a twig at her. "You know our task could go much more quickly if you talk *while* you gather?"

"Pssh. That's no fun. What rush are you in to get back to that awful house?"

"I'm in no hurry at all," I said with sadness. And embarrassment. I hated being in the four walls. I didn't want others to think I actually wanted to be there. But I couldn't act as though it upset me—that would bring dishonor to my father. So instead, I busied myself each day in the village. As soon as I saw the glow of the rising sun, I sprinted from the house to meet Wenona. In the afternoons, I walked the woods and the riverbank by myself, looking for medicines. Mapping them in my mind. We had good amounts of dandelion, cottonwood, oak, and sweetgrass. I'd found mushrooms and a little Chaga. I still had licorice from the camp in the Northwoods. Aunt Mika had her collection of plants. The Medicine Man had enough sweetgrass to burn as he prayed for our village. But what if someone was wounded? Or caught a terrible cough? I had yet to find coneflower or butterfly weed. We needed them. But what could I do? Father said we were forbidden to ride off the reservation. For now, I listened to the calls of the plants in my heart's ears. *I hear you, Great Mystery,* I called back.

Wenona and I walked westward on the banks of the Long River. Our totes were growing heavy, so we made our way back inland at a bend. Along our way, we found a low-lying meadow I hadn't seen before. Silver frost on the grass rose into a steamy mist from the warming sun. The meadow was filled with our horses, their powerful necks bending and pulling mouthfuls of long grasses. It was a peaceful sight, majestic and ever-changing as the earth was.

I was surprised to see a young man I didn't recognize among our horses. I estimated he was six winters older than me. He looked taller and stronger than Breaking Up or Brown Wing. He was focused on one horse, trotting around him at the edge of the meadow. Two long necklaces bounced off his chest as he jogged in a circle, the horse trotting parallel to him, falling in line with the circle he made. The horse tossed its head and shook its dark mane—it seemed they were having a silent conversation. Striking and strong; the man's focus as appealing as his looks. A curiosity stirred from my depths and set a twinkling net of interest on my heart. Wenona noticed me watching him, and laughed. "Ahhh . . . someone's first time seeing the handsome new arrival to camp?"

I blushed but continued to watch him moving through the grey fog. It was like my eyes were hungry. "Who is he?"

Wenona moved closer, loving the opportunity to gossip. She whispered as we watched the man and the horse move together in perfect circles. "He's the Man Who Sings to Horses. Tashunke . . . Tash." Tashunke. The moment I heard his name, something in the sky of my heart opened. It felt like rain was falling on dry grass. "He's Lakota." A far western tribe of the Seven Council Fires we belonged to. My cousin continued to explain that when he was a young boy, his family was killed in an attack from Blackfoot. Tashunke escaped and wandered for many moons, followed by the band's herd of horses. Eventually, he encountered a camp of Dakota near the Long River. He was a member of our Seven Council Fires, so they could take him in if the tribe agreed. After little deliberation, it was decided the boy must be smiled upon by Wankan Tanka. My cousin's eyes lit up. "He survived an attack of the Blackfoot *and* was followed by the horses." So, Tash lived among the tribe of Chief Sleepy Eyes for years, but the Great Spirit called him East and just like when he was young and his horses followed. He'd moved among the different tribes of Dakota, until, Wenona and I both looked at Tashunke, "the Long River had guided him to us."

Tash slowed to a walk, stretched out an arm and dropped his shoulder. The horse slowed, tossed its head again, and walked inward towards him. Tashunke stood tall at the center of the circle, arms at his sides, his palms facing up. The horse gently stepped through the misty grass, eventually standing with its nose breathing clouds into Tash's face. In a moment of magical beauty, the animal world, spirit world, and human meeting as one, the horse bent its head down, and pressed the star of its forehead against Tash's chest, right upon Tashunke's heart. Tash raised his open palms and placed them on both sides of the horse's strong jaw. He nuzzled his own head between the horse's ears. An act of gratitude and connection for them both. *He really does sing to horses*, I thought.

To my dismay, Tashunke turned then and looked, spotting us. I cringed with embarrassment. His ability with horses was so incredible to witness, and the connection between him and horse so intimate and responsive, that our presence suddenly felt an intrusion to his talents. I looked away, and awkwardly grabbed for my firewood tote. "Let's be on our way, cousin," I whispered with urgency.

Wenona picked up her tote and chuckled. "Oh my . . . it seems this may be the horse man's first time seeing my beautiful cousin."

"Shh." I scolded her boldness. But I did dare a quick glance back at Tash. His gaze was still upon me. For a second, I felt his pull. I turned my head down in modesty. Like the horse, all my instincts wanted to turn in towards him.

Wenona and I made our way through the grasses, entering camp circle. I moved through, saying my "good mornings" to Uncle Chaska and others who greeted me. I shifted my heavy tote to my other arm and looked up to see the square outline of our white man's house at the top of the bluff in front of me. A breeze blew against my face. I hated that house. I was desperate to escape those walls, and now the Man Who Sings to Horses offered a new call to return to camp circle.

December 5, 1861

Many moons passed in the white man's house. I hoped I'd adjust, at least be able to sleep, but I never stopped feeling like a fish trapped in a net. The windows were the least bad part of this house. The creaking floors were the worst. Such foolish design for a dwelling; nothing like the double lining of the tipi which ventilates us in the summer and insulates us in the coldest night of winter. Sleep never found me in these walls. I ached for rest each night, but my mind never settled for more than an hour or two. To pass the long hours, I'd pull on my father's buffalo cloak and sit on the crate at the window, looking out at the faint flickers of campfires in the valley below.

Earlier that day I'd sat with Wenona and Dina in the tipi, while the men played a lively gambling game. Tashunke was in the circle of men, as my father had welcomed him to stay with our camp. His horsemanship was an asset for our people. I'd seen Tash occasionally since that fall day in the meadow, but I wasn't sure if he ever noticed me. Each time I saw him, my heart fluttered like a chickadee's wings. Today I'd seen a jagged scar on Tash's upper lip; another marker of his history. I wanted to know about the scar. I wanted to know everything about him. Every other young man in our village, I'd known since birth. But Tashunke was a mystery.

I felt discreet excitement to be so close to him as the men rolled their dice and made their bets. Others hollered with delight and disappointment, but Tashunke was mostly quiet, though I thought I could read at the corners of his mouth and the edges of his lips when he was amused. It would be improper for me to watch the men directly, so I acted as if I was enraptured with the story Dina was telling. I was always aware of Tash's presence as if he were the summer sun. I prayed for him to notice me, dared to let myself hope he'd perhaps consider me for a wife. Wenona said I was wasting hope; Tash was a wandering warrior with a wealth of horses and had no need to tie himself to a single tribe. She wanted me to consider Little Rapids's best friend, Red Otter. But I felt Red Otter was not a sharp thinker and too quick to follow the influence of a group.

Someday soon, a man would make an offer to take me as his wife. If I approved, Father would surely accept. I'd begun a list in my mind: Red Otter, no. Runs Against Something Crawling, no. Too brutish. Maybe a man from Traveling Hail's band? Live among my mother's people, and finally leave the white man's house. I tried to taper my preoccupations with Tashunke by considering my cousin's dismissal, but it only made my heart dive deeper with a longing to know the wandering man followed by horses.

It was Tashunke's turn and the tipi filled with energy. I silently hoped for his success. I heard the dice tumble on the ground and looked over to see the result. The men watched the rolling dice come to a stop, all facing up. Tashunke had a perfect roll. A roar came from the men; even Dina and Wenona let out a laugh. I couldn't hold back my smile as I looked up at Tash. Our eyes locked for a moment. Tashunke's reflex had been to look to me when he won. I immediately looked away to maintain my decorum. But when our eyes connected, I felt as if I had plunged underwater in an April lake just after the ice has gone. Thrill and chill. Overwhelm. Feeling fully alive. That's how he felt to me.

It was the opposite of being in this soulless structure tonight; I was trapped in this white man's house. The flat ceiling echoed every sound. The cold of the Hard Moon filled the walls. My nose was chilled, and I pulled father's buffalo hide cloak up over my head, cocooning myself. My stomach growled. The hunting party had only taken deer this fall. No moose, buffalo or bear. And we hadn't been able to collect as many berries, roots, and squash as we usually did. Our food supply was rationed, limited. Father said that our payment from the white man would be coming soon; it should have already arrived. Our bellies would soon be filled . . . but my stomach was growling for more than food. I craved the tipi back. Wanted nearness. I desired to roam and find Puffball, more medicinal plants. We'd need the Puffball for Wenona's labor. I stared out the window at the very far tipi, at the outside of camp circle. It was Tash's tipi. Where he lived alone. I let myself feel it fully . . . I wanted the Man Who Sings to Horses. I wanted Tashunke. I prayed for him to make an offer to my father. I wondered what my father would do . . . make a dramatic proclamation of some kind. Bind Tashunke to our tribe. Would Tash ever consider it? Or did he like wandering alone? I needed my future life to be outside of these walls. In a warm glowing tipi. But here I was, the fish in the net. As I watched the far-off light of my people, my stomach growled again in the darkness.

EIGHT

Emma Heard

October 5, 1861

O ur wagon wheels crunched over crisp fallen leaves, then slowed to a halt in front of Turner Hall. The yellow of a waning moon shone through ominous bands of clouds. Otto leaped down from the front bench of the wagon and began to unhitch Kit and Kamish, who were steaming from the brisk trot over the cool prairie. We could hear the welcoming bellows of the accordion. A shiver of anticipation ran through me; the harvest dance was finally here. Pa walked around the side of the wagon and hoisted little Catherine over the side, then took Ma's hand as she held baby Peter and carefully stepped down the side ladder. Pa exclaimed, "Now, if this isn't the exact night Psalm 65 was referring to." He quoted the verse, *"You crown the year with your bounty; your wagon tracks overflow with abundance."* The harvest had indeed been abundant, our root cellar was stocked floor to ceiling with braided garlic, salted ham, potatoes, kohlrabi, squash, jars of canned apples, pickles and green beans. Ma and Pa lingered hand in hand, reveling the lovely sight of the hall illuminated for the harvest dance.

Uncle Allen hopped down the ladder, worn violin case in tow. I looked to Ida: the excitement behind her eyes matched mine. I was glad to see my sister so jubilant. She was truly stunning. Ida's porcelain skin blushed like a pink apple from the chilly ride. Her dress was enchanted, made of a blue fabric called *A Ladies Midnight Calico*. A matching ribbon softly tied up half her golden hair. She was, in every way but one, turning into the ideal of a lady. She could sew and mend, churn butter quicker than I, was thorough while canning, and always found more eggs in the chicken coop than anyone else. Ida was strong. Hardworking. She made submission look enjoyable. My moment of awe at my sister twisted with edges of envy. Ida was impossibly perfect. Except for that one thing, one thing she couldn't help. The empty abyss in the place her voice should be. I'd always fought back the embers of jealousy in my sister's shadow. Though she was mute, she more than made up for it with her diligence, her accommodations, her beauty. Perhaps the world loved her more *because* she never voiced any disagreements. I should learn to mind my opinions, shut myself down into a perfectly pleasing woman.

We'd both sewn new dresses for the occasion, but my calico was brown—an unremarkable russet blended into the fading autumn world around us. Quite different than Ida's meticulous frock. While she had worked diligently, I'd sewed my dress in haste, rushing to get back to my reading. I'd just started a new law book and spending evenings sewing rather than studying was dreadful. Ida had measured precisely, keenly sewn, and gently stitched each seam. Even when Ida's hand cramped from hours of stitching, she simply sighed and gently massaged her aching palm, before continuing on. The patience I missed in my measuring was glaring. The sleeves now sat too short upon my arms. My exposed wrists were a reminder of the little things that made me all too different from my older sister. I'd loved my studies at the time but now felt embarrassed at my underwhelming appearance. I attempted to comfort myself by remembering how pointless it was to hope to feel special tonight. My role was to look after the youngest children while the adults indulged in their festivities. At best, I'd be watchful to make sure baby Peter did not spit up on my only calico. I hoped I'd get to spend a bit of time in the ballroom before my relegated task. I resolved to make the best of things.

Regardless of my dismal assignment, I truly couldn't wait to see inside the decorated Turner Hall. My sister and I made our way over the creaking planks of the wagon and down the ladder. I teased Ida: "Did you hem your dress to the perfect length for your waltz step?"

She shook her head as if to say "certainly not." Every time my envy flared for my sister, I remembered her terrible affliction, whatever horrible mystery had stolen her voice. I was flooded with a wave of guilt. My poor sister was a silent angel; my soundless confidant whose only fault was working too hard and doing things too well. To let jealousy consume me would make me a monster. And, I should be grateful to Ida—because she was so proficient in her chores, it made it easier for me to help in Pa's office. Ida hooked her arm around mine. Like the moon above, my jealousy waned, and the thrill of the evening overtook me. We skipped forward, in our Sunday-best boots, my heart beat cheerfully in step.

We made our way through the arched stone entryway. Arrangements of disfigured gourds, auburn squash, robust pumpkins, and crossed corn stalks decorated the entry. Candles of all sizes lit the way into the glowing central ballroom. I squeezed my sister's arm, and she gasped with elation to enter the space. The ballroom was beautiful, overflowing with a spirit of comradery and bounty. Mrs. Kuhn and Mrs. Schein rushed to greet us. They wore matching golden goose broaches atop their dresses to distinguish themselves. "The Sisters Heard. Welcome to the harvest dance and Celebration." Ida raised her eyebrows and nodded her head in appreciation.

"My sister and I are grateful to the Ladies of Ulm for the invitation to such a magnificent event," I said. Speaking for Ida was as instinctive as setting the water to boil in the morning. It was my automatic duty done without self-reflection or contemplation of a different way of being. Tonight, just the same as when I was five and Ida was six. And I expected it would remain that way until the end of time. Unless I *actually* left to teach. I didn't know a day without my mute sister; I could not imagine the world beyond her. My sister might well have been my right arm, I might well have been her voice box. We were stitched into each other's functioning. My insides turned with upset; to leave my sister would be unbearably painful. And my cruelty. If I were to leave, Ida would basically have her voice stolen again. Was my dream worth further injuring my sweetest sister?

"Emma, it's my understanding that you're assisting with the children tonight. You'll be in the front room," Mrs. Kuhn directed. My shoulders fell. I had just entered the beautiful space and already was being sent away. Ida looked at me with a genuine pity; she knew how disappointed I was about my unfortunate assignment. I viewed the dazzling room. Skirts were billowed as women twirled. Foam sloshed over the top of beer steins held by men clustered in boisterous groups. Everyone beamed with happiness. I suddenly felt like a girl about to cry. I wanted to run away, to hide in the corner, to refuse to be sent away. But I was well-practiced at silencing that internal whining voice. When I was little, Ma would hold her hand over my mouth when I was displeased, and scold, "You contain yourself until you can act like a lady." Ida didn't need a hand over her mouth, something deep inside of her learned to hold herself back long ago. Sometimes when I looked in Ida's eyes, I felt as if there were something I didn't quite know hidden deep within. A voice, perhaps, her voice my ears longed to hear. Mrs. Schein must have noticed the longing in my eyes, as she offered a brief reprieve. "Edith, we must let the girl try a dumpling before beginning her duties. There." Mrs. Schein pointed to the back corner.

I swallowed my distress and replied with a quiet, "Thank you so, Mrs. Schein."

I dropped my arm from Ida's side. I didn't look at her as I strode towards the back corner. Another Lady of Ulm, Mrs. Mayo, a physician's wife, greeted us as she scooped two steaming apple dumplings into a tin bowl. "Hello, Heard girls. Ida, this dress is exquisite. You look as if you are going out for a night in St. Paul." Mrs. Mayo said warmly, her golden brooch shimmering in the candlelight. She passed us the bowl to share and said, "Enjoy."

The perimeter of the room was lined with square bales of straw. We took a seat on a bale in the back. My resentment about missing out on the festivities surged. I wiggled in my too-small dress. It felt as restrictive as my duties. I took one bite of the lovely dumpling sprinkled with cinnamon and dripping in syrup. The familiar spice of fall danced in my mouth. It was so delightful I closed my eyes to savor the flavor. I battled feelings of delight and pain, knowing these would be my few special moments of the night. Not wanting to be greedy, I enjoyed the single sweet bite and passed the dish to my sister. She took the bowl and lightly tapped on my leg. I knew she was urging me to find a way to join her in the ballroom. "I can't! The children need looking after." I shook my head in irritation. She took my hand and squeezed. Though Ida couldn't communicate with words, we always seemed to understand one another. The tiniest changes in pressure meant something different between us; now I knew she cared. It wasn't Ida's fault I would miss out. I softened and squeezed gently back. She picked up the spoon to taste the dumplings. "They're delicious, aren't they?" I said. She continued eating.

I was always careful to contain my self-pity around Ida. She would never be able to call out that dinner was ready, sing lullabies to a babe in her arms, or burst into laughter. I couldn't remember when Ida had been a babbling baby or a toddler calling out to her twin. Nor do I remember the long trip to America where her voice slipped away, day by day, until one day she went silent forever. I do remember being small, Ida and I tucked beneath our quilt, and Ma saying fervent prayers that Ida's voice be restored. I used to sneak open my eyes, checking to see if my sister was consumed as the burning bush. She never was. I wondered if God heard our prayers. If he'd ever heard my prayers.

I could bear one evening of disappointment. There'd be another harvest dance next fall. I would sew a better dress, carefully measure the fabric, plan a matching ribbon for a bow in my hair. Or maybe by next year my dream would come true—I'd be away, working as a teacher! How proud I would be, to go from being relegated to watch over the sleeping children's room at the harvest dance to being an actual educator. Perhaps, I'd even be in a big city. I imagined dances happening every week in Iowa City . . . bustling streets, grand ballrooms. I'd make friends with other schoolteachers. It'd be so difficult to leave my sister. But sitting next to her even now, I still felt isolated. Who was I to this family? To this entire prairie town? If I were a teacher, my lonesomeness here could someday be a faraway memory.

I tucked my hands under my legs, feeling the scratchy straw beneath me. In the middle of the dance floor, Mr. Ulrich and Mr. Ayer sat, pulling their accordions wide then crunching them shut with joyous melodies. Uncle Allen was next to them, rosining up his bow. The music illuminated our faded memories of the homeland. German polka merrily floated through the space as dancing pairs crowded the floor. Ma and Pa talked to the Theobalds; laughing in unison. Otto was nearby, mixing with a group of other older boys. I recognized the girls near them, sitting on bales of hay, chattering and making eyes at the boys.

Soon, striding across the ballroom floor towards us was Otto's friend, a plain-looking fellow named Oskar Theobald. I tugged at my short sleeves. He made a warmhearted compliment, "Good evening, ladies. I do say, Emma and Ida must be the twins, not Otto."

Ida finished a bite of dumpling as we gave each other a quick glance. Oskar stood on long gangly legs, shifting his weight nervously. I didn't rescue him from the awkward silence. His gaze was fixed on Ida. "Ida, your Ma mentioned you were interested in some dancing this evening?" I sighed, my parents always found a way to push Ida to the front. She was their most prized daughter. I could feel the undercurrent of worry in my parent's behavior around my sister; they wanted her to make her way in this world. I never took up their thoughts, never mind any of their worries. I'd make my own way in this world while they weren't minding me.

Ida looked at me. I read the sparkle in her eyes and inelegantly interjected on her behalf, "Well, I don't believe the evening is called the Harvest Sit on the Hay, is it?" They both looked at me, the little sister, with pitiful bemusement. I motioned towards the opposite side of the room, "It's called the harvest *dance!*" In agreement, Oskar bowed and stretched out a hand to help Ida up. She reached up for his hand and passed me back the bowl as they headed for the dancefloor. Invisible to the eye but palpable between the melodies were the stirring desires of young adults whose slightest glances were heavy with longing.

The dance floor felt like it was miles away, a separate world I had missed an invitation to. I picked up the spoon to comfort myself with another bite of dumpling, only to find the bowl empty. Ida had finished every bite. I watched her take her first twirl on the dancefloor. Envy again ran through me. Perhaps, I realized, I was actually the one who was unable to speak about what I wanted. I was unfulfilled. I comforted myself with thoughts of my letter, tucked away in a mail stagecoach saddle bag, or sitting in a mailbag in some darkened Iowa General Store. I prayed my letter would bring me the potential that this ballroom couldn't.

The front room smelled earthy and damp; a single oil lantern sat on a dresser. A young German woman, who barely spoke a lick of English, was overseeing the room when I entered. I was carrying Peter, but she shoved another baby in my arms, bluntly demanding, "TAKE!" as she excused herself. I was alone, surrounded by children asleep on their parents' wool coats. I settled on the chilly window bench, holding baby Peter in one arm and an unfamiliar infant in the other. Their tiny warm bodies nestled into mine. The sounds of amusement from the ballroom rang distant from my lonely seat. A wave of discontent rushed over me. How could I be so close yet so far away from the most wondrous festivities of the year? I anticipated how awkward I'd feel tomorrow at church as everyone recalled their favorite memories of the dance. It was doubtful anyone would even remember I'd been present; perhaps it was for the better if no one remembered me at all.

I startled as the door burst open and light streamed in. Mrs. Ulrich, round as the pumpkins in the entryway, shuffled into the room. She mumbled, "I imagine some quiet would do me good," as she plopped herself on the floor. I was surprised at her pleasant and casual disposition; she was usually such a serious woman. A sticky sweet smell clouded the room; I remembered her fondness for black-berry brandy. The liquor had smoothed her temperament, not to the point of clouded judgment, but relaxation. She motioned for me to pass her the children. I was stunned. Was she willing to watch over the room?

"Get on, Emma. My knees can't keep up with dancing like they used to. And your sister shouldn't get to have all the fun." I was sur-prised. I never thought Mrs. Ulrich noticed the dynamic between my sister and me when we helped wash her laundry. Perhaps, the difficult woman was more perceptive than I realized.

I replied, "Thank you ten thousand times," as I passed her the children, who melted into her pillowlike body.

I reentered the ballroom. Uncle Allen was up out of his seat, chin tucked into his fiddle, pulling the bow with enthusiasm while people hollered with enjoyment. It was as animated as I ever saw my mild-mannered uncle. Couples danced round. Ma hurried over from the dance floor, cheeks flushed. "Emma girl!" The spirited fun made her unusually affectionate, and she gave me a kiss atop my forehead. "Are the children okay?"

"Yes, they're sleeping. Mrs. Ulrich is with them," I assured her.

"Oh, dear. Mrs. Ulrich will likely fall asleep, as well," my mother said with slight concern. I was scared Ma would point me back to look after the children. But the song changed, and her face lifted with glee. "I danced to this as a young girl. Come with me." She pulled me onto the dance floor. She stood clapping and hopping, dancing a polka I was unacquainted with. "Emma, move with me," she said and began teaching me the steps. She wasn't my demanding mother giving instruction on the farm. She was Anna. The song had transported her back to being a young girl in Germany. She took my hand. I laughed with her as I tripped over my feet.

The room buzzed around us. Ida and Otto stood with friends. Elderly neighbors sat on bales of hay, watching the younger folk. The hearty twanging smell of sauerkraut and dumplings wafted through the space. I was so grateful to be in the midst of the magic. My anger in the other room now felt embarrassing. There were so many cheery faces, it was almost like being at church, but also a bit the opposite. There was no lecturing sermon, no sin fretted about. Everyone was together in joyful spirit and thanksgiving. In the corner stood Pastor Vogel. He was speaking with a rugged-looking young man, slightly older than Otto. I didn't recognize him. Pa ran over and jigged in front of us. I burst with amusement at his fanciful footwork. My cheeks ached from laughter; I looked at my beautiful mother and handsome father dancing with me, and it was a precious moment in which I felt so special to be their daughter.

Suddenly, the spirit of the room lifted even higher. Uncle Allen's fiddle sang out familiar notes: it was the Polka Do-Si-Do! The dance-floor roared with enjoyment as we recognized the tune. The dance was an eight-count partner square-dance. We skipped in time, finding our partners, right arm out and bent up toward the rafters, adjoining arms, and dancing around, kicking our heels, moving in little duos round and round in the same direction. Every eight counts, we spun in wonderful disorder, finding a new companion for the next series. Curly-haired Farmer Krause and I matched first, then I paired with Hanna, a friend from school.

The momentum of the song whirled me around the room. Another tilt in the music was our prompt to change partners. I was spinning amusingly about when a man's arm seamlessly connected with mine. Our forearms aligned, and his rough hand took mine. In a moment quicker than a quarter note, our eyes met, and the lively room slowed around us. A shiver ran through my body down into the heels of my boots. It was the strong-featured stranger who had been talking to Pastor Vogel in the corner. His dark brown eyes were unfamiliar and mesmerizing; my legs weakened as the eight-count pulled me forward. It felt as if the accordion was squeezing inside my chest. The entire night transformed in one locked arm spin. Our moment was one I had never shared with any man before. As quickly as the music connected us, the beat paused, partners changed, and it took us apart.

Mrs. Schein hooked my arm, and with force spun me in a circle as she belly-laughed with amusement. I scanned the room to spot where the young man had gone, but he disappeared in the dizzying swirl of swapping partners. I couldn't find him in the mix. The song finished; we all clapped in unison. Mr. Ulrich and Mr. Ayer nodded as their accordions pressed the rich reedy harmony of a slow three count waltz. Older adults coupled up for the formal dance.

I walked over and sat on an open bale. I was breathless, still scan-ning for the young man. My heart filled with curiosity and interest.

Otto sat beside me, knocking into my side. His energetic charm had only grown in all the attention of the evening. He beamed, "Who're you looking for, sister? You appear as if you've just seen Jesus Christ in the flesh." Jesus had never captivated me in the way this man did. The room was full of townspeople; I wasn't able to find the stranger in the crowd. The moment was just a minute ago. Was it real?

A wave of woozy disenchantment blended with my trembling heartstrings. "I'm not sure what I am looking for, Otto. Perhaps I've had a bit too much spinning for one evening."

"Too much spinning? No such thing," my brother said as he pulled me to my feet and twirled me around. I laughed but still wished to lock with the stranger's deep brown eyes again. It was such an unfamiliar feeling. Such a forceful connection striking in an instant, then gone. I wondered if I had just dreamed the encounter; maybe I'd confused myself. I pushed away the impractical feelings and refocused on the easygoing waltz with Otto. I knew my brother would be waltzing in this room at every harvest dance for years to come. I didn't know where I would be in the coming years. I felt I was destined for something different. Part of me wished I could settle into the dance that was life here. Learn the steps. Comply as Otto and Ida seem to do so easily. A warmth spread through me at the thought of my siblings. How could I love people so much that I was willing to walk away from?

NINE

Oenikika

December 31, 1861

Snow sizzled as it hit the hot kettle. Aunt Mika, Owl Woman and I sat with the morning mending, while Wenona stirred a heavy ladle through the steaming kettle at the centerfire of her tipi. The tipi flap was pushed open, a frigid wind blew into the room. Tashunke's large body crouched at the opening. My lungs took in the chilled air as energy hummed in my chest at the sight of him. Why would he come to a tipi of women? Was it possible he was coming to ask me to walk with him? Breaking Up had asked just yesterday and I'd grudgingly gone. For a second, I let myself wish Tashunke would ask me.

"Good morning," he said to the group. "My mare suffered a sprain."

I swallowed; I felt a sting of disappointment that he hadn't come to walk with me.

He continued to speak. "I am hoping for a medicine that would help her."

A hope lifted my spirit when I realized he sought the thing I cared about most—plants of healing. My heart stirred impossibly as

Tashunke's eyes were upon me. But Wenona looked to her mother, the keeper of medicine.

Aunt Mika sighed. "I have nothing." The reservation hadn't many plants and the winter had been hard.

My mind spun as I thought through the medicines in my baskets. "I have comfrey," I said, confidently. Tash nodded and stepped back, closing the tipi door. I quickly stood and grabbed my long buffalo robe; I'd need to fetch the plants from the house on the bluff.

"Too bad Breaking Up or Red Otter didn't think to ask her for medicine," Wenona clucked to my grandmother and Aunt. "Then they'd actually get the attention of my impossible to win cousin."

I pulled my hair back and drew up my hood, as I explained, "Comfrey is important. It will help with a sprain." But I couldn't help but match the twinkle in my cousin's eyes as I departed; my family's warm laughter trailed me as I stepped into the chilly brightness of the winter day.

Tashunke stood outside his tipi at the far edge of camp circle, holding the lead of a palomino mare. My moccasins sent up puffs of snow with every step towards them as I carried a cup of the comfrey paste. My hands had trembled as I had mixed the plants and warm water up in our white man's house. I'd shared healing medicines before . . . but bringing them to Tashunke made me nervous in a way I'd never felt. I didn't feel annoyed, encroached upon, anxious for space as I did with the other young men. With Tash, I felt . . . excited. Eager. But I couldn't focus on those preoccupying feelings. I must think of my task. Focus on healing. Center myself.

As I neared Tash and his horse, I could see the mare was pained in her front right hoof, lifting it out of the snow.

"This is Wicapi," he said.

I stood near Tash, opening my beaver-fur mittened hands to

reveal the cup of comfrey. Wicapi reached her neck out, leaning her soft nose to the warm mug I was holding. Her nostrils took in the smell of the medicine, then moved to my face, rubbing her nose to my cheek.

"This is Oenikika," Tash explained to his mare.

She moved her nose over me again. Her sniffs felt like an evaluation. I was standing in a sacred space; Tashunke's and her connection was a precious place I was being allowed to enter. Finally, her head hung calmly between us, and her bothersome leg became the focus.

I crouched with the cup and took off my mittens. I used two fingers to spread the comfrey paste over the swollen leg above her hoof and wrapped a piece of leather around the medicine, securing it with a bit of buffalo tendon tie. I held my hand upon the leather, closed my eyes, and prayed.

Pushing up to stand, I looked to Wicapi. Her dark eyes closed heavy with relaxation, as if she were starting to sleep. Tashunke rubbed her tired face.

"Thank you," Tash said, his face serious and intense. His gratitude felt like he'd genuinely appreciated my help. My calling. Me.

My legs felt unusually weak as I adjusted my stance in the snow. For a moment, I nervously wanted to fill the space between us . . . explain the comfrey. That it should soon help Wicapi bear weight. Reduce her inflammation. But my breath clouded out in the chilly air, and I watched the man and his horse stand connected. He knew his horse; he didn't need a long explanation from me to understand her.

I patted her shoulder as I departed. Walking away, my heart stirred with an invigorating encouragement. Tashunke had sought me out. Something inside of me seemed to know, he understood me too.

January 20, 1862

Women stood, huddled with our backs to the harsh wind. I pulled my thick cloak in tighter around me and leaned into Aunt Mika. Today was finally the day of the food distribution from the treaty agreement. The missionary Riggs had confirmed delivery; he'd translated for my father when they rode together to the white man's trading place. This Riggs was well-liked by my father. Riggs rarely mentioned the white man's God to him. It was pleasant but unusual; still, I didn't trust it. We had gathered for food delivery like this four times already, each time assured, *guaranteed*, that the whites would arrive with provisions. Yet the white traders never showed; their words were as empty as my stomach. We'd been stretching our dried berries and venison as our only nourishment for the past five moons. Owl Woman was frail and unable to keep warm. I'd given her my portions of dried venison this morning. Brown Wing had asked my father for permission to leave the reservation to go hunting; Little Crow denied him, saying we needed to keep our word to stay on the reservation. But I saw how my father's eyes moved back and forth in the sky. I knew he was having many thoughts, probably considering what he would do if the traders didn't show again today with their promised provisions. I hoped the supply would have plenty of meat. That's what we needed in winter.

Chief Wabasha and Chief Traveling Hail arrived on horseback from the east with some of their men. The two were opposites, Chief Wabasha was dressed like a white man as most of his band had "converted" to farming ways. He'd been gaining influence and power among some of our people. Our men immediately began laughing among themselves at the sight of Wabasha in pants and boots. It was poor manners to make fun of a chief, so I did not find their immature mocking amusing. Internally, I was defensive. My father, the chief, lived in a white man's house. If they would disrespect Wabasha, they could do the same to my father.

Chief Traveling Hail, my mother's brother, though living on the reservation, had rejected the farming ways as he wanted to remain in traditional life. He was dressed in his powwow cloak, decorated with quills and beads. I knew right away it was a message to my father and Chief Wabasha as if to say "I am the most Dakota chief of you all!" Father walked between the two contrasting chiefs. He knew the tension was building . . . everyone's stomachs hungry. I knew Father would try to keep the peace. Though I didn't show it, something inside of me felt proud seeing my uncle in his beautiful cloak. While my father hadn't started farming, he had given up our tipi, and I felt betrayal in that. I didn't want to convert to the white man's ways. Their house. Their clothing. Their farming. Their religion. I watched Uncle Traveling Hail. His intensity. It felt like he understood my instincts, my desire to reunite our people.

The chiefs stood together with the other men, and the women gathered, waiting for the distribution. I hated the feeling . . . our dependence on this delivery. On the white men. I knew the feeling of riding free. I was independent in my soul; anything but freedom for our people made me sick to my stomach. But yet I stood here today awaiting another white man promise as the frigid winds felt like they blew right through my cloak. Our hunger was stronger than the cold. Seeing Tashunke cloaked in his magnificent black bear blanket didn't even bring me the brightness it usually did. We waited and waited, anxiously anticipating nourishment, as the winter sun slowly crept across the sky.

Just as I was about to give up hope, two enormous horses pulling a sleigh emerged at the top of the bluff. It moved closer and glided to a stop in front of us. We could see the back was stacked high with crates. The tension in my spirit loosened, my heart lifted with relief—food and supplies were finally here. One of the white men, a rat-looking man with a mustache, spoke harshly with Missionary Riggs in their language. The second man, a giant counterpart to the rat, carelessly kicked crates off the back of the sled. I stood aghast; this delivery was precious, and the man kicked at them like meaningless discards. Riggs walked towards my father, shaking his head, appearing frustrated with his encounter with his own kind. After all the crates were offloaded, the two men sat at the front of the sleigh and cued the horses forward. The sled circled back to the northeast.

Left in front of us were a dozen toppled crates, lying about in the frozen earth. We all stood a moment. We follow tradition: the men hunted, women gathered and prepared. I was unsure what we should do in this situation . . . Should the men take the crates? Was this the same as hunting? Or was this gathering for the women? Everyone seemed to look to Little Crow, me included. My father nodded to Aunt Mika, Wenona, and me. The women would unpack the crates. Wenona and I walked to a container and pried it open. Icy frost clung to a hard block of frozen meat. My stomach rolled with hunger. Our provision was finally here. Wenona wiped at it with her fox mittens. The frozen grayish meat had yellow lumps all over. What kind of meat was this? Pale with creamy yellow bulges . . . Suddenly, my eyes made sense of the sight. The yellow bumps were maggots frozen into the meat. This couldn't be! The meat was rotten. Inedible. Soon as it would thaw, the smell alone would poison our camp. Wenona and I looked at each other in disbelief. We were desperate for this food. Wenona continued to frantically scrape off the icy burn built up along the crate. She revealed some kind of plants which had been packed along with the meat. Those too were now a brown frozen mush into the bottom of the crate. This food was rancid. Completely spoiled. As if it had sat out for months, been remembered in the winter, and brought here without any care.

"Liars." Wenona hissed into the air as we watched the sleigh disappear over the top of the slope. As others around us popped off the tops of their crates, their eyes all rose and looked about in hopeless misery. The delivery we had been so eager for would be of no help. There was not enough food for the long winter. My heart felt as hollow as my stomach. My body shivered in the unrelenting cold. I thought of Owl Woman; we had to get her food. Our people had never been in this position. A frantic thought ran through my mind. I remembered where the squirrels had buried their acorns . . . Could I scrape through the snow and frozen earth and find them for my grandmother?

Chief Traveling Hail hollered at Chief Wabasha, "We needed you on the hunting mission this fall! Instead you sat, digging at the earth like a foolish rodent. Now, what do you have to show for your farming?" Wabasha shook his head. I trembled with my own disgrace, as I had just thought to find food like a foolish rodent. Traveling Hail continued fiercely, "The white man's promises are the worms in the stomach of our people."

"What do I tell Kimimela and Wolfchaser? They're so hungry. I promised . . ." Wenona's voice choked in her words. I'd never seen Wenona cry before. I worried about her stomach, as well. She was eating for two; she must be the hungriest of us all.

"We will find more food. We will," I said to Wenona with as much certainty as I could muster. Though I had no actual plan, I had determination. As much determination as a foolish rodent. I would do whatever it took to provide for the youngest and oldest among us.

My heart pounded. This was not sufficient. My father finished discussing this matter seriously with Riggs, who must be translating his exchange with the Rat Trader. I hated that we had to depend on a white man to understand the white man. But I was thankful we had this missionary in these desperate times. He would attempt to make himself useful.

Aunt Mika pleaded with her brother, "Can we use the gold payment to purchase food from the white man?"

"The gold payment was kept from us. To pay off debts . . . Debts they say we owe. It is unclear where these came from. Our next payment comes in the spring." The other chiefs jumped up in anger. It was outrageous. Every payment that had been promised for our move to the reservation was kept from us.

"Spring? My people will starve," Traveling Hail exclaimed.

"The Great White Father has lied. We will send a hunting party to the far west." Little Crow looked to the other two chiefs; it was unclear if my father meant he would violate the treaty and go off the reservation, or ride so far west the hunting party went beyond the white man's land. I suspected he phrased it vaguely on purpose. "Traveling Hail and Wabasha, send your best hunters at sunrise."

The men and women began to mix, wandering crate to hopeless crate, hoping one held something—anything—of sustenance. I stared at the container in front of me. Fear began to itch under my skin. Crawl out from my inside of me. My entire being was rejecting this new existence. Our people were truly at risk on this reservation. The four walls of the crate, they had trapped what was supposed to give us life. What could have sustained us. I would never trust the white man's four walls. I had to get out.

As I was growing more despondent, Aunt Mika came to me. "Niece, Chief Wabasha says there is a grove of birch trees a half days ride south of his village. I proposed we would split any chaga we find growing at their roots. Will you ride with me?"

Chaga, the hard-woody fungus that grows thick on the birch. It wouldn't fill our stomachs for long, but it was rich in nutrients. It could hold us over until the hunting party returned. I didn't need a moment to think. "I'll find an ax," I said with determination to my aunt.

"I'll prepare the horses," she replied.

I saw my father across the group and began moving towards the chief, ready to ask for an ax. But a man wrapped in a long bear blanket crossed in front of me. I stopped and looked up at Tashunke.

Desperation and conviction awoke a boldness in me. "I am going in search of chaga. I'll need an . . ." and before I could finish my request, Tashunke was reaching inside his cloak and pulling out a painted ax. I nodded as I accepted the tool for my mission; my hand felt the warmth of his as it brushed in the handoff in the frozen hopeless morning and I glanced at his face in thanks. As I began to step away, a different set of eyes caught with mine.

My father was at a distance, but he was looking straight at Tashunke and me. In the terrible morning, I hoped he saw me. A daughter determined. A daughter focused upon her people. A daughter who knew what she needed.

TEN

Emma Heard

January 18, 1862

It wasn't long after the harvest dance that the first winter storm took town in a fury. The world was buried in a thick blanket of white, tree branches bending under the heavy snow. Long coats, flannel scarves, and lined wool mittens were taken out of trunks for the season. On this bright January day, it took all of my focus to stroke my pen carefully, depositing the ink in perfect looped symmetry on the fibrous paper. I had assured my father that my penmanship, refined in Miss Knudsen's classroom, was sufficient to help him with record keeping in the office. With the influx of settlers on the prairie, copies of land patents, records, and deeds were demanded at a wrist-breaking pace. My father's left-handedness slowed him; any aggravating smear of the dark ink made him holler in frustration. My cleaning and tidying had significantly improved the office; my offer to assist him in record keeping was taken up with little hesitation. I felt a bit selfish, continuing in the office. But Ma and Ida moved through the day's chores in flawless synchronicity. Now when I helped at home, I felt even more inept in Ida's wake. In the rhythm of the day's chores,

I tangled up their flow. It was a similar teamwork with my father. We had a pattern to our day, a routine for my assistance. And I felt strong in the office, something inside of me was solid and able. The work kept my mind going through the maddeningly dull months of winter. Homestead plots on the prairie had been divided and purchased. Requests for land continued to pour in; even more settlers expected by spring. Reams of paper with the preprinted contract, delivered to "THE OFFICE OF ATTORNEY HEARD" read:

THE UNITED STATES OF AMERICA

Certificate No. _____

To all whom these Presents shall come, Greeting:

Whereas, _____ has been deposited in the GENERAL LAND OFFICE of the United States a Certificate of the Register of the Land Office at _____ whereby it appears:

Warrant No. _____ for _____ acres in favor of

_____

with evidence that the same has been duly located upon

_____.

According to the Official Plat of the Survey of said Lands returned to the GENERAL LAND OFFICE by the SURVEYOR GENERAL _____

NOW KNOW YE, That there is therefore granted by the UNITED STATES unto said _____

_____

tract of Land above described: TO HAVE AND TO HOLD the said tract of Land with the appurtenances thereof unto the said _____

heirs and assigns forever.

In testimony, whereof, I _____

PRESIDENT OF THE UNITED STATES OF AMERICA
have caused the letters to be made Patent and Seal of the
General Land office to be hereunto affixed. GIVEN under my
hand, at the City of Washington the _____ of _____
in the year of our Lord one thousand eight hundred and ____ ,
and of the Independence of the United States of the _____

_____

BY THE PRESIDENT:

By _____ Sec'y _____ Recorder of the General
Land Office

My father documented individual purchase details in the blank
spaces. I would then record a copy for the landowner. The origi-
nal was sent east to be signed by the president himself. My father
explained proudly, "This patent is a contract as good to God as to
man. It will last till the end of time, without question. Any alter-
ation or addendum must be reviewed and approved by an attorney.
This is the absolute power of law; its dignity is what separates man
from beast." The pages as presented were as powerful as the scrip-
tures of the Holy Bible. The responsibility of these documents was
tremendous. My privilege to participate, even just as a recorder, was
wondrous. It felt as if I were in the classroom again, but with an independence to my diligent work. I was no longer a little girl sitting at a
school desk now, both my feet sat sturdily on the floor as I worked. I
was growing in so many ways.

In secret, I felt the penmanship practice on these contracts would be useful if I were to be a teacher someday. I wondered where my letter to Miss Knudsen had found itself. It had been long months of waiting with no reply. I read *Leaves of Grass* every night to comfort myself. I stared at the beautiful hardcover—*my* book. Proof Miss Knudsen had been real—not a figment of my imagination, real as the words on the page. I was beginning to have a creeping fear that the correspondence was altogether lost. Or that she did not agree that my merits qualified me for the profession. Perhaps she still remembered the mistakes I had made in my lessons; I couldn't forget the day I misspelled "exemplary" as "examplery" in my oral exam. My fourteen-year-old cheeks flamed with embarrassment; they flamed with the memory now. If I were a teacher, I could never misspell such simple words in front of my classroom. Maybe Miss Knudsen wished Ida could speak, Ida would be the loveliest teacher. I felt a wave of guilt at my inherent abilities allowing me chances my sister would never know. Places she'd never go. But Miss Knudsen had made *me* feel like the special one. The little things; quietly advancing me in my lessons to the grade above my own. She'd given me her own Walt Whitman book. How I wished she could see me now—stacks of completed legal documents at my side. I desperately wanted her to know how I had studied my father's law books every evening. She'd be proud of each chance I had taken to learn. But there was little hope of a response in the coming months; ponies struggled to carry mail through the debilitating snowdrifts of the plains, and dark blizzards overtook the sky with no warning, so in the winter the mail delivery was infrequent or halted altogether. At church, I prayed my aspiration of becoming a teacher would someday be possible. Now I worried that prayer was going as unanswered as Ma's despairing petitions over my silent sister.

By December, I'd moved the far table in the office closer to the fireplace. Winter's frigidity seeped in; I scooted my chair close to the warm hearth as I worked on my duplicate patent. Ma hadn't objected to my increased duties in Pa's office. While farm chores didn't cease during winter, they certainly slowed, and Pa was convinced my contributions would make the law office profitable through the bleak wintertime months. My worth was measurable. I felt special boarding the sleigh with my father each dark winter morn.

The forsaken north winds shrieked through the barren town and blasted the office windows with swirls of confused snow. My mind drifted back to the glowing October dance floor. I could still feel the stranger's warm hand on mine. His eyes were intelligent and wild. The moment was still so vivid. I'd looked about the pews in church, hoping to catch a glimpse of him. My distracting memory had turned me silly: once, in early November, I ran out like a fool to the cornfield to see which men Otto was talking to. To no avail. Embarrassed, I pretended I thought they had called my name. I was sixteen years old, preoccupied by a do-si-do spin from months ago. The man remained the stranger I could only know in a brief memory. But how useless to waste my mind on such matters. What I really wanted was to teach, anyway.

I wrestled with my two secret hopes: becoming a teacher and finding out the identity of my dance partner. These things that had lit a fire inside of me were now as frozen as the snow-buried tundra. The thought of the mail moving again atop a springing green prairie felt like a lifetime away. But I would forge ahead, making flawless copies of land patents, the patchworked prairie being divvied up into perfect squares. I looped the final script and set another finished contract on my growing stack.

April 5, 1862

Though winter's will had seemed unending, eventually the days lengthened, and the edges of rooftops dripped with snowmelt. I was in the office; Father was busy discussing road maintenance with a small group. I excused myself to venture out for a midday break. I wondered if the new issue of land patent forms would be delivered soon. Father and I had worked through nearly the entire ream in the winter months. I walked down the street past Turner Hall. I had been hopeful to see a response arrive from Miss Knudsen now that the mail was running regularly. But there was no word from Iowa City. I gladdened myself with the lovely weather. The spring sun had reemerged, and its rays kissed my face as I pulled back my bonnet, basking in its return. The sun instantly heated the top of my hair. The spring season was reviving the town that had been in hibernation. I was relishing my break when I heard a familiar voice call out, "Emma!"

With my hand at my brow to block the bright sun, I saw three young ladies sitting in rocking chairs on the porch of the Kuhn's impressive Victorian home. I waved and called out, "Good morning."

Hanna Kuhn beckoned for me to join them. "We were *just* talking about you," she said with a slight smile, Elsa and Charlotte seemed to be in on something too. "We've not seen a single one of you Heards in the last week."

"You must know we're preparing for planting season. Everyone has been mightily busy," I explained.

"Obviously, we most want to see Otto." Charlotte boldly stated. They all giggled. I self-consciously joined in too. In the last few months, Charlotte managed to work Otto into every conversation we had. And today, she wasn't shy about why. I again felt like the awkward little sister. Otto and Ida were on the cusp of adulthood. Besides the one fleeting moment on the dance floor, I hadn't tipped into this world yet.

"He'll be busy with planting for another few days" I said, "at least." I was used to the "group think" of these three. Some days it felt like too much to be in their presence. But other days, they were entertaining, and I couldn't help but laugh along with their snide observations and cheeky comments.

"I hope he'll say hello at Sunday service," Hanna responded.

"Pass that along to him from us," Charlotte said.

Charlotte's particular fondness for Otto was exhausting. I didn't feel it necessary to continue discussing my older brother. I turned to Elsa and asked, "How are things at the brewery this spring?" Schein's brewery was one of the most profitable businesses in all of Minnesota territory, maybe even on the whole frontier. "When times are going well a man needs a beer, and if times are worse he needs two," Pa would say. "Those are some promising economics."

"Quite well, I do believe," Elsa said warmly. As always, I wished Elsa wasn't flanked by Charlotte and Hanna. Her eyes were eternally kind and when she laughed, even at the mean jokes, it seemed more about a lighthearted amusement than a cruel attempt to make herself feel better than anyone else. "Pa is hosting a meeting at the courthouse next week. My entire family will be there. Make sure you all come. Ida too."

At the edge of the block, a chestnut-colored Thoroughbred turned from State Street onto our stretch of Washington Street. The girls turned their heads and I leaned against the porch rail. Something was foreign yet familiar about the sight of this rider. The horse's shod feet sunk in the soggy roadway as its steps made a slow clip-clopping sound. The young man looked more like a fur trader of lore than any farmer in the area. His long buffalo leather coat was open in the mid-morning heat, revealing a white shirt unbuttoned halfway down his chest. His skin was tan, his hair a dirty blonde. His chin was covered with the stubble of a man who lived in the woods.

"It's Stephen Riggs," Hanna whispered under her breath to us. As he made his way down the block, he cast his gaze up toward the porch. In an instant the world seemed to slow. One of his strong hands held the reins, the other rested on the worn leather of his saddle horn. I immediately recognized him. It was the man whose hand had matched mine, spinning round, months ago. I felt a dizzying stir. I was torn between hiding, not wanting to be seen, and greatly wanting to look in his eyes again.

"G'morn, ladies," he said, lifting his hand to tip his wide-brimmed hat.

"G'mornin, Missionary," Charlotte hollered back with a twinkle in her eye. The man nodded to us all, but in the quickest blink as he scanned the group politely, his eyes connected with mine. I knew him without doubt, but I couldn't tell if he had any memory of the girl in the russet-colored dress. The spring warmth danced between us as the name "Stephen Riggs" imprinted inside of me. But time continued on; he and his steed made their way down the block.

He was barely out of earshot when Charlotte snickered, "And all you ladiesss," she mimicked his inflection, "realize that he is *married* to Jesus. Every missionary marries the Lord God before they go live with the Indians," she said with a snobbish certainty. I seared with annoyance; she always acted like she knew more than anyone else. And she had little understanding of who this man really was. In reality, I did not know him either. But I felt like my shared moment with him months ago had some kind of truth in it.

While they laughed in unison, I grappled with the fact he wasn't a fictional character of my exaggerated recollection. There he was. In the flesh. Riding down the middle of the street. Perhaps he wouldn't remain a stranger. Spring awakened the vivid memory I had thought was lost in the winter wind. I laughed along to mask my internal overwhelm. But I realized that as I shared the laughter—I must appear to be a town girl, standing on this porch. He would think me shallow and spoiled. I shuddered as the group carried on.

"Well, that's just plain incorrect. It's the Catholic nuns who marry Jesus, Charlotte," Elsa corrected her.

"Someone didn't pay enough attention to Pastor Vogel's teaching on Religions of the World." Hanna giggled.

"Oh please, do not act as if you heed that old man's lessons any differently than I do." Charlotte rolled her eyes. "I want to wipe the crusty spit from the corners of his mouth when he preaches."

We laughed again. Ma would smack me right across the face if she heard me laugh at someone making fun of a man of God. I was ashamed that I shared in the humor. I wasn't an overindulged town girl. I was from the Heard farm. Although recently I had been spending the most time in my father's office. So maybe I wasn't entirely a farm girl anymore. I wasn't sure exactly how to define myself; it didn't seem I quite fit anywhere. I looked down the block and caught sight of Riggs turning at the next block. My sense of myself was as muddled as the mushy spring road.

I excused myself and stepped down the porch stairs. I wanted to get back to the office. I knew who I was and what I needed to do when I was there; I was my father's helper. The solid feel of the pen scratching over paper. Someone important. If I had a classroom, I could live in this feeling. A teacher knows who they are. If I were a teacher, I would finally know myself.

ELEVEN

Oenikika

May 13, 1862

A soft rain fell outside as Owl Woman and I prepared the evening meal at the fireplace. I'd never been so grateful for the Moon of the Green Leaves. The hard winter had worn on us all; but under this moon strength returned to my bones and the earth was warm and providing again. The midwinter hunt had brought us a few deer and antelope; Aunt Mika and I had successfully collected chaga . . . the Great Spirit provided just enough to keep us alive after the Liars' Delivery. I watched as Owl Woman's shaky hands struggled to flip the fish in the sizzling pan.

"Let me help," I said lovingly as I turned the browning filets. I was quick to look for ways to help her these days. Something about the winter had changed Grandmother; her back now curved like a hunter's bow, pulled to an arch before the arrow's release. Even in the spring light, Owl Woman's eyes looked eternally tired. I knew Grandmother was getting older, but she had been like time itself, moving slowly and steadily. Each day familiar and indistinguishable from the last. But as I stepped back now and watched the beautiful

Owl Woman, I could see many winters of her life had passed, this last one the longest. I filled with adoration when I looked at her. Our caretaking roles had unspokenly shifted; I now took the lead. Somewhere inside of me, I knew our shared moments were precious as the colors of a fleeting sunset. Time has pulled her, as it pulls us all, steadily closer to the earth.

Little Crow sat at the window, watching the evening drizzle, eating his fish. We had prepared his serving first, as is custom. The sunset burst through a break in the clouds, lighting the room in an orangey radiance as the rain continued to dance on the rooftop. I plated Grandmother's meal and passed it to her, then fixed my own. I savored the flakey white fish, grateful for the nourishment. At the start of each mealtime, I felt a rush of anxiety, as if the food in front of me could disappear. I couldn't forget how hollow my stomach had been just a few moon cycles ago. I had always known the seasons to shift the availability of our resources . . . but this winter the white man's lies had made the sharpness of the winter season worse than anything we'd ever known. At the spring thaw, we took back some of our power. The three of us tonight enjoying a quiet meal was almost perfect. Except for the white man's walls and the lingering memories of just how hungry we'd been . . .

My father stood up abruptly at the window and looked outside. As I heard a horse whinny, Father walked across the room and out the door. Who'd be visiting in a sunset rain? I looked at Owl Woman and crinkled my brow, questioning. She looked back and said, "Be a modest woman and remain seated. This is for your father to decide." Her response confused me . . . Grandmother had never called me a woman before. What was she sensing?

In a swift moment of comprehension, my heart froze in my chest . . . Could it be an offer? Grandmother had sensed something, giving me quick womanly guidance to stay calm and in place. My hands began to tremble holding my plate. Though my stomach suddenly wasn't hungry, I knew better than to waste a single bite, and quickly finished the last morsels. The moment was so overwhelming. I adjusted my skirt to lie smoothly under my legs and sat up. I couldn't bear my curiosity . . . who was here? *Please, not Red Otter* . . . he'd been lingering near the riverside when I gathered water every day. If Wenona had said anything to encourage it, I'd be furious. She knew I had no fondness for him. The door swung open, and I couldn't help but lean to my side and peer out. I saw my father standing on the porch, and beyond him, a hand was holding onto a rope leading a magnificent bay horse. I could see the hand . . . I couldn't take it. I must know! Desperately, I leaned myself over, practically tipping completely onto my side until I could see him. Tashunke. My mind searched and my soul hoped . . . If he wanted to speak with Father about hunting or another matter, he'd do it when the men were smoking pipe. Could he want to make an offer? Why else would he come up the bluff in the evening? A horse was a generous offering for a wife, especially in difficult times like these. I could barely believe it . . . I tipped farther yet and fell to my elbow where I saw that each of Tashunke's hands held onto lead ropes. A gray horse was at his other side. *Two* horses. My heart fluttered in my chest, more than a chickadee flapping its wings—as if an entire flock of chickadees lifted to the air, taking flight, at once. It was incredible. I had prayed for this moment, and here it had found me so unexpectedly on a rainy evening.

I sat back upright, wishing I could open my ears wider to hear Tashunke and Father's discussion . . . I could hear my father's even tone, his voice speaking slowly, casually, but I couldn't make out the words of their conversation. "This is not for you to hear, Oenikika. Be a respectful daughter." Owl Woman patted the ground next to her, calling me over. I scooted towards her, my body tense, awaiting my father's acceptance of the offer. "Who is the suitor?" my grandmother whispered.

"Tashunke," I said quietly. It was so wonderful. My eyes brimmed with hopeful tears. "With *two* horses." She nodded favorably. She knew my hope.

Moments dragged on as I sat in obedience. I began to fear . . . my father was not immediately accepting Tash's impressive offer. Chief Little Crow was *slowly* taking his time to evaluate, as always. I simmered with frustration. Father had to accept this offer. I'd given him no indication I was displeased or unwilling to partner with Tashunke. I wanted to leap out of my seat on the floor and tell Tash we, *I*, accepted him. But that was not my place, so I sat in excruciating stillness on the floor, contemplating the wonderfully generous offer of two horses from the most talented man who'd entered our territory. This could be the perfect opportunity to bind him with our tribe. It should be a simple "Yes." If Father rejected him, Tashunke could continue on his way and leave us. The stakes were raised in my heart even more impossibly. My father *must* accept. The vermilion orange of sunset disappeared, the dimming sky changing the room to a dull gray.

Father walked closer back to the doorway . . . I could hear him telling a familiar story and my heart trembled. "It is the bird who sings too loudly in the first warm day breaking winter. The bird sings, it is so beautiful . . . Everyone wants to believe winter is gone. But we know our winter. It takes more than one warm day to break. Soon another storm rolls across the sky and buries the world again in snow. We know the first to sing are the foolish birds who will not survive." I'd heard this story before, and the tears in my eyes changed from hope to devastation. Father turned around to face Tashunke to deliver a final message. "Your chief does not accept this offer."

My spirit felt like it was crumbling, caving in, my whole being devastated. Father stood while Grandmother and I sat; the white man's house filled with definitive silence. I stared ahead, in disbelief, at the planks of the floor. I couldn't look at him. My father was trapping me here forever. As the rain fell harder outside, I heard his footsteps move back out the doorway. The rooftop pounded with hefty drops that matched the pounding in my spirit. It took everything in me to keep from crying out. I finally stood, picked up my plate and Grandmother's, quickly rinsed them in the washtub. My hands moved over the dishes while my mind slipped farther into hopeless thoughts. This will ruin me. The walls have ruined the woman I could be. My father did not understand. I stacked the plates in their place. My legs felt weak, and my eyes couldn't hold back the tears. I was done.

"I am ill. I'm going to sleep early," I said, as I collapsed on my bed in the corner. I did feel ill. Tashunke had asked for me. He'd seen me. It was all I had yearned for . . . and we would never be. My hope curled into a snake around my heart. Twisting, tightening. I pulled up my blankets, turned my back to the room, and trembled in devastation. Why did Father tell the story about the bird who sings on the first warm day of winter? Had he rejected Tashunke just because it was the first offer for me? Two horses! What more could my father want?

I heard Owl Woman as she shuffled nearer and eased herself down beside me. She tenderly ran her hands through my hair, the edges of her weathered hands catching my tears, pulling them back into my hairline. I'd never actually heard of a father denying an offer for a willing daughter. I could not believe this was my fate. Grandmother leaned into my ear. "Hold on, Oenikika. Trust your father."

"He doesn't understand, Grandmother," I said. This was beyond disappointment. I felt anger. Father was taking everything of meaning in my life. My village. My people. And now, taking away my future as a wife to Tashunke. It was not as a good daughter would do, to have such rage at her father. But I hated him in this moment. Soon as I felt the fire, I knew why the Medicine Man says peace is the power of the healer. Rage would burn up my connection to the healing earth. Then the shame buried me. To be a bad daughter. I was ruining myself. My sorrow and rage were dragging me deep into hopelessness.

"Hold on," she repeated as she stroked my hair. My heart ached. Why must Father make *everything* into a lesson? Be the most powerful man, always. In each interaction using his influence. *He keeps me here. These walls keep me here. These walls suffocate my life.*

"Tashunke understands me," I said as tears stung my eyes, and I remembered how free and hopeful I once felt riding through open grassland. "I want to ride again." *I'll never feel that way again.* Grandmother didn't leave my side as anguish pulled me under and swallowed me whole. I pulled my buffalo blankets up to my face, and my pillow grew damp as it collected my sadness. Grief crawled around me, and somewhere in the hopelessness, sleep took my hand and pulled me far away.

My eyes opened wide as the earliest ray of dawn light shone through the side window. My first thought was, as it is every morning, *I am in the white man's house.* But today my second thought was just as devastating: *Father rejected Tashunke's offer.* It hit me like an arrow into my stomach. I rolled over in bed, not hopping to my feet as I usually did. I couldn't bear to gather firewood today. How embarrassed I'd be if I encountered Tashunke. What an insult for his offer to be rejected. I couldn't explain myself to Tash . . . explain what my feelings actually were. I had to abide by Little Crow. I was powerless to do anything to reverse my father's choice. And I couldn't face Wenona or Aunt Mika. I would surely crumble to tears. A weak girl. Tears began brimming in the edges of my eyes as all the feelings swarmed back into my body. Shockingly, as if I were dreaming, I heard a voice call out in the bright morning from beyond the front door.

"Chief Little Crow. I've come to add to my offer."

I immediately sat up in my bed, a rush of hope washing over me. Tashunke had returned. Grandmother groggily pushed her disheveled hair from her face as she leaned on an elbow from her spotted deer hide blankets. My father rose and moved towards the door.

He pulled it open and brilliant light poured in. My eyes adjusted and from my bed, I could see Tashunke standing confidently, holding two lead ropes in each hand. Four horses. His extraordinary bear hide stretched across the porch railing. With a giddy wave of excitement, I pushed back my blankets and sat tall. I'd never heard of so much being offered for a wife. I hadn't considered that Tashunke might return, offer *more*.

My father crossed his arms across his chest, surveying the addition to the offering. My heart pleaded for his acceptance; I held my breath as I waited for his response. Surprisingly, he twisted back and looked directly at me. My spirit asked with my eyes, "Father, *please*."

I could see my father's gentle, thoughtful eyes transform to the sharp look of Chief Little Crow as he held my gaze. I began to fear he would reject Tashunke again. Instead, he turned back and faced Tashunke. "The offer pleases your chief and his daughter, Oenikika. The Breath of Life. She will take you as her husband."

It would be. My heart surged, I looked to Owl Woman who smiled widely. She raised her eyebrows at me, as if to say, "What did I tell you?" It was more than I could have conceived . . . a husband who paid so much honor to his chief. And I'd be returning to the tipi! Tashunke had pulled me back to the life I knew while also pulling me forward to something beautifully new, becoming a wife.

May 15, 1862

Owl Woman combed my hair then added a few tiny braids. She twisted in stems of the little white flowers into the hidden braids, so it appeared as if the flowers themselves were blooming from me. Tashunke was on his way to retrieve me; I would move to his tipi tonight. Grandmother helped me as I changed into my favorite ceremony dress, with fringe along the arms and the bottom hem. Pink beads covered the bodice, with light blue beads intricately stitched into star shapes among the pink. Grandmother gave me a kiss upon my forehead, and my preparation was complete.

I emerged from the white man's house in my regalia. I felt decorated, beautiful, and most of all, loved. My family had gathered to send me off. Uncle Chaska and Little Rapids stood beside Father on the porch. Wenona and Aunt Mika prepared Ahone, painted with blue lines and circles, a deer hide blanket atop her back. Little Kimimela watched, learning the ways of women. Soon as Kimi saw me emerge from the white man's house she ran to me, reaching her fingers out to touch my fringes. "Ahh ahh." Wenona walked over and tenderly pulled back her daughter's hands. Wenona's belly had grown but it was nowhere near as full as it was with the twins. She explained: "Auntie O is coming back to camp circle. She is now the wife of the Man Who Sings to Horses." My niece nodded in her understanding.

"Can I visit your tipi?" Kimi asked sweetly.

I crouched down to meet my niece at her level. "Oh, I hope you do. Every day." I tickled her nose with my own. Kimi ran her hand over one of my fine braids. I let her take in my ceremonial appearance, hoping she'd have this moment to look forward to herself someday. Her big dark eyes surveyed me, my fringe, my beads. My sweet niece was so observant of the world; a trait that would serve her well.

"Auntie's eyes are happy again," she said.

Hearing her comment brought a wave of emotion I didn't realize I'd been holding in. The constant wearing on my spirit that living in the four walls had on me had shown. I'd feared that would be my feeling forever. But even Kimimela could see the change in my spirit. My family had to adjust the tradition of walking from tipi to tipi; today I was moving from the white man's house to tipi. The sunset stretched across the length of the horizon; the sky was painted with my hopefulness, the entire earth welcoming me back after my captivity. Tonight, I was set free.

"*All* of us are happy. When one family member has joy, we all do," Wenona explained as she hugged her daughter close. We did share a peaceful joy. Even Father looked proud and pleased tonight. It was a special moment, sharing sundown with my family on the bluff.

Tashunke arrived just as the last of the setting sun was gulped by tomorrow. His palomino bore bright blue bands of paint through its white sandy mane and down its front legs, to match those of Ahone. I took in the beauty of his horse but kept my eyes averted, as was customary. My aunt and cousin helped hoist me onto Ahone's back, where I sat unusually, with both legs to one side to accommodate me in my dress. Ahone moved forward next to Tashunke, and in the deepening blues of twilight we moved out together at a steady walk.

As we departed, my family called out, "Yi Yi Yi!" in celebration. A smile burst wide across my face. I was overjoyed moving across the bluff. I could see the welcoming tipis of camp and many people standing about, watching Tashunke and me in our ceremonial procession. I sat a bit taller on Ahone's back, feeling both pride and gratitude. Tashunke and I rode side by side in companionable silence until we arrived. Tashunke led his horse wide about the village. Ahone followed and we came to a halt at the very far side of the circle at the tipi, Tashunke's tipi, the one I had watched from the white man's windows for many nights.

He pushed open the door flap and I stepped inside. For the first time, it was just me and my husband. I took a seat quietly on the women's side, which was bare. I suspected I may be the first female to *ever* be in this tipi. He'd never taken a wife before and his family had been gone for years. We were alone together. It was good manners for a wife to wait to speak in the tipi until her husband spoke to her. Just as it was good manners for a husband to speak to his wife, ask her opinions, and regard her feelings. He moved back to the tipi door, to take our horses to pasture for the night, but before he ducked himself back out, Tashunke spoke to welcome me, his voice deep and pure. "I am glad to have you here. What was mine alone is now ours." Ours . . . It didn't seem real, yet. It seemed like I was in a dream, a wonderful one I didn't want to wake up from. Tashunke left and I was alone. I got up and shyly investigated the space: our supplies, one pot and kettle, a single cup and water ladle. It was simple in its trappings. There had been no need for more. A lone man had occupied the tipi for many years; it was clear no woman had ever made it her own. He hadn't decorated the walls with paintings, memories, or dedication colors to the Great Spirit. I was used to the tipi grandmother had created; its walls painted bottom to top. I smiled, thinking of the eagle Brown Wing had painted and the yellow sun I naughtily added when we were little. Owl Woman had scolded that we painted without permission, but she'd never washed them away. I thought of the bead bags, the kettles, the tanning tools; the items of women's work. In Wenona's tipi, little dolls, cradle boards, and hoof toys fill the space. I let my senses take in his area, let my soul settle. I was Tashunke's wife. We would work together to make this space ours. The sound of laughter and chiding came from beyond the tipi walls. The sounds of camp. A part of my heart that had been sick for so long was soothed. I was home.

I sat alone and took in that which was so familiar but still felt so new. I thought of the four walls, how far they were from this tipi and felt guilt. There was an ache inside me to think of Owl Woman who remained in the white man's house. And my heart stung further to think of my father . . . How could he choose to remain in there? It was just two moons ago I fell asleep crying, believing my father had ruined me forever. And now here I sat, in my future. An offer of the highest honor to take me as a wife. Perhaps my father did have a wisdom I couldn't yet understand. But I couldn't quite let go of my resentment. I would never understand my father. But I needed to push those preoccupations out of my mind. My duty now was not as a daughter, but rather as a wife. I needed to focus upon Tashunke, learn his wants and needs. Paint his body for ceremony. Braid his hair. It was a noble honor to be a wife. I was the wife of the Man Who Sings to Horses.

The late evening was growing darker when Tashunke reentered the tipi. His presence made my body warm with eagerness. He'd been in my mind for so long with little time actually near him. I felt the anxiousness I did at mealtime now when I remember the harsh winter; could his wonderfulness be pulled away at any moment? I'd never forget the feeling of having Tashunke's offer rejected by my father. Maybe that's the lesson Little Crow was trying to teach . . . how precious it is to be joined with the one your heart seeks. Tashunke's presence was larger than life; his handsomeness striking. I was allowed to look at him as his wife in the tipi. But my heart felt such overwhelm at the sight of him, that I instinctively averted my eyes. He took an awkward seat across from me, averting his eyes as well. It felt too impossibly pleasing to finally take each other in.

"Is it acceptable to my wife to return to a tipi?" he asked. Acceptable? I wanted to laugh, it was amazing. But conceivably Tashunke had thought of me living in the white man's house as something I had wanted. I assure him that it was not the case.

"The tipi is everything I hoped for," I felt the need to clarify, elaborate that I had yearned for him too. "This—" I finally looked into Tash's eyes, "—is everything I hoped for."

His expression changed . . . he started to smile but it seemed as if his scar caught his grin from stretching across his face. It seemed to pull him back as if the mark itself didn't want to let him get too happy. But I was satisfied, seeing my husband pleased.

"Can I prepare an evening meal for you?" I asked, ready to take on a wifely duty.

He shook his head. "I ate rabbit earlier." His eyes scanned mine.

"Has my wife eaten? I can hunt in the dark, the moon is full." He was eager to meet my needs.

"No, no. I cooked for grandmother and the chief," I replied. He was anxious to meet my needs, and I his.

"Very well." He nodded. "A celebration fire is burning. I will attend to show my honor to take you as my wife." His strong legs lifted him smoothly to stand. I rose with him. He opened the tipi flap, revealing the wonderful gathering at the center of camp.

The night air vibrated with happiness, even the stars overhead seemed brighter. After moving to the reservation and the hard winter, I felt like Tash and I joining in marriage had brought a new outlook to our tribe. It was a reassurance of tradition. Even on a reservation, we could hold onto our ways. People were gathered at the fire. I tucked my ceremonial skirt round my legs as I took a seat on the ground next to Dina and Scarlet Woman, who'd brought their beading to do by firelight.

"Oenikika. We celebrate you and Tashunke tonight," Dina said warmly as she pulled a string of red beads along with Cut Nose's regalia cloak.

"We made you a little gift, I'll bring it later," Scarlet Woman added.

"I have so much happiness to be with Tashunke and living again in the village," I said as I looked into the wild flames. It was as if I were returning to a happy memory. From the opposite side of the fire, Kimimela and Wolfchaser came running through still filled with excitement from the ceremonial activities earlier in the day. Wolfchaser ran past me, while Kimi came crashing into my lap with a giggling laugh. Wenona strode in, and sat beside me, leaning her back against the long log behind us. She tickled her daughter's side. "Remember to walk near a grand fire, little one." Kimi nodded in acceptance of her mother's teaching, as a good daughter does.

Wenona sighed and tipped her head to my shoulder. "My heart feels better to know you've returned."

"Mine too," I replied as I set my cheek lovingly against Wenona's head. But I quickly lifted it when I saw Mato's dark frame approaching. Father held the lead rope and Owl Woman slid her hunched body down from Mato's tall back. My heart lifted with gladness when I saw them.

Owl Woman shuffled her way over to the women and Wenona gave her a hand as Grandmother sat. "I told Little Crow, load me up! Bring me to my granddaughter's celebration fire. I don't know how many more I'll be blessed with," she said with a gummy smile, as she looked straight at little Kimimela and proclaimed, "I'm old." We all laughed and enjoyed the cheerfulness we shared.

Aunt Mika leaned herself in between Wenona and me and stuck out her hands. She was holding two beaver pelts and a long patch of leather. Her eyes looked into mine with a sparkle. "What is this, Auntie?" I asked.

"I have prayed to the Great Spirit. I believe it is my calling to create a medicine bag for you." Her eyes glistened with tears as she explained her calling. It was a great honor to carry a medicine bag, often reserved for the Medicine Man, the spiritual overseer of a tribe. Our Medicine Man lived alone, just beyond Red Iron's camp at the far West of the Long River.

"I am allowed such a wonder?" I ran my fingers along the soft beaver pelt.

"You're now fully a woman among our people, and you have the power of the healer in your blood," she said, referencing her own healing abilities and those also held by my mother. My mother. The piercing loneliness of my love for her hit my heart in this special night. I wondered what she would have done today . . . helped change me into my dress? Sat next to me now? Mika continued, "And the Great Spirit has signaled it is your time. Look how the stars twinkle tonight. They favor something. I believe they indicate protection for you and Tashunke."

I looked up at the dark sky and the constellations that did seem to dance. Protection of the stars. Protection from what exactly, I wondered? Tonight, we were so safe. All gathered close. Our stomachs were not aching from hunger, but the memory of starvation still walked among us. I would be grateful to the stars if they protected Tashunke and I from ever feeling that way again.

"I am honored," I said to my aunt. Fully a woman now that I was a wife. Fully a healer with the blessing of a medicine bag. Gratitude to the Great Mystery sunk deep into my bones. I looked across the gathering toward the men. Little Crow was telling a story, Uncle Chaska at one side, and my husband at the other. Tash stood confident, arms crossed. He looked like he belonged. We were joined. I wondered if he'd felt that belonging before . . . perhaps it'd been a very long time. A time before that scar that holds back his smile. My heart loved him; and my heart flooded with love for our people.

Dina's lovely voice started singing the woman's song, the Balancing of Men and Women. Her voice rang out, and without missing a beat, mine joined with Wenona, Grandmother, Mika, and Scarlet Woman. The song was our joy and our intention. Our prayer and our reflection. My spirit flowed with the sound. And I sang out with the women to the Man Who Sings to Horses, and indeed, in that moment I felt the return of balancing.

In the wonder of that night and under the protection of those stars, little did I know what was coming for me. What was coming for us all.

TWELVE

Emma Heard

Saturday, August 16, 1862

My lunch tin sat empty on the table; I'd already eaten my hard-boiled egg and apple. The sweltering summer heat was a reminder that I had been assisting in father's office for over a year now. While the summer season required more of my presence on the farm, I still rode into town with my father several times a week. The space had transformed from his private study to feeling a bit my own. There was another hook in the wall, for my bonnet and petticoat. The table nearest the door was "mine." It wasn't quite a sense of belonging, as my father worked in silence and kept to himself for the most part. But I felt some shelter in the office; a feeling of physical respite from the tasks of the farm. And a growing intellectual freedom. I was becoming much more acquainted with legal terminology. I continued to read my way through the bookshelves, educating myself on different topics and using small scraps of paper to flag information I thought my father might find useful.

Pa sat in his desk chair, sweat dripping, studying a recent trial transcript sent to him from Mankato. The room was roasting.

"Emma, I'm awaiting the next portion of these transcripts. Please see if the mail has come."

I set down the ink well I was refilling. "Of course." Checking for mail was routine now; I used to get excited about the task. Back in the spring, I still had hope for a reply from my former teacher, but spring turned to summer, and my hopefulness withered. I sighed, anticipating another unpleasant encounter with Myrick. My frequent visits had made the dreadful man ever more comfortable pressing upon my space, my femininity. I'd never tell my father of my discomfort around the store clerk; I could not bear to risk making myself a distraction or a liability. If I were never to get my opportunity to be a teacher, continuing to assist in the law office was my only relief from long days on the farm; I would do nothing to jeopardize these precious hours and access to my reading material. I'd worked hard to prove my value in the office and was not about to let a greasy man get in the way of my potential. I could handle him and his slimy annoyances. I wished I had a tail, like our heifer, so I could swat him away as the cow did to the persistent flies around her. I grabbed my bonnet off its hook and went out.

A muggy and moody wind whipped my skirt. I tied my bonnet tightly under my chin. Bruno, in his shabby overalls, walked by with purpose as Captain trotted steadfast at his heel. He held something, carefully cupped in his hands.

"Hello, Bruno. I say it's likely to storm," I called. The sun still burned hot and high; but in late summer, the prairie sky would often blossom with furious storms in the late afternoon. It felt like the vibrating tea kettle on the stovetop; the final pressured moments before the release. "What are you holding so carefully there, my friend?"

"Found 'em in the road." Bruno opened his hands and showed me a wiggling caterpillar. "I'm saving his life. He was crawling right in the middle road."

"Ahhh." I viewed the grown man's precious insect friend. "As you may know, Bruno, that is a Monarch caterpillar. See the lovely yellow and black stripes. Soon, he will transform into a handsome butterfly. You're saving both a caterpillar and a butterfly," I said with a warm-hearted sparkle in my eye.

He gasped in astonishment. "I'm saving a caterpillar *and* a butterfly!" he exclaimed with genuine gladness. Without another word, he stomped off on his rescue mission.

"Place him on the milkweed by my father's office," I hollered after him. I watched the kind man and his loyal canine make their way down the road. Bruno's thoughtfulness was encouraging. He lived as if the world wasn't here to serve him. I reflected as to whether I could do the same. I wanted to believe God would smile upon a hardworking Emma, educating children. It didn't seem to matter anymore; God hadn't heard my prayers over the loud howls of the winter wind. There was an empty space inside of me; a void of no reply from Miss Knudsen or my prayers echoed with shame for my silly dreams.

I walked on to Myrick's. I paused and patted my kerchief delicately along my brow, glistening from the short walk in the August heat. I needed a moment to steel myself before another encounter with Myrick. I took a deep breath, anticipating the noxious clerk. But when I entered, Myrick was occupied, presenting rolls of fabric to Mrs. Mayo. I headed to the back of the store where Hermann, Myrick's rough assistant who was usually at the Indian Agency store, stood behind the counter. Hermann leaned forward against the counter, a large wad of chewing tobacco bowing out his lower lip. He was an intimidating and gargantuan man, with a bushy black beard and ill-tempered eyes. It was rumored Hermann had killed a man back east, before moving to the prairie. He squirted a dark glob into a mason jar held to his bristly chin, half full of the thick nauseating liquid. Though both men were foul, I would rather deal with a cantankerous oversized man than a perverted shrew one. And I would deal with any man I had to for the sake of the precious intellectual freedoms my work in town earned me. In my deduction, most men seemed to have one of three characteristics: slick, distracted, or rough. I'd find ways to manage, or in the worst cases, protect myself, around any of the three.

"What's it you want?" Hermann asked gruffly.

"I'm here to collect the post for August Heard," I said with importance. My tactic in town was direct confidence. Being delicate as a late-summer daisy may help make a man like me, but it wasn't about to get him to respect me. The work of my father's office was important enough to demand the latter. I wasn't here to be an object of their desires; such matters would only get in the way of my efficiency. Hermann grunted as he turned and scanned the square wooden grid of mail cubbies. I was curious as to why both he and Myrick were in the General Store together. Who'd be manning the Indian Trading Post? I'd witnessed Myrick's untrustworthy trading tactics and Hermann was a rumored murderer. The two were trouble. I knew better than to ask many questions. Still, I couldn't help but wonder.

Finding the "H" cubby, Hermann grabbed the pile of envelopes, sorting through with a gristly voice repeating, "Heard, Heard, Heard." He looked up, scanned me up and down, and asked, "Which one are ya? Ida or Emma? I can't tell yous two apart." It was as if we were two calves in a corral he was aiming to separate. His up-and-down glance was cold, not seedy and prying like Myrick's. I never understood how anyone could confuse me with my magnificent older sister. And the fact alone that I was *speaking* to him seemed an identifier enough.

"I am Miss Emma Heard," I clarified.

He set down the small stack of mail on the countertop. Placing a dirty envelope atop, he said, "One's in for you."

My eyes locked on the letter. Miss Knudsen's familiar cursive, once a daily sight across the classroom blackboard, was scrawled across the front of the envelope. I froze. It was here. It was here! Her response. My breath caught in my throat and my eyes blinked in disbelief. Hermann's enormous hands shoved the pile forward. I tried to contain my smile. My hands trembled as they reached across the counter.

"Wonderful. Just wonderful. Thank you so," I said. I felt like hugging the disinterested giant. Air filled my lungs, filled my entire body, as I ballooned with happiness. What a marvelous surprise!

I rushed out of the store. The letter was here. I desperately wanted to tear it open. I shuffled one way across the general store porch, only to see Dr. Mayo and Mr. Kuhn. I needed to open the letter in secret. I ran to the other side of the porch. No, how foolish. I couldn't open it here at the busiest store in town. I was disoriented by my excitement. This was something I must review in private. When the moment was proper. I resolved to hide the letter and open it this evening. My thrilled steps barreled down the porch stairs and rushed back to the office.

I spoke to God. "You heard me. I worried so—that you didn't want me to be a teacher. Believed me selfish. I began to doubt." I felt a panging guilt in the back of my consciousness. "I doubted this dream you put on my heart was actually from you. I feared I was selfish." The initial pang of guilt was that I had doubted the Lord heard my prayer. But the second felt more like a full out kick from Kit in my stomach. The guilt of being willing to leave my family. Wanting to leave this town. Wanting my own grand chalkboard to fill with lessons I'd created. I hugged the pile of mail to my chest.

I needed to conceal the letter before I reentered my father's office. I entered through the large front doors of the courthouse, rather than through the back door as usual. I stood in the small, dark hallway and set the mail on the floor. I untied my dressy town apron, my fingers working quickly to unbutton the front of my shirt. I grabbed the letter and slid it into the center of my chest beneath my light layered chemise. It sat snug between my skin and corset. Hurriedly, I rebuttoned my dress and tied up my apron. I pulled my bonnet loose and grabbed the rest of the mail from the floor. I shimmied in my dress, testing the security of the envelope against my body. It stayed in place. The adventure of the moment, a moment I had assumed would never come, excited me so. I opened the side door and went into the office.

My father looked up, surprised. "Well, I wasn't expecting you to come in that way. I'd like to head back to the farm immediately. We don't want to get caught in a storm. I've already hitched up Kit." Grabbing his hat, he asked, "Did the transcript arrive?"

"Oh. Ahhh . . ." I hemmed and hawed a moment as I looked at the small pile of mail in my hands. I hadn't even thought about the transcript with my exciting distractions. But transcripts were large and heavy, never folded. It couldn't be in the thin envelopes in my hand. "No. No, transcript," I said with a self-conscious laugh. My father looked at me for a lingering moment. I worried my odd behavior was making him suspicious. I placed the mail on the table and said, "It would be wise to beat the storm."

I took my place to the right of my father on the front bench of the wagon. Kit swung her head back and forth as she pulled us forward along the familiar route. As we headed down the main street, a tall wall of dark bottomed clouds grew on the horizon. I felt the edges of the hidden envelope against my body. I couldn't wait to tear it open. This little letter had made such a long journey, and soon, it would be at its final destination. We made our way down the block towards a group of men gathered at the edge of town. As we got closer, Pa muttered under his breath, "Ahh, this better not be trouble."

Six Indians and wild ungroomed ponies were in a cluster. Three men stood in front, and three more behind remained on horseback. Some of the men's bodies appeared gaunt compared to the Indian men I had seen a year ago. Their faces too, with desperate eyes and hollow cheeks, were troubling. I'd always understood that Indians were the fiercest hunters on the prairie; a group of Indians could ride alongside buffalo, swiftly taking down the animals in seconds. This group in front of me bore a fierce semblance to a wolfpack—I hadn't seen any buffalo on our prairie. Perhaps their hunting had been less successful recently? But it was summer season, surely crops could sustain them. They must have some organized farming. Standing with the group was the Indian Missionary, Riggs. He held the reins of the chestnut Thoroughbred I'd seen him riding into town on in the spring. His tanned face looked serious. I wanted to watch him, understand him, but the hostile scene demanded better of me.

Andrew Myrick and his assistant Hermann stood across from the natives and the missionary. Myrick was chewing on a handful of peanuts, obnoxiously spitting bits of shell into the air. Hermann appeared even more a giant beside the weaselly clerk. I pressed my hand to my bodice, an instinctive reaction to safeguard my letter as we approached the tense group. I'd never seen this many Dakota at once. Part of me wished to know the matter, curiosity being such a strong impulse. But a different part of me prayed Pa would urge Kit onward, letting us home as quickly as possible. I had a precious message burning inside my bodice. Instead, Pa slowed Kit and tipped his hat. "Gentlemen." His eyes scanned the group.

Myrick motioned for Pa to join them. "Attorney Heard will talk some goddamn sense into these Injuns," he said as he spit another blast of shells to his side. Hermann shifted his position, revealing revolvers in two holsters at his waist. He stared at the Indians who outnumbered them, ready to shoot at a moment's notice. My body, slightly damp with sweat, chilled with nerves at the foreboding scene. I feared that Myrick had done something to aggravate our unfamiliar Dakota neighbors. My Pa was a practical man; logic and reason prevailed with him. If anyone could mediate, surely, he could.

Pa passed me the reins. Kit snorted, likely frustrated that her routine trot home was interrupted. The mare pushed forward, and I held tight. The cart rocked but I was strong enough to keep her in place. Pa vaulted down from the wagon and walked across the dusty grass.

"If I can be of assistance to anyone—" my father nodded assuredly at all parties, "—I'm more than glad to be."

Thunder rumbled in the distance.

Riggs, who was helping to translate, explained the tension. "My friend, Chief Little Crow, here—" he pointed to the distinguished looking Indian in the center of the front line, "—rode to the Trading Post this afternoon. We found it padlocked with no one manning it. Obviously, this is concerning, as the tribe is due—*overdue*—annuity payment. I believe it's outlined in the treaty agreement you helped create, Attorney." Riggs was reasonable in his presentation of what appeared to be the facts. But his emphasis that my father had personally helped create the treaty did put the onus on Father to address the issue.

My insides squirmed. I felt defensive of the legal agreement with the natives that my father helped establish. Through treaties, land deeds, patents, and most of the work of his office, my father had helped create Minnesota. Helped create America! This was a point of pride; creating treaties was an honor of a dignified profession. The American Government simply *had* to honor its commitment to pay the tribe; that couldn't really be in question, could it? I wondered where that missing annuity payment could be. The mail had been flowing again for months. My own letter had arrived. But surely the man I had spun around a dance floor with could understand that my father couldn't just summon the payment.

"Indeed. You are correct, Missionary Riggs; biannual payment structure was outlined in the treaty agreement. Just a matter of Washington sending the money, is all. Simply out of my hands, I'm afraid." My father looked back at me in the wagon. "Say, Emma, was there any mail today postmarked from Washington?" he asked, as if perhaps there was some simple solution to the disagreement at hand.

I was caught off guard that he called on me. Involving me in such matters was unbelievable. My father, grown accustomed to me assisting in his office, perhaps forgot that I was merely a six-teen-year-old girl. Regardless of my surprise, I had been the one to gather the mail today and would undoubtedly remember what letters we'd just received. I felt a pulse of searing responsibility. A sharp corner of the envelope dug into my stomach. I had been entirely captivated by my letter from Miss Knudsen when I collected the mail. I hadn't checked any of the other envelopes. Even when Pa questioned about the arrival of the trial transcript, I was too distracted to actually read the other postmarks. Should I reveal that I did not have the slightest clue whom the letters were from? The gaze of the store clerks and the stares of the Indians fastened on me created excruciating pressure. I knew for certain that Riggs saw me now. He looked at me earnestly. I wished I could give an answer that would resolve all the pain in the group. My chest tightened with uneasiness. It was undeniable to me that the Indians had been treated unlawfully. I wasn't overly interested in the foreign-ap-pearing men or their people. But the lack of payment, which was a violation of contract, seemed as black and white as the ink on the treaty paper. A dreadful, staining wrong was happening in front of me. And I felt powerless, in my person and in my circumstance, to do much of anything about it. My father tilted his head, expecting me to recall such basic information. I decided to answer as fairly as I could. "I . . . I can't be certain . . ." I said meekly.

"What's that?" my father seemed exasperated. My throat swelled under the pressure. I simply shook my head to indicate I didn't know. I was a ghost of the confident woman I'd acted like in the store just an hour ago. My competence, my intelligence, were shadowed by my feeble voice and small frame.

My father turned to the group. "If there are any updates from Washington, we will get you that information. I'll see to it personally."

My father's vague assurances rang hollow. Even I realized how empty the promise would be to the men with hungry eyes. Something quite horrible, something quite unfair I worried, was happening to the men across from me. The party responsible for payment, the United States government, was far away from this cluster gathered at the edge of the westernmost prairie. I sensed Missionary Riggs was desperate for something of goodwill, something real, for these men. Empty words and promises couldn't fill a hungry belly. My body softened, filling with sympathy for the men trapped in the binding lasso of an unfulfilled treaty.

The chief respectfully waited for my father to finish speaking. But he did not need interpretation, he could tell this attorney's words wouldn't give them access to the food they needed. Little Crow began speaking in Dakota, a clear deliberate response. Riggs stared at the chief, listening intently. The missionary's eyes dropped to the ground. The chief finished his message and was quiet, expecting Riggs to translate. Instead, Riggs stood in silent censorship, appearing to be deeply contemplating whether to interpret the words aloud to the group. The quiet moments dragged on.

"What the hell are you here for if you ain't going to tell us what he said?" Myrick finally snapped, insulting the missionary. He dropped the rest of his uneaten peanuts on the ground, crushing them beneath his boot in front of the hungry men across from him. Anger seethed through me. My buried discomfort from Myrick's putrid eyes fixed upon my body, his slick words licking over me the past year, rose to the surface. My quiet discomfort morphed to a flaring hatred for this pompous, entitled store clerk.

Riggs swallowed. He began translating Little Crow's slowly delivered words, "We have waited a long time. The money is ours, yet it is kept from us. We cannot get it. We have no food, but there are stores filled with food. We ask that you make some arrangement by which we can get food until our payment arrives." Riggs paused and looked away from the storekeepers, unable to make eye contact. Perhaps he was as repulsed as I was.

Riggs continued sharing the chief's words, staring at the dry grass in the center of the group, "If you do not help, we may take our own way to keep ourselves from starving." Riggs took a slight pause and finished, "When men are hungry, they help themselves."

The threat hung in the air. Little Crow stared, with piercing confident eyes, directly at Myrick. Though their situation was desperate, I felt Little Crow to be a powerful keeper of his own kingdom. Inside, my senses were stinging with warning. It was critical to do something, anything, to remedy the lapse in payment and issue some food and supplies. It seemed a basic fairness.

All faces turned to Myrick to wait for his reply. Instead, he rotated on his heels, kicking up the discarded peanuts, walking away from the group and back towards town.

My father interjected, "Come on, Mr. Myrick. Have the decency to let them know your decision. Will you open the storehouse to feed them? The annuity is surely on its way." I was relieved my father was a reasonable man compared to the insolent clerk. Surely, he recognized a broken contract must be addressed and hungry men to be fed from their own supplies currently sitting behind a padlock.

Andrew Myrick twisted back and faced the group. His rat face puckered with hatred, "So far as I am concerned—" Myrick stared coldly at the chief, "—let them eat grass or their own shit if they're hungry."

I gasped, moving my hand up quickly to cover my mouth, at both the language and the inhumane sentiment. Riggs too reacted to the insult. He crouched to his knees, shook his head and looked toward the storming western sky. After a moment, he turned back around and shook his head in direct disbelief of the trader. I sat horrified, realizing Riggs would have to interpret and repeat the awful words to the Indians he lived amongst.

Lightning flashed across the sky.

Myrick taunted, "Make yourself useful, translator."

The mercilessness of the clerk sickened me. Riggs had a bewildered look in his eyes. "I do not wish to repeat such words." The missionary's morals were so far from Myrick's; it seemed an unfair task to have a man of God repeat the horrific message. Little Crow said something to Riggs, likely asking what the storekeeper had said. Though conscious of their severity, Riggs must have decided a lack of honesty to the men he lived amongst was a greater sin. He interpreted. Riggs stared at Myrick as he repeated in Dakota language Myrick's response regarding opening the storehouse. Little Crow's eyes were fixed on the storekeeper. The group stood in silence. Myrick, the cruel fool, spun smugly once again on his bootheel and continued his walk back towards his shop. Hermann glanced at the group and then began his own saunter back to town. The message was clear. I was stunned. The moment to do something, anything was ruined. As crushed as the peanut shells in the dusty trampled prairie grass.

In unison, the Indians cried out with shrieking yelps. The howling screams sent a shiver down my spine. Kit skittered, and I gripped the reins as my heart beat in rhythm with her frantic hooves. Swiftly, the Dakota chief and his men mounted their ponies and took off southwest at full gallop. My father stood, arms crossed across his chest, watching arrogant Myrick walk down the street. I glimpsed back at Riggs from my rocking wagon. He was centered on me in the chaotic moment. Staring into his brown eyes again, there was no magic as there had been at the dance, just a mutual understanding that damage had been done. He saw it, same as I did. They had warned us. I feared that storehouse padlock wasn't strong enough to hold back a wronged tribe. Hungry men needed to be fed. And an entire storehouse of goods, goods legally intended for the Indians, were being withheld. I wouldn't be surprised if those horses were hurtling straight for it now.

A lightning bolt came down. Thunder crashed behind it. Pa excused himself and hopped back up in the wagon. "Get on, Kit," he said with a flick of his wrist. "We don't want to get caught in this storm." Judging by the darkness sweeping across the plain, it felt like it was coming right for us. The chief's words, Riggs's voice, rang in my ears. If hungry men would help themselves, I worried what *angry* men would do. What they could be justified in doing . . .

Evening supper's usual discussion was interrupted with frequent flashes of lightning and cracks of thunder that sounded as if they'd split the roof in two. Pa and I had been caught in the downpour on our ride home. Soaked to the bone, I ran through the front door, hunched over in an effort to protect my secret letter. I prayed it had stayed dry. I sprinted up the center steps, went to the small wardrobe I shared with Ida, and peeled off my soaking layers. By some miracle, the envelope was waterless. For hiding, I tucked it between the pages of *Leaves of Grass* and set it at the bottom of the wardrobe, then changed into my dry nightdress.

It felt peculiar, sitting at the table, eating dinner in my nightdress. But the feeling wasn't just from the clothing. Upstairs, Miss Knudsen's letter seemed to be shouting from the wardrobe. I looked about the table, but everyone was busied with metal spoons scraping against tin plates. Otto and Uncle Allen gobbled their well-earned dinner after a long day of work on the farm. Ida sat across from Ma at the end of the table, spooning overflowing bites of applesauce into Peter's mouth. My glaring secret was safe. Pa was the first to bring up the encounter we stumbled upon on our way home.

"I fear Myrick may be getting a bit bold in his dealings with Indians at the trading post," he said.

"Now, what makes you say such things, August?" my mother asked.

Pa briefly glanced at me, and I understood the look meant I wasn't to share the specifics of what we witnessed. "Sounds as if those Indians are still overdue on their treaty payment. Myrick's in charge of the Dakota food and supplies in the storehouse at the post. He's padlocked it 'til payment comes in."

The dramatic encounter still rattled in my body. Whooping shouts of Indians haunted my conscience. Something inside of me connected with their screams of outrage. The Dakota had always been strange people at the fringe of our world. In my encounters, the Indians seemed reasonable. Just different. And more human the more I got used to their differences from us. The Dakota seemed sensible and even *wise*, in my evaluation. Myrick, quite the opposite, behaved as if the world was his to take and use for his own gratification.

I couldn't resist but comment. "That cruel man is keeping starving Indians from the food that's due them."

Ma corrected me. "Emma. What an unsympathetic assessment. Myrick deserves to get paid for his goods."

Rain beat against the farmhouse walls. Sometimes it seemed as if my mother's eyes looked out upon an entirely different world than my own. Focusing on Myrick's needs was the opposite of what mattered to me. Ma didn't know how I carefully danced around the man. She didn't see his twisted face tell hungry men to eat grass. Even if she did, I felt she'd rather me be the delicate daisy, sitting quietly in a planted row, than the strong oak tree of a woman I was growing into.

Otto reached his arm across the table for another piece of cornbread. "It's not Myrick's fault," he agreed.

Sometimes I wished I could quiet the boldness of my thoughts. But lately, important matters couldn't be muted in my mind or on my tongue. "I believe Myrick's storehouse will be raided soon." I looked up to see if my father shared my concern. The furious hoofbeats of the wild ponies galloping away from us. There was such intensity; it seemed as if Myrick's back might well have had a target on it.

"Emma!" My mother was shocked. As if me saying it aloud was prophetic.

"I simply fear it," I explained. "It would be dreadful . . ." I covered up my thought and acted as if it was based in concern. How could my father not acknowledge the actions of the inhumane store clerk? Or the failure of the United States government to keep their promises made? Their treaty? Otto laughed aloud at my outrageousness, coughing as he choked on a dry bit of cornbread. Ida's eyes darted back and forth between my parents. My siblings didn't share my level of interest, of care, about the topic. It didn't seem anyone did.

"Nonsense to dwell on this." My father dismissed the conversation. "We'll hope the annuity payment arrives soon. This mess will resolve itself."

I prayed he was accurate in his assessment. Our bellies were full. A few days or weeks didn't seem long to us, but I wasn't sure if our neighbors could bear it the same.

After helping with dishes, everyone settled into their usual evening routine. Ma set Peter and Catherine to sleep. Ida was in her rocking chair, crocheting. Ma and Ida spent their evenings, mending basket between them, in perfect synched rocking. I hated mending. I quietly excused myself up to the loft. My reading in bed in the evening was commonplace, so no one suspected what a special treasure awaited me.

I snuck my book out of the wardrobe and lit the lantern on the nightstand. Crawling into bed, I pulled my blue quilt up over my knees, shielding myself in case Ida or Otto were to come upstairs while I was reading the letter. My hair was still damp as I leaned back against the pillow; the rain pattered on the rooftop above me. I set my treasured book against my bent legs, opening it to the pages the letter sat between. The envelope was dirty and tattered from what appeared to be an especially long journey on the mail stagecoach. It looked like it may have been around the world and back. All happenings earlier in the day swept from my mind. Everything that mattered was this moment. I gently ran my finger along the top edge, tearing as noiselessly as possible. I opened the folded letter, my eyes desperately scanning the page. I was shocked at the posted date in the upper right-hand corner, nearly ten months ago!

October 15, 1861

Dear Miss Emma Heard,

I thank you kindly for your delightful correspondence.

My heart is gladdened to know that you are looking to consider the life of an educator. As Europeans and Easterners alike flood our wondrous Prairie, the demands for additional schoolteachers has increased substantially. Towns are repeatedly disappointed as teacher postings remain vacant each fall. I can assure you the profession is rewarding and worthwhile.

As you have requested, here are details on the process: Teaching certification is issued each August. Send your inquiry to:

Americas Teaching Association:

Request for Certification

Chicago Illinois

Any requests received before mid-August will be considered. At this time, I will additionally mail them a letter of recommendation on your behalf.

How are Otto and Ida? I pray all are in good health. It seems a lifetime ago I had the luck of teaching in the special Minnesota town of New Ulm. Please update me kindly on your certification and how your family is fairing. Life is quite fair in Iowa City. I do hope the Prairie agrees and no snow encumbers the delivery of my letter.

Your teacher and friend,
Miss Dorothea Knudsen

I read and reread the letter up and down, each sentence again and again. It was so wonderful. And so simple. To only mail a request to Chicago! Where a recommendation already stands on my behalf? My heart nearly burst out of my chest. I bit onto my hand, so as not to make a sound while I screeched internally with elation. But the timing. The dreadful timing. It was mid-August at this very moment. I would need to write the letter immediately. Tomorrow. Another bolt of lightning struck, matching my internal buzzing. A door to my destiny had opened. This prairie had been tilled to create our life here and I finally saw what hope it held for me. Nothing—no storm, no season, no man—could stand in my way.

THIRTEEN

Oenikika

June 16, 1862

The white man has gone back on their word. Again. Our tribe had been moved onto an even smaller reservation; a greater annuity payment for future generations "was guaranteed." We now were kept to the south side of the Long River; the whites had started moving into the north. I scoffed when I heard of the new treaty. The land from the first treaty, the land *promised* for Dakota to eternity, already taken away. How could my father ever agree to another treaty with the Liars? It made something in me question whether my father held as much power with the white men as I assumed. Still, I hoped our situation would improve with the arrival of the annuity payment, scheduled for this moon—The Moon When the Chokecherries are Black is usually a sturdy, reliable moon, the season of ripening. The time was finally ripe to bring the overdue payment. We'd buy supplies and food. Preparations for the winter. I tried to view the actual experience of moving as a blessing for Tashunke and me, as it was my first time taking down and setting up our tipi myself, a tradition that was a consistent part of life for wives for generations. I loved our home; I'd brought in gifts from Dina and Scarlet Woman and used spring berries to paint two blue circles around the top of the tipi. The blue felt like bringing in the sky. Open and hopeful in a way this reservation was not.

I wished for Owl Woman to come see how I'd set up . . . double-check that my tent poles were pounded at the most secure angle, as she always used to do. Hopefully, Father would bring her to evening fire; I could show her then. Anxiety tightened in my chest. My father remained with her in the white man's house, which was now off the reservation. Upon their square of eighty acres. Acres. As if the land could be cut up and quartered like the quick cleaning of a doe. Though at the time I resented the sight of it, at least on the north reservation I could step out of the tipi and see their house on the bluff. Now on the smaller south reservation, I couldn't see them at all. Couldn't quickly ride up with water or firewood for Grandmother. Maybe it'd be best for Owl Woman to come live with Tashunke and me. I could care for her. I picked up my medicine bag and hung it on the hook Tash had made me on the north tipi pole. I liked that it hung proudly; completing the space. I was sure Owl Woman would be pleased with how I'd arranged things. As I stood admiring the set-up, Tash ducked inside, with two jackrabbits in his hands.

"We don't go hungry today." My husband passed me the day's food. I knew Tash was disappointed he hadn't found larger game. But I was grateful my husband had honed his sharpshooting from all his independent hunting. Earlier in the season, Tashunke had spoken with Riggs, who helped arrange a trade of Tash's old shotgun for a rifle. Now we didn't need to pick tiny bits of shot out of rabbit and pheasant.

"I rode past Wabasha's camp. The Farmer Dakota's gardens and fields are budding. Your grandmother's too," Tash shared. Jealousy flared inside of me, imagining bountiful gardens at the time of harvest. There'd be so much food. Less worry for the winter. I questioned, feeling a bit guilty, if the Farmer Dakota had made a better plan than we who remained committed to traditional ways had. Crops would feed when the hunting was sparse, and the hunting was getting worse by the day.

"Did you stop at the house?" I asked. I was contemplating if I should bring my portion of jackrabbit to Owl Woman.

"I did. Your father took a grouse this morning." His quick answer knew I was really asking about my worry for Grandmother's food supply.

"Very well." I set to prepare our one meal of the day. Though we were blessed to find food today, I already feared for tomorrow. I should set out in search of berries. Our constant preoccupation with finding food took all our time. Maybe instead of bringing Owl Woman to live with us, I thought for the first time, perhaps Tash and I should move our tipi to Little Crow's land. Help my grandmother farm. We could share the crops. We'd be apart from camp circle. But if the hunting parties could not follow where the animals roam, what would we do? Is this what my father had been planning for?

I tried to fix my mind on the goodness that remained. Yesterday, I'd found puffball while seeking out mushrooms for a meal. I tucked them into a pouch in my medicine bag, careful not to break them open. Today my body ached from the work of yesterday, and now I feared I had risked too much by exhausting myself. Without secure food, energy was precious. But to get energy we needed to search for food. When neither was available, the fear came.

We ate the rabbit stewed with a little mushroom and water. It was warm in the tipi, so we sat outside. Tash liked to face west. And I liked to sit with my husband. I was growing more accustomed to his handsomeness and the details of his face, his body, were etched in my mind. I loved the roughness of his palms, where his hands had changed from the long hours holding reins. His muscled arms. He was so powerfully alive. The scar down through his top lip was as familiar as the easy sound of his voice. Impossible to imagine him in any other way. And he always wore two necklaces around his neck . . . Thin strings of leather, each tied around a smooth round stone. I was curious if this was a custom of his people. I had seen our men sometimes wearing bear claws or buffalo horn necklaces for ceremony, but never a stone. And those were only worn for ceremonies.

"Husband, your stone necklaces. When did you first put these on?" I asked.

Tashunke looked ahead, his serious expression deeper than usual. I worried if I'd asked something that upset him. "I tied them myself as a boy. In my days I rode alone. They remind me of my mother and sister." I stayed quiet and kept my ears open to hear his heart. Grandmother says listening is the wisest thing to do when someone is sharing their pain. "I couldn't shield them. The weight of their memory is carried with me." He stared out at the open plain.

Tashunke had never spoken of his past; all I knew was what Wenona had told me. He was a young boy and his tribe was attacked by the Blackfoot. Now I learn through his necklaces, that his mother and sister were killed. I was heartbroken for my strong husband. Even as a little boy, a man's instinct and greatest role as a warrior is to protect his women. What a loyal son and brother, to carry his love with him. I looked upon my husband. I wanted to hold him in the places that hurt. I loved him. I knew Tashunke was talented and handsome but was continuing to learn the depth of his thoughtfulness and care. He was the wisest and strongest kind of man—one with a heart he lets beat.

"I saw the necklaces were beautiful. Now, even more so how I see them upon you."

A friendly fox stuck its face out from a thicket, sneaking a smell of our finished meal. I felt my body buzz from the nourishment. The fox ducked its head back in, as another tiny creature came bounding for us.

Kimimela's bare feet raced as she announced, "Auntie. Grandmother Mika says to tell you . . . the time has come." At my niece's words, worry overtook me. Wenona's belly had not become full as a woman who is in her time. Her cheeks weren't yet to a plumpness. The baby was not ready . . . but I leaped to my feet and ducked back into the tipi. I grabbed for my medicine bag, pulling the long strap over my shoulder. I led Kimimela back, trying not to rush. I wanted to enter the birthing with the steady peace of a healer. Not the worry of a cousin. Little Rapids paced outside their tipi. I reassured myself, *We have the puffball*, but soon as I entered the tipi, the look in Wenona's and Mika's eyes made me nervous.

"Can I paint my face in celebration?" Kimi eagerly asked.

"Not yet . . ." I quietly explained to my niece, who was excited and not appreciating the gravity of this circumstance, that there was a risk we may be grieving instead of celebrating. Childbirth was a dangerous sacred time for a woman. I should know—I was living proof a birth could bring deathly devastation. I passed Kimi her favorite doll and told her, "Sit quietly, rock your dolly, and pray to Wankan Tanka."

The labor was difficult, as if my cousin's body wanted to both hold the baby in and needed the baby out at the very same time. I was close by when Aunt Mika's steady hands received the newborn at the moment of her arrival. At the separation, I quickly applied the puffball to the mother–child cord. The infant was impossibly tiny, fitting in Aunt Mika's hands. Her cries were weak. There was not the instant rush of relief and joy usual at the sound of a crying babe. Instead, worry lingered. This world seemed too big, and the baby girl far too small.

My mind anxiously raced to think of any plants that could be of help. We needed to summon the Medicine Man to start calling out to the spirit world to strengthen the child. Aunt Mika's face appeared solemn as she passed the newest arrival of our family to Wenona's devoted arms. The eyes of the mother took in her preciously tiny daughter with unwavering love. Those long moons of the hard winter, our stomachs starving—this baby hadn't had the nourishment to grow strong. I remembered the anger and ruin in Wenona's eyes after we pried open the Liar's Delivery. I looked upon the fragile baby girl, her teeny arms spiderwebbed with blue veins.

"Kayawi," Wenona whispered lovingly. Kayawi, Girl Shielded as the Turtle. A name giving strength and protection. My heart surged with love for the newest arrival to our people and my eyes filled with tears. Each birth was a miracle. We would fight for her.

I turned to my niece, who was still seated holding her doll, her wide eyes showing she understood something was amiss. This was a delicate moment and my heart was resolute. "Kimimela, go paint your face. Celebrate the arrival of your sister."

July 12, 1862

In the midmorning sun, Dina passed me a tanning scraper. Scarlet Woman held taut the edge of a beaver pelt and tied a tanning rope posted into the ground to hold it in place. Grasshoppers leaped onto the pelt immediately, I shooed them away with my hand as I pressed down. In the Moon of the Red Blooming Lilies, the creatures that crawl were blooming more than anything else . . . locusts had overrun camp. In just a matter of hours, they destroyed the plants growing at the house; Owl Woman's hard work had been nibbled down to stubs. The crops of Chief Wabasha's farming village were devastated. Another food source destroyed. So discouraging. *This is why we must remain in the ways of hunting.* I tried to assure myself. Usually, Wenona would be here helping with the tanning but she stayed in her tipi. Always holding tiny Kayawi, the baby's little chest still working hard to breathe. The medicine man meditated for two days as he burned sweetgrass. He said Wankan Tanka will make a decision within the next moon cycle. But Wenona wasn't finishing the mother's tea I brewed for her each day. I pressed my worry into the hide, pressing to clean it smooth, working the skin until it was supple and soft. Wolfchasher and Bonko wrestled in the long grass beyond our tanning work.

"Auntie, I am hungry," Wolfchaser said as he knelt near me at the tanning station.

"Hopefully the hunting party returns soon," I said brightly, though I too was hungry. I hoped for the hunting party to violate the treaty; we needed much more food. It was time to start making jerky for the winter. A few rabbits and the occasional deer were barely keeping us going . . . and now we had no white man's crops. There were no preparations for winter. My father had been so adamant to keep our word, remain on the reservation. But the white man hadn't kept their word. There was *still* no annuity payment, there had been no food delivery, and the reservation had been decreased. We needed buffalo. The men needed to go wherever the buffalo called them; not where the whites told us to stay.

"Look at me." Bonko walked over from the tall grass, holding up two handfuls of moss to his chin as if he had a white man's beard. "I'm Riggs!" Scarlet Woman, Dina and I burst into laughter. As our laughter quieted, I heard the sound of men's voices. Were they already back? Perhaps they had come upon a herd in the morning, taken many animals quickly. Thank goodness. I turned to look across camp, but as soon as I saw them, I knew good fortune was not the case.

Cut Nose was stumbling. Cousin Brown Wing was behind him, holding a bottle of the white man's drink. Killing Ghost, Breaking Up, Runs Against Something When Crawling, and Red Otter were wrestling like children. They had been drinking. This group must have abandoned the hunt and decided to find trouble. A chill of fear ran through me; I'd heard of the white man's drink turning men into blind fools, mean and terrorizing. I wished my father and Tashunke were here. But it was us women and children alone. Some of the men walked as if they were dizzy. Their voices carried through camp uncharacteristically loudly.

Dina and Scarlet Woman looked worried and fearful. I was uncertain what to do . . . remain working on the tanning? Should we sneak away? Hide the children? Wolfchaser laid on the ground near my feet, pretending two pinecones were dogs barking at one another. Brown Wing walked towards us. I was nervous as he approached, but I tried to appear focused on my tanning. Wolfchaser played with the pinecones, making barking sounds. His Uncle Brown Wing crouched near us. "You know what our people did before our dogs we have now?" Brown Wings words were slurred. His question was harmless, but I watched my cousin with careful eyes. Wolfchaser shook his head no. Brown Wing explained, "Little boys would go steal a wolf pup from a mother wolf's den." Wolfchaser's eyes opened in astonishment, and he looked at me to verify if his uncle was telling him a tall tale.

I nodded at Wolfchaser. "It's true. Boys your age would go into a den. It required much courage for a young brave." Wolfchaser looked scared and thrilled. Brown Wing smiled wide, unusual for his typically serious disposition.

But the moment was soon poisoned, as Cut Nose staggered towards us. His eyes were glassy and an eerie meanness was pungent upon him. "That was when we could be real men. Not trapped by the white man as these pathetic boys are now." Cut Nose kicked at Wolfchaser but lost his footing. Cut Nose tumbled and fell atop the pulled beaver pelt. It was so taut it tore in two as he came crashing through.

The women shrieked and Wolfchaser skittered back, terrified. Dina and Scarlet Woman looked both mortified and furious. Scarlet Woman took Bonko and led him away from the scene. I pulled Wolfchaser behind me. Dina sat up straight, never moving an inch from her seat. "Your wives cast you out from the tipi." I sat, shocked. It was a rare occurrence but a husband could be cast out for treating a wife improperly. But never in public. I looked at Cut Nose, his dark hair tangled, body sweating unusually, lying in a tangled mess of a destroyed pelt. Instead of remorse, Cut Nose laughed an ugly laugh.

I was terrified. Cut Nose kicked at Wolfchaser, a child! The men were not in their right minds. Cut Nose laid in his disgrace and continued to laugh. All of the women and children scurried into hiding for the rest of the afternoon. I hid in Wenona's tipi, stitched a pair of Little Rapids leggings, and listened to the conversations of the drunk men outside. The men continued to drink the white man's brown water and were out of their minds.

"We cannot hunt as we used to," I heard the men complain as the bottle sloshed among them.

Another grumbled, "No animals anyway."

Their belligerent voices argued over what do about the missing annuity payments. I wondered if there was any plant antidote, any medicine to undo the state they were in. They complained about the trading post big man who intimidated people. My heart feared listening to their complaints, their voices trailing off then starting again. But what I worried about most was the legitimacy in their arguments. The lack of food. The confines of the reservation weren't realistic for our way of life. It was destroying us. These were all the things I was terrified of. I too felt we were being wronged by the white men. Was part of me as foolish as these men? Or did the drink just loosen them enough to let out their legitimate anger? Their fear?

When the sun finally lowered, and a thin ray of light shone through the small opening at the bottom of the tipi, I heard the hoofbeats. The hunting party was back. Finally, support to deal with the men who had horrified camp for the entire day. I looked out and saw Tash and

Uncle Chaska with bucks across the backs of each of their horses. Two deer! Finally, meat. I stepped out of the tipi cautiously, ready to receive my husband and begin preparing. I was intimidated by the madness of the drinking men who were scattered on the ground. Laying on their bellies and backs, as if they were too dizzy to stand. I'd never seen anything like it. Men uncaring for their dignity. Their sense of basic kinship manners erased by the brown liquid.

Chaska, Little Rapids, Tashunke, and Father rode to the middle of camp and dismounted in front of their less accomplished counterparts. Cut Nose turned on his belly, and his glassy eyes seemed full of spite, "Ahh, the Great Hunters have returned."

"What children put foolishness of drink ahead of the tribe's needs? You have not even attempted a hunt." Uncle Chaska stared at his own son Brown Wing, who sat up and cowered. I knew my cousin knew better. Once he came to his senses, his heart would enflame with embarrassment to be seen in such a state.

Tashunke appeared quietly irritated; he was a man of integrity like my father. My husband would not want to engage with such shameful men; Tash nudged Wicapi forward. Her back legs were streaked with the blood of the buck and my stomach moaned in anticipation of a filling meal tonight. I was already planning how I'd prepare the venison and hoping we'd have some left for the start of our winter preparation. I rubbed my hand on Wicapi's soft nose, then moved to her back legs. Tashunke hopped off and stood beside me as we prepared to pull the heavy, lifeless deer to the ground. As I was grabbing the hindquarter, Cut Nose stumbled into me and attempted to grab the leg of the carcass from my hand. I jumped back in shock and surprise. It was a violation to make such aggressive contact with a woman.

Quicker than a lightning strike, Tash and Little Crow moved beside Cut Nose. Their voices followed as the thunder does, in unison calling out, "Do not touch my wife!" and "Do not touch my daughter!" Tash's eyes flared with protective anger. My father looked stern and intimidating. He was making a statement. The chief must be respected.

Cut Nose laughed insultingly. "Ahhh. Chief Little Crow eats from his garden. He doesn't need a deer."

"The birds and locusts are eating more of his garden than he ever will," Runs Against Something When Crawling said from the ground beyond us. My eyes went wide in disbelief. Red Otter laughed, seemingly unable to stop himself. Their disrespect was overwhelming. A chief was never spoken to in such a manner.

"What kind of men lay like a lazy woman past the dawn. This deer gave his life, we've shown it gratitude," Father responded. His voice was strong and gruff as he pointed at all the men. "You show shame and disgrace. This meat will not be shared. You are *banished* to Fool's Lodge 'til the next moon."

The Fool's Lodge was a terrible village of rejected and punished men, a place of casting out for all the tribes. I looked about at the reckless young men, slowly sitting up from their day's stupor. I saw the tears in Scarlet Woman's eyes before she pulled her head back in their tipi. Father didn't even know Cut Nose had already been banished from his tipi by his wives. Scarlet Woman, Dina, and Bonko would have no food, no provider. I looked at our deer, my stomach hungry, and knew I could make do with a little less.

Cut Nose and the young men got to their feet and began their way out of camp. With more sharpness than I thought possible for the drunk man, Cut Nose turned around. "What chief lives in a white man's house? Puts his tribe on a reservation? Twice."

My father did not respond. Instead, Little Crow held a cold stare. Letting Cut Nose turn again and continue in his shame. But the message had been heard. I felt protective of my father. And guilty; I too had questioned his choices. My father's eyes stayed on the disrespectful men. I wondered what options he really had as chief. Especially when his own men were being disempowered in a new way. By the bottle.

"Thank you for protecting me," I said to Tashunke and my father. Father nodded and walked back to Mato. I felt relieved that the drunk men were finally gone.

"It's been a long day. For us both," I said to Tashunke. He passed me the sharp blade to begin butchering. Before he walked away, I asked, "Husband, I will share a portion?" as I nodded my head toward Dina and Scarlet Woman's tent.

"My wife is wise, always considering others," he responded affirmatively.

I walked with a backstrap towards their tipi. I said, "No man's foolishness, white or Dakota, should make a woman go hungry."

Friday August 15, 1862

Tash and I seated ourselves in the soft grass of the hillside; it'd become our nightly ritual to watch the horses in the blue of twilight. My legs stretched out exhausted; with little food my body tired so quickly. I worried about using the little energy we had to make the nightly walk. But this time was some of the only good we had left on the reservation. As we took our seats, Wicapi raised her blonde head and nickered into the night air, calling out to us. The horses munched away in the meadow below. Fireflies flickered and floated between their legs. My husband watched his herd keenly. A foal couldn't wiggle its nose at the other side of meadow without Tash noticing. He'd trained the horses, they were responsive to him in a way I hadn't known was possible. I imagined he felt with the horses as I did with my healing plants. Alive. Fully connected to the Great Mystery. Wicapi made her way towards us; she liked to be near Tash. Just as I did.

Tonight, in the Moon of the Swatted Tail, the air sat heavy with heat. It would storm soon. I prayed a storm would break up the fish in the river, who had buried themselves out in the deep cool water. Wenona especially needed the nourishment; she had fallen ill with discouragement that baby Kayawi wasn't growing. Wenona's body wasn't producing milk as it did with the twins. I brewed her mother's tea—but no medicine could remedy the requirements of a mother's stomach. If we didn't get our food delivery and payment tomorrow, I worried for Wenona and the baby. We were approaching the end of the moon the Medicine Man said would either call for the baby or let her remain for us. We needed this food. And I feared for Owl Woman, who grew frailer by the day. I hated how much fear and worry persisted in my thoughts. We all walk on to the Happy Hunting Land someday . . . I was not supposed to fear death. I could understand that someday, Grandmother will walk on. But Baby Kayawi; she was robbed before she was born. The threat of her death wasn't natural in the cycle of life. It was a tipping of the scale by the white man. We had to get away from them. Could we escape the reservation? All flee together? Would the tribes to the west of us accept an entire nation of Dakota people? Were these the questions my father asked himself? There was no simple answer. And all we could focus on each day was finding enough food to last to the next.

I chatted quietly about my hope for fish to Tashunke while I rubbed bear grease mixed with goldenseal across his arms to repel mosquitos. "Even if the fish don't move, you and father are going with Riggs to the Rat Trader tomorrow. We'll have our food delivery and payment," I said hopefully. I felt like I did when talking with Wenona, how easily I shared my thoughts and feelings with my husband.

"Riggs appears trustworthy. He says Wankan Tanka and his God may be the same; I see that too. If he remains with our tribe, we could have a ceremony for a Dakota name for our friend," my husband suggested with sincerity. A naming ceremony for a white man . . . unheard of. But I thought about my father living in the white man's house. A convert. How much converting was pushed upon our people . . . if a good white man existed, perhaps we should convert him to our ways.

I looked over at my husband. "Man Who Sings to Horses. Tashunke. My soul understood your name the moment I saw you," I said lovingly, remembering my husband in the silvery fog of a meadow.

He stared out into the deepening twilight. Bats swooped and crickets chirped their summer song. "Oenikika. The Breath of Life." He paused. "I cannot see you in any other name. Your father named you well."

Hearing him say my name, recognizing that my father alone had named me, summoned the hurting child that still lived within me. The understanding of my beginning, that my birth brought so much pain. It'd been a quiet shame I'd held my entire life. I'd never spoken of this sadness, always keeping it in. But something about my husband's strength and the emerging blanket of stars above us made me feel safe.

"My name remembers my shame. The worst part of my being." I let out a shaky breath as I told my husband, "My birth *took* my mother's life." I pressed my hands to the earth; just saying *mother* made me draw back to her. I looked at the beautiful world around us. "My name, Breath of Life, will always remind me of what I took away." A spring of warm sadness bubbled up from my depths, I wanted to know my mother so badly, and yet I was the one who removed her. Having our world moved to a reservation, made smaller and ever smaller, had taken me from the many places I had felt her spirit. The valleys of coneflower. The chilly waters of the licorice creek. Places that held her were stolen. I'd lost her again.

"That's not what I see when I look at you," Tash said. "I see life." He nodded, then continued, "I first noticed you in a meadow. That afternoon when I returned to my tipi, for the first time I realized how empty it was. When I saw you, I saw the hope of life."

He had indeed noticed me in the meadow that morning I walked with Wenona. The chickadees of my heart took flight again. I felt seen by my husband. Loved. My body was weak with hunger, but my heart was filled with untiring love. For him. For our people. The night grew darker and the constellations began their slow crawl across the sky. I thought we'd return to the tipi, and I began to stand. But Tashunke spoke, and I took my place near him again.

"I will share the dream I had. A vision."

I was eager to listen. He'd never shared a dream with me before. Our bond as husband and wife was growing like an oak tree. The roots sunk deep into the soil while the branches stretched into the sky, soaking in the life-giving sun. The spirit of the tree both secure in the earth and hopeful towards the sky. That's how learning Tash felt.

"In my dream, the hardest winter came, even more difficult than last. Ice formed over our tipi; we could not go in for shelter." His voice sounded troubled as if this dream had actually occurred. "My wife took her heart out of her chest, sunk in her fingers, tearing it in two. You put both pieces of your heart upon my feet to keep them warm." He continued, "The winter storm raged. I told you 'Hold on!' and put you on Wicapi's back. Your heart kept me warm enough to keep going. It never ended—we just kept moving towards the sunset together."

The breath of something powerful, something true, washed through me and the hairs on my arms stood on end. I ran my hand up my arm, feeling the reality of my husband's dream. I looked back at him. "The Great Spirit brought you truth. I'd give you my heart."

FOURTEEN

Emma Heard

Sunday, August 17, 1862

Today was the most dreadfully tedious of my life. I was so eager to write my letter of request to the Teacher's Association, that the expectation of attending Sunday church was unbearable. I sat in the stiff pew, my legs bouncing in my anxiety to get a pen and paper in my hands. Whomever built this bench made sure sinner and saint alike would never get fully comfortable in the presence of God.

I prayed gratitude for God's grace in Miss Knudsen's miraculous reply. But my gratefulness kept being interrupted with my burning desire to get home and write to the teacher's board in Chicago. I watched Pastor Vogel at the pulpit, cloaked in his green velvet robe. Distracting drops of sweat rolled off his face and dropped onto the open Bible in front of him.

"GOD," he boomed, "is educating with the agony of our sins." The overheated congregation stared back in silence. Farmer Krause, broke the silence, gutturally clearing his nasal passage. I dug my nails into my palms.

I looked about the oppressive sanctuary, noticing a Dakota man in the back pew. He was dressed as we were, but sat straightly upright, dark hair parted clean down the middle, a long face composed with stoic dignity. He seemed to be taking in the sermon with more attention and focus than anyone else. My spine tingled with a buzz when I recognized him. Chief Little Crow! I was stunned. The leader of the Dakota, sitting amongst us.

I turned back to face the front, trying not to gawk. I'd seen him derided by Myrick just a day ago. Now, he sat behind me in mindful consideration of Pastor Vogel's longwinded sermon. Had I overestimated the intensity of the interaction yesterday? Little Crow calm and thoughtful; he didn't appear a man ready to storm a storehouse and steal what's rightfully his, as I had feared. Pa mentioned that two of the primary efforts outlined in the treaty with the Indians was to help them learn to farm and help them find God. Seeing the chief in church, I thought, perhaps the resolution could be as simple as a few seeds of corn and faith.

A swirling curiosity overcame me . . . was handsome Missionary Riggs in attendance today? Perhaps, he had brought the chief. In my desire, I dared to turn back again and survey the pews. Mr. and Mrs. Kuhn stared drearily ahead. Hanna Kuhn raised her eyes in a flash of fun at me, enjoying my waywardness. I made a half-smirk back, as if I was in on the adolescent defiance Hanna was insinuating. But all I wanted was to glimpse the Missionary's face again. The other benches were empty. No luck; Riggs wasn't here. I exhaled the disappointment. What was wrong with me to feel such discontent over the absence of a man? It was nonsense. I readjusted in my uncomfortable seat.

I stared ahead and thought of the regal chief sitting thoughtful in the last bench. What did he think of us settlers? Could he understand Pastor Vogel's English words? Our Christian message and morals? Did he see us as honest people or did we appear hypocrites? Last week Pastor Vogel spoke about taking care of the least among us. If human beings were starving across the river, did their circumstance reflect the obligation of our faith? I couldn't even be sure of exactly who we were at times.

After ninety minutes, the long-winded sermon ended. I looked again to the back, only to see a vacancy where the chief had been. We rose from the creaky pews and made our way out the center aisle. We children rushed back out to the wagon, all aching to head home. It was a brutal blow when Pa announced we'd ride out to Leavenworth for a late luncheon with the Eastlicks, who had recently settled on a 50-acre plot at the northern turn in the Cottonwood River. I'd have to wait to write my letter. Ma scolded our unenthusiastic expressions and said, "There's nothing in the world as important as being a good neighbor."

Otto, in rare obstinance, replied, "Soon as I shake the neighbor's hand, I'm going for a dip in the river."

The afternoon passed slowly. We Heard children made our way to the riverbank; Otto offered a sliver of entertainment by swan diving into the refreshing river water. I held Peter and paced in the shade of a willow tree, jealous of Otto's freedom. I whispered into Peter's ear, "Want to hear a secret, Little Brother?" I tickled my nose against his soft curls. "Someday, your sister is going to be a teacher." My baby brother giggled, and I tried to relax with him. I'd just have to write my letter tomorrow.

I looked south across the gently flowing Cottonwood, toward the Dakota reservation. Identical green willows dangled their long arms into the current. Little Crow had looked contemplative today; I was curious what his thoughts held. The Dakota were so close. Our worlds both overlapped and repelled each other. From the stacks of land patents I'd copied, I knew that settlers would soon have every single plot of land around that reservation. The incoming settlers felt like a winding vice; the pressure for land was overwhelming. Little Crow had to feel it too. Did he pray, to our God or his own, for peaceful coexistence with the strangers? Was his fortune, or those of his people—our neighbors—any of my responsibility, really? I protectively pulled Peter closer as I shook off the shadow of bad feelings.

Finally, the sun angled lower in the sky, and we waved "Auf Wiedersen" to the Eastlicks.

Settled into the bed I shared with Ida, I let out a sigh. The entire day felt a setback. Ida looked at me, a quizzical look on her face.

"It's nothing" I whispered. But Ida sensed my preoccupation.

"It is just so dreadfully hot," I said as I flipped the quilt off of me. Ida waved one finger in the air, her signal that she agreed. A "no" or disagreement was shaking two fingers. She too pulled the quilt off herself.

"I would've given anything to jump in that river." I said.

She tiredly waved her finger; agreeing, then closed her blue eyes. We were mirror images, curled facing one another in our bed. The heavy heat of the summer night gripped me. I tossed atop the straw tick, my unfulfilled goal running through my mind. It seemed impossible for me to settle till my letter was written and my future secured.

PART TWO

FIFTEEN

Oenikika

Monday, August 18, 1862, 12:05 a.m.

My eyes couldn't fully open. They were swollen; as if all the tears I cried had flowed back into my eyes and were trapped under my skin. In the total darkness of night, Tashunke's stirring woke me. I turned over, kicked our blanket off my legs, and closed my heavy eyes. My entire being was exhausted from grief, and my throat pained from my cries of mourning for baby Kayawi. But I felt Tash's weight rise from bed. Getting up in the night was odd for my husband, whose routines and habits I'd been absorbing. I opened my eyes once again and tried to make sense of the blackness in our tipi. Tash pulled on his leggings.

"Husband?" my scratchy voice asked.

"They're riding to approach Chief Little Crow. It's a war call," Tashunke explained. A call to war? I sat up immediately as my body surged awake. Now? The humid night air felt suddenly thick with tension as I slipped my feet into my moccasins. I wanted to understand what was happening. I'd been so consumed in Wenona's grieving tent over the last days . . . Had I missed some event? Who would rouse a war call in the middle of the night? The men usually deliberated these decisions at war council; this midnight commotion was unusual. Perhaps they would finally break into the storehouse, I thought; after all, Cut Nose had challenged my father to do it already. Wisely, Father wouldn't be pressured into such a perilous and important decision.

The rumble of hoofbeats vibrated across the earth; many riders were on the move. My heart swelled with protectiveness for my father. How many warriors were surrounding the house? Summoning the chief from a deep sleep . . . was this a tactic to catch him off guard? And dear Owl Woman would be woken from her bed by men calling for war. How overwhelming! My instincts beckoned me; a granddaughter must be steadfast at her grandmother's side. Women were not typically present at a war council. But then again, a typical war council was not called in the middle of the night. At the chief's house. And these were not typical circumstances—failed treaties, missing payments, reservations. This was not a usual foe. What white man warriors could be met at battle? All I'd seen were farmers. We were too weak for a war right now. We needed food. Supplies. I did not have enough medicine.

"You're riding out now?" I asked. Tashunke nodded affirmatively.

"I will join you." It was a bold assertion, rare for a wife. My husband watched as I pulled my day dress over my head. More hoofbeats barreled past; it seemed bands from the west were riding along the river, heading to the meeting. There may be hundreds of warriors gathered by the time we arrived. I recognized my husband may not want to bring his wife out in the midst of the chaos. But all the more reason for me to be at my grandmother's side.

"They're meeting at my father's," I said." Owl Woman should not be alone in such a gathering of the men."

"Wicapi will carry us both. Move quickly."

Wicapi trotted through the shallows of the Long River to the north side of the reservation where my father's house remained. I wrapped my arms around Tash's sturdy waist as a sliver of the Moon of the Harvest shone above. A war council—the reasoning for warfare would be discussed, every man sharing his opinion. Then my father would contemplate, decide whether to head to battle, and the tribe would yield to his influence. Though I feared because Chief Little Crow had been so disrespected recently . . . Would our men *actually* yield if my father decided now was not the time for war? There was more than enough reason to take the storehouse . . . I actually hoped my father would before all the food spoiled and went rancid, as it had been delivered last winter. But a war with the white men? I had nowhere near enough medicine prepared. The typical plants for battle wounds were off the reservation. My father had worked so hard for peace with the Great White Father. He'd never give up his position of favor with their chief.

"Where does my husband stand on the war call?"

"I saw my people killed. War is not in my heart," he explained. "But I am loyal to Chief Little Crow."

My husband was thoughtful; I was grateful for his sturdiness. He wasn't one of the fools clinging to the bottle. He wasn't a Dakota in the white man's trousers, plowing a field. Tashunke was strong as the sun and steady as the moon. Though he wasn't from our band by birth, in spirit he lived the Dakota way. If we went to war, Tashunke would ride as a warrior. I clung tighter to his waist. Wartime was a time of honor for men and deep fear for wives. As a child, I hated the anxiety I felt when my father was out on the warpath with the Ojibwe. A woman should be proud of their warrior brothers, sons, fathers, or husbands. But I was always quietly terrified. I'd watched Aunt Mika tend to injured braves—their wounds horrible and devastating. I saw the cruel pain battle inflicted no matter how courageous a warrior was. I wanted my husband and father at home, in the village. My father had been protecting us from this. Shielding us, even when he rode to the Great White Father. I reassured myself as I leaned my cheek against Tash's back. My husband and father would both oppose the war call.

I could barely see my father's house among the warriors and their horses, hundreds of them; swarming with energy. The braves danced and sang, showing the War Council gathered inside that they were ready to be released to battle. Brown Wing was among them; his feet stepped to the rhythm of the war dance, but when our eyes connected, I saw something concerning in his countenance—a look of worry in his eyes. The rest of the braves were wound up, calling with powerful, angry voices, the opposite of fear. What was my cousin feeling among the men? The hairs at the back of my neck stood up in alarm. I felt like a deer on alert in a field. Something was amiss . . . The truth was in their formidable voices. And yet truth, also, in my cousin's worried eyes. Tash guided me quickly through the men toward the house; I followed closely behind him. I flinched as the war cry overwhelmed my ears. Every disappointment over the past moons was awakened, feeding the braves their fury. Their wrath was not aimed at me, but to be near such a powerful force sent shivers of wonder and fear down my spine. It was intimidating. This was more than a war council. The entire war party was already assembled, primed, ready to be broken free.

We got through the pack and to the house. Tashunke opened the door; inside my former home, the men of importance now gathered for the council meeting. Chief Little Crow nodded at Tashunke, accepting his arrival. My father didn't look upon me, though I knew he was aware of my presence behind my husband. I was relieved Father didn't send me out immediately, shame me for being present at a meeting of the men. I hoped he secretly understood why I'd come as I scurried to Owl Woman's side. She was sitting up in her bed, trembling with her deer blanket pulled around her. My sweet grandmother. A mothering energy arose within me, to care and comfort her. I whispered, trying to be discreet and took Grandmother's hand in mine. It was shaking as I'd never felt before. I held it firmly, hoping I was not trembling myself.

"I had nowhere to go," she said to me with sadness in her voice. It must have shaken her to the core to be woken from her slumber, surrounded by powerful men, and angry braves forcefully stirring around her home; being a woman in the midst of this would have been contrary to all her reflexes.

"I didn't want you to be alone," I said as I squeezed her hand. Her faded brown eyes, brimming with tears, looked into mine. Her lonely gaze held pain from more than just this moment . . . The look reminded me of how isolated she had been upon this bluff. Though the last months were difficult, Tash and I had reveled in each other. We'd found our routine as a married couple. The night I dropped my water cup in the fire, and we shared our first full laugh together in the darkness. During all the small moments of happiness I'd shared with Tash, Grandmother had still been here in the four walls. Tomorrow I'd come for her. She'd spend the full day in the village every day. She never needed to feel this overwhelmed and alone at her old age. That was no way for an elder to feel. Owl Woman sputtered a rattling cough. I placed my hand upon her back; she was burning with fever. Instantly, I was wrought with concern. I ran my hand over her back to comfort her, feeling the deep curve of her spine. She coughed again, a rattle from deep inside her lungs. I looked about for the water pail, but it was on the other side of the room. It would not be appropriate for me to move across the space now. Tash and I must take her back to our tipi tonight after the war council dismissed the call. I could care for Grandmother tonight, ride in search of artemisia for fever and butterfly weed for her cough in the morning. But . . .

I filled with dread as I remembered—I'd never found either of those plants on the reservation. Tomorrow I'd search again with new determination. *I must.* I exhaled my worry quietly, as I continued to rub Owl Woman's back. There was nothing as important as being a good relative. I watched my resilient husband standing in his quiet contemplation. Being a good wife. A good daughter. Niece. Cousin, I reminded myself. All the people that made me who I am. The people the Great Spirit had blessed me to be bound to.

I sat cross-legged, leaned in closer to Owl Woman and took in the gathering. Men formed a circle around flickering torchlights. Tash stood next to Little Rapids and Uncle Chaska. My mother's brother, Chief Traveling Hail, sat opposite my father, near the fireplace. Chief Wabasha, dressed in his white man pants and shirt, stood at the other side of Uncle Chaska. The door opened; the sounds of singing engulfed the room and Chief Red Iron appeared; Father nodded, accepting him to the council. Other prominent men from various camps stood near the walls, some so close to grandmother their moccasins dirtied her blanket. They went around the room, each man sharing his view on war.

"I do not favor."

"I do favor. They lie and cheat."

I couldn't believe the sight of so many prominent men in a white man's house. A *war council* meeting in the four walls. It was a grand irony. I still hated being inside such a strange structure, but now, with my life in a tipi, I looked upon it with a new understanding for my father. He was trying to navigate these uncertain times. Out the window, the braves were dancing, their cries for war continued. It seemed like their song was only intensifying.

I swallowed, my throat pained with grief and nervousness, as I asked my Grandmother, "Why meet tonight?"

She coughed, then whispered, "Brown Wing, Breaking Up, Killing Ghost, and Runs Against Something When Crawling . . . this afternoon." I thought of Brown Wing's scared eyes . . . What could they have done? "They unwisely killed five white men and women. In a dare."

Killed five people? Brown Wing? Again, a breath of truth rushed down my spine in warning, alerting me; this was horrendous.

She shook her head. "A dare over chicken eggs."

"No," I whispered aghast. There was so much to be upset with our pale-faced neighbors about . . . But for my own cousin and our men to be so unwise! To kill innocent men and women. Brown Wing and the others would need to pay with blood. There was no way around it. The white men would come calling for my cousin. Tears of devastation filled my eyes. Why! Why be so terribly stupid, Brown Wing? His niece died yesterday. Obey kinship, stay and grieve. Then there would have been no recklessness. I thought Grandmother had told me everything, but she continued.

"The boys rode back to Fool's Lodge. Every man there rode to your uncle, Chief Traveling Hail. And now, they're here, asking Chief Little Crow to go to war." Her weary eyes met mine, a sickness overtaking her just as a fateful moment was overtaking our tribe.

No. This was like a pot atop a fire, rolling with an angry boil. My cousin and his friends had gone too far. The whole lot of Fool's Lodge riding to Chief Traveling Hail? Who they knew was the most angry and ill-tempered chief towards the whites . . . this was intentional, to bypass my father, mobilize a larger group. I simmered with irritation. This was a manipulation, trying to sidestep our usual traditions of deciding to go to war—our council tradition that revolved around logic *purposely* designed to manage emotion-based war calls and avoid hasty rushes to attack an enemy. The outcast men of Fool's Lodge were trying to pressure my father. It was a challenge in power as much as a cry for justice, a call to protect the reckless acts of my cousin.

Owl Woman shuddered as another cough crawled its way out of

her chest. In mourning today, she had coughed, but I thought her throat was hurting from crying out, as mine was. How unwise of me not to notice. Not to be in tune with the world around me. It seemed like the whole earth had shaken as the moon rose tonight . . . And for sweet cousin, Brown Wing. *How proudly you had stood manning our centerfires. How little Wolfchaser looked to you as if you live among the stars.* I couldn't bear the thought of turning Brown Wing in to the whites . . . it sickened me. The hunting had been so sparse, his manhood breaking. Why must he turn to such recklessness? Now my father must pick . . . a war he'd been protecting our people from or turning in the young men of his tribe. In any other circumstance, turning them in would have been the simple wiser choice. But here, now, with hundreds of spirited braves longing to reclaim what had been taken—simple was trampled as the grass under the warriors dancing feet. So many moments had led us here. And now, after a dare over chicken eggs, it seemed as if the entire fate of our people hung in the heavy summer air.

"Tell precisely what you're seeking," my father requested.

"Protect our men, Brown Wing and the others. *Kill* all the whites!" my uncle, Chief Traveling Hail, said fiercely. A cheer came from warriors outside, who were clearly listening through the thin walls.

I knew my father favored compromise and intellect; he'd been in a long dealing with the Great White Father. He wouldn't abandon his diplomacy easily, but, if there ever was a moment to go to war, to attack, to take back everything that our ancestors knew . . . this was it. The white traders had lied and lied again. Our people had been at the brink of starvation. Even now, my stomach was hollow. The Great White Father failed in his promises. A chief could not respect such a foe, a coward who hides behind a piece of paper. The Dakota pray strength for their enemy; that's how we stand tall in our victory in battle. Could we even take on such people without morality? It was a circumstance we'd never faced before.

"You're the greatest chief, where you lead, everyone follows," one man stated. They were appealing to my father, calling for his approval, his leadership. A far cry from the disrespectful behavior of drunk Cut Nose and the other young men towards their chief just days ago.

"They lie to the Dakota, they're no good on their promises. Tell us to eat grass." Little Rapids chimed in. My cousin's husband must be feeling rage after his daughter's death. I didn't blame him. Tears of grief returned to my eyes, for the frailest among us. Next to me, Grandmother's chest rattled again. The old and the young were dependent on the wisdom of the chief. The actions of us, who were in our prime and still able. We held responsibility in this room.

"Our hands are already bloody," Little Rapids continued.

Chief Wabasha, favoring peace, interjected, "Does blood wash off blood?"

"If we go to war, you pour out a stream of Dakota blood upon the earth," my Uncle Chaska agreed. My throat caught tighter with sorrow. I pained to see my uncle make such a sensible statement; doing so would mean that his own son would surely be turned in, killed by the whites for what he'd done. I looked over from my uncle to Tash; the two necklaces upon his chest . . . his people had been killed. My husband knew, as much as anyone, the precious consequences of what was being called for.

Before any others could add to the debate, my father strode into the middle of the room. His eyes were cunning as the crow he was named for, his steps both graceful and commanding as he spoke. "You are like dogs that run mad and snap at their own shadows. The white men are like locusts when they fly so thick, they block the sun." Little Crow's voice forceful and persuasive. "Kill one, two, ten, and *ten times* as many will come to kill you."

The men inside the house were captivated as my father commanded their consideration. The sound of the war cries outside shifted to a steady chanting, a war drum had begun pounding in evocative rhythm. All eyes were upon the chief as he walked steadily around the center of the room, stirring the energy of his influence. My father was at the most powerful I'd ever seen him and my chest pounded with the intensity of the moment. I was both afraid and hopeful. Terrified of what we could do. Terrified of what would happen if we didn't do anything. The fatefulness of my father's decision . . . What it meant for him as chief. What it meant for us all. I held on to Grandmother's knobby hands tighter.

He continued, "Yes, the whites fight far away among themselves. But their soldiers are thick as the tamaracks in the swamps of the Ojibwe." Father shook his head. He had seen the power of the white men to our east. He walked towards Chief Traveling Hail. Chief Little Crow leaned forward and spoke directly to the chief making the call to war. "Your eyes are full of smoke. You will *die* like rabbits when the wolves hunt them in the Hard Moon."

I could barely breathe, filling with unease at the memory of winter . . . relentless wolves upon the skittering jackrabbits on the snow. The bright red stains of their kill sites.

Father turned his back to Traveling Hail and went to the center of the room. It was decided. There would be no war. Chief Wabasha and Uncle Chaska looked to each other, confident that the wisdom of the peace-seeking older generation had prevailed. But surprisingly, my father did not take a seat; he did not conclude with his stirring call for restraint. Instead he continued to walk about the room, rubbing his chin in deep contemplation. What could he be considering? He had been compelling. Decisive. We would die like rabbits in a war with the whites . . . I looked down in the silence, respectful of the deliberation. I stared at Owl Woman's spotted deer hide under me. I remembered playing under it as a child with Wenona and Brown Wing during the cold of a fall evening by the Sandy Lake. It'd been many winters since; so long since that time of innocence. Life had become so hard. I could still feel the swelling of grief around my eyes as I blinked. How hard I cried out in Kayawi's death.

The room was quiet but the warriors outside continued their steady war beat. The gravity of this gathering felt like too much upon my spirit. I closed my eyes; I wanted to be free as we used to be, free as children playing under Grandmother's blanket. Free riding upon the plain. Free gathering medicine. That's where my mind escaped to for a moment, a summer breeze upon my face. My medicine bag full and ready; a speedy recovery for my grandmother. Perhaps, I would have found medicine for Kayawi. A plump baby would wiggle and giggle in Wenona's arms. Owl Woman would smile her gummy smile at the two. The generations gathered as we always had . . .

I opened my eyes; the glow of torches flickered upon my father. I felt overwhelmed with pride of my people; the strength of the deep contemplation of the powerful men standing here. Our history. How mighty we used to be when we'd migrate in mass across the prairie. A shiver of haunting love ran through me. Baby Kayawi. Her tiny perfect fingers. How hard her little chest had fought and fought until it could no more. Wenona's heavy tears. How our cries of grief had felt trapped atop us in the hot summer air. The war drum called out to my pain. *BOOM, boom boom, BOOM, boom boom.* The braves' voices continued to sing, their feet stomping to the beat. The noise suddenly sounded as if it were surging into the house. I felt its sway. My heart stirred as their voices sang louder, like rapids in a growing roar on the river. My spirit grew hungry for dominance, the painted horses of war, the eagle staff, our men's war striped faces. The power of how we used to feel.

For the first time in many moons, the air was alive with the united strength of our people. Our potential. Our past and our future rang out in the warrior's voices. I heard Brown Wing's sharp trilling call stunningly take the singing higher. Everything inside of me wanted to hold on to his voice. Protect my cousin. He'd done wrong but everything that'd been taken from him, from us, screamed out in my heart. The whites couldn't take him too. I wanted to protect our people. Protect him. The war cry sang out. My father faced toward me, and I saw the slightest flicker in his eyes. The warriors' calls felt like a current swirling tighter around the white man's house. Father continued to circle. I knew the chief could sense the flood of power outside. He knew the blood already spilled. He could feel the undeniable power we still held in our spirit. Our world sat upon his lips. Waiting for his final decision.

Chief Little Crow turned and in the fire of his eyes, I saw both the sharpness of a chief and the beating heart of the man I knew was my father. The current had shifted. My father spread out his arms. He called out loudly, so the braves outside the white man's walls could hear him. "Taoyateduta is not a coward. He will die with you!"

The surge of the war song erupted. Chief Traveling Hail leaped to his feet. Cheering! Fierce war whoops engulfed the white man's house. The battle drumbeat pounded even louder. Father stood proud as the power of a thousand warriors roared around him. I held onto Owl Woman in fear and awe . . . Our people were rising up, flooding back out upon the plains. We were going to war.

SIXTEEN

Emma Heard

Monday, August 18, 1862, 9:00 a.m.

Though I got little sleep in the sticky night, a miracle met me in the morning. Ma wanted to take Peter and Catherine into town for new shoes. Otto and Uncle Allen were spending the morning raising beams at the Lamplighter Saloon. Ida and I were free to stay home. I could start my teaching application immediately. Pa hitched Kit and Kamish to the wagon and the crew set off for town in the sprightly August morn. I squealed with delight as the wagon dropped out of sight. What brilliant relief. My sister grabbed her straw basket, heading to gather eggs. Of course, Ida, with her perfect sense of duty, would set to her chores immediately. But my irritation lessened as I realized it was all the better for me that she was going; I could write my letter alone. I assured her I'd be out to help shortly.

I was finally, *miraculously,* alone. I tiptoed like a mischievous child, sneaking paper and an envelope from my father's desk. I grabbed his inkwell and pen. The hairs on my neck prickled as I felt a strange sense of something creeping and looked back at the door. The house was perfectly still. Perhaps my guilt was making me spook. Guilt, joy, and excitement wrestled within me: writing to the board was a permanent choice, one I could not come back from. I might as well be saying farewell to my family with these pen strokes. My chest ached but I turned determinedly toward this new future. I carried my stolen supplies upstairs and sat upon the edge of the bed, placing the supplies atop my nightstand. From my seat, I could see out the sizeable 16-paned loft window. I watched Ida enter the henhouse. Harmless clouds drifted carefree across the sky. I walked to the wardrobe, taking Whitman's *Leaves of Grass* out from the bottom. How far I had come since I first read this, years ago. I opened to the pages holding Miss Knudsen's letter. The page I'd read so many times before felt different now.

Not I, nor anyone else can travel that road for you.
You must travel it by yourself.
It is not far. It is within reach.
Perhaps you have been on it since you were born, and did not know.
Perhaps it is everywhere—on water and land.

My mind stretched in self-reflection; this was *my* life. Each layer of new experience was folded into past layers of understanding myself and the world around me, each fold inching me along, incorporating perspective. I thought of Baby Peter's sweet eyes looking up at me yesterday. If I left to teach, how much of his life would I miss? Sadness churned within me. The sorrow and pain were layers I'd need to learn to fold into myself, as well. My hopes had taken root inside of me. To pull them out now would be to destroy the deepest part of myself. My mother's teachings rang in my mind. "A task that isn't easy will be worth it." Teaching would be worth it, I just knew it . . . though I also knew Mother wouldn't approve of me being a professional woman. I truly felt God was calling me to this very moment. Taking my pen in my hand, I dipped into the ink and set to replying with confident and self-assured strokes.

Dearest Teachers' Association,
I am writing for consideration of certification

I paused to plunge my pointed nib back in the inkwell. Movement caught my eye out the window. It took a few seconds for my eyes to focus, to comprehend what I was seeing. A group of men on horseback. Indian men. Four of them. They rode up around the backside of the barn and into the yard. Painted bodies dismounted their ponies, smeared in matching colors. War paint. War? Yesterday, Little Crow sat in settler clothing under a church steeple. But I recognized the bright war paint streaks from the animated stories Otto told, of whooping bands of Dakota and Ojibwe attacking one another. I'd always assumed the details of Otto's tall tales were exaggerated but the paint was real, here in front of me. The hairs up and down my arm raised; my throat seized. I fell to my knees at the edge of the bed. I crawled, shaking, to the window and peered out in terror. What were they doing at our home? I needed Pa, needed him to grab his gun and help us. But Pa and his gun would be halfway to town by now. My eyes scanned the yard and in the worst timing, I spotted Ida, shutting the coop door. I couldn't believe it. She was blissfully, terribly unaware of the Indians just behind her. I scrambled on the floor, wanting to bolt and somehow warn my sister of the intruders. My boots caught and tangled in my long skirt; I stumbled in my effort to stand. The men were yelling, shrill pointed screams. I scrambled on all fours back to the window. When the Indians had whooped on the outskirts of town, the frustration behind the noise was understandable. But the cries in the yard now sounded soulless, the chilling calls of men out for blood. My own voice seized in my throat. I wanted to scream in horror. What could I do? Help was miles away. Instinctively, I shrank as small as possible, a spectator unable to move or think.

Upon hearing the bloodcurdling noise, Ida frenziedly sprinted back for the house, her basket tipping freshly picked eggs out behind her. But the distance to the house was too great, the Indians too quick. The men were upon her in an instant; crushing her into the ground. They seemed less like men and more like predators atop their prey. They twisted and pulled her thrashing body round to face them. One warrior was straddling her. Another covered her mouth, assuming Ida could scream, smothering her face. A third man grabbed for her flailing arms. She was overpowered. I felt a surging reflex, all the awfulness of my alerted senses when near Myrick, all magnified in front of me. Upon my wholesome sister was a cruel foulness. Deep in my womanly purity, I knew what was happening. They were going to rape her. I all so intensely anticipated Ida's violation inside of myself. Her boots had flown off in the impact and lay next to the discarded basket. Bare feet struggled under her captors; her heels kicked and pushed violently into the grass. The man over her clawed at her, ripping her shirt.

I stiffened; it seemed like my spirit was leaving my physical being as I watched my terrified sister pinned under the possessed men. They'd find me. I'd be next. My body heaved in a convulsion of terror. Ida had been curled identical to me in bed last night. We laid as mirror images. And I felt a terror that we would be bound to each other in this day. There seemed no getaway route on this open prairie. The men were too fast. Then, the worst thought: Ida and I would mirror each other in our final moments. My eyes blurred; death like a clawing beast.

A fourth warrior suddenly moved across the yard. He raced to the cluster on the ground, his long hair flying out behind him. He raised an axe as he approached the group. My stomach retched; my sister was about to be hacked apart by the incoming man. Instead, the warrior swiftly kicked off the Indian straddling my sister. He tumbled to the ground. The other men released her. Ida struggled, crawling like an injured animal. The warrior with the ax stood between her and the three other men. The braves yipped at the defending warrior but didn't take him on, instead, they sprinted to the barn.

My sister got to her feet, grabbing at the tattered pieces of her shirt attempting to cover herself. I suffered powerlessly; I desperately wanted to shield, to protect, my degraded sister. But in cowardice or self-preservation, I clung to the windowsill and watched as Ida stood vulnerable in disoriented terror. She scrambled and ran for the house. The man followed her. A flooding wave of panic stabbed my stomach like a pitchfork into a haystack. I was reconnected to my body, a wave of fear refilling my consciousness. They were coming for the house. I had to get to my sister and save us. But how?

I clambered up from the ground, horror buckled my knees, knocking into my nightstand. The inkwell tipped, spilling dark ink atop my hand and my dress. Frantically, I tried to think of a place we could hide. Together under Ma and Pa's bed? But the Indians knew Ida was here. What if they came back for her? What if they wanted to raid the house? Of course, they'd invade the house next. I raced down the stairs, though everything in me wished to remain hidden in the loft. But I had to get to my sister.

I tore open the front door. As it swung wide, Ida raced up, her eyes those of a petrified creature desperate to stay alive. I screamed, "IDA!" with a power I didn't know my throat possessed. She sprinted and fell into me, collapsing in my arms. We toppled into each other in the doorway. My face cracked against the hard edge of the door frame. The impact twisted my vision, and the world went black for a single hollow moment. When my eyes opened, to my horror, I saw the warrior standing in front of us on the porch. He was strong-jawed, with a scar across his upper lip. I stared at the scar, transfixed, as our fate fell in his hands. His eyes looked steadily into mine, and in the chaos, he gave a clear command: "Go."

My keen intellect slackened impossibly. It felt as if my mind stopped turning. Gears that wouldn't catch. *Go. He said to go.* An English word, go. I felt dim and slow. I puzzled at the two long bands of crimson paint running from his forehead, over his cheeks. Ida lay cowering next to me. The injury in my head quivered; a wave of pain streaked from my temple. Shrieks sounded from the barn across the yard; the brutal men were near. The warrior urgently repeated, "GO." He pointed his sturdy arm, painted with red stripes, in the direction of town. The gears in my mind caught, and I realized his command was our chance at survival. We must run! I dug my nails into my sister's arms and pulled her up. The seconds swirled in my drive to live. I yanked Ida as we raced across the porch. I took a final look at the warrior who spared us, feeling a strange churning mix of gratitude and dread. Then we took off at a run, a terrible, tripping, scrambling forward. I didn't look back.

Our legs were hell-bent, rushing through tall grass. We sprinted down the ravine and labored up, falling, then used our arms to continue up the hillside. There was not enough prairie to separate us from the Indians. There could never be enough distance from them. *Go.* His voice like a raven-haired ghost tickling a whisper into my ear, sending me forward. The grasses whipped my legs, whipped my face. A wave of nausea filled me as my legs churned ahead.

Ida's fear made her move limp and loose, like Catherine's rag doll. She clung to me slackly. I felt trickles of something falling off my face. I pressed my hand to my chin and looked to see my fingers covered in red. Blood. It dripped from the edge of my jaw, I could feel it rolling down my neck. Thick and warm. I felt dirty. Dusty, and dirty, the blood syrupy over my skin. I looked down, seeing brilliant red splotches on the front of my dress. Distracted, I stepped into a vermin hole and sent us both tumbling into the grass. Ida and I lay on the ground, stunned, gasping to catch our breath. I knew we must keep moving. I had to get to my family. We could not let them return to the farm.

"We must move toward the trail," I said, "must warn Ma and Pa." Ida made a grunting sound. Her face was filthy and scuffed. Her top was torn, and there were scratches across her chest. Her hands shook as she lifted the bottom of her ripped skirt, looking at her bleeding feet. Her heels were stripped raw in her desperate kicking to free herself. Her damaged body was next to me, but it seemed like her mind was somewhere far away. Still pinned down in the yard.

The vacancy in her eyes suddenly worried me even more than her injuries. Fierce love for my sister coursed through my veins and I swelled with willpower to continue. I gripped her hand tightly. The Indians could be anywhere. They'd come out of nowhere, and I was terrified they would soon be upon us again. We took off, at a pace just below a run. It was at least two more miles to town.

We ran parallel to the road, yet off to the side a short distance, ready to take cover if needed. I used the back of my hand to wipe the blood from my brow. My hand was smeared with blood and ink, black and red intermingled in stain across my shirt and skirt. The ink. I had been writing the letter when this all started. I beheld my injured sister trotting desperately beside me and filled with self-hatred. If I hadn't been so eager to write my letter, I would have been out helping her with chores. I could have protected her. They could've taken me instead; watching my sister get attacked was worse than anything they could do to me. What cowardice to sit at the windowsill. My heart pinched sharply, and the sting of tears bit at my eyes. My emotions made it even harder to breathe; each breathe I took felt too shallow. I gasped as we ran, narrow breaths of suffocating shame that my self-interest had protected me and put my blameless sister in harm's way. I wanted to let my self-disgust consume me. But my legs were determined to keep moving, I couldn't let anyone else in my family get hurt.

We continued across the prairie. I could barely believe it when I saw Kit's white starred forehead, Kamish's straw-colored mane, bouncing in merry step up the road. Our wagon. My voice couldn't catch up to the moment. Instead, I broke into a stumbling run.

"PA!"

Pa and Otto's heads turned in unison, their recognition turned to a moment of puzzlement, then horror. Instantly, Otto hurdled over the side of the wagon. Uncle Allen launched his lean body out the back. My brother sprinted to us with an athletic fury.

The edges of the sky blurred.

My brother looked so solid and healthy. So safe. My mind went sluggish.

I'd never seen such a serious look on my older brother's face. He paused as he approached and took in the sight of us. Uncle Allen, in an unusual moment of leadership, gave direction to his stunned nephew, "Help me get them to the wagon, Otto." With strong arms, Otto scooped Ida up. She laid her head into her twin brother's chest and closed her eyes. Her face trembled as heavy silent tears finally spilled down her dirty cheeks.

Uncle Allen looked straight into my eyes and gently said, "I'm gon' pick you up now, Emma girl." I nodded, confused. Ida was hurt, not me. Uncle Allen lifted me over his back. Floating atop his shoulder, I watched the ground bounce beneath me as he strode back to the wagon. The bouncing swirled, my vision twisted into something peculiar, and without warning my stomach heaved, and I vomited. The side of my head ripped with pain at the surge. Pieces of upheaval strung in my hair and dribbled down the back of my uncle's leg.

"I'm sorry," I said softly. A swell of embarrassment. Silent guilt for Ida's pain. A wave of devastating sadness. It all blurred.

"I've got ya now," he assured me and patted my back like when I was a little girl. Something of my innocence had left today. My head pounded with every step.

Next, I knew, I was lying on the back bench of the wagon. Uncle Allen held his handkerchief to the right side of my face. Ida sat ghost-like leaning against Otto. He held both arms around her, bracing her. Confusion whirled as the gears in my mind felt once again disconnected. I turned to the side; Ma's worried face was beside me. Kneeling on the rocking wagon floor, her terrified eyes were even with mine. I hated seeing her so upset.

"Emma, darling, what happened? Did they attack you?" Ma clutched my hand, demanding understanding.

"Not me." I couldn't bear to put words to what I had seen them doing to Ida.

"Darling, you've been hit on the side of your face. They hurt you. Ida too." I couldn't tell if she was asking a question or telling me what occurred.

Marbles filled my throat, the words burned. "Not me. They tried . . . hurting her." Tears went over the edges of my eyes. I couldn't dam them back, and there was so much I couldn't put words to.

Pa turned around from the front bench, his face wide with worry. "How bad are they, Anna?"

"Emma's come to. Just get back to town swiftly." She paused a moment, staring with concern at Ida, whose usual silence now felt haunting.

"I'm so glad you found us," I said, as tears poured down my cheeks. I could taste the salty tears mixed with the metallic taste of blood.

"As am I," she said, tenderly wiping a tear.

"How'd you turn back for us so soon?" I asked.

"When we learned there was trouble, we headed back to get you girls. The doors to the general store were locked . . . Mr. Ayers told us that Indians were attacking the trading post." She hesitated and looked up to Uncle Allen, appearing to debate whether to tell me the rest. "I suppose you've witnessed enough to be in the know. Those savages murdered Myrick."

Uncle Allen added flatly, as if the detail was stuck in his brain, "Stuffed his mouth with grass." Ma shook her head against my hand as she cradled it, appalled at the inexplicable brutality.

I turned away from her and looked back up at the rocking sky above. Stuffed with grass. Uncle Allen and my mother wouldn't understand the origin of that merciless action. But my understanding of the attack, the violence, suddenly all settled into place. The dead man's heartless words rolled in my memory. "Let them eat grass or their own shit if they're hungry." Myrick didn't just put a target on his back. He'd put the target on us all. Though it all connected, my mind swirled in the senselessness, and I dizzied with confusion again. Little Crow's thoughtful face flashed in my mind. He looked so calm. His stoic lifted chin. Pain raged through my brow, deep into my head, and stabbed down to my core.

Pa hollered back, "Final hill into town girls, hold on." Though Ma gripped my hand and safety was closer than ever, inside I didn't know what to hold onto.

SEVENTEEN

Oenikika

Tuesday, August 19, 1862

Over the sound of the injured men moaning, my ears were keenly alert to Owl Woman's breath. She laid in a state of delirium with her mouth open; the whistle of wheezing came with each exhale. There was a new sharpness to the sound; I feared her condition was worsening. I waved the flies away from her face and placed my hand upon her forehead. Her skin was still damp and warm; the fever persisted. What could I do to aid her? If she worsened further, I should begin my focus upon helping her to the other side. One of the greatest discernments a healer must make is when to help with the transition to the Happy Hunting Grounds in the Hereafter . . . and I hadn't enough experience to strengthen this discernment yet. I wasn't ready to let go of Grandmother; I selfishly prayed the Spirit wasn't summoning her. If I just had my plants, she could be healed. I looked about in overwhelmed unease. A canopy had been strung between four sturdy maples at the edge of camp, a staging area for the injured. Our camp had tripled in size; all the tipis of eastern camps had congregated at our village. Better coordination for battle. While the men were at war, I was focused entirely on my calling, tending to the growing number of injured. A warrior, Nine Tails, laid on the blanket beyond grandmother, grimacing as he attempted to reposition himself. Bloody fluid ran down his chest from a hole that was ripped open in his shoulder. Nine Tails and others had been shot by the white man. Another brave had fallen from his horse, his leg twisted and broken.

"Be still, Nine Tails. I'll grind you more oak for the wound. Then we move you," I called out as I reached into the lower right pocket of my medicine bag. I used my fingernails to scrape every fragment of bark from the bottom. This was the very last of it. "No," I muttered in frustration under my breath, not wanting the sick around me to be aware of just how depleted the medicines were. Wartime without access to our prairie. Without access to our plants. I placed the oak in a blending bowl, crushing it to a dust. Grandmother coughed violently as if there were mud stuck deep inside her lungs. *Don't give up, Owl Woman.* But my heart fretted; how would I know when she needed to transition beyond? If only I had medicine. How could I find them? When could I gather? I'd need permission to venture out and I couldn't make a case to my father while he was away at war. I looked beyond the healing tent. The top of the Medicine Man's tipi curled with smoke from burning sweetgrass. When he emerged from his meditation, I'd bring him to pray at Grandmother's side.

I walked with the bowl and knelt next to Nine Tails. Slowly, I sifted the ground oak through my fingers, letting the fine mill fall over his mangled shoulder. I didn't know the man, but spoke to him in a low, soothing voice, as I imagined his mother once had when he was a child. "This will quicken your recovery. Oak shields the wounds of a warrior," I said as if I were confident that he would heal. But I wasn't. The injury was terrible; the bullet had blasted apart the center of his shoulder. His arm would never work again. I tried to appear calm and confident; what the vulnerable needed to see in the healer who tends them. It was an honor to be among our fighters. The most exceptional pride a Dakota man could take was as a warrior, riding into battle. And the utmost warriors are those who face injury and most holy of *all*, those who give their life for our tribe. If, after the oak treatment, Nine Tails's wound began to rot, and survival was not possible, then we'd prepare him for a fearless transition to the other side. He could be reunited with the people of his tribe who'd already passed. A place of no more suffering.

I pinched a final sprinkle of the ground oak over Nine Tails's wound and my mind ran over everything that had happened since the war council. Once the decision was made, the men summoned the fighting spirit of the bear and the eagle. I'd filled with pride seeing my father wearing his necklace of buffalo horns and majestic war bonnet decorated with eagle feathers, mink tails, and painted leather tied in knots. Mato's black body was painted with white stripes for the honor of carrying the chief among chiefs to the attack. Our best marksman rode with honed arrows. Warriors were armed with rifles, shotguns; the strongest men carried arrowhead spears and buffalo shields. As the sun rose, Father led a thousand riders, my husband among them, toward the storehouse. They returned, victorious, with crates upon crates of food and supplies from the Rat Trader. I filled with pride and satisfaction—it was everything that had been withheld from us. In an instant, our village overflowed with food and supplies.

Some warriors tied strips of scalps to the front of their tipis; a sign of pride in their bravery to touch an enemy. After the war, we would take these and bury them in our sacred ceremony honoring our enemy. Cut Nose already had the most scalps . . . some of the bloody strips of flesh had the long blonde hair of a woman. A few appeared like the fine hair of a young child. I worried Cut Nose was a foolish fighter, senseless in attack. Honor came when we fought a fierce enemy . . . and these scalps were those of the weak. This war wasn't intended for the weak whites; we needed to find the powerful among them. The men that lie and make the treaties. That's where our true battle was.

When my father saw the light-haired scalps of children, he yelled out in anger, "No women or young are to be attacked. And none with white hair and blue eyes. Fool." Cut Nose just laughed proudly, but my father went on, "The whites worship a God of white hair. Their angels have blue eyes. They will send their warriors in swarms if we kill these kinds." In war, my father was strategic. Focused. The braves, meanwhile, were unruly, riding in small groups in any direction—as if they wanted to attack for the sake of attack. Father was trying to wrangle the braves—focus the war effort not on settler homes, but upon the village. Little Crow had directed Tashunke to manage the horses and commanded me to take care of the sick. I was not to ride out of our camp. No one was.

Uncle Chaska dropped off a crate of food at the healing tent. He and most of Wabasha's men maintained their commitment to peace and refused to participate in the war. It was a shocking feeling to be surrounded by a surplus of food. I was reassured that we *had* done the right thing to go to war and retrieve what was ours. But while our food was finally secure . . . I sighed with concern looking at my medicine bag laying collapsed and empty. What would we do? I'd searched every inch of camp and the riverfront, to no avail.

A warrior arrived at the edge of the tent. His eyes looked dazed, and I soon saw—the lower part of his calf was gashed so deeply through I was shocked he was able to walk. Aunt Mika ran to receive him. Panic ran through me; I'd just used the very last of the bark in the medicine bag and I knew every oak tree in camp had been stripped bare. We'd have nothing but prayers to offer this warrior who'd just hobbled an unimaginably painful journey to seek our help.

Aunt Mika moved quickly to my side and whispered, "What remains of the medicine?"

"Very little. Only mint leaves," I said shakily, unable to hide the worry in my voice. "I should ride out and search for more . . . at least to the oaks at the south edge of the reservation . . . maybe even farther." I looked up to see how she responded. I was testing Mika, seeing her response to my slight suggestion to ride beyond the reservation. I wanted her to say, *Yes, niece! Ride quickly.* But instead, she refused.

"No. Your father instructed us to remain here. We don't know where the enemy is."

"Look at the crates . . . our men were successful in battle," I replied, more snap in my voice than I intended. We'd continue to be victorious—*if* we had supplies and medicine. Our gaze moved in unison to grandmother, as Owl Woman's cough rattled in the space between us. My aunt looked up towards the horizon. She was a healer too . . . Didn't she hear the plants calling to us? Couldn't she feel the need of the sick among us? Her own mother? We *had* to find more medicine.

Instead of agreeing, she sighed and finally said, "Prepare mint tea."

I filled with a questioning irritation. Mint tea? That would be of no help. It wasn't what my instincts were telling me. "That's for a full stomach," I argued. These were grave injuries. Mint is a delightful plant, but the Great Spirit doesn't intend it for these grim matters.

"Speak a prayer of hope into the leaves," my aunt said as she stood up and leaned into my ear. "Then tell the wounded that tea eases pain. And it will give them hope."

"Mint eases pain?" I asked, uncertain.

"That's what *hope* does. It takes away a bit of our pain."

I reached into the medicine bag, grabbed the very last of our plants, and began my prayer. But my heart heard the calling of the plants. I needed to do more than hope. Perhaps when the Medicine Man emerged and began his rituals in the healing tent I could sneak away. I knew I needed to ride.

August 19, 1862

I was at the edge of sleep when I rose, realizing someone had pushed back the tipi door. "Husband," I called out. Each sight of him during wartime made me awash with relief.

Tash sat near the door, dunking his cup in the water pail. "I'm exchanging the exhausted horses for fresh ones. I will soon head back," he said as he stretched his muscular legs out in front of him, flexing his feet and pointing his toes. His body was sore. Though I was tired from my day of caring for the wounded, I imagined my husband was even wearier than I. The men had been fiercely battling day and night, and my husband's position of expertise was prized. Horsemanship was an honored skill among men. His role required him to make frequent sprints between battle and the village. I quietly appreciated it as it seemed to keep Tashunke away from the front line of attack.

I observed him. "Your war paint faded during the battle."

"My wife may paint me."

"Certainly, I will." My voice was calm. But inside I was brightened. It was an honor as a wife to be asked to paint. I retrieved the paint dish of red clay and knelt before him. I put some cool water upon the clay and used my fingers to mix it to a creamy thickness. I prayed a prayer of bravery and discernment as I slid the cool mixture over the ridges of his cheeks. His breath was warm upon my hand. I looked into his deep brown eyes as I pulled two streaks down the curves of his arms. I painted two circles under the stones of his necklaces. Though sore and weary, he still looked brilliant and strong. "Your past gives you wisdom in battle," I said, grateful for his wholeness. I'd seen the bullet holes from the white man's rifles, been surrounded by the broken bodies of wartime. I feared what I'd do if Tash appeared at the healing tent. I'd have nothing to offer him. What would I be able to do to mend those bodies, to call upon the Spirit for hope and healing? I needed to find medicine.

"My wife has worry in her eyes." He looked at me carefully. Could he sense my worry for the wounded? My husband was a keen listener and I felt safe to confide in him.

"I try to summon peace within me. I pray in everything I do." I tried to reassure him. "But I worry when I do not have my plants. Owl Woman is very ill. And the wounded . . . there will be many more to tend to. A great battle is coming?" I asked my husband about the rumors.

"Your father says we attack the white village. If we work together, we should be victorious. But some of the braves are unfocused."

"There will be injury in battle. I must find plants soon. I want to ride off . . ." I stopped when I saw the serious look in my husband's eyes.

"You were instructed by the chief to remain in the village. There are terrible battles to the north."

"But sacrifice for others is what makes us powerful. That's what makes you a brave warrior. There may be risk in riding to find medicine. But it's worth it for our people. Especially now." I spoke with certainty, as I explained my motivation.

Tashunke sat in his stoic silence. Our first disagreement. My eyes went back and forth across his face, seeking any understanding of him. He didn't immediately command me with power as my father did but sat in deep contemplation. I fell quiet, worrying I'd upset him. I put aside the paint and knelt in humble silence.

"It's too dangerous." He responded with genuine care. I appreciated his worry, but I knew my calling. Still, I also knew the obligation, the honor, required of a daughter. Of a wife. I sighed quietly as I resigned myself—I couldn't ride out and break my kinship duty. Tash took my hand in his, squeezed it lovingly, then gracefully rose up and slipped out of our tipi. Back to battle. The hush of night filled in around me as I laid down. I prayed *Speak to me in my dreams. Please give me a vision, Great Mystery.*

August 20, 1862

I woke in the darkness but could sense in my body that morning was nearing. I rolled over a void of blankets beside me. The battle continued. My memory was empty of dreams, I rose in disappointment. A day of no medicine to offer the injured—I'd continue to pray; that's all I could do. Today, I wouldn't even have any mint to pray over. How was Owl Woman? I quickly dressed myself and splashed water upon my face. I'd go to her first.

I emerged from our tent as the Moon of the Harvest hung low overhead. The faint edge of morning brightened the horizon. To my right stood a surprise—a horse. A strong, beautiful bay mare tied to the maple tree outside our tipi. My medicine bag was secured in a gentle loop round her neck. She was ready for a ride. I felt so much joy I nearly leaped out of my moccasins! Tash must have prepared her for me before he went back to battle. What a gift to be understood by my husband. I filled with relief and hope as I moved swiftly. I didn't think twice about the approval of Mika or Father . . . This was the opportunity I'd prayed for. I would ride.

I was grateful I'd woken early; fewer people to notice me slipping off. As soon as we cleared the forest to the south of camp, the mare kicked to a gallop, and we were free with brilliant purpose. We moved steadily; we'd need to cover much ground to collect all the plants my heart hoped for. The early morning light shone upon the tall grass. I looked about. What was there to fear? Still, I startled as two grouse burst out in front of me. I jumped back with surprise, but most surprising of all was the laugh that escaped my throat. I was exactly where I was called to be. There was nothing to fear.

It felt wonderful to be back out upon the earth that knows no reservation. First, I rode south to collect artemisia and butterfly weed for Grandmother, at the rocky banks of the Golden River. As my medicine bag and my soul grew in tandem, I was grateful for a husband who could see my calling. I patted my horse's shoulder, also thankful for her strength; Tash knew she was the right horse for the task. The heat of the day grew, but I remained focused. I found purple mallow for internal pain. Then barberry for the wounds. Though the sun was dipping lower in the western sky, I had one plant left I knew I must find. When I finally saw the coneflower, tears filled my eyes. Beautiful. I'd missed these fields so much. I acknowledged their magnificence as I gathered the plant into my medicine bag. "I've missed you so," I spoke to the expansive meadow of dazzling purples and pinks the Spirit usually saves for a sunset, glowing in the flowers around me. "We're trying to return to you," I explained of our absence. "Wait for us." I could barely curl my bag closed; it was so full. Every satchel tied at my waist was bursting with medicine.

Night had fallen by the time I returned to camp. I'd ridden longer than I intended . . . but it's where the plants called me. Though my body was sore, as I hadn't ridden all day in many moons, my tired legs moved with newfound confidence to the tent of the ailing.

"Oenikika," Aunt Mika exclaimed with both relief and exasperation.

"Auntie, we needed a little more hope," I said, explaining my absence as I unfurled my bag and showed her the overflowing pockets of plants, then opened the satchels tied upon my hips. Mika shook her head, indicating her disapproval of my disappearance, but her eyes glistened with appreciative tears. She knew, as did I, our wounded and sick needed these plants. We both quickly went to work distributing medicine through the tent. In a kettle over the campfire,

I started a decoction of the butterfly weed. Once it had simmered to proper intensity, I scooped it with a cup and knelt at Owl Woman's side.

"Grandmother, this will comfort your cough." I helped hold her head up from her pillow as she slowly sipped the liquid. The risk of leaving the reservation, disobeying my father . . . it was worth it watching Owl Woman's wrinkled mouth take in the soothing medicine. My soul was satisfied.

Slowly, drink by drink, the butterfly weed tea disappeared from the cup. Owl Woman laid her wearied head back and reached out for me. In the comfort of my grandmother's hand, my own tiredness washed over me. I curled on the grass at her side. Gratitude relaxed me and my eyes began to feel heavy. A slow, steady prayer filled my heart . . . healing for my relatives . . . healing for the men around me . . . protection . . . tomorrow, I wouldn't need to feign hopefulness. I had everything my heart needed.

EIGHTEEN

Emma Heard

Monday, August 18, 1862

Upon arrival to the protection of New Ulm, Ida and I were rushed into the Kuhn's home. Mrs. Kuhn and Hanna took Ma and us girls upstairs. A pounding soreness came when I stood. I'd never been to the second level of their house. I sat against the wall in the bedroom, still holding Uncle Allen's kerchief to my head. Ma and Mrs. Kuhn filled a tub with water and tended to Ida first. An ache settled in my right temple as I took in the space. The Kuhn's bedroom was covered in ornate wallpapered walls and elegant drapes. The morning's horrors seemed like a dream. Ida's feet kicking into the grass. It all was a flickering memory of a dream that pulled to my mind in vivid flashes.

I could feel Hanna's eyes watching me; some mix of curiosity and pity. I couldn't bring myself to look at her . . . and I didn't want to be seen. My stomach still churned with sickening waves, my bloody shirt clung to my chest. My mind flashed again: my cowardly white knuckles clinging to the windowsill. It seemed Hanna could see my shame upon me. Ida sat, wrapped in a towel. Ma beckoned with her hand, and tapped the edge of the tin tub, calling me over. I peeled off the sticky layers of my grimy clothing and sunk myself into the lukewarm water. It felt like a protected embrace, cleansing away the dreadfulness. Ma gently squeezed warm sponges over me, tenderly minding bruises forming on my knees and arms.

"They've hurt you. But this will heal. Head wounds bleed tremendously like this," Ma said quietly.

"I hurt myself. I fell." I wanted to clarify—*I* wasn't the one who had been attacked. Pounced upon like Ida had been. But Ma looked at me with a soft frustration. I couldn't "agree" that *they*, the Indians, had hurt me. I fell. Even in my most fragile times I struggled to be agreeable, as she wished.

"Oh, Emma. And your sister? Did she fall too?" Ma lightly challenged my explanation. Her eyes searched mine. I knew she could sense the awful acts of the morning. She must be feeling as helpless as I had. I didn't know what I should say about Ida. They had tried to rape her . . . but it had been inexplicably interrupted. The man with the scar had intervened in time.

"No. They did . . . attack her," I said. Guilt wrung my stomach in the tepid water. I hated myself for letting harm come to my sister. But Ma held my hand, rubbing away the blood and easing away most of the ink. I stared at the ink. Would mother ask questions? Get upset her daughter was writing to her former teacher, even at a time like this? But she just rubbed with the washcloth, the ink disappearing in whirling watery tendrils. She must have been preoccupied on the safety of her daughters. I was grateful that she was gentle with me. Mrs. Kuhn began bandaging Ida's heels. Ida was dressed entirely in new garments. Hanna brought her white blouse for me. Ma tightly looped a bandage around my head; the tension was painful but necessary.

"We'll stay in town 'til Pa can get a plan sorted," Ma said. "We won't be going back to the farm until things have calmed."

Mrs. Kuhn pointed to the bed. "You girls may rest yourselves."

Ida and I laid back in unison. The bed was soft. I felt as if someone had put a heavy winter coat over me—exhaustion cloaked me. The curtains were tugged closed, and the room darkened. Ida's hand reached out and found mine. My sister, safe. The familiarity of lying in a bed, as we had done almost every night of our life, a wonderful sanctuary after the threat of the morning. It had been so terrifying.

I had to acknowledge what I'd seen Ida go through. What they tried to do to her. "I'm so sorry, sister. I hate myself for not . . . protecting you." I hoped she didn't resent me, her younger sister always off doing her own thing. Didn't hate me for failing her this morning in my preoccupation.

She waved two fingers across my palm. Her way of saying no, it wasn't my fault. There wasn't any more to say. Sleep pulled at my body with a power I couldn't outrun. I held on securely to Ida's hand and let myself succumb.

I awoke to pain shooting through the side of my head. An unfamiliar room. A candle. A painted chamber pot. Cobalt paint swirls upon a glazed pot. We were not in our bedroom. I sat up in alarm and remembered I was at the Kuhns'.

"Keep sleeping, Emma," Ma said. I couldn't tell what hour it was. What day it was. The candle cast a small circle of warm light about my mother, who sat rolling bandages upon the floor. "Your father's helping to organize a defense. I'll stay with you girls 'til the morning." She sat watchfully. My spirit settled; my body craved more sleep. I drifted to the deep.

Tuesday, August 19, 1862

Early morning light poured through a small gap in the curtains, shining through lacy drapes. I sat up in bed; Ida turned over next to me, still asleep. I looked about. A neat stack of rolled bandages sat where Ma had been overnight. I jumped slightly when I realized two people were lying on the floor beyond the end of the bed. One was a woman with bandages around her arms. Another was a man with what appeared to be a broken arrow protruding out his thigh. More injured. The attack. I realized the woman was Lavina Eastlick. The woman whom we'd visited after church just a day—or two?—ago. The world had been upended so quickly. I quietly lifted myself from bed. The sleep had made me stronger.

I peered out the window—the town was inundated with settlers taking refuge. Wagons, lumber, and logs formed a perimeter around the innermost buildings. I recognized Otto, working to create the barricade. But the window held the same sized panes as the windows I had looked out into our yard. As the warriors crushed Ida into the ground.

I ached as my mind felt captured again in the memory.

A whisper broke my thoughts. "Emma." Ma cracked the door open, waving for me to come out into the hallway. I walked lightly out.

"What's happening, Ma? Are Indians coming for us?"

"We can't be certain. They've hit all around the prairie. People've been coming in all night while you were sleeping. They killed so many." She touched the side of my head. "Hurt you."

I pulled back slightly from her touch; so often there was the wedge of miscommunication between us. Frustrated that she didn't understand, "They *hurt* Ida," I explained, "I simply fell." I didn't explain Ida sprinting into me at a full terrified run. There was a lump in my throat at the word *hurt*. How could I ever put into words all the fear? Describe men attacking my sister? I felt protective over Ida to describe such a thing to anyone. Even our mother. It was too awful. As if letting the words out would stain Ma, as well. I wished Ida could explain it how she wanted to . . . If only she could speak. Say what happened. They were about to rape her. It was happening.

I heard movement below us on the lower floor. A shocking number of people huddled in bunches, stood along the walls. Many more had sought refuge while I slumbered. I wondered what else I had missed in my sleep.

"Where's Pa?"

"In his office. It's within the barricade. Most of the men are checking in there."

My inner drive kicked in. "I'll stop by. I'd like to see how I can be of assistance." I'd spent the last year in Pa's law office—gravity pulled me there. I needed to push out the anxiety that lingered in my veins. Being in the office would be a respite. I thought of Ida sleeping in the bed a wash of guilt flooded my heart. Last I separated from her, she was going out to the chicken coop. "Or perhaps I should stay near Ida. She can't wake up alone."

Ma shook her head, her eyes full of worry. I knew she didn't want me to leave her sight. But she surprised me when she said, "I'm not leaving Ida's side. Your father would benefit from you checking in. You're in that office as much as he is." I looked at her eyes, the lines of worry at their edges. Had she missed me in my hours of work in the office? An understanding I hadn't expected settled in the space between us.

Footsteps upon the staircase interrupted our discussion; Dr. Mayo walked upstairs. "Oh, thank goodness. In here, Dr. Mayo," Ma said while pointing the way. "And Emma . . ." she said.

"I'm feeling much better. I promise. I'm checking in with Pa and will be right back."

Her expression softened, but the anxiety remained in her eyes. "Right back," she replied.

I made my way swiftly down the staircase, weaving through the cluster of refugees, anxious to get out of the crowded house. But as soon as I stepped out to the street, I felt a wave of apprehension at no longer being in the safety of a brick building. A wide-eyed family hobbled past. "A doctor's that way." I pointed back to the Kuhns'. Fear nipped at my heels. The street that had once felt so familiar now made me feel vulnerable. Survival knew no pride; I took off at a run to my father's office.

Oskar Theobald and his father walked out of Pa's office, which had become an improvised command post for the town's defense. Three other men entered in front of me; I snuck in behind them. The men hushed with the arrival of a woman, my bandage round my head a reminder of the attack.

"Emma." My father's warm voice called out, his eyes glimmering. I'd never seen it before, but he appeared to be crying. "You look much better . . ." He took a breath and pulled his mouth tight.

Mr. Kuhn interrupted. "Women and children ought to stay in the brick buildings, Heard." He said *women and children* as if he couldn't decide which I was.

"Ma said I must check in with you," I reassured my father. Though my knees were still weak with fear, I wanted to contribute, do something. Ida needed a warm bed and brick walls. I needed a way to repent for my failure to protect her yesterday.

"Emma will head back soon. I do need to check in with her as my office assistant," my father explained to Mr. Kuhn. I felt a brightening of pride to be referred to as his assistant. "Emma, is your mind sound and straight?"

"It is." Hearing my own confident voice was an internal recentering. It was as though I had been a vase knocked on a tabletop, spinning, overwhelmed with fear, about to fall and shatter. But I'd grabbed onto the self-reliance that still lived inside of me. And I stood myself back upright and solid.

"Good. We need all the help we can get." He stood up and readied himself to go outside, "The Dakota are raging on a warpath. This is now your task." He shoved the large open record book across his desk. "I've started a log. A log to keep track . . ." His fingers brushed over the open book. The columns read—ALIVE, WOUNDED, MISSING, and DEAD. ". . . of the damage." I took the book. Pa was wise to make a record. But it was an incredible responsibility to charge his daughter with.

Otto burst in the office, full of adrenaline. Incredible, since he'd been working all night. "The barricade is complete. Sister," Otto said as he noticed me; then he glanced at my father. "She doesn't belong here. She belongs under shelter." His war duties had awakened a manly sensibility in my usually playful older brother.

"Emma's taking over the record. She can complete her task in the shelter of Kuhn's or Turner Hall," Pa said definitively.

Otto nodded. "Is the military sending troops to help?"

"They're too busy fighting the goddamn rebels in the south. No army-man will be helping anytime soon," Mr. Kuhn interjected angrily.

"We still haven't many men," Pa explained. We all looked about the room and out to the street. It was a ragtag group. These were men used to tending crops and sharing a pint of beer, now called to defend our little prairie town. A civilian army. Despite the lack of experience, the men seemed to be working together in organized chaos. "Or many weapons. Maybe 30 shotguns, and 25 rifles. *Total.*"

We looked out the window towards the street and watched as Bruno walked by, holding a pitchfork; Captain's tail held high. A tremor of fear shuddered through me as I realized the limitations of our situation. Bruno armed with a pitchfork didn't seem any defense at all. I looked at my brother's brave face. The determination upon my father's. They would be on the front lines if the Dakota came for the town. I wanted to break out, escape, take my family somewhere safe and far away. But I knew Otto and Pa were two of the fittest men in the bunch. If any of us were to survive, Pa and Otto would have to give their all. Letting them go. Putting myself to work. This was our only prayer.

Father turned and faced me. "Emma girl. Get the facts—talk to every party you can. Find who's accounted for." Otto tossed Pa his long rifle. Pa grabbed it clear out of the air with his right hand. He'd transformed from a contemplative lawyer, armed with quill and ink, to an arms-bearing man ready to defend his family and town.

The world stabilized again with a sense of duty when I picked up the pen and ink. I wouldn't fail Ida while holding a pen, not this time. I'd do my part. This log could be so important—the official record of this moment. Accuracy, thoroughness. Every single person mattered. That was how I would navigate the chaos of our world being under attack. My heart skipped a beat; how long would we be barricaded? Did we have supplies to survive? I flashed back to the terror at the window ledge as the Dakota rampaged our barn. The unsettled feeling that had coursed through me at the edge of town, when I held Kit's skittering steps and the Indians whooped. This moment was what my heart had been warning me about. My head ached as the alarm pulsed through me. But at least the feeling meant I was still alive.

I quickly developed a system of recording names: I titled 52 pages and would file each family or person alphabetically. I'd place an "X" in one of four columns: ALIVE & WELL, WOUNDED, DECEASED, MISSING. I started in the back of the office; Farmer Krause was there cleaning a gun. I decided an introduction was necessary to make clear my role.

"I'm working as the Official Recorder for the town of New Ulm. Please aide me—how may I account for members of your family?" It was a formal approach, removed from the emotional reality of the task.

Farmer Krause cleared his throat, then looked at me with broken eyes.

"Just me."

"Mrs. Krause and your daughter are. . ." This job suddenly felt both tremendously important and excruciatingly awful. This was awful. To make him say aloud, the reality of what had happened. To mark it down. The permanence of loss. I felt terrified for us all, barely barricaded. An enraged group of Natives on a warpath. What if Pa and the men couldn't hold off the Dakota? What if we were all killed, anyway? Would someone find this record, see we had been attempting to save ourselves? A few of us had survived longer than the others?

"Butchered." A sob ripped through his voice. I'd never heard a man make such a sound. "I was out in the fields—they were doing laundry. I raced toward them when I heard . . . but I was too late. Scalped them. Savages!"

Scalped? Was that the gruesome act I imagined it to be? My hands quivered in nervousness. Was that what the Dakota would have done to Ida and me? My mind was frozen in fear. I stared at the weeping farmer for too long a moment. This broken man. He hadn't been able to protect his wife and daughter. Just as I hadn't been able to protect Ida. Shame loosened its grip on my stomach, I felt a bit less alone staring at the curly-haired farmer.

I quietly replied, "I'm so very sorry." I opened my log to "K" and wrote KRAUSE, CHRISTOPH and checked under Alive. Under that, MRS. KRAUSE and DAUGHTER KRAUSE I held my pen for a moment above the paper. Setting the pen down, I made a first wobbly-lined "X," and then another, under the deceased column. I had to keep my mind sane—this record was the most intelligent thing I could do. It was an act of decency. A stand against brutality. I could count and tally. Record. Not let my brain be held captive by the memories.

I made my way through the men, logging accounts of the survivors then left for the Kuhns'. I carried the hefty logbook as I ran up the street. Images of scalped, bleeding children, pulled out innards, and mouths stuffed with grass ran through my mind as my legs carried me forward. The move between buildings was a terrifying risk. I turned back into the Kuhn's. Some families cowered together; others kept themselves busy casting bullets or preparing bandages. In the kitchen, I started with kind-faced Mrs. Duta, who I recognized from a farm just north of our own. I introduced myself and explained my task.

Mrs. Duta paused from rolling a length of bandage. She looked up at me. "We're all alive, somehow. Mr. Duta was already in the corn-field. The children and I hid with him when we saw 'em comin."

"So glad to hear that," I said as I busied myself flipping to the "D" page, making checks in the ALIVE column. But when I looked back up, I saw Mrs. Duta's sizable cheeks were trembling.

"I've done something quite terrible," she confessed. I couldn't imagine what she was about to say. I held the woman's pained gaze. "Our dog, Walter, was running back and forth from the house to our hiding spot in the rows of corn. I was so afraid he was 'bout to give us away . . ." Her head dropped but she went on. "I strangled him. Pulled my apron tie tight round his neck." I looked at it now, cinched around her broad waist. "He only wanted to protect us," she said between sobs. My mind fuzzed. Horrific. Mrs. Duta strangling her own dog. I felt myself pull back the slightest, not with judgment of the poor woman, but in shock of what it had taken for her to get to safety and save her family. "Forgive me," Mrs. Duta cried.

"You did what you needed to save your family, Mrs. Duta," I said. She let out a shaky breath. I pressed my hand atop hers, then stood. My job was to collect the record. Accurately. I couldn't let myself become consumed in the stories. I must find the truth and mark an X. I must keep my mind in sanity.

I repeated this motto in my mind—*Find the truth, mark an X*—as I interviewed people. At one point, groups crowded around me, eager to tell their stories. I held my breath like a fortress in my rib-cage. I needed to stay focused and strong. Mrs. Ayers could barely be contained in her account. She claimed everyone to the north, south, east, and west of her was massacred. I asked if she had seen them or how she knew. She said she'd heard it! And commanded me to write it down. I braced myself against her pressure. I couldn't let the record get muddled with hearsay. The record must reflect the facts. By the time I got upstairs rumors about the atrocities were spreading faster than a prairie fire. Lena Lundberg stated that an infant had been nailed to a tree. I stood in gaping shock. When I asked the name of the child, she said she'd just overheard it, didn't actually know a name. I immediately fell back in relief. A hysteria was growing among the gathering. My mind would collapse if I gave in to such ravings, to the waves of fear washing through the group. My terror had kept me from rescuing my sister yesterday. I would be stronger today.

After working through the groups in two of the three upstairs bedrooms, I took a seat for a moments rest on the floor in the upstairs hallway. Ma stood at the end of the hall, discreetly discussing some matter with Dr. Mayo. Soon as she finished the discussion, she made her way to me and sank down in her own exhaustion.

"Ida's still resting. . . Emma, please tell me, just what the attack was upon your sister. I fear, looking at the state of her torn skirt, it was something horrifying."

I couldn't look at Ma. I didn't want to say it aloud. But I tried. "I'm not sure how to explain it. They were atop her." Ma let out a small groan and covered her mouth. I continued, "But one of them kicked the others off. He . . . *defended* her," I said in disbelief, although I had observed it.

"Kicked off? So, the act was . . ." my mother paused. "The act was interrupted?"

"Yes." I still shuddered in the thought of the violation. But he stopped them. I was grateful for that. I was surprised Ma didn't care more about the defender. He stood out in my mind. I hadn't pictured an angel to have long black hair, but something about that warrior felt like divine intervention.

"Thank the Lord above. The doctor saw worrisome bruising upon her legs. Oh, Emma, you helped save your sister," she said. But I hadn't done nearly enough to protect Ida. She was still so hurt. So terrified. Bruising all over her. I wanted to lash out at those awful men. Hurt them as they had hurt her. "You need not tell others about what was upon Ida. This is a private matter." It was another complication for the hidden world of women. I'd carefully learned what to be quiet about, what matters bore a secrecy laced with shame reserved for our gender. With a simple hushed sentence, my mother reminded me, this was one of them.

Ma pushed back my hair and looked with care at the side of my head. "It doesn't appear we need to change your bandage . . . A good sign. But are you certain you're able to do this?" She patted the logbook resting upon my lap. Ma's honey-colored hair fell softly around her face. It suddenly felt odd to be with her, watch her move about a home that wasn't ours. She took a quiet command; nursing the injured. I was seeing her exist for the first time beyond the farm. Realizing she was someone beyond our family.

"It's important," I assured her. "I've finished logging everyone upstairs. Except there." I nodded to the bedroom I'd slept in.

"Lavina Eastlick is awake now," Ma said. "She's been through quite a lot, I fear. Her mind has not yet returned."

"I'll check in with her," I said with purpose, hoping it masked the dread that ran through me before each check-in.

"Quickly and quietly," Ma advised. I turned the ornate knob and entered the darkened room. Ida remained where she'd been this morning. Mrs. Eastlick was sitting in a chair, staring blankly. Bandages were wrapped up and down her arms.

"Mrs. Eastlick? I'm here to take account of you and the family," I whispered as I knelt beside her, opening my log, and quietly giving her my introductory speech. She looked at me vacantly. "Do you remember me, Lavina? Emma Heard?"

An eerie sound bubbled from her throat. It strangely grew into a full laugh as she leaned forward and covered her mouth. I sat back. Tears had been cried in front of me; I'd seen feelings of shame. Horror. Outrage. But it was most unsettling to hear the incongruent sound of laughter. Enclosed to an experience all her own, Lavina began rocking herself, laughter coming in waves. "Well, I . . . see you're wounded," I said, wanting to excuse myself as quickly as possible from the discomfort. She surprised me when she finally spoke.

"They're all dead. Dead. My babies," she said this without looking at me. The laughter disappeared, and she sunk into a rocking emptiness. A void settled round us. Just days before I had been bored at their homestead. What an indulgent unimaginable feeling now. We'd sat together. It was unfathomable. We'd all been together. I felt a new pain of empathy watching the crazed woman in front of me. I couldn't bring myself to make the permanent X's in the death column in her sight. I closed the book.

"I am so very sorry. They were such nice boys," I said in an awkward attempt at comfort. The past tense *were* glared unintentionally sharp off my tongue.

"My sweet boys," Lavina said to herself. Grief took the woman somewhere far away—like she was teetering on the brink of two worlds: reality was sharp and painful, and memories a disappearing relief that slipped too quickly off the edges off the mind.

I moved toward the door. The Kuhns' home was brewing with fear; death crept between the spaces among the living. I needed to gather myself. I made my way out of the house and stepped onto the front porch. I felt oddly numb to the heat of late afternoon; my ability to feel had gone somewhere far away. A yell came from the end of the block. My body flinched at the sound. Towards the south, a familiar chestnut-colored horse galloped toward town and the barricade. Mr.

Schein, manning the south gate, held a gun shakily pointed at the incomer.

"Hold fire, Schein," Otto hollered with authority. "It's just the Indian missionary." In the pandemonium of the last day, I hadn't even considered what fate had befallen the man who had stolen so many of my thoughts. The lone white man living among the Dakota. How had he survived? My heart turned in relief that Riggs was within the slight protection that town offered. I remembered Riggs's gaze centered upon me after Myrick had threatened Little Crow. I'd felt an understanding. I wanted him, his perspective with us.

The horse came to a halt. Otto and other men made their way to the newcomer. In an act of boldness, I walked out to the gathering as well. At a time as dire as this, I, as the official recorder, felt as justified as the men in keeping up with incoming information. Riggs quickly dismounted, then lifted his hat, pushing back his golden-brown hair mopped with sweat. Still out of breath, he stated, "I'm sure you're well aware of the attack at Fort Ridgley and Indian Trading Post."

"Damn well aware, Missionary." Mr. Schein interrupted, unimpressed.

Pa made his way to the front and asked, "What do you know, Riggs?"

Riggs wiped a hand down the center of his face, pushing sweat down his cheeks and through the scruff of a weeks-old beard. He nodded, a look of defeat on his brow. "They'll be comin' this way. Soon." The circle of men shuffled in anticipation and fear. "I'd expect a full-scale attack on New Ulm tonight." My body stiffened. Full-scale? What had we been experiencing so far? A tingling reached down to my toes and my hands grew cold.

"How many of them are coming?" my father immediately asked, wanting to plan, predict, protect. "We'll be outnumbered?"

Fear cut at the inside of my throat. New Ulm was the very edge of the western prairie. Beyond us was wilderness. The Indians' world.

My mind surged back to the flowing waters of the Cottonwood. We hadn't just overlapped with the Dakota. We had stretched ourselves into their world and now they encircled us. We'd gone too far.

Riggs's dark eyes scanned the shabby group of farmer soldiers. "Outnumbered, unquestionably." My heart dropped again to hear of our vulnerability. "But half the Dakota didn't want to attack. And some were just seeking food." It made sense in my understanding. But the missionary's explanation was too sympathetic for this audience.

"If someone's hungry they don't scalp infants. Scalp our women!" Mr. Ayers challenged. I'd heard some accounts of scalping in my recording. But none of infants. I gripped my logbook tightly, curling it into the nook of my arm.

Riggs's expression settled with a sincerity. He saw us for the clustered terrified group we were. "It's a good number on the warpath. I'm saying if you hold on, you might outlast 'em. They all don't want to fight."

"We're ready," Otto said with conviction, tapping the butt of his rifle into the dirt.

"I'll cork 'em good if they come near me. Or Captain," Bruno said with childish enthusiasm as he lifted his pitchfork to show he was ready to go.

"I came to bear warning. I don't want any harm coming to either side. But I know it's too late for that."

"It's far too late for that." My father dismissed any harmonious intentions as superfluous and impractical. Taking command, he directed, "We'll make a perimeter behind the barricade. Split into groups of three, we'll switch stations, rotate provisions, and sleep every third shift."

I suddenly began feeling out of place among the men.

Mr. Ayers expressed his worry. "They'll try to burn us out. We need fire plans. And as many bullets as can be made."

Fire, too? My mind couldn't keep up with all the ways we were set to die.

"Women are casting bullets fast as they can in Turner Hall."

With that, Otto took my arm to escort me back to shelter. I took a final look at Riggs standing tall beside his horse. I glimpsed Pa's serious face. Our lives all fell in their hands. I listened desperately as Otto walked me away.

"If they breach the barricade?" someone asked.

"I'm placing explosives throughout the buildings within the barricades. Those Injun's won't get to take a single damn thing from us if we destroy ourselves first."

Destroy ourselves first? The plan was a horrifying thought. Fear sank its fingers down my throat and around my stomach. At least this time, when the Indians attack, Ida and I won't be alone. I grabbed my hand onto my brother's steady arm and moved quickly as I could to be in the place a daughter wants to be when she's scared. Next to her ma.

Determined women busied themselves casting bullets, brewing coffee, tending the wounded. Every so often, panic would flood through the group of us gathered at Kuhn's. False alarms, any sound, really, that could mean our final moment had come, would take the house with shrieking and dread. Each wave of fear in the daylight was a false alarm. But quick as day turned to night, Riggs's prediction became our reality. A full-scale attack. We could hear gunshots in the streets and feel the bullets pelting the side of the building.

I sheltered in the upstairs bedroom with Ma, Ida, Catherine, and baby Peter. In the dark, I sat close to Ma, running my fingers back and forth along the lace edge of her dress sleeve. Mrs. Eastlick sat in her chair; four injured men lay on the floor. A single candle stood on a nightstand; the light kept a tiny flicker of saneness in the hours dragging in the darkness beyond us. Fear sat in my body for so long I numbed into a hollow shell. Time was interrupted only with the echoes of gunshots outside and moans from the injured men inside.

Mrs. Eastlick sat like a ghost. I tried to keep my eyes averted from her. She was a reminder of the horror that could happen, what little of life could be left for a survivor. The bodies of the injured men smelled peculiar. I scooted closer to Ma, who led our room in prayer. Over and over we repeated the familiar words: "Lord protect, the men, the children and us all. Keep us safe in your good name." The booms rang from every side; the attack sounded as if it fully encircled the town. I thought of Pastor Vogel's descriptions of hell. Unable to escape, consuming, everlasting.

As an injured man across from me let out a guttural wail; I pressed my fingers into my ears, but my mind couldn't be shut off so easily. What would I have done had the gun been on the gunhooks at the farm? Would I have been able to fire? Shoot the Indians dead in our yard? I wanted a sense of power and protection. My loathing for the man atop Ida made my arm eager for the weight of a long barrel; my finger craved the smooth hook of a trigger. But what of the concern in the warrior's eyes, the scar, his word lingered in my memory. *GO!* They weren't as purely evil as my recollection wanted me to believe. That warrior had protected us. My urge to destroy shifted to an angry confusion.

I opened the logbook in my lap; the "H" page of the book fell open. I realized I had neglected to record the status of our own family. I set to marking bold Xs under Alive for August, Anna, Otto . . . Ida. I stopped. The scene in the yard flashed in my mind. My stomach flipped. Should I check Alive or Wounded? Part of me wanted to simply check Alive for my sister and continue along. As if marking an X on a paper would let us move on in life as well, as if no heinous act had ever been attempted upon her. I looked across the dark room. Ida gently pulled her fingers through Catherine's fine blonde curls.

Ida's bandaged feet stuck out the bottom of her skirt. The scars would tell the truth. I must, as well. I scanned back to Ida's line and made the X under Wounded. As I set the pen down, it triggered another memory. The pen in my hand. My letter to the Board of Teachers. I'd actually believed God intended such a promised future for me. The world had changed since I sat to write so hopefully. The application deadline would undoubtedly come and pass. The idea of becoming a teacher was so optimistic it stood out as foolish now. The darkness gripped my once hopeful dream; it died within me in the long night. The future stopped existing; all I had was this terrible moment.

All night we sat powerless; intermittent lengths of silence were as unbearable as the reverberations of the blasts. There was no way to interpret the sounds, make sense of our fate. Mrs. Eastlick, who'd taken Catherine's rag doll, sat holding it close to her chest, rocking it in her bandaged arms. Grief had brought on a peculiar madness that I couldn't look away from. Ma, needing something other than the same prayer after long hours, said into the blackness, "Let's sing a hymn of faith." Her soft voice rang through the echoes of war,

What tho' my joys and comforts die?
The Lord my Saviour liveth;
What tho' the darkness gather round?
Songs in the night he giveth.

I joined in until a new sound filled the room. A pounding. Rattling on the rooftop. Ida, Ma, and I looked at each other as we realized the meaning—rain. No buildings could burn in such a downpour! It was as if an army from the sky had arrived to protect us. As if heaven itself had opened for us. Ma started the verse again, and for the first time, our voices brightened in the darkness.

Thursday, August 21, 1862

After the long hours of the night, Ma finally could take the gloom no more, and she pushed back a curtain. Rain beat against the windows, as we looked down at the street. Men were soaked and running about; some appeared to be coming up to the house. We paused in anticipation of an update. A voice shouted up to us from downstairs, "They've retreated." A roar of cheers erupted through the crowded house. I looked at Ma's face, which for the first time in the ordeal, broke with tears. The rain had protected us, and the Indians had been held off. We'd survived.

I needed out of that room. The odor of the injured was too thick; I couldn't take it another minute. I went downstairs and filled a mug of hot coffee. I wanted to see my father, Uncle Allen, or Otto. I ventured out onto the porch, uneasy to leave the safety of the house, but more anxious to seek an update from the men. The cup steamed in the damp chill of the morning rain. Puddles rippled as raindrops splashed down in a steady stream. Such sweet relief. Pa sat in a rocking chair at the end of the porch, head bent forward in exhaustion. I teared up in my happiness to see him alive. My father had bravely stood guard through the past two days.

"I prayed for you the whole night long, Pa."

"This rain's falling from heaven. We wouldn't have held 'em much longer." He looked down the sloppy street. His eyes stopped upon on a small cart tucked between two buildings across from us. The cart was loaded with something; a bulky shape covered with a piece of canvas. A set of legs stuck out, ragged pants covering fixed ankles, boots bent straight up, unmoving. A casualty of the night had been moved to this wagon. Beside the cart sat Captain. Sitting loyally in the pouring rain.

My heart tremored as I comprehended the sight. "Bruno? Pa? Is that Bruno?" I asked, praying I was wrong.

Pa said nothing but I knew. Bruno was dead.

I wanted to look away, but my eyes were fixed with heartbreak watching the faithful collie shaking as the cold rain fell. Bruno wouldn't harm a caterpillar. I doubted he was even able to comprehend what was going on in the attack. He was so vulnerable. We should've kept him in Kuhn's or Turner Hall. Put him somewhere safe. Sweet, kind Bruno.

Pa explained, "A group of us were lying on our bellies along the barricade. Indians just beyond it. Bruno spooked and stood up to run. They covered him in arrows and bullets. He went quick." Tears dropped heavy from my stinging eyes. They were insufficient to let out all the pain. Of course, Bruno would be scared. The terror of the last few days had overtaken us all. Every few minutes we could hear screams of panic during the night—and we had brick walls protecting us. I stared out into the falling rain. Could this rain actually be falling from heaven? Heaven was so far from this. What place would ever feel safe again?

Looking out, there was movement at the edge of town. I squinted, eventually making out four riders, holding lanterns, surrounding a stagecoach. A uniformed man sat on the wagon seat. Was it the army finally arriving? My father got to his feet and moved down the porch stairs, his body still ready to fight at a moment's notice. In my curiosity, I followed him to the bottom step. The rain fell vertically, splattering. Men rushed to create an opening in the barricade, and the formal procession rolled its grand way up the center of the street.

We approached the protected wagon. A young man sat in the middle, upon the small bench. "We were diverted this way," he hollered. "Annuity's supposed to go to Fort Ridgley."

"Annuity?" my father asked. The chilling rain soaked my dress.

"All the way from Washington. The annuity payment for the Dakota." The young man couldn't help himself; he pridefully showed off his valuable load. He opened the side door of the wagon, revealing a massive chest. When he opened the hinged top, we could see a heap of gold coins. The unexpected treasure glowed in the somber morning.

"I'll be damned," Pa whispered.

It was the Dakotas' long overdue annuity payment. A massive amount of gold. We had assumed it would never come. The sight was beyond my comprehension. I jumped when the man snapped the chest shut.

"Where's safekeeping?" he asked.

The payment had been on its way just as the Dakota could take no more. Unimaginable. If only they'd known. If only we'd known! I was overcome with dismay. The uncanny timing. The *safe*keeping for the gold! The rain poured, soaking me in disbelief. It was too much for comprehension; all I could do was laugh. All logic evaporating at that moment. I suddenly understood Mrs. Eastlick's laughter, the craze, though her whole family gone. Incomprehensible. We were awash with bewildering humanness. Rain beat upon my face. I let the craziness swallow me. The world had gone mad.

NINETEEN

Oenikika

Wednesday, August 20, 1862

I walked in the serene glow of a full moon. A warm wind stirred around me, beckoning me to the lakeshore. The lake of wild rice. I filled with a peaceful gladness at returning to this place of my childhood. The damp sandy shore was cool under my feet. A bark canoe, filled with spectacular fur blankets of our ancestors, floated within reach. I took the blankets into my hands to admire—a silky beaver pelt, a hide with the speckles of a fawn, and the plush of a red fox. They were magnificent; yet soft and comforting. Climbing into the canoe, I folded a blanket and placed it under me as I took a seat. A strong spirit compelled me . . . but I was not supposed to be alone in this canoe. My voice called out. I could hear myself calling. But what name I was saying? I was calling a man—it was his time. Finally, a shadowy figure emerged from the dark forest behind me. Who was he? He crawled into the canoe and laid down, like a child, pulling the blankets around him.

A quiet urging stirred in me. He was going to the Happy Hunting Land. The green reeds rustled as I paddled us towards the open center of the lake. The winds blew stronger, yet the water was unmoving as my oar dipped into its dark stillness. How could this be so? Still water with wind? Ahh, my soul realized: *The Great Mystery is guiding.* I sat back and let the wind push us forward. Unexpectedly, a woman's deep soothing voice called from the wild rice. . .

"He's coming to be with me now, beloved daughter." My breath caught with hope. Mother? The Woman of the Winter Sun! I looked about with yearning; where was she? But it was just the stalks of wild rice looking back at me, rippling. Tears of adoration formed in my eyes. I longed to be with her. Nearer.

"Can I see you, Mother?"

"You see me all the time," she said with amusement.

"Can I *be* with you?" I asked, hopefully.

"It's not your time. There's much more healing left for you to do, Oenikika. You'll remain." *I'll remain.* "But if he doubts, you will let him know he did indeed die in battle. With the greatest honor."

I nodded. This was the discernment of a healer who needs to help someone transition. I was gaining an understanding of my duties. A shiver ran down my spine, as I sensed the spirit of my mother receding back into the darkness of the reeds. Swiftly the winds changed. My hair swirled. I covered the man with the ornate blankets as the canoe moved shockingly *towards* the wind. How was this possible? The tranquil water reflected the magnificence of the moon and stars above. I set my oar aside and let the winds of Mystery pull us out upon the open water.

My soul focused on the silent man in front of me; my purpose was certain: help him to the other side. "You aren't alone when you leave. And you won't be alone when you arrive in the Happy Hunting Land." The winds whirled as the stars began to twinkle and the moon beamed with brilliance. His time had come. Though the man's body remained covered in the canoe, his spirit streamed out above the water. He hovered like a wispy silver cloud. My soul filled in pure drenching love as his spirit flew from the water and towards the moon.

In an instant, the winds stilled, and he was gone.

I woke with a shock, gasping for air as if I'd been pulled up from the depths. I'd been dreaming so vividly that tears had run in trails down my cheeks. The dream had such clarity—waking did not. Where was I? Not in the tipi. Grandmother laid at my side; my hand still held hers. I laid back down as I realized I'd fallen asleep at the healing tent. That dream was a vision. I'd asked the spirit to speak to me in my dreams . . . And it did. But Death was not what I'd expected to see. I felt unsettled . . . I craved more guidance. *Spirit, you are so close, reveal more of yourself.* A dreamer must accept whatever dreams were sent to them. Mika had explained a healer would some-day know the wisdom of each dream. Someday I'd understand why I was brought such a vision.

A soft pitter-patter whispered above, and I stared at the canopy stretched overhead. Rain was falling. My heart warmed as I remem-bered the voice of my mother. It was the most comforting sound I'd ever heard. I wanted to close my eyes and return to the dream. Could I reach out in the reeds and touch her? And the man whose spirit left . . . who was he? Why would the spirit bring me this vision but not reveal his identity? Streaks of rain fell harder in the night beyond me.

Abruptly, my entire body tensed. My husband! I never saw Tashunke when I returned with the medicines. He never woke me during the night. He would have woken me when he exchanged horses for battle. A terrible chilling fear sunk into my bones. Where was my husband?

Thursday, August 21, 1862

The soil around the village had turned to a slippery mush in the chaos and rain. Warriors galloped through camp, furious with their failure. I was completely soaked, as I stumbled about in the gray wrath. I twisted to look at each face that passed, hoping to see my husband. His solidness would emerge from the chaos. It always did. He was my steadiness. But all I saw was gray fright. Anger. Worry was consuming; I could think of nothing else. I spotted Little Rapids trotting by. He would know where my husband was. I ran to him and called out, "Cousin. Have you seen Tashunke?"

"No," he said without care, and in the disorder after a lost battle he would not stop to talk with a woman further. Worry turned to alarm, and I spun in frantic fear. Hopelessness sunk its claws into my lungs. What had happened to Tashunke! Devastation wrenched itself as I looked at the mess of camp . . . Horses without riders barreled past. Braves cried out angry trilling calls; the war party was disorganized. Men rode in packs north, south, west. I turned about again, and then I saw her, standing in the pouring rain: Wicapi.

I ran to my husband's mare. Her palomino hair dripped as the rain fell atop us. The red handprints of warpaint Tashunke had made upon her shoulders were disappearing as quickly as my hope. Her dark eyes looked into mine.

"Where is he?" I whispered as my soul begged the mare to show me something. But Wicapi just stared back with sadness in her brown eyes. I knew she would never leave him if he were alive. "No," I cried out as the reality of his absence soaked in. Wicapi pressed her forehead into my chest, as my heart exploded, and my voice cried out to the angry skies above . . . "No." I fell to my knees and clung to the mare. We both were incomplete without him. I thought of the last time I had seen my husband. I was painting him in our tipi. As he listened to *my* concerns. He worried about the risks for me to ride by myself. My heart had been so preoccupied with the plants. We both focused upon my call to healing. I looked up at Wicapi's empty back. Where a rider should be sitting tall. Tears fell into the rain streaming down my face. I gasped—my dream from last night. My dream of helping a man to the other side. Had my mother been calling for my husband? Was that the moment he had crossed over? In the night?

Mud swamped up my shins as I cowered under Wicapi. My stomach turned as the sickening worst reality of wartime was no longer a fear. I felt hollow remembering Chief Wabasha's warning at the war council—Dakota blood would pour out upon the earth. I stared at a muddy puddle in a hoofprint in front of me collecting rain. Drop. Drop. Each splash an impossible abyss I sunk deeper into.

A voice interrupted my hopelessness: "Rise up." I was taken aback and squinted up at my father, atop Mato, the feathers of his war bonnet funneling the drumming rain towards his face. It poured off the angles of him in a stream. His eyes were grave.

I pulled myself together to address my leader. Chief Little Crow averted his eyes and looked about the frenzied camp. I felt as if he couldn't bear to truly look at his daughter, weeping for her husband in the rain. "Tashunke? Father," I yelled out over the sound of the downpour—I wanted him to care. Where was his warrior? His son? I wanted to keep yelling. To scream. I felt as if the ground had let out under me and my entire world was sinking. My spirit tearing out from my insides. My heart was gone.

"We *all* ride west. Immediately." West. The War Chief was moving us; we'd surely lost our position of power. We'd failed to take the white man's village. This was a retreat. The whites would be coming for us. Why weren't the braves moving together? Organizing a defense? Our power wasn't united. I wanted to stay, lay myself down, in the last place I had seen my husband. My heart could *never* leave here. My memory went again to the dream . . . the peace as the canoe glided over the water. His spirit traveling out over the still water. My husband was gone. I felt as if I was permanently exhaling . . . my breath would never fill again.

My father called out again, commanding me. "Oenikika. We move on."

PART THREE

TWENTY

Oenikika

August 31, 1862

While the men debated, my gaze fixed on a single strand of grass lightly waving in front of me. Earlier today, a white man rode waving a white cloth and delivered a letter. The white's war chief, Henry Sibley, was a day's ride away. The message: they would destroy us with all the power of the United States Army *unless* we surrendered. If we surrendered, they guaranteed no harm would come.

I stared at the green grass, lost in thought. *No harm will come.* What a meaningless message. So much harm has already come. Baby Kayawi dead. The braves that died in the healing tent, the many more who passed on when we tried to move them during our retreat. And my husband. My heart pinched painfully inside of me. I stared at the strand of grass and tried to remember the wonder I used to feel being in the world. Now I just existed. Wonder was gone . . . hope was gone. There was an emptiness inside of me without Tash; a raw pain that exhausted me. This was why we have our four days of wailing and the formal mourning for a death. Families must circle together—share pain, open up, let it out so it doesn't bury you. But we fled so quickly, and I never had my time to cry out. No one had seen Tashunke die. He'd just disappeared. Some men said Tash could be out riding with the others in disorganized attack. But I knew my husband would never do such a thing. He would never leave Wicapi. Never leave me.

I sat near Owl Woman under the shade of a lone elm. There were far fewer trees on this part of the prairie; we'd ridden west for days. Owl Woman's fever had broken, but her body was still weak. Mika and Wenona leaned against the trunk as Kimimela and Wolfchaser slept using their mother's legs as pillows. Wenona was a shell of the jovial joking cousin I'd known; the death of Kayawi had enraged her husband and sent her into a lonely faraway world in her mind. Little Rapids had abandoned her and the children, disappearing with Brown Wing and others to continue raiding. Pointless raiding that didn't serve the war mission or their families. Dina and Scarlet Woman sat quietly; Bonko lay in melancholy. Cut Nose had left them, as well, impulsively riding to kill the white man who'd brought the letter.

We'd moved in mass; a thousand of us, mostly women and children and the men of peace. Many braves had scattered after the lost battle. We'd retreated so far hoping to escape the reach of the white men. But the white flag waving rider made it clear we had failed. My eyes finally left the strand of grass, and I watched the men debate as a numbness settled in behind my heartache.

Father scoffed at the message. "No surrender. We are *still* strong." If my father didn't want to surrender, we would all die tomorrow. A deadened sense of defeat filled me. After all the pain, the suffering, the starvation, our rising up together. We'd be massacred upon this flat land we'd run to. Like wolves upon rabbits in the hard moon. Just as he'd predicted.

"Enough blood has been spilled." Chief Wabasha compelled Little Crow to see differently. Of course, Wabasha wanted to submit. He'd never been willing to stand up for our tribe. He'd wanted to farm. To become a white man. Irritation punctured my numbness.

"We ride and summon other chiefs from the Seven Councils—chiefs from faraway north and west. They have not encountered the white man yet, but they will. If we can organize with them . . ." Little Crow explained a strategy. *That* was a fair consideration: to find the tribes of the Seven Council fires. A few braves nodded in allegiance. But how would we move a thousand of us, especially the slow-moving women and children, before the oncoming white warriors reached us?

"If we surrender peacefully then *no* harm comes," Uncle Chaska reiterated the white man's message as if he actually trusted them . . . and maybe, Chaska and Wabasha had a chance at peaceful surrender. They'd never fought a single day in battle. Along with us women and children, the whites could spare them. But Chief Little Crow that led the attack? No. My father would be killed, most certainly. The white men had deceived, lied, and manipulated when he had done nothing but follow the treaty as expected. They would *destroy* him for standing up.

Father looked about at our camp. Supplies were dwindling; most men had abandoned camp for the reckless pillaging, and this left very few men to go out hunting. He'd been deserted by the braves who called for this war in the first place. There were a few left who stood at his side; only a small fraction of those who once swirled united outside our house during the midnight call to war. My insides squeezed in anxiety. All seemed lost. Once again, my father was in an impossible position.

"Those who wish to surrender may do so of their choosing. But the chief rides on," Little Crow declared.

Chaska and Chief Wabasha looked to one another. "I'll pray for your journey," my uncle responded. In a quick moment, it was decided. Our chief was riding on for his people. The masses would surrender.

My chest felt as if grief was a rock from the riverside, placed heavy in the center of me. My father leaving. I understood why my husband had worn the necklaces in memory of his family. This heartache was a weight that would be upon me forever. I knew the white man's walls were not for me. My husband was gone; the battle with the whites had taken him from me forever. I couldn't stand the idea of submitting to people who had taken someone so powerful and lovely and . . . tears filled my eyes as they did whenever I let myself recall the wonder of my husband. I looked at my father: A chief with no tribe. Only a small contingency of mounted braves left at his side. It was like we were a boulder dropped off a cliff. Exploding as it hits the ground. Something that had been so strong—broken suddenly into pieces. Could he really ride off? Leave us? Leave me?

"Grandmother, what will we do?"

She grunted and shifted herself on the ground. "My body is old now. I need an easier path, one with no harm." Owl Woman sat hunched. Aunt Mika looked at her mother in caring agreement. But my heart wrestled itself. My family was going in two separate directions. I didn't believe there was an easier path. But they would surrender. I couldn't comprehend the world without my grandmother. Her sweet nurturing love. How I was called to care for her. But I couldn't comprehend the world without my father, either. He'd been the guiding North Star for our tribe, our family, for me.

Owl Woman looked at me seriously, rolling her lips back and forth over her gums, contemplating. My insides wrenched. I felt paralyzed between the two choices—to surrender or ride on. What would Tash have wanted? My soul wished I had my husband here to help me understand my world.

Finally, Grandmother asked me, "And what does the chief's daughter feel called to do?"

The *chief's daughter*. With Owl Woman's gentle but intentional words, the spirit of kinship stirred within me. Though no longer a wife, I was still a daughter. I knew what I would do. I looked back into

Owl Woman's eyes, the woman who'd been my mother figure for my entire life. She did what a mother does and nudged my wings to fly. I reached inside myself, somewhere below the numbness of grief. Even if I couldn't fully feel it, my strength still remained somewhere deep inside of me. A glimmer of purpose lighted my darkness.

I rose to stand. "I will ride with our chief," I said confidently. Heads turned in surprise. A woman speaking so boldly. But I was called in kinship to serve my father. I could prepare food. Aid our small contingency in the continued fight for our people. I had too much left to give to the world to let the white man take me captive. Chief Little Crow didn't miss the chance to show the audience his approval of my choice.

"A daughter who brings her father honor! We leave before the last of the daylight." To ride the prairie without the protection of a tribe would be dangerous, but the risk of death was better than surrender.

Ahone was packed. Though I knew the power of my choice, the rock of grief still pinned my soul as I wrapped my arms in goodbye around Grandmother. Then my aunt. My cousin. I was able to hide my aching heart until my niece clung to my neck and wouldn't let go. It was the cruelest goodbye of all. To take another thing from a young girl who'd already lost so much in her little world. I was at the edge of dissolving into sadness when Wenona pried Kimimela's thin arms off of me and held her weeping daughter. I rose quickly and I didn't look back. I couldn't look back.

A chill of fear for my loved ones set through my spine; as soon as the sun was in the sky tomorrow, they'd surrender to the white man. It made me ill with anger and hardened my hurting heart. Anger gave me power above my defenseless sadness. I took in a long look at our people. Hundreds of tipis set up on the open plains. Smoke of camp-fires curling into the air. Beyond, all our tribes' horses. A sight I may never see again. I walked to Ahone and pulled my husband's ax from the carrying sleeve. There was only one thing left to do.

I walked to the edge of camp and stood above the ashes of an abandoned fire. It once burned bright and mighty, but these charred logs of ruin were all that remained. I knelt down and sunk my hands deep into the ash. The core was still warm. Up to my wrists, my hands were covered in black soot. I put my fingers to the bottoms of my eyes and scratched my fingernails straight down my cheeks through my jawline . . . my delicate skin tore under my sharp nails. I felt a warm wetness mix into the ash. My blood upon the blackness of grief that lived in me now. My breath quickened in my chest but I would not sob. I imagined white riders approaching on the horizon. Coming for our people. No! I filled with rage and fury. You cannot steal one more part of my soul. In a crazed agony of sadness and outrage, my blackened hands grabbed Tashunke's hatchet. I walked with determination towards the field of our picketed horses. Our beautiful powerful herd, bound. Tied up. Mounts of such value, waiting to be taken by the white men just like our people were going to be. Like everything in our world had been.

I refused to let surrender be the destiny of the horses that had belonged to my husband. The horses that sang in harmony with him. They were part of his spirit, ours, and I felt a charge over their fate. His horses surveyed me with questioning eyes as I approached. My steps weren't peaceful and soft as usual. I was raging. Tashunke was never coming back. The white man couldn't have one more piece of him.

I ran to Wicapi. She shook her golden head against the picket rope with fright. With all the power in my heart and all the fury in my soul, I swung the ax overhead and hurled it down with all my might. I sliced the rope. Wicapi stumbled free, tripping, running. I ran towards her screaming. I wanted my pain to scare her; I needed her to run. Escape. Go far from here. Roaming gave her a chance. A chance our people didn't have. And I walked down the line of my husband's horses shrieking and slicing; hoping they had enough fright to abandon what was lost. The horses barreled away, sprinting into the rolling fields. This time, my husband was not a spirit form disappearing over a lake. The galloping hoofbeats of Tashunke's memory thundered over the grasses. I watched him go.

My hands shook holding his ax as I watched the last stallion gallop out of sight. I turned back. My father, sitting upon Mato, was waiting. He nodded. Ashes and blood stained my face. My heart was hollow. We could leave.

TWENTY-ONE

Emma Heard

September 3, 1862

Dusty light streamed into the grand courthouse. A gavel thudded resoundingly upon the wooden desk; the war trials were commencing. I was equipped with pen and paper. My nerves rang with the gavel's echo. Today, I wielded more power than I'd ever anticipated.

So much had occurred in the last two weeks. I still felt the horror when I remembered . . . Bruno's boots. Mrs. Duta's apron. Mrs. Eastlick rocking. And I couldn't shake the image of Ida in the yard from my mind. The gash on the side of my head was still painful, but healing. The ache felt like the memories trying to scratch their way out; when would we heal from our internal wounds? Another sickening memory: the unbelievable arrival of the annuity payment; a treasure of gold that would never reach Indian hands, as it was now set for depredation claims.

In another matter of unlikely timing, Colonel Henry Sibley rode into town with two companies of the Minnesota 7th Infantry in that afternoon rain. 1,500 soldiers, who had been in training in St. Paul to fight the rebels, were instead sent to our defense. My entire body had gone limp with relief when the troops formed a human perimeter around our town. I hadn't even realized how much fear I'd been holding in. Seeing the soldiers let me breathe again. Upon sight of our organized defenders, Otto hollered with pride. He'd protected his town. His sisters. I was able to return to my task keeping of what was now called the "Survivor's Record." Under the increased protection from Sibley's troops, my mind was able to focus, and I worked systematically to collect accounts. It was no longer a task to distract me from our doom but the stepping stone to rebuilding life.

Sibley, a mustachioed former fur trader, knew the Dakota well. So well, it was rumored that he had a daughter living somewhere among them. My father had worked with Sibley on the Dakota treaty years ago. Pa called him a "mighty good land man," as Sibley had become one of the wealthiest men in the entire state from his transactions with the Indians. One day, as we remained barricaded in New Ulm, I sat on a bench in front of Turner Hall, working on the Survivor's Record. Sibley walked over in polished knee-high boots and asked, "Heard's daughter?" I nodded, shocked that someone so important knew my identity. He grabbed the record book with his gloved hands. I held my breath as he flipped rapidly through the pages. "Very well." His approval made my heart stop. My work mattered, noticed by the most powerful man in our city. I was useful; I was *good*. I looked upon the open pages of my record, feeling as if something of order in the world resettled into place. If I worked hard and used my mind, good could prevail. The date for the teacher's application had come and gone but perhaps God had found a different purpose for me in protecting and rebuilding this town.

Soon additional troops arrived from the Minnesota 3rd Infantry to supplement Sibley. Thousands of trained soldiers were necessary to conquer the Indians. It seemed all the more astonishing that the few men of New Ulm had been able to hold off two days of attack. Now,

Sibley overtook the Dakota efficiently. Some warriors were killed and many escaped, while mostly non-hostiles surrendered at the edge of the state. They were brought to a massive corral northeast of New Ulm where they were carefully guarded day and night, not only to block their escape but because so many townspeople were out for revenge.

Last week, Major General John Pope, a grumbly bear of a man, took federal control of military operations. I'd once thought Colonel Sibley's status to be impressive. But Pope, frock coat gleaming down the front with gold adornments and grand shining buttons, was both impressive and imposing. He took command immediately. Sibley, who had little real experience in battle, was submissive to his superior officer. Pa told me Lincoln had actually reassigned Pope to New Ulm after he'd suffered a massive defeat in the south, the reassignment an insult as much as a punishment. But Pope carried himself with absolute authority.

Nothing about the general belonged in New Ulm. Even the uppity steps of his Tennessee Walker sent a message of superiority. Upon his arrival, General Pope explained, "I can't stand to be in the uncivilized backwaters of this country. I'll be making this quick." As soon as he arrived, he was looking to leave. "We'll try the savages by Military Commission. Get through them all before the snow flies." General Pope spent much of his day in an oversized canvas tent, puffing away on his pipe, appearing both distinguished and disgruntled. The general's simple dismissal irritated me. He didn't seem to truly care about what had happened here; his intention for dealing with the matter seemed more for himself than to address what was best for our town. I felt a defensiveness towards our "protector." Sibley hadn't any experience with military commissions; he enlisted the help of my father, a civilian lawyer, to help organize the military proceedings.

As Colonel Sibley and my father discussed trial plans and assigned roles, I busied myself with the Survivor's Log, but secretly listened in on their discussions. Sibley often deferred to my father's legal knowledgeability. The commission would be composed of Colonel Olin, Crooks, Grant, and Bailey—who all had fought as soldiers against the Dakota. Father was nominated to the commission as civilian soldier. Missionary Riggs would serve as interpreter. Sibley's army recorder had been shot in the right arm; he'd be unable to serve as court recorder. Just a few days ago I sat, transcribing away, in the Survivor's Log. When I looked up, Colonel Sibley's eyes were upon me. I lifted my pen from the page. They couldn't be considering . . .

My father broke the silence. "Emma is my daughter and dutiful assistant. In honest evaluation, her accuracy and penmanship are superior to any man's."

Sibley wiggled his mustache. "I suppose those are the most important factors in considering a court recorder. It would allow the men to stay focused upon the most important matters." I couldn't find words of agreement or rebuttal. My stomach turned in a wave of nervous disbelief. A court recorder? Me? In a simple affirmation, Sibley made it official. "She'll do."

Those plans brought us to today: the opening day of the trials. The courtroom was alive with energy. I could hardly believe my role—an actual recorder in a military commission. God had indeed found purpose for me. I was anxious for my duties; I wanted to execute them perfectly. I'd never seen a trial before; much less been part of one. My father and the others formed a panel of five sitting at the mahogany table in the front of the courtroom. Sibley, the commissioner, served as something like the moderator and judge. He was stationed in the raised seat above us.

I sat at a small table off to the side. I'd spent the morning nervously preparing; extra pens, nibs, inkwells, and blank pages sat on the ground. I was ready as could be. My job was to transcribe every word uttered during trial proceedings. Just as I had approached my task with the Survivor's Log in the past weeks, I approached this record with an extreme and equal sense of duty. I wanted to make my father proud. If I wasn't meant to be a teacher, I could devote myself to this. I reassured myself, as I gripped my pen tightly, ready to record every detail of such a prestigious courtroom.

As the gavel dropped, Sibley's voice called out, "We are here to try summarily the Indians, now nearly 400 prisoners, and pass judgment upon them, if found guilty of murder . . . and other outrages upon the whites." The entire commission, my father included, had just been in battle with the Dakota men they now sat to try. Once enemies, now they must judge their enemy fairly. The presumption of innocence until proven guilty was the core of American law. I wondered how the commission, even my father, could presume any Indian innocent?

Missionary Riggs opened a door behind Sibley and walked in a shackled Dakota man. My heart pounded upon sight of an Indian, my terror from the yard flooded back in, as if body knew the memory before my mind could make sense of it. It was the last I had seen them. I stared at him; anger ran through my veins. Part of me felt satisfied to see the man in shackles. He couldn't hurt Ida, hurt anyone now. As I continued to study the man, I realized I didn't actually recognize him. How could I know what he did or didn't do in the attacks? The face I would never forget, the man with the scar, reappeared in my memory. His voice: "Go." I inhaled through my constricted throat. My head swirled with the mess of recollections. I must refocus upon my task at hand. Once again, there was nothing more important than recording the facts.

"Here we have—" Sibley looked down through his spectacles, "—Red Otter?"

Riggs spoke to the man in Dakota. "Yes, I am, proudly, Red Otter." Riggs translated. I scrawled every word. I glanced up at Riggs; this must be uniquely terrible for him to now translate the trial of the men he had lived among.

"This man is believed to have participated in the raiding at the

Outpost on Monday, August 18, 1862. And is suspected of *murdering* the well-regarded trader Andrew Myrick, as recorded in the Survivor's Log. We call witnesses forth those who can attest to this Indian's plundering crimes."

My head spun at hearing my own log referenced at trial. I was disgusted to hear Myrick described as "well-respected." It seemed like just yesterday and yet an entire lifetime ago that Myrick stood behind the desk at his own general store. In a way, he was a reason all of this started in the first place.

A couple who lived near the post approached the bench. Both declared they had seen *this very Indian!* These "witnesses" reminded me of the hysterical reports made to me while recording in the log. I was suspicious of their adamant memory. Riggs struggled to keep Red Otter updated on their testimony. Without any witnesses called on Otter's behalf, the commission quickly moved to vote. The five men discussed quietly amongst themselves for a minute. Then down the line, each seated man pronounced a verdict: "Guilty." My own father's voice echoing last.

My heart flipped. I thought justice would feel more satisfying. I looked about the sterile courtroom. General Pope stood to the side. He pulled his gleaming pocket watch from his jacket and checked the time. A smug, satisfied grin spread across his face. Hearing a death sentence was the first he'd looked happy since his arrival. I was repulsed by the man. These proceedings were nothing like what the law books outlined. I squeezed the pen, my fingers already stiffening from so much transcription. I wrote solemnly as Sibley's voice summarized the verdict and gave the sentence: "Guilty of the specification. He is sentenced to be hanged by the neck until he is dead." I looked up briefly. It was all decided so quickly. Red Otter stared at Riggs, as he translated the decision. I felt for the missionary's horrible duty.

I set my hand back to my task, once again recording a death. But this time, a death that hadn't happened yet, but was *planned* for the future. I hesitated briefly before forcing myself to scrawl, "hanged by the neck until he is dead." The ink on the hanging bottom loop of the "G" bled into the page. I sat up in my seat, my eyes wide. Could this really be all there was to our trials? All the texts I had read. The complexity of law. Rules. Truth. This felt something the opposite, a swift conclusion. My head swirled in confusion. I suddenly felt profoundly out of place, not for my femininity, my youth, but for my internal conscience. A keen voice inside of me issued an alarm, the same internal conscience that had whispered a warning when I watched Myrick's messy dealing with the Indians. But what could I do?

The military court tried twelve men. And my pen wrote the fates of ten men sentenced to die, two others sentenced to imprisonment. My mind flashed to the day of the attack, the dark ink and bright blood that stained my hands. Though I was clean today, the same feeling of filth felt upon me. The court record was open, the dark looping script calling for the blood of the Indians. I stared at my own besmirched handwriting as the first day of trials ended with the echo of a slamming gavel. I felt heavy as the sound. The reality of justice rang empty. Tomorrow, we would start again.

September 5, 1862

In one snappy blow of a northwest wind, the season changed. The breath of fall crept along the farmhouse, pushed its way through the smallest cracks in the wall and seeped under the door. A fire roared in the hearth. I looked about and took in the normalcy, the things I'd taken for granted. After long days in the courthouse, it was a simple satisfaction to be home in the evenings. Pa, Otto, and Uncle Allen's presence felt like protection; their rifles always within reach. After the Indians were defeated and caged, we'd returned home. The house was, miraculously not too damaged. Some flour and coffee taken, our pigs gone. But they hadn't touched the root cellar. My body had shivered upon return when I saw the front door still standing open. The moment I'd last opened it, Ida was sprinting towards the house, the Indians here. Ida was stone-faced when she walked back through the doorway, appearing as if nothing had ever happened. But during the nights, I felt her tossing next to me in her sleep, having nightmares, probably. She had to be remembering it too. Shame had grabbed me at the sight of ink spilled over the unfinished letter on my nightstand. Though it was just weeks ago, I could barely remember how simple my hope had been. I needed to let Miss Knudsen know of my disappointing change of plans. The Teacher's Association had required commitment by August. We were now into September; there was no way an application could reach them in time. Besides, with all that'd happened, it would be foolish to consider leaving. The court proceedings could take months. And Ida. Separating from her not wise. After what we'd been through, my instincts yearned to be close to her. Safe with her. Still, something inside of me broke with sharp disappointment. Letting go of my secret dream.

I carried a candle as I walked upstairs and took a seat with a blank piece of paper at my nightstand. I set to write to Miss Knudsen, informing her that I'd missed the deadline. It had been silly for me to hope for a different life, anyway.

September 5, 1862

Dearest teacher and friend,

This is not the update I'd expected to pen. I first offer my sincere apologies. Your recommendation to the Board of Teachers, while making my heart burst at the generosity, has gone unsupplemented by my own failures. You've likely heard of the Indian warpath in New Ulm and surrounding countryside. Glory to God, our entire family has survived. However, this is the explanation for my failure to apply to the board within the August deadline. After experiencing wartime, I believe it'd be selfish to leave my family to pursue my independent dream of becoming an educator. I express both my regrets and apologies.

Furthermore, I've been assisting in my father's office. I am currently serving as court recorder in the trials that have commenced since the Dakota's great defeat at the hands of the United States Army. I am uncertain what my future holds, especially as I currently serve in such an unexpected role.

I am terribly sorry to disappoint you, as I likely have. I can tell you, receiving your response was one of the greatest delights I've known.

With apologies and sincerity,

Emma Heard

I folded the paper, letting go of a part of myself; teaching now a past dream shed from me. Ida crawled into bed next to me. I thought to hide my letter on the nightstand from her, but so much had happened, hiding my past hopes didn't feel necessary. Ida had been difficult to read lately; her silence felt open to misinterpretation. Though I'd vowed to be by her side, my duties with the survivor's log and trial did sometimes take me away from her. I felt guilt that I was always being pulled to some calling that seemed very different than hers. Though we laid next to each other each night, Ida seemed far away. I wanted to understand her; she was my mirror, my counterpart. "Sister, how are you feeling?"

She waved her finger in the air, a sign she was fine. Her ambivalence was underwhelming. Such an incredible amount was happening in the world around us. I wanted to connect with her—and wanted her to *want* to connect with me. I felt an urge to recall our shared experience. "That day repeats in my mind. It all happened so quickly." I wanted Ida's understanding. But something of frustration flared in her eyes, as if she didn't care to interact with me at all. Her lack of engagement was irritating. Even her silence suddenly became annoying. "You can't act as if you don't remember," I said angrily. She needed to let me have space to discuss it. Explain my guilt. That I would've done anything I could to save us. But instead, I'd frozen . . .

Ida shrugged her shoulders with a dismissive apathy. My heart raged at her denial. She waved two fingers, "No."

"Well, *I* remember." I pushed her with my words: "The warrior whose command saved us. Do you remember?" I demanded her acknowledgment. Her corroboration. Anything to help the experience make sense. Her refusal was infuriating. She looked at me with an expression that said *no more*. She rose from bed and went downstairs. The cold ire of abandonment simmered. Why wouldn't she acknowledge what'd happened? And she didn't even seem to care about all the work I was doing in the courthouse. How dare she. A swirl of emotions spun my thoughts even faster. And coming up from a dark depth was a selfish and overwhelming disappointment. I'd been so foolish to think I could be a teacher . . . Hopelessness crushed in upon me. The feelings boiled together until hot tears swelled in my eyes. I was alone. Ida was pushing me away. My heart's hand couldn't find hers. My deep desire to understand, to find truth was taking me away from her. I looked back at my letter. I was resigned to stay with my family. Yet, here I sat. Alone.

September 10, 1862

The orange of sunrise glowed in the office window; it would be another long day of trials. I took quietly to my usual seat at the far table, willing myself as small as possible in the path of powerful men. The panel, Sibley, and General Pope gathered in the law office ahead of the trial. I'd grown used to the routine of assembling in the office, then lengthy hours of trial, and a quiet ride home with my father. Maybe I'd even grown used to my frustration with the trials. The commission was like a threshing machine at harvest time. Efficiently churning in, cutting down, spitting out.

The townspeople were fully supportive of the commission's proceedings. The headline of the newspaper on Father's desk read "DEATH TO THE BARBARIANS." There was now a bounty placed on any Indians remaining in the state. I quietly read the front page, knowing not to comment or ask questions. My appropriate conduct was to be a silent automaton. I was the recorder only; there for precise transcription. But I wasn't as mindless as my duties; every day my silent frustration grew. I questioned if I could continue working in a law office, after seeing the truth of how powerful men manipulated the implementation of law. It seemed to me the Dakota had been willing to abide by a treaty; it was our own government's failure to honor the treaty that was the impetus for this disaster.

"You know most of these are the Dakota who surrendered. The rascals who started the uprising are riding free in the far west," Sibley explained to General Pope, who was pacing near the windows with a surly step.

I braced myself. Pope's voice bit through the air. "*Exterminate* them all! If you find the slightest occasion for it—sentence an execution. Women and children were murdered. What defense have they? Send a message." The room went silent. My stomach tightened. The clock struck seven, and with that, we proceeded into the courthouse.

I looked around the space I previously admired as grand. I'd once believed, as Pa said, that the implementation of law was our ultimate distinguishing human characteristic. But with each day of the trial, each conviction with scant evidence, each execution order, my pen felt something devious and sharp, the law malleable and misused. Once again, I was a cowardly spectator, clinging to a windowsill. As I moved down the center aisle, my chest filled with dread.

I settled in my wooden chair at the front of the courthouse, my fingers aching as I picked up my pen. The trials began at a rapid pace; I wrote furiously to keep up. I'd get a brief moment of reprieve when Riggs walked a sentenced man out; only too soon he'd walk another new accused to the doomed seat. The day passed in repetitive announcements of "GUILTY." Another seventeen Dakota men went before the commission, ten sentenced to die. General Pope stood in the back of the courthouse and gave a heartless nod of approval to Sibley at the tenth hanging announced. This general tallied each execution as if it was his own battle won. He was twisting the process. Where was innocence until guilt was proven? The court failed to ensure due process. No one cared about understanding the facts. Finding the truth.

The courthouse emptied for the day; the men of the commission walked out. I was relieved to separate from them. I was dedicated to my task and remained at my desk, taking time to review my record. I was powerless during the proceedings and wanted to be sure my one quiet bit of power, the court record, was as strong as I could make it. That it reflected the truth, and the failures, of what happened in this room. Alone in the quiet courthouse, I reread my pages. I heard a click of a door and lifted my head to see Missionary Riggs entering the room. My heart paused. I felt the magical instant connection to him as our first encounter, but it was dulled under our terrible reality. No matter the rush of feeling within me, my question for him was a practical one. It was a chance to ask him for clarification.

"Excuse me, Riggs? *Missionary* Riggs, my apologies," I shook my head, embarrassed that my casual nature may reveal how much his familiar name ran through my brain. "Would you have a moment to clarify a Dakota name spelling for the court record? It's difficult to keep straight."

He made his way in my direction without saying a word. He dragged a chair across the floor and scooted in close to me. I shivered. Riggs's wide hand slid down the pages. He stopped at each Dakota name, occasionally correcting my spelling.

"Thank you so," I whispered as I delicately edited in the corrections. He was earnest in his review. It seemed he was joining me in seeking clarity. My instincts, for the first time, didn't feel so alone in this space. I watched his hands moving down the page; the warmth of the ballroom at the harvest dance ran through my body.

"This seems the closest anyone's wanted to get to the truth," Riggs said under his breath.

I looked at him, trying to read his face.

"This cannot be an easy assignment for you," I said. My heart had broken for him. I'd watched him translate the death sentences, day after day, to the Dakota people he'd been living among. He, like me, had an important role but so little power in these proceedings. I wanted to understand him more.

Instead of agreeing, Riggs pointed to a Dakota name, Chaska, at the top of the page. "He never so much as mounted a horse. Didn't fight a minute. You realize they don't have most of the men who started the fighting? Many are the ones who surrendered." He put both hands against his head. "I praised Chaska's desire to be peaceful. Not to fight." He let out a shaky sigh. Riggs was facing his own internal battle. I had only considered that he was familiar with the Dakota. I hadn't appreciated that he, in fact, was trying to protect them. Now, instead of protecting them, he was literally telling them of their execution orders. My own morality had been frustrated by the violation of justice. But Riggs was sentencing his friends to death. My own understanding of the trials expanded, and a solemn sadness stretched out inside my chest. What were we part of? What an extraordinary horror this was.

I felt an instinct to comfort him with a touch. But I didn't; I knew to be decorous. I struggled to find the right words to meet Riggs in his depths. Finally, I said a quiet, "Thank you kindly, for helping me." He sat up straighter, his hair pulled wild at the sides.

"Thank *you* for caring about accuracy. Maybe we will get a piece of the facts in the record." He looked at me as he said "we." I held onto the word that joined us. I was no longer alone in my feelings of frustration; Riggs felt the injustice too. His strikingly handsome face sent a wave of nerves into my stomach. But I also appreciated his understanding. Feeling suddenly awkward, I busied myself by collecting my pens. Riggs helped, picking up my inkwells, and we carried the supplies back to the office. My father sat in his chair, reading. He looked up at Riggs and I entering the office together, a flash of questioning in his eyes. He was likely wondering why his daughter was alone with the young missionary.

"The missionary was helping me with spelling accuracy in the record," I explained truthfully. But something about my connection with Riggs made me feel bashful. Though the time reviewing the record together was innocent, there was a spark that I didn't want my father to sense.

"Ahh," my father said. "I'm learning something . . . all military trials require Presidential approval prior to any executions. We'll need Lincoln to sign off on all these."

"That is an interesting development," Riggs responded.

"That will take time," I said.

"General Pope won't be pleased," Pa said. There was a quiet understanding between the three of us. "I need to continue my research, though." I resigned myself to additional hours in the office.

"I'm glad to walk her home," Riggs offered. I turned in surprise, my heart flooded with a tingling of nervous excitement. Riggs was *glad* to walk me home? Had he felt the connection, as I had? I'd never made the trip between the office and home with anyone other than Pa.

Pa glanced at me, then gave his fatherly permission. "I suppose that would be sensible. Emma, would you like to walk, or would you rather stay here and study?"

I was surprised Father asked my preference. The chance to talk further with Riggs made my thoughts leap with delight. I wanted to hear more of his perspective, walking accompanied as a young woman, not sitting a child beside my father. But I hid my girlish eagerness and acted as though I was pleased with the practicality of getting home earlier.

"I'll be back in time to help Ma prepare supper." A chore I had never cared for, but a good excuse. I moved for my coat on the wall.

"Very well. See her there *safely*." Pa nodded with seriousness at Riggs.

"Certainly," Riggs said, as he opened the hallway door and grabbed his rifle off a hook. I looked at the handsome gun-slinging missionary; what an unusual and unexpected walk home. I slipped an arm, sore from my labors, through my coat sleeve and wrapped a chunky scarf round my neck. I felt like I was walking through a new door in my life.

I turned back to Father. "See you this evening, Pa." He nodded and blinked with a softness in his eyes. It felt odd to leave him. But the familiar journey home had an energizing sense of adventure that I couldn't resist tonight.

My breath came out as a fog in the crisp autumn air. Riggs and I walked side by side under the wide sky of twilight. The first steps pressed butterflies into my stomach. I was nervous about filling the space between us, but Riggs slowed his steps to match mine; easy conversation flowed. When Pa talked on the way home, he'd educate me, explain lessons of law in long monologues. Or we'd sit in silence. But Riggs was thoughtful and asked me questions about myself. I felt like my heart and mind were a boat being steadily pulled to shore, each topic, a rope Riggs could pull me in with. I was more settled, more connected, with each step. He shared of his family. Four brothers, all lawyers, on the east coast; he'd actually met Lincoln through them. The president was a family friend. I was taken aback in quiet awe. In that courtroom, Riggs was unassuming as he served the defeated Dakota, while other men, like General Pope, puffed their chest and manipulated for power. All the while, it was the missionary himself that was the most well-connected of the bunch. I could tell, even though he was carefully humble, that Riggs came from a powerful family in the East.

"How'd you find yourself here?" I asked.

"First time was a rail trip, west . . . a holiday tour, of sorts. I expected fun—but being here in this openness . . ." he motioned to the water-colored sunset streaking the length of the western horizon. "The lessons of the Bible I'd heard my whole life but never really felt. Once I was here, I felt it. This openness was God," he said with comfort in his voice, his expression soft. *Openness* was God. Like how my mind felt reading. Open. I was all the more intrigued by Riggs. "When I had the opportunity of some adventure back on the prairie, I said, 'sign me up.'" We laughed together when Riggs said, "And who would believe my choice to head west to serve God and my country would be considered an act of rebellion by my parents?"

The sound of our laughter intermingled, rang out across the prairie. It had been so long since I felt these pure feelings of delight inside of me. After weeks of war and war trials; it felt like something inside my being was breathing again.

The blue hour of twilight hung heavy in the sky when seemingly out of nowhere, a creeping sense of fear went slinking up my spine. I realized I hadn't walked this trail since the day of the attacks. I looked at the long rifle strapped over Riggs's broad shoulders. He caught me staring at it. I explained, embarrassed, "I apologize, I've been fearful in a way I can't shake since . . . the attack."

"Of course." He validated my feeling. "I saw the wound on the side of your head. I was worried about what'd happened to you."

He had noticed my wound? I always assumed I was invisible as I sat silently in the courtroom. I felt oddly overwhelmed to think of being noticed. "Oh, that wasn't from the attack. I simply fell. Well, during the attack." I fumbled my words, self-conscious.

"It looked painful. I noticed it right after I rode through the barricades," he said glancing at me. He had noticed me weeks ago? Cared about my pain amid the chaos? I didn't know how to respond. His deep voice broke the silence. "It's understandable you're fearful. But remember—I guaranteed your safe passage home to your father. I'm going to see to that." Riggs's brown eyes shimmered with an honest charm.

His sincerity was like a warm blanket in a chilling world. I settled back into the walk. We shared our worry regarding the rapid pace of the trials; his concerns matched mine. I felt understood in a new way. I'd always thought Ida knew me best in the world. But something of my mind and my hopes were more fully alive with Riggs than they ever were with Ida. When I spotted the glowing windowpanes of the farmhouse, the four-mile walk suddenly seemed all too short. Though my nerves flipped to imagine him sitting at the dining room table with Otto and Uncle Allen, and what questions Ma would have seeing me arrive home with a strange man, I thought it polite to invite Riggs in to warm up before he walked back.

He declined. "I'm plenty toasty. Have a nice supper."

I was relieved to have less to explain to my family. "Thank you for escorting me, Missionary," I said as he turned back the way we had come.

I felt toasty too. I wondered if I was feeling more than friend-ship. But why would a missionary possibly be interested in a seven-teen-year-old farm girl? We were just a court recorder and a court interpreter, connecting over the trial proceedings. But I suddenly felt less alone in that courtroom. Riggs saw what I saw. He understood.

Over the frosting grass, I moved towards the house, when his voice called out: "Emma!" I turned, loving how my name sounded on his tongue. He hollered with a glow in his voice, "Call me Riggs."

TWENTY-TWO

Oenikika

September 30, 1862

Ducks flew low in the somber sky. While an inner wisdom guided the birds south, our necessity moved us north. The other braves scouted out ahead of us. Father was continuing on to villages of the far away chiefs—trying to coordinate a resistance to the white man. I was self-conscious entering the new villages as if people could see the rawness of loss upon me. My face still bore my grief, the lacerations where I'd torn my face with my hands of ashes. But I also had pride riding in the wake of the revered Chief Little Crow. My pain showed just how worthy my father's call was. Though we were welcomed by all, when the subject turned to warnings of the white man's trouble, people seemed uncertain, as if the white woe was a sickness Little Crow was carrying with him. Always the other bands decided that they didn't want to take on the trouble Little Crow warned of; no chiefs joined a renewed war effort. I wanted them to take us in; live in the protection and acceptance of a tribe. Leaving the villages, I was frustrated by the rejection. And below my irritation was jealousy. I was jealous of their innocence, their easy maintenance of tradition.

Their tipis arranged in peaceful circles—yet to be tainted by the reach of the whites. Why would they want to join a war effort now? Until the day the white man wanted the lake they lived near or the stretch of the prairie they roamed—*then* these tribes would finally realize what Little Crow was trying to protect them from. Someday they'd know the pain I already felt.

Despite the repeated rejection, we rode on. A lone chief wandering with his only daughter, and a few loyal braves scattered beyond us. Father was always ahead of me, only turning back to give direction or declare where we'd stop. I rode in solemn silence over miles of open prairie. As the ducks quacked overhead, I thought of Bonko and Wolfchaser wrestling. All the easy afternoons I'd passed tanning hides alongside Dina and Scarlet Woman. Grandmother's hands pulling through my hair. My husband's warmth next to me. It was unbearable hurt thinking of Tashunke; I craved his memory, but it hit with such sickening sharpness. I looked ahead to my father, Mato's strong legs lifting through the tall grass. What had it been like for him to lose my mother? To have a newborn daughter to take care of? The burden I'd been . . . though Owl Woman and other women of our clan helped, I'd imagine just the sight of me as an infant—what pain I must have caused him.

In the evening, I set up the tipi Tashunke and I used to share. It was lonely for me at the fire, without Wenona, Mika, and the other women. But I was proud I had not surrendered to the white man. The braves camped beyond me on the prairie. Scattered, not like a village. Father spoke with the braves in the evenings. But after, he often sat with me—told the stories of our family, sometimes asking me to repeat them as if he were testing me. I was beginning to feel differently towards my father. I'd previously regarded Little Crow as difficult, unknowable. But I'd seen so much, lost so much in these past moons. I'd watched him make impossible choices. I'd chosen to ride with him. Where would we be two winters from now? How long could we wander? I feared the white's retaliation . . . they would surely search for the chief among chiefs who'd led the charge to war. We needed to find a tribe to take us in. I didn't want to keep wandering alone, like a lone buffalo. Being separated from a herd was vulnerable. We needed the power of our people.

October 5, 1862

In the chill of the Moon When the Wind Shakes Off the Leaves, Father and I sat close to the evening fire. The aroma of the roasted squash I'd prepared for the evening meal still lingered in the air. I sat quietly, as always, enduring my undercurrent of sadness. The days of our journey blurred together. Grief was like a prairie fire blazing; it consumed everything that was, leaving only a black flatness from what used to be. I wondered if I'd ever feel life again.

Father surprised me with a question.

"What does my daughter remember of my return from meeting with the Great White Father?"

"I remember when you made Grandmother and I ride on from the village and up to the white man's house of the four walls," I stated, not sure of what answer he wanted from me.

Father was animated, speaking as if there was a group of men around him, not a daughter who was not made for spirited debate with a chief. He continued, "What was *your chief* intending?"

I sighed; my soul ached to recall those days. Hoping to appease him I responded, "I could never know the mind of a chief," but he continued to stare at me. I remembered I had felt those many moons in the white man's house. "I fear the things that separate us from the Great Spirit."

He stood up then declared, "The chief was not afraid! Because in the worst moments of life—the Great Mystery created goodness.

Wisdom. When my wrists were shot—I gained the honor of being chief."

He stared deep into the fire. "In the death of your mother . . ." My body sat in perfect stillness. He'd never in my life said a word about my mother to me. "The Mystery blessed me with my daughter."

My eyes widened. *Blessed* with a daughter. He'd never said this before. I felt relief to hear my father just mention her. My mother. I had a mother. I thought of her voice—comforting, steady, calling out from the wild rice in my dream. I longed for it, for her. And I only knew her in my dreams. I looked up at my father. How much worse must it be for those who'd had the blessing of knowing her. A shiver of shame ran through my body. This was not how my birth story felt to *me*.

The fire crackled between us.

"I've hated my birth story—the pain I caused. What shame upon a daughter. It would have been better for me to never have been born. To spare such hurt. To not have taken her." This was the closest I'd ever come to apologizing to my father for what I'd stolen from him. His wife.

I couldn't look up at him. I kept my head down. The quiet moment seemed to echo with my truth I'd finally shared. My insides seared with the pain that had burned for so long.

"No. The Great Spirit brought life through death. That was a miracle. You were my miracle, *Breath of Life*. The name of my daughter. Oenikika."

My father's words flooded over me. My soul could not bear such love. After years of frustration with him. After the grief of losing my husband. It would be easier to keep my heart hollow and continue to mourn. I kept my head down and my throat seemed stuck with stones.

"Why do you think I rejected Tashunke's first offer for you?" he asked me.

I remembered my raging, believing my father had ruined my life, that he didn't understand me. I shook my head. I couldn't speak. It took everything to contain the overflowing emotions inside.

"Tashunke could never have offered enough horses for you," Father declared with pride. "I had to make sure *he* knew you were worth everything."

My heart unraveled hearing my father's explanation. What both men had done in their love for me. Tears brimmed at my eyes; I focused on my breath. *He had to know you were worth everything.* My father loved me. A log cracked and fell to the fire, sending a swirl of sparks to the night sky.

We stayed silent for a long while.

"The grand rainstorms of summer . . . with the wind, sheets of rain. Have you ever seen a herd of buffalo when such a storm approaches?" Little Crow asked.

I let out a long shaky breath as my mind searched my memories. It'd been too long since I'd seen the massive herds of buffalo that used to roam when I was small. Finally, I lifted my eyes and shook my head, no.

"When the other animals run from the storm, to hide—" he nodded his head and gave a fierce smile, "—the Buffalo turn and *face* the storm. As one herd, they run towards it. Through it."

As my father described this, I suddenly understood him not as a stubborn leader, but as my *father,* who had made difficult choices out of love. For the purpose of protecting his people. And his daughter.

"We face the storm and are not afraid," he finished with an assured look in his eye.

I smiled and blinked back the tears in my eyes, looking at the chief with new admiration. I was my father's daughter. We would continue. *As one herd.* Our mission was to unite the Seven Council Fires.

TWENTY-THREE

Emma Heard

October 14, 1862

The first fingers of dawn light reached up at the horizon; Pa yawned next to me on the wagon bench and I wrapped my warming blanket closer around me. Dull piles of fall leaves sat on the wagon floor, beneath me. I watched as I rolled my boots over the dry leaves. Crinkling them into dissolving flakes—tiny brown pieces, nothing like the brilliant auburn leaves they once were. Stupidly wonderful fall. Beauty that distracts us from the fact the world was about to fade and die. I sighed as I looked back up at the autumn morning. I felt a creature exhausted. It'd been long weeks of working as the court recorder in the military trials; my back ached on the early morning rides to the courthouse. I was relieved that today marked the final day of trials. My exhaustion made my disillusionment with the proceedings harder to keep at bay. Rolling across the prairie, closer to that courthouse, frustration flooded into my bones.

"General Pope doesn't care about justice. Or our town. This is all just a feather in *his* cap," I complained to Pa in a huff.

In a rare moment of anger, Pa raised his voice to cut me off. "My daughter will never complain of a superior in such a manner. The court recorder must know not to speak so foolishly."

The bite in his tone stung my struggling conscience. I knew my father was putting his reputation on the line to allow me, a girl, to take on such a prestigious official duty. And I did feel slightly guilty that my reactions betrayed the "honorable" court I was serving. But my guilt never managed to outweigh the outrage I felt of the proceeding of what I believed was a sham trial.

"Why isn't a revised treaty with the Indians considered? At least with the non-hostiles? Is our only option to kill off the entirety of the Dakota people?"

"Emma Heard," my father said, exasperated. Kamish snorted and Kit's tail flicked. "I've considered the same treaty option. But this is beyond my opinion; it's in the hands of powerful men in our government. I have 500 land contracts already stacked for next year. There's simply no stopping the necessity of westward expansion."

Land contracts? What did that have to do with the trials? I questioned, looking at my father's face, but he kept focused on the golden grassland ahead. I was shocked. I hadn't even considered that these trials were functioning as ways to remove the Indians from their land and clear space for settlers.

"That's dreadful," I said emphatically. A terrible thought flashed through my mind: had the failure to send the annuity payment been an attempt to force the Dakota's hand?

"Emma. Learn the wisdom of holding your tongue." He seemed irritated with my reaction, and perhaps, I supposed, he questioned whether he had shared too much with his daughter. "Absolutely *no more*," Pa said sternly.

Pa enjoyed the benefit of my intelligence when I assisted him. But to have quick thoughts and opinions of my own? That was an unacceptable step too far. I wished for another walk with Riggs. I was desperate to discuss all we'd witnessed. I had a sense Riggs would appreciate the unfairness. Not scold me to hold my tongue. Discontented, I shuffled my feet and kicked the bits off leaves off the side of the wagon. Let them scatter behind us. Dying bits of something that was once hopeful disappeared into the world behind me.

I took my seat at the front side of the courtroom. The disgruntled General Pope walked up and down the center aisle, never satisfied with the pace of the proceedings. His tongue may well have been a whip; how it thrashed upon Sibley, all of us, breaking us to work our way through the defendants ever more quickly. Just before we entered the courtroom today, Pope commanded we finish the trials of the remaining forty Indians. *Forty* trials in under eight hours. A final grueling day. I watched my father settle into his seat on the panel. He was the person who'd educated me on the sanctity of the rule of law. Though Pa often deferred to imprisonment over execution, I'd heard him agree to punishment by death more times than I could count. I couldn't shake Pa's explanation from my mind. *A necessity of the West*? Was that how he rationalized these proceedings? As an inevitable need for land? We'd execute human beings to make space for others?

I could finish; I just had to make it through forty more verdicts. The trials took off at a rapid pace; my pen scratched the paper furiously. Dakota man after Dakota man rotated in. So many warriors tried they blended together in my mind. Impossible to keep track of, except for this record. Hundreds of executions to bolster Pope's name in military history. No witnesses on behalf of any Dakota were called, and no defense was active on behalf of the Dakota. Another verdict was called out.

"Guilty of the charge. This Indian is to be hanged by the neck until he is dead." I recorded the words and turned to the back of the log and added another name to the execution list. The pen fumbled from my hand during my transcription; the least of the egregious failures, among the greater miscarriages of justice, witnessed in this courtroom. The three-hundred-second name. I took a deep breath as I quickly scanned the list. Three-hundred-two Dakota sentenced to death. President Lincoln still had final approval of the execution orders, a fact that deeply irritated General Pope. I prayed that when President Lincoln reviewed the words of the trial transcripts, the words I had written, that he'd have a discerning mind, hold a higher standard for the conduct of law than General Pope. Riggs had told me that Lincoln was fair-minded. I looked at the trial transcript, praying, "Dear Lord, let the truth be clearer than the words on these pages."

Pain radiated from my wrist; turning into a tingling numbness through my fingers as I flipped back to a fresh page in my log. I detailed a "#392" in the upper left corner of the page. This was the very last man, the three-hundred-ninety-second and final trial. Riggs walked the bound Indian in, motioning to the defendant's seat. *The guilty seat*, I called it in my mind. I admired Riggs, how he always looked the Dakota men in the eyes. Treated them with dignity. It reminded me that each of the men who took that seat, were, at the end of the day, human. I imagined Riggs felt as much in a predicament as I did; in a horrible system, we had to be strong to do our one small duty well. I transcribed with honesty. He translated to the Dakota with honesty. It seemed all we could do.

I looked back to my record and wrote Sibley's opening statement, "The final trial of this day and of the entire commission is Tashunke. CHARGES: It is said between eighteenth and twenty-third of August, 1862, he did join and participate in the various murders, robberies, and outrages by the Dakota Indians on the Minnesota Frontier." It was the same overarching charges I had written 392 times before. My arm prickled as my fingers could barely keep grip of the pen; it was all almost done.

When I looked up again, I caught sight of the final Indian, Tashunke. I saw his scarred lip and a gasp of astonishment escaped my throat . . . it was him. The memory was branded inside of me; my cheeks burned as I recognized him.

The warrior who'd saved us.

That horrible day flashed in my mind. The yard. The porch. His painted arms. This warrior had safeguarded Ida. Why was he on trial? There was no way he hurt anyone. Was there? I looked at him longer. He was a striking man. Though shackled; he looked about with dignity. I just couldn't imagine him murdering, plundering, after experiencing his protection. But were my few moments of interactions with him really enough to judge? He was a *warrior*, after all. Tears of overwhelm flooded my eyes. Here I sat, a member of the commission, alive *because* of him, while his own fate was being contemplated by the court. I looked back at the record, blinking hard.

Riggs translated Tashunke's testimony: "I was not at the battle of New Ulm. I was standing a way off. Tending the horses. I never fired my gun during the war."

My heart pounded as I recorded the words. I knew Tashunke must be upstanding; it had taken character to protect us from his own people.

A farmer witness came to the stand, who'd been able to recognize a remarkable number of Dakota in the past months. "I know this Indian," he said. "He used to be a good Indian. But I heard he stole a horse in the Big Woods."

I didn't think the witness was credible. He was only mentioning a stolen horse because Tashunke said he tended to horses. I couldn't keep from shaking my head.

I feared the court would move swiftly with such information, and sure enough, by the time I looked up from my writing, Sibley was announcing the verdict, "Guilty of the charge. Tashunke is to be hanged by the neck until he is dead." I'd grown almost numb to hearing these verdicts, but this final "Guilty," directed at a man I knew, felt like a stab to my gut.

I recorded every fraudulent word, just as I'd recorded every fraudulent moment of this military commission. My handwriting suddenly repulsed me. Riggs spoke quietly in Dakota to Tashunke as he walked him past me. I wished I could command Tashunke to "Go." As he had done for me. A new guilt bubbled up. I hadn't been able to protect Ida. He had. I knew something of this Tashunke's character. He'd acted in opposition to the wrong his men were committing. I looked down at my pen, my handwriting on the page in front of me. I feared I was something the opposite of him. I was complicit in the wrongs of my own people. I wanted to scream. My insides were bursting against this process, against Tashunke's verdict. I wanted my screams to ring out in rebellion off the courthouse walls; louder than any "guilty." But as I looked about in my anger, my eyes caught Pa's and my feelings scattered frantically back into hiding. "*The wisdom to hold your tongue*" rang in the memory of my ears.

The final gavel struck the wooden desk, reverberating off the walls. It was decided. I flipped to the last page in my log.

Execution order #303: Tashunke.

Later that evening, as Ida was sitting in her rocking chair, I pulled up Ma's rocker close alongside her. I whispered quietly. "Ida, the warrior who . . . *helped* us that day . . ." Ida looked at me with exasperation in her eyes. She hated when I brought up those events. It was easier to ignore the memories, the feelings of powerlessness. The violation. But I didn't care about offending her sensibilities tonight. It was too important to verify the man's identity. "Do you remember him having a scar upon his lip?"

Ida leaned her head against the back of her chair, staring straight ahead. I feared she was going to get up and walk away. But instead, she nodded, then raised a single finger in the air. I caught my breath. She confirmed it. Tashunke was indeed the warrior who saved us. The warrior who was now sentenced to die. The confirmation ripped through me and the burden of truth anchored in my chest. Why must I learn this now? After the verdict. He was to be executed and I was powerless to do a thing about it.

October 29, 1862

An unfamiliar sound, a voice, awoke me in the dead of night. Soft moonlight streamed in the upstairs window. All seemed well but my body tingled with an alertness. Since August, I was keen to sounds, ready to protect myself at any moment. Slowly, I eased myself up in bed. Ida's face rested on the pillow next to me. Otto, in his bed at the opposite side of our large open room, appeared sound asleep, as well. The gunmetal of his new double-barreled shotgun gleamed in the darkness. A gift from Colonel Sibley; the United States government's acknowledgment of his valiant efforts in the defense of New Ulm. Otto always kept it within arm's reach, even when he slept. His presence, the gun itself, reassured me. But what had I heard? Something had awoken me.

Suddenly I heard the words again, "No! No, nonono." The voice was coming from *my* bed. I looked at my sister. Her dark eyelashes fluttered at her closed eyes. She tossed slightly. Her lips were moving. The sound. The voice. Words. It couldn't be. Ida talking in her sleep. Ida *talking*. Her golden eyebrows furrowed, Ida pleaded aloud, "Please, no."

I would have been less surprised to see Kit speaking in his stall. It was *impossible* for my sister to talk. But there she lay, dreaming, something free inside her throat. I sat frozen, stunned. Her tone, the sound of her gentle voice soaking into my mind. I'd never heard it before. I wanted to hold on to it. It seemed a miracle. Should I wake her? I hesitated, not wanting to interrupt this moment. She continued to murmur quietly. A skeptical question pierced my elation . . . had she always had this ability? She used to be able to speak as a small child. But she'd stopped on the journey to Minnesota territory. The doctor had said she must be mute. Ida stopped talking because she was unable. There was no way someone could go a lifetime without speaking, by choice. So, she must have been cured, I told myself. It was marvelous, *unbelievable*, to hear her soft voice.

Then something ugly flared within me. Every time I'd spoken on her behalf, each decision I'd made, each assignment—the children's room at the harvest dance. All my guilt. If she had been physically able to speak this entire time . . . why hadn't she? It had to be because she couldn't. But I was watching her speak now. Did she know she could? Had she simply forgotten? I shook my head; how could someone *forget* they had a voice? If you have a voice, you use it.

Eventually Ida settled, the dream passed. I laid awake, staring at the warped oval knots in the boards of the wooden planks of the ceiling. My mind, twisted as the knots, questioned the miracle of hearing her voice. A moment suddenly shone through my memory, brilliant. Running from the house that day. Our sprinting, terror, fear. When we fell in the grass, Ida had grunted. Made a sound. She *had* made a sound. And the warrior covering her mouth—was she, in fact, screaming? My body felt sick. Everything about this world had fallen apart in my understanding. Who was my sister? Didn't she want to scream out?

Nothing was what I thought. After the trials, could I even believe in the work of the law office anymore? My sense of myself, my sense of safety, dangled so precariously in the world. My own sister, my mirror. I thought I knew her so well. It was wonderful. A miracle. But also troubling and inexplicable. How? I turned over to take another look at her sleeping face. She laid quietly sleeping; angelic as ever. But the silence between us was deafening.

There was no time to confront Ida about what I had witnessed. As Ida and I were waking Pa announced he and I would go into town as soon as possible. I stared while Ida quietly ate her breakfast at the table. I felt a peculiar fury. SPEAK! I wanted to yell at her. But I merely glanced back at her as we headed out the door. Ida remained in her seat, looking small as she gave a meek smile at our departure. *Don't you know you can say goodbye?* I felt desperate. I wanted her to help herself. Our family had always just accepted her silence. Why hadn't we pushed her more to try to talk? Had her voice been right there our entire lives? The anger loosened inside of me, and sadness rushed in behind it. Ida wouldn't get to work in town today. How much of her own life had been lost along with her voice?

As soon as we arrived in town, we received the news: Lincoln had approved just 39 executions. Pa had received a copy of the list of the condemned. I unfolded the pages, searching the names. "Please. Please." I quietly pleaded to God. But there it was. "TASHUNKE. CONDEMNED." I felt like I'd been punched. My breath came out in a devastated sigh. I had prayed that Lincoln would miraculously read between the lines of the transcript. That the President, in charge of Tashunke's fate, could somehow know what I knew. The months of trials made me sick to my stomach. So many men still sentenced to hang, at least one of them innocent. Angry conversations could be heard from passersby outside Pa's office. They were as upset as I was, but for quite the contrary reason. They wanted every single one of the 303 death-sentenced Dakota to hang. For them, the president's choice had been a betrayal. All the pain of August raged. There had been so much loss. My heart choked to comprehend all the wrongs that had occurred. So much had been taken away. I thought of Bruno, his gentle innocence, the terror he must have felt in battle. Perhaps I needed to accept the other thirty-eight executions as revenge; blood for blood.

My memories were interrupted when Mrs. Kuhn stopped in, announcing that the Ladies of Ulm were wearing their golden brooches every day as a sign of solidarity. "Hang the HEATHENS! If Anna has an item similar, we'd encourage her to wear it." She glanced my way, "Or you, Emma. We know what they did to you and your sister." I didn't say a thing in response. What did Mrs. Kuhn "know" of what had happened to me, or to Ida? I was irritated at her assumptions. To her, the scar on my head likely represented the attack of a bloodthirsty Indian; she'd probably assumed I was hit with a tomahawk. This was the very kind of misunderstanding that fueled the mob. The townspeople were hellbent on total vengeance, upset at the president for commuting the sentences of hundreds.

In the uproar, I saw Riggs walk by, and I ran out after him. I called out his name. I needed to be near him in a moment like this. With him, I felt understood, like stepping under a shared umbrella in the middle of a downpour.

"I'm not sure what to make of Lincoln's decision," I explained.

"Revenge is a stronger motivation than the influence of justice," he said defeatedly, "Even thirty-nine executions are too many. I know these Dakota. A few sentenced did wrong. But most of these men convicted are truly not guilty of any war crimes."

I wished I could hug Riggs's words around me. When he brought up knowing the Dakota well, I felt I had to ask about the thing that had been eating away inside of me.

"I want to ask you . . . about Tashunke. What kind of man is he?" I asked.

Riggs stared at me. I wondered if anyone had ever even asked him his own impressions regarding the men he knew so well. "A very fine one. Serious and hardworking. He has a gift with horses . . . any of his participation in battles was to help with the horses. He told me as much. And I believe him."

His words had confirmed what my gut knew. "So, you don't believe he murdered anyone?"

"I do not." He shook his head in disbelief that his friend was sentenced to death. "I came to this prairie trusting in God. It's been feeling harder to hold onto faith. Tashunke was—" his voice choked with sadness as he corrected himself, "Tashunke *is* a good man."

My heart dropped in the weight of Riggs's confirming words. The anchor of truth was setting deeper inside of me. How would I hold onto faith when Tashunke would be sent to the gallows for caring for horses? After he had protected me? Rescued Ida? The Dakota man had done the exact opposite of what he was accused and condemned for.

In the final moments of warmth from the late autumnal sun, a small miracle floated past: a monarch butterfly, waving its untroubled wings. It gently spun a circle between Riggs and I, as if it were riding upon our understanding. A memory netted my mind . . . Bruno's hands uncupping to reveal his precious rescue. Could this butterfly be the very caterpillar sweet Bruno had saved? My heart fluttered in bittersweet awe as I marveled the stained-glass orange-and-black markings upon the monarch's wings. Was this a sign? As I watched the beautiful creature, so recently transformed, a warm stream of faith began softening the hardening in my heart.

In the past weeks, I had changed as much as this butterfly. And last night, Ida speaking from her dreams next to me was a truth I couldn't come back from knowing. Ida wouldn't . . . *couldn't* use her voice. But I was going to use mine. And suddenly, I knew with conviction exactly what I had to do next. Anything I could to not let another good man die. I looked straight into Riggs's eyes, and with a strength I felt sure of, I said, "Tashunke saved my life. We cannot let him die."

TWENTY-FOUR

Oenikika

November 1, 1862

The horses fed in the valley of the sloping hill below us. The braves had ridden ahead to the north; Father and I rode west—we'd meet them by the next moon at the north river. The earth was crunchy underfoot; icy patches covered the brown grass. But the midmorning sun was generous, highlighting our good fortune of finding a late season apple tree. What kindness of the Great Mystery, to bring us to apples not destroyed by worms or eaten by deer. Father walked ahead as sparrows chirped in the branches above. From here, rather than riding north as we'd been, we'd turn and ride west. I hoped we'd finally venture to the land Tashunke was from. His people would want justice for Tashunke, and a tribe may feel compelled to join the war cause. I stretched up, twisted another brilliant apple from its stem and set it in my growing satchel. We'd have so many I could simmer them together, store them for our journey—a sudden BOOM! blasted through the bright morning air.

I fell to the ground as my vision blurred, apples scattering around me.

My ears rang.

What . . . had . . .

Disoriented, I turned over.

Father lay on the ground, his legs bent bizarrely under him. What had happened? My ears rang as I stared at my father who was lying perfectly still, face up. I crawled on my hands and knees to his side. That sound . . . A gunshot?

I looked about, up to the apple tree. A bluebird sat carefree upon a bobbing branch. My mind couldn't make sense. "Father?" I asked in disbelief as a dark red circle of blood spread out of his stomach.

Little Crow gritted his teeth and gave a guttural moan. His eyes opened wide, trying to find the enemy that had already torn him apart. I scanned our surroundings. A sparrow tipped its head. I turned, and in the far-off horizon, I made out two figures. Men. Another sound cracked through the air and I ducked in fear. A branch midway up the tree exploded; falling pieces rained upon us. My father laid his head back down, the color draining from his face. I wiped away the tiny bits of bark that had fallen upon his cheeks and into his eyes. The sparrows were gone. Reality set upon me. Two white men on foot. They were far off . . . But still, we hadn't much time. Their aim would only get more accurate as they closed in. Could my father walk? Could I move him? Foolishly, I'd left my medicine bag tied to Ahone. I need every medicine ever created. My mind spun. How was this possible? We'd ridden so far. He'd faced the enemy in war. How had we come under fire, midmorning, picking apples? My heart skittered with panic. Overwhelm made me unsteady. I looked down, the deepening crimson upon his stomach was pouring out as if it were a spring. My daughter spirit wanted to cling to him. I needed my father in this world. But my healer spirit knew he was mortally wounded. I looked at the horizon. The two men still just specks in the far-off distance. What should I do?

"A chief should die in battle," Father said. He spoke weakly, his hands moving over his stomach in frustration, smearing in the bright life spilling out of him. Suddenly, the memory of my death dream struck my heart with the precision of a lightning bolt. A healer will know the moment to reveal the wisdom of her dreams. *If he doubts, let him know he did indeed die in battle.* The moment was here. This was the intention for my vision. This single impossible moment; my father dying. I spoke with all the clarity and strength I could muster. "This is the battle. The fight for our tribe, for *all* Dakota people, continues." I swallowed hard and tried to steady my voice, summon all my strength.

"You aren't alone now," I said. I took my father's bloody hand in mine. "And you will not be alone in the Happy Hunting Ground. The Woman of the Winter Sun waits to receive you." Tears came to my eyes, remembering how beautifully her voice had called for him. I cowered low to the ground to protect myself as much as I could, and pushed back the danger that roared at the back of my mind . . . The men moving closer with every passing moment. I looked upon my father and felt the fullness of love and the empowering energy of the Great Spirit that lived within me. I wanted to hold his pain for him. Ease him onward. I closed my eyes and remembered the brilliance of the dream . . . every detail intended for him.

"Feel the comforting fur blankets of our ancestors. Feel the calm of the Great Mystery around you." When I opened my eyes, my father stared at with me intensity, as if he clung to every word. With a deep breath, I beckoned the assurance of my healer vision. "Your spirit is called above the still water. The warm wind carries you."

Father's hand trembled, slippery, in mine as his strong dark eyes looked up from me to the brightness beyond us. He stared at the sky as his whole body began to shake. He was going quickly. I held his hand tighter. Suddenly, his expression transformed, shifted lighter, as if he were seeing a new spectacular sight. I twisted to see what he was looking at, only to see silver wispy clouds of morning in the sky. His grip on my hand loosened. I turned back; my father's fierce eyes glazed with emptiness, reflecting the peaceful clouds above. The chief, my father, was dead. His glory passed to the Hereafter. My heart broke in two . . . all his fight, all his perseverance, his wisdom— no longer for this world.

Lovingly, I took his crooked wrists and placed them across his chest. "Blessing to our greatest chief. The highest honor awaits you who bravely died in battle," I said reverently. I knew I didn't have long but I buried my head in his shoulder for a moment. Taking in his closeness, the strength of my father, for the last time.

The blast of another gunshot boomed. And without one more precious moment of goodbye, I ran for my life, sprinting toward Ahone as fast as my legs could carry me.

TWENTY-FIVE

Emma Heard

November 5, 1862

The cold settled in as if it had something to prove; today I remembered the true bite of winter. Icy bits of snow pelted the farmhouse windows. It was my first day at home helping with chores since the trials finished. Ida bundled herself near the back door of the kitchen, tucking her hands into mittens before grabbing the wicker egg basket from its shelf. I hoped that during chores today, I could finally speak privately with Ida.

"They're still laying?" I asked. Ida shrugged. I immediately felt an urge to help my sister gather eggs; I couldn't imagine how terrifying it must be for her to walk out of the hen house every day, after what happened in August. I was guilt-ridden for all the time I'd been away. "Let me," I said as I stood up and grabbed my coat and my muffler, my favorite one Ida had made for me. My sister crinkled her eyes as if to say, "If you insist," when I took the basket from her hands. I'd been agonizing to understand Ida since the middle of the night a week ago. When her voice punctured the space, the understanding, between us.

"Would you girls bring in some firewood, please?" Ma hollered.

"Yes, Ma," I called back as I tucked the handle of the basket into the nook of my elbow. I'd been anxious to see if Ida would share with me about her ability to speak. Was it a recent development that she'd been keeping to herself? Unsure of what to do with her newfound voice? Or did she not realize she was able? Or worse . . . did she not *want* to speak, even though she could? All the options ran through my mind. I hoped she'd share with me, once she realized I knew. But I also feared for the worst . . . That my knowing would push her away. Or anger her. Perhaps she wouldn't believe me, wouldn't *want* to believe me. I was nervous but resolute. I had to let Ida know what I'd witnessed. As we walked out the back door, a despairing wind whipped sharply around us; we pushed headlong into the gale. I pulled the edge of my scarf down under my chin. My heart shivered in anticipation of my words. Finally, I let them out into the winter air.

"Ida." I touched her coat sleeve. She turned toward me, crunching her eyes against the winter wind. "I need to ask you about something. Something . . . miraculous." I fumbled with my words. Each statement felt like dancing on a thin sheet of ice, about to fall through into the unknown. It was an unfamiliar type of vulnerability with my sister. We'd never discussed the fact she didn't speak.

I treaded farther out onto that thin ice. "Ida . . . I heard you. The other night, you were speaking. You were *talking* in your sleep." It was impossible and amazing and entirely incomprehensible. I feared she would think me crazy. I studied her beautiful face, which stood frozen, gauging her reaction to my bold declaration. Telling the truth was a daring act on my part. Just like after her attack, our escape, I wanted her connection. I wanted her to help me make sense of what I witnessed. But the only reaction was the shrieking howl of the wind.

After a long pause, Ida put her mittens up at the edges of her face, hiding from me. It seemed I'd upset her. Or perhaps, surprised her? I'd felt so many feelings upon hearing her voice . . . maybe she was feeling those now. My sister and I had been puzzle pieces our whole lives, fitting together perfectly. I could have answered any question on her behalf. In the past year, though, we'd been floating apart. Hearing Ida's voice had been extraordinary; I prayed it would bring us together again. But instead, she kept her face covered.

I wanted desperately to look into my sister's eyes; I wanted to understand her. I wanted her to explain it. Get upset. Become over-joyed. Show me something. Connect with me in some way. *Any* way. I grabbed onto the edges of her elbows and tipped my head low, so she could see me under her cupped hands.

"Ida. You can speak. You were talking in your dreams. You *can*." It could be life-changing for her. My breath was heavy with the power of those words. I felt a fierce fire light inside me; this was so import-ant. My heart wanted to push hers. Shove her. Wake her up. I wanted her to speak again. I longed to hear her soft lovely voice again. But she shook her head back and forth, appearing almost embarrassed. Found out . . .

In the heat of my reaction, I challenged her. "Talk. Try it. Say something now." But as soon as I said it, I knew she would not. My sister's face bore a look of overwhelming fear. A terrified refusal. She continued shaking her head, no. Sorrow washed through me. Ida could physically speak. But my sister could not will herself to use her voice. I could see it in her. It was too terrifying. I looked into her eyes as tears welled in mine. "You can speak. You know it, don't you?" I asked in a heartbroken whisper.

For a suspended moment, we stared into each other. The love between us was there, stretching over the growing distance between us. I felt her pain. Tears welled in her eyes. But I knew the truth. She could speak. But wouldn't. I would have stood with her forever in that whipping wind. I loved her so much. But she broke the moment, shaking her head as she pulled back from me. This was too much for her. It was too much for me too. But necessary. I wanted the honesty. I wanted my sister to know: her voice, her secret, her abilities, inabilities, whatever it was . . . anything would be safe between us. Even though it seemed unbelievable that my sister wouldn't speak by choice, something about that truth unexpectedly fit in my understanding of Ida.

Ida moved forward towards the woodpile, eyes averted. I stepped up and stayed next to her. I didn't care if my sister could talk or wouldn't. I loved her. She looked back at me, appearing defensive. Guarded.

"Ida," I said whole-heartedly, "Your voice was the greatest sound I've ever heard."

Her face softened. I held her gaze. My lovely, complicated, older sister. She was everything I had impossibly thought I should be for so long. Hardworking, obedient, sweet. All my silent jealousy of her. My resentment. My guilt. But helping Ida exist in the world no longer felt like my sole responsibility. She lived in a world of selective silence. That was not a world for me. I had dreams. I had thoughts and opinions I wouldn't hold back. *My* voice must exist. A renewed sense of determination set inside of me.

There was no knot I could undo that would free her voice; nothing between us to push against. I was ready, now, to let her be. I'd said what I needed to, and I was becoming who I needed to be. And with that, something for me shifted in the space between us. I grabbed her hand, and our mittens squeezed. I lifted the egg basket, indicating I would head to the coop.

With a final sincerity, I let her know, "I'm here if you'd ever want to . . . want to talk." She nodded, her bright blue eyes glistened in the grey world around us. She knew, I knew. Though my chin still trembled, I pushed into the wind and stepped forward by myself.

November 6, 1862

As the clock struck noon, my stomach growled in unison with the sound of the chimes; it was finally time for my lunch. Though my father had been absent from the office this morning I still planned to take my break in the empty courthouse, as I often did. I set aside the land patent copies and picked up my lunch tin. I took a seat in the back row of the courthouse and pulled out a biscuit. This room had been the center of our universe these past months. But as quickly as it had filled with power, it now sat vacant. I came here to be alone, to try to make sense of my thoughts. But it was also a place to meet Riggs—I'd mentioned I'd try to take my lunch here; and if he could, to meet me. We planned to discuss an appeal for Tashunke.

Over the past week, a plan had formed in my mind. I just needed Riggs's agreement. As I heard the door handle click, a wave of nervousness tingled down my spine. He was here. My heart and my mind were anxious for him. While the townspeople angrily demanded more Dakota to be hanged, Riggs was the only person who knew of my hope to do the opposite. It was our chance to do the right thing, one right turn, as time moved us inevitably towards the executions scheduled for December 26. We had just over one month to pull off this plan.

Riggs moved down the bench toward me. His scruffy beard made him look even older than his twenty-four years. Though we were alone, he came close to me so we could speak quietly.

"Finally," he said. He must have been as eager as I was to discuss a plan to save Tashunke. Or maybe, he was as glad to see me. Behind his dark eyelashes, there was such a brightness in Riggs's eyes. I felt seen. I also felt shy, suddenly. His arm was stretched across the back of the bench. He touched lightly on my shoulder and said, "I've wanted to hear your thoughts."

His prompting touch and encouragement loosened my nerves. I spilled out everything that'd been wheeling in my mind.

"I want to appeal Tashunke's conviction to Lincoln. I believe the expedient nature of these trials would make it *prudent* for the president to take into consideration the word of an additional eye-witness," I explained. Riggs took in my words. I'd felt so convicted; my plan meant so much. I was bursting at the brim to share it. Anxious for his approval. "I'll serve as the witness. I'll write out my testimony. And you can attest to Tashunke's character?" If Riggs added his personal impression, it could show the trial had missed critical information. Between the two of us, I felt we had a strong case.

"Yes. Of course, I would attest to his character. It destroys me to think of Tashunke shackled, waiting for his death. But what then? We mail the letter? You think it'll reach the president before the hangings?"

"I thought . . ." The final, and most imperative, part of the plan required an immense personal ask of Riggs. I took a deep breath before explaining the crucial piece of the puzzle, "it'd be most effective if you'd appeal to your friend, our president, *directly.*"

I wanted Riggs to go to Washington D.C. and deliver my witness statement in person. I felt guilty asking Riggs to use his acquaintance with Lincoln as leverage on behalf of Tashunke. But something inside of me knew it was our best chance at commuting Tashunke's sentence.

Riggs sat in silence. The courtroom bench creaked as he shifted in his seat. I tingled with nervousness, worried I was asking too much. Perhaps this would be where Riggs would show he was too good to be true. He wouldn't risk his reputation, stretch his family's connection for the sake of one man. I could hide my testimony in a letter. Riggs would be leaving, riding off—there was a much greater chance his reputation would suffer more than my own. Was I too idealistic asking so much of this man? I wished Riggs could have been at our farmhouse the day of the attacks. To have witnessed what Tashunke had risked saving my life. *I* owed this appeal to Tashunke. Riggs did not. But it was imperative . . . he had to see to my testimony's safe passage. The mail stagecoach would not be reliable or speedy enough at this point of the season. And we needed Riggs to explain the heart of the matter to the highest power in our land, his family friend Abraham Lincoln. I knew Riggs's sincerity; his first-hand experience could enlighten the president. With an affirmative nod, Riggs replied, "I'll send word ahead to my brother. I believe he'd be able to arrange the meeting."

A swell of grateful joy filled me. My plan had become our mission! And before I knew what I was doing, I wrapped my arms around Riggs's neck. Just as I realized what I had done, I felt his arm stretch around me. We embraced for a moment. Long enough for me to take in the smell of his leather coat mingling with the warmth of his skin. I leaned myself back before my senses could pull me in any further. He made me feel wildly alive. I couldn't believe I had just thrown my arms around him; I was warm with embarrassment.

"Ah, I'm simply overwhelmed at how glad I am. I'd been hoping you'd be willing," I said, buzzing with self-consciousness. I feared he'd think me childish, overzealous. But he had embraced me in return . . . he must be feeling something, too. The more I was with him, the more I wanted him near. His willingness to go to such lengths for what he believed in. The weight of our mission settled in my mind. Somewhere Tashunke sat shackled while I could embrace someone. It wasn't fair. I wouldn't let them take his life when he had given me mine.

"Just as I had stopped believing in miracles. I think this may be our chance at one," Riggs said optimistically. After so much darkness, I too felt a new light of hope in the world.

A note lay on my office table. My father's familiar handwriting read:

"Planning with Sibley. Will retrieve you at four o'clock, sharp." I'd have the office to myself for the next three hours; the moment to draft my testimony had found me quickly.

I pulled my oil lamp close, and turned up the wick, illuminating a blank page before me. I carefully set to writing the words . . .

Dear Mr. President,

I do hereby swear and attest that the following is true:

On the morning of August 18, 1862, my sister Ida and I were tending our family farm. Four Dakota men arrived on horseback. Three of the men attacked my sister, pinning her in the yard. It was Tashunke, who intervened on her behalf . . .

My mind went back to that day. Fearful memories stung my body. But this time, my pen became my powerful weapon of justice. Seeing the ink of my truth on the page was like drawing a circle of protection around Ida, me, and Tashunke. A circle of hope for our future.

November 15, 1862

Church service concluded. We remained in the sanctuary, socializing in the aisles. As we mingled, Pastor Vogel's loud voice boomed, "That's fantastic, boy. You're doing God's work," as he patted Otto's shoulder. I supposed Otto had shared about his new role, helping the army build the platform for the hangings. General Pope called it his "stage"; he'd even moved the location upriver to the larger town of Mankato so even more spectators could gather to watch the executions. Thirty-nine hangings were scheduled for December 26; but it would be thirty-eight if I could do anything about it. Time was moving too quickly; and it seemed Riggs and I were trying to swim upstream from the rapids of revenge that pushed the rest of the town towards the date as if it was an extension of the Christmas holiday. A reason to celebrate. It was hard to see Otto appearing so enthusiastic about helping construct the hanging stage. He evidently enjoyed the approval of Pope and the proximity to Colonel Sibley. I wished I could pull him back. How did he enjoy such a morbid activity? Did he not understand he was creating a platform for death? He approached it with the same amount of contemplation as if he were building a new lean-to for the barn. The comradery of the military men seemed all-consuming. Otto had refined his sharpshooting in the battle with the Indians, was convinced he could take on the southern rebels too, if given the chance. My charming brother, partaking in the grimmest of activities; I couldn't stand it. The war had taken away even more than the losses in battle. It had changed us, our minds, hearts, attitudes.

I dizzied with anxiety whenever I thought of Tashunke. My responsibility to right the wrong. I looked at the crucifix at the front of the church. Would Jesus Christ look with favor upon me? I didn't know how much I could atone for with one appeal. But I felt sure God compelled me to try. I wouldn't be able to forgive myself if Tashunke was hung. Thinking of it made me sick. Each day of my life would go on because of him.

I held baby Peter and stood behind Ma, gossiping with the ladies.

"I don't think he's saved a single heathen soul," Mrs. Carrothers announced with conviction.

Mrs. Kuhn agreed. "I'm certainly suspicious of the man. He is far too sympathetic to those Indians." I realized instantly that they were talking about Riggs. My heart throbbed, as I filled with defensiveness. Riggs was a righteous man of God. He lived in his faith. How could his counsel, his dedication, sitting at the side of the condemned until their last breath be anything but service? I seethed with anger.

"He's from the Eastern states. Full of Indian sympathizers. Easy for them to say on the East coast. They've already been exterminated there. They have no understanding of the horrors we survived," Mrs. Carrothers explained. The group of women clucked together in agreement. My hatred of their ignorance flared and then fell into trepidation. I stood in silence, my secret plan—my "Indian sympathizing" secret plan . . . The stakes were high, higher than I'd perhaps realized. Hearing the group talk like this about Riggs made me understand what outsiders we were. What would the town do to us, if they found out our plan?

"I hope Pastor Vogel has the influence to get Riggs removed from this station. We don't want that kind of missionary here," Mrs. Carrothers stated.

I slowly stepped back from the gathering. They would run Riggs out of town. For serving the Dakota? The women didn't even know about our plan to seek a commuted sentence. What would they do then? Hang him alongside the Dakota? I couldn't listen anymore.

"Continue to wear your brooches," Mrs. Kuhn cried, "Till we see every last one hang."

I took a seat in a pew and I bounced Peter in my lap. Ida was running up the center aisle, chasing little Catherine. A handsome young farmer, Rudolph Richter, was also running after his toddler son. Rudolph had been widowed in August. I remembered his tears when he told me his wife had been killed by the Dakota. Rudolph's son ran to Ida, arms up. She picked up the motherless little boy and placed him on her hip. Catherine shrieked and ran round Ida's legs. Farmer Richter approached Ida. I couldn't hear what Rudolph was asking, but Ida was nodding; responding to his questions. Instinctively, I felt the urge to help translate. But I held back. I'd once thought myself so necessary to Ida's functioning. But she was more resilient than I realized. She had every ability to help herself. She could speak if she needed to. There was a tingling of hope for my sister. Maybe she was feeling the same excitement with Rudolph that I did with Riggs.

Rudolph looked at his towheaded boy, who seemed to be soaking up Ida's loving embrace. Rudolph ran his hand over the boy's hair, smiling. Ida smiled too. She looked blissful. To a stranger, they'd appear to be a happy family. This distance seemed the right length between us. Space to love my sister and let her live life, as she'd choose. My heart trembled for myself. If it was discovered that I'd tried to lessen Tashunke's sentence . . . what would they do to me? Would I bring shame to my entire family? Otto was so proud among the army men. How would it'd look to have his own sister be an Indian sympathizer? My father might never allow me in his office again. I looked at baby Peter. What memory would he have of me? A sister who'd betrayed her town? Her family? Or a sister who'd bravely used her voice for what she'd believed was right? Regardless of my fears, I'd made my choice. I remembered Tashunke. He was a righteous man; standing up to his own people who were committing wrongs. I'd do the same for him.

November 16, 1862

It was after evening supper; my voice trembled when I volunteered to do the nightly milking, as planned. My chest pounded in nervousness. Riggs was to come meet me and retrieve my testimony—tonight. All our efforts came down to this moment. I picked up my worn copy of *Leaves of Grass*, and with shaky hands, pulled out the folded letter from its pages. It was the most important thing I'd ever done. My testimony would be in the president's consideration. I was risking my reputation. My parents' approval. I couldn't think of how it would look to be found out . . . The court recorder, using her own words to try to lessen the sentence of an *Indian*. I would undoubtedly be banished from my father's office. And Riggs would be "reassigned," cast out from town. I comforted myself with the thought that at least if I were ever found out, I'd be in good company. I tried to steady myself. I finally understood Tashunke's determination when he saved Ida. I had that determination, that conviction now. In my very bones. This appeal must be made. I read Walt Whitman's words,

"What you are here—that life exists, and identity; That the powerful play goes on, and you will contribute a verse."

I closed my eyes, placed my hands atop the envelope, and made Whitman's words my prayer, "Lord, in this powerful play, let these words be my verse."

I moved swiftly through the house and out into the night. Across the prairie, I could make out the silhouette of a man on horseback at the horizon. I filled with new hope and fear to see Riggs there. Time seemed to move quickly, but each second was heavy. He was ready for the handoff. I couldn't contain my anxious anticipation, and I trotted faster across the expanse. I wished for his arms around me again; they were the only thing that could steady the world at this moment. As I approached, Riggs dismounted, and said, "Hello, there."

All our previous encounters had been somewhat happenstance. But this moment was precisely coordinated. Seeing him made my heart stop.

"Hello." I took in the sight of Riggs, his worn coat, a buffalo blanket, and a cap pulled over his ears. He was ready for a long ride.

"A private mail stagecoach, per the order of Emma Heard," he said with a smile as he patted his steed on the rump. But I was too nervous to laugh. I was anxious to get my testimony on its way. I wanted it in Riggs's hands. I trusted him with it. With my truth. The hope itself, of sending this letter on behalf of Tashunke, was almost unbearable. If we succeeded, his life would be spared. And if we failed . . . Tashunke would be executed in the shadow of Christmas. My heart ached to imagine Riggs risking this long journey. He'd ride through the night to get to St. Paul. Then make his way through the woods of Wisconsin to a train in Chicago and then east. I felt guilty that I had asked him to do this, but Riggs assured me he could handle the travel. The plan was such a long shot, but a shot we had to take.

"Here," I said as I pulled my testimony from my coat's breast pocket. The white envelope glowed in the moonlight. Riggs took and tucked it away. I could barely believe the next time this letter was passed, it would be into the hands of the President of the United States.

The function of Riggs and I meeting had been accomplished but we both lingered in the cold. I wanted to stay with him longer. I didn't know when I'd see him next. My knees weakened as I looked at Riggs's handsome face. We stood, not as court recorder and court interpreter. Not even as co-conspirators. But as two people who needed each other to feel a little less alone in the world.

"Please," I finally said, "be so careful on your journey." I shivered suddenly in the chill of the evening. He stepped forward and rubbed his gloved hands up and down my upper arms in an effort to warm me. It was intimate but natural. I leaned into him. In a moment of vulnerability, I let him know, "I'll be thinking of you every moment. Until you're back safely."

As I tipped my head up to look in his dark eyes, his hand gently took the back of my neck and pulled me close. Before I could say another word, his warm lips tenderly pressed into mine. His rugged earnestness hit me like lightning. It felt as if the stars swirled above us in that moment. My body craved his warmth; it was a refuge in the frozen world beyond us. His scruff scratched against my skin. I heard the crinkle of the envelope in his breast pocket as he pulled me in. All my nervousness and excitement spun together in the purity of our connection; our passion and our purpose crashed into each other. I wanted to stay near him; never let him go. But our shared mission was more important than our desire. I stepped back, overwhelmed at our kiss. It was more than I could take and yet all I wanted in our last moment together. Would he bring good news when he returned? Or would our best efforts together not be enough? He must make haste; accomplish the important assignment that brought us together. "Take this," I said as I wrapped my favorite scarf around his exposed neck. "Until I see you again."

He tucked his nose into a fold of the scarf, and breathed deeply, as if he was taking me in. "You'll be keeping me warm for the miles to come, Emma Heard." He mounted his horse and slipped into the darkness. Watching him go, my heart beat against my coat, in the empty place where the envelope had been. Now my words beat against a different heart. His. As I stood in the silence of the open winter plain, I prayed they would be strong enough to be heard in the noise of this world. Strong enough to change a man's fate.

TWENTY-SIX

Oenikika

November 17, 1862

Grief swirled inside me in its many ways. Sometimes it was cavernous, winding as a burrow, wrenching in its turns. Sometimes I tiptoed within my own heart, fragile as the November ice creeping out on the lake. And sometimes, the heartache was as beautiful as the soft falling snow. Wonder quietly suspended in the air around me, then covered my world, changing everything I saw.

Vultures trailed me high in the winter sky, looping with loneliness, sensing the spirit of death that walked alongside me. Mato's steadfast steps led us west while Ahone carried me. Besides the horses, I was by myself upon this frozen earth. I'd ridden north, hoping to find the braves who'd ridden ahead. Hoping they'd somehow heard the gunshots. The shots that still echoed in my ears. I'd ridden back south. Then north again searching for the river. Never finding anything of hope. And now west—the direction my father said would have the largest bands of our greater tribe. The reins slipped frequently from my fatigued hands and Mato guided us when I could not bear to sit up in the saddle any longer. I curled myself into Ahone, pulled my coverings around me, cocooned myself. In the protection of my cocoon, I could feel the stinging upon the skin of my cheeks, raw and chapped, from my days of crying for my father. While my skin was still painful, my sobbing was done. Now I entered the customary winters of grieving for my father and my husband. Though I was by myself, I was not alone. Their spirits were with me in my father's buffalo cloak tied around my neck. In Tashunke's black bear blanket covering my body, shielding me from the biting wind. The world had grown so cold—the last warmth I felt was standing under an apple tree. But that warmth was just a fleeting memory, as everything of goodness was in my mind now. Leaving Father's side, I'd sprinted in terror, leapt on Ahone, sending the horses barreling towards the western horizon. I had looked back to see if the men who'd been shooting were following, but what I saw was worse than if they had been at my heels. The white men were dragging Little Crow's lifeless body away. I wanted to turn back, rip my precious father from their cruel soulless hands. Give him a proper death ceremony. But instead, I kept galloping west—as a devastated, angry, blood-curdling scream burst out of me. It kept coming out of me. Endless. A scream no one else on this earth ever heard.

When I sat up, my eyes squinted and strained, the world a blur of white. I looked down to my mare, watched her shoulder blades and muscles moving together and tried to steady my vision. I pulled my hand out of my mitten and felt the warmth of her body. The stains upon the saddle . . . The once bright red spots faded to dark brown. The smears of my father's blood. He was real just a few moons ago. I shuddered with sorrow. I wished that I hadn't been forced to leave his side. I wished I'd had time to straighten his legs. Changed his moccasins so he was ready for his walk to the otherworld. I'd just needed a few more moments with him. Why did they have to take him? Why did they need to drag him away? My mind weakened with the memories and the horizon started to spin. As I passed clusters of sagebrush, catching the drifts of the blown snow, I heard whispers in the wind.

Look to the animals to learn how to survive. My father's voice.

Keep moving towards the sunset. Tashunke.

You see me all the time. My mother.

Delirium fell like a gentle rain upon me . . . could they be nearby? I wanted their company. Wanted their voices. I needed to reach out. Hold onto them. I looked ahead, and I saw the familiar sight of my father ahead of me. His tall straight back, long hair bouncing, riding Mato. "Father," I called with a hoarse voice as a gust of wind blasted into me. When I looked again, Mato was riderless in front of me. My present reality and the Hereafter were so close, it felt like the two worlds were touching. Spinning me in a winter mirage. Was this snow-drifted world the afterlife? I turned my head and saw Tashunke, his muscular legs pushing through the hard crust of snow, walking beside me. My heart burst in love. "Husband," I called out in delight as I reached for him. But as my hand stretched in front of me, Tashunke disappeared. Leaning, I looked for his tracks in the snow. I tipped in the saddle and fell crashing off Ahone onto the hard earth.

I stared up at the dimming gray sky; the Moon When Winter Begins was above me, farther away than usual. *Even the moon leaves me,* I thought. I sat up. Ahead was an ancient willow. Its leafless skeleton stretched toward the sky while frosted, weeping arms dangled and hung about a mammoth trunk frozen to Mother Earth. I felt woozy as I climbed to stand. Confused. I moved through the snow towards the tree. In a wearied haze, I set my tipi into the willow tree and grabbed my medicine bag, still full. The horses scratched at the snow, exposing bits of brown grass to munch on. I was too tired to eat. I fell atop my blankets and clung to my plants. Exhaustion buried atop me like an avalanche. I nuzzled into the bark of the old willow. I closed my eyes and thought of Aunt Mika, crafting me the precious bag I clung to. Owl Woman . . . Wenona. Tashunke. My heart was a spiderweb of love tied to everyone I once knew. Memories of them sparkled in my soul like drops of dew in a sunrise, illuminating the beautiful invisible strands that connected us still.

My favorite smell, the sugary smell of simmering sap, danced in my nose. The scent of my childhood. The warm wind stirred around me; I immediately recognized—I'd returned to the dream. The lake of wild rice. Peace filled, I walked to the bark canoe and pulled the comforting blankets of our ancestors around me. My voice called out.

I could hear myself calling.

"Taoyateduta." It was his time. I called louder, "Taoyateduta. Chief Little Crow."

From the dark woods behind me a young man, a child, and my father, all embodied in one walked out. His image was a blend of his entire being; all phases of his life somehow visible at once. "Father," I said, as I welcomed him, and he quietly crawled into the canoe. His wrists were straight and strong, as if he'd never been shot. His stomach, uninjured. He was completing his journey to the Happy Hunting Grounds.

The reeds rustled as the wind pulled us out upon the water. I remembered hopefully; this was when she had spoken to me . . .

"Mother?" I asked into the darkness.

"You've been a wise healer, my beloved daughter," her voice said. I filled with pride to have done well in her eyes as the hurting parts of me broke open. I wanted my mother's refuge. I wanted her love. I'd been so alone.

"I don't know how to be without our people. I need you, Mother."

"Just like the winter world still needs the sun. I see you, Oenikika. Your heart holds the beating drum of the Dakota. That can never be stilled, and you will never be alone." As my mother spoke, Father's spirit left the canoe and hovered above the water between us. Bands of wispy clouds passed in front of the moon. The winds stilled between the three of us.

"He has found you?" I asked.

"Yes, your father is with me."

"Can I be with my mother and father?" My voice cracked as I asked. I felt like a young child, wanting the comforting arms of my parents.

"There's a river of life still left for you, Oenikika. You'll remain," she said with calm assurance.

I'll remain.

I was alone in the middle of the lake. Alone again. "Mother, where do I go now?" I asked, questioning which shore I should paddle to.

"Your husband's dream has given you all the direction you need. You do not need any more instruction from this side. It lives within you."

"Tashunke! Has he found you?" I asked urgently. But the Moon When Winter Begins stared back at me and my question echoed into the stillness.

I woke with a jolt, my cheeks screaming in pain. My salty tears burned the skin of my wind-chapped face. I'd first experienced this dream the night Tashunke disappeared. I assumed it was for him. But I now knew—this vision had been for my father. There was an aching incompleteness inside me. . . what had happened to my husband? How could my heart have never had the chance to say goodbye? How come I could not reach out to him . . . find answers when I called out in the hereafter?

I rested my weary head against the willow tree. In death, life persists. In life, death persists. The circle continues. I remain.

November 25, 1862

Day after day, a crow flew west ahead of me. The earth changed here and became different than any place I'd ever been. I was growing worried; had I ridden too far? Was I still in the territory of our Seven Council Fires? Hills with orangey-red bands of earth rising out of the white snow surrounded me. I followed hoofprints in the snow. Buffalo had moved through; I followed their trail. Mato stopped at a ridgeline. Ahone carried us to the edge. A river cut through the red earth. And along the river stood the recognizable shape of tipis. Many tipis. A village. I put my hands to my face and shook my head as shaky breaths of disbelief filled me. Could it be real? I uncovered my face and the village remained. My heart burst with anticipation. Finally, I'd found our western bands.

I hopped from Ahone's back and readied myself to approach. This tribe could reject a lone rider. Suspicious. A woman traveling by herself in the winter. I wanted to present myself with dignity. I unhooked my father's eagle staff from Mato and took it in my right hand . . . there would be no other bands for miles. *Please accept me.* I felt as I had in my dream, anxious for the relief of being near my mother. To be within this village, their safety and protection. I needed shelter and support. I mounted Ahone, sat up as tall as I could and raised my chin. Mato fell in line behind Ahone and me, the eagle feathers bouncing with our quick trot. I wished my father were here. As I approached, cloaked villagers emerged and met me on the eastern front of their camp. I pulled the horses to a halt. My heart was a pummeling drum in my chest. Men gathered closest to me as women huddled behind them. Their questioning eyes surveyed me. I announced myself.

"I am the wife of the Man Who Sings to Horses and daughter of Chief Little Crow of the easternmost band of Dakota in the Seven Council Fires. I am seeking shelter," I said hoping to sound confident, summoning all my bravery. It was strange to hear my own voice after so many days of silence. I hoped no one could see my weakness; my hand holding the reins shook.

"And where is the chief?" a man's voice called out.

I swallowed, my throat pained with grief, but I spoke of my father with pride, "Chief Little Crow died with the highest honor in battle. Many of our warriors have died." I looked among the men; it was unclear who their chief was—especially as they stood wrapped in blankets.

"In battle with which tribe?" a voice questioned. These men were testing my story. How unusual to have a lone woman ride this far by herself. It amazed me that no one here had encountered the storm cloud of the white man, in the way we had.

"The whites. They've spread like locusts flying in thick clouds on the summer prairie," I explained, calling the spirit of my father. I imagined his voice, his warning, his wisdom during the war council.

The men murmured and debated among themselves while the women looked at me with judging eyes peering out of their cloaks. I feared what would happen if they rejected me. I wouldn't survive an entire winter alone. I couldn't survive many more nights alone. Mato tossed his head, his dark mane shaking. I was my father's daughter. I would speak with the chief's intellect. I boldly continued, calling out my warning, in the space between us. "The white men are thick as tamaracks in the swamps of the Ojibwe. I will share what I have seen. Tell you of their tactics. Help you prepare to protect your people." I hoped they saw my face. My scars. My aloneness. I hoped they saw the power in *my* journey.

"It is not a woman's place to speak of war. Especially not one so young."

Young. I closed my eyes and remembered everything the last winters of my life had shown me. Freedom and captivity. The white man's walls. My medicine rides. I'd seen warriors die from battle and ridden at the side of the greatest chief. I'd been chosen by the Man Who Sings to Horses. And I'd journeyed alone over incredible distances while maintaining our traditions. I was gaining wisdom. I required acceptance of a tribe who saw my value. I studied the group. One man stood quietly in the center. He was younger than the others; Tash's age, perhaps. But the others looked to him, their eyes repeatedly checking for his reactions. I recognized the keenness in the young man's eyes. It was the same look of my father. He was their leader.

I waited until I felt his eyes upon me. All their eyes upon me again. And I spoke from my heart with determination.

"I am Oenikika! Of whom the Great Mystery has blessed with visions and healing. I come bearing medicine and intentions of peaceful tradition and protection for all Dakota of the Seven Council Fires. I have witnessed the Great War against an enemy you do not know. But certainly, you will soon. If you do not want the blessing of my abilities, I ask for safe passage to continue towards the sunset." My hand trembled with nerves holding my father's staff. I breathed to steady myself, confident in my purpose upon this earth.

The young leader walked forward and nodded, then pointed his arm out of his cloak to the edge of the camp. His voice called out, "Chief Crazy Horse accepts you."

Relief dulled the sharp edges of survival that had kept me going for so many moons. I would have shelter. It was a tribe not my own . . . But I was accepted. I had spoken bold and precise—just as my father would have. I stayed sitting tall and nudged Ahone forward as we moved towards our future.

TWENTY-SEVEN

Emma Heard

Wednesday, December 25, 1862

In the glimmer of lanterns lit for the Christmas night service, my footsteps made perfect pointed outlines in the dusting of snow on the church steps. My mind ached for distraction. The days felt unbearably long waiting for word from Riggs. I missed him. Missed when we held onto each other, on to our plan, with hopefulness. It'd been almost six weeks since he rode east, and the hangings were scheduled for tomorrow morning. His extended absence seemed a terrible sign; I filled with dread at the thought of Tashunke's fate. His death mandated for tomorrow. With Riggs gone and my testimony with him, there was nothing for me to hold on to. I'd put everything into my testimony letter. Anxiety tingled through the chill of the evening. I had no more power to change anything. I looked at the glittering snow falling onto my woolen coat sleeve. How could there still be such beauty in the world tonight if we're going to stand at a mass execution tomorrow?

My family walked into the church in front of me. I could hardly bear to go inside. Each movement forward was one I couldn't come back from. I peered into the glowing entryway. All the familiar faces . . . so many people I felt so different from. I heard Hanna Kuhn ask, "What is *he* doing here?" with a sniff of disdain. I turned towards the yard, and before my mind could fully comprehend the sight of him, my boots leapt off the steps and were running across the snow.

I could barely contain myself. Riggs was back! He appeared exhausted. I couldn't read if he held good news on Tashunke's appeal or otherwise. I wrung my mittens together, as relief, hope, and trepidation tangled inside of me. I remembered his departure, our brief kiss. My heart leapt high as my boots had off the steps with the memory. I wanted his energy around me again. I wanted him to share everything that had happened. How had our mission fared? I wanted him to take my hand . . . bring me in close. It was so wonderful to see him, but my anxious hope for Tashunke was unbearable. If the president hadn't reduced Tashunke's sentence, there'd be no changing what would happen tomorrow.

"You're back," I said with disbelief. Seeing him again felt like a miracle. I scanned his face, looking for longing. Had he missed me? Needed me as I had needed him in these long weeks?

"Had to return this," he said with a tired teasing. He unwound my navy scarf from his neck. I took it caringly; it was now even more precious after its service to Riggs.

"Riggs?" I questioned, "How. . . what did Lincoln say? Did he reduce the sentence?"

Riggs nodded. "I've already met with the jailers. Tashunke was pardoned," he stated. His words were unexpected.

"Pardoned," I said, shocked. "Pardoned *entirely*?"

"I delivered the presidential request for immediate release," Riggs said. "Tashunke's free."

Free. His words lifted into the snowfall with an impossible lightness. I hadn't even thought to consider a full pardon. But it made sense. If our testimony was true—which it was—President Lincoln had every reason to dismiss the charges entirely. It was even better than I had hoped. My heart almost broke in relief. Tears welled at my eyes, prickling in the cold.

"Oh, Riggs. That is miraculous. You did it." I said with elation. I wanted to hug him. This was everything we had worked for. Yet another shocking glimpse into the workings of this world. A man either dead or completely free. Guilt or innocence. The world wanted black and white. All I could see were shades of gray in the winter world around us.

I could tell the trip took everything Riggs had. He could barely stand he looked so tired. He'd been on a different journey than I in the past weeks. I felt guilty looking at his exhaustion. I wondered what he'd seen. What he'd said to the president. Did his own family know what he was trying to do? How would they feel? I thought of the east coast being full of Indian-sympathizers, as Mrs. Carrothers had said . . . suddenly, I wondered what that could be like. To be in a town that actually shared my values.

The lovely moment was interrupted. "Emma." My mother's sharp voice cut through the winter air. The service was starting. I looked back at Riggs, ignoring my urge to hug him, but held myself back. We were in the sight of others. He gave a tired nod, urging me to go inside. I could only imagine how it looked—me running to him. If my mother knew of our embrace, our kiss, I'd be outcast for being a hussy as much as an Indian sympathizer.

"Come along, we have much to celebrate this Christmas," I said to him, still reveling in the afterglow of such fantastic news. Riggs didn't seem to match my enthusiasm. The exhaustion on his face now also looked like defeat. How could he be down after achieving such a wonder? I deflated as I realized how short lived our wonder would be . . . though Tashunke was free, the executions were inescapable. I feared I had just experienced one moment of joy as I sank into the reality of tomorrow. And the edge in my mother's voice made me nervous. It had been indulgent of me to run to him as I had. As I walked away, I thought about him entering the church, the controversy surrounding him. They viewed him as an Indian sympathizer and no one even knew about the pardon yet. He had to be welcome; it was Christmas. Surely, he would be treated with respect, in *church*, tonight.

But as I moved into the warm entryway, my mother's voice hissed in my ear. "Do not embarrass our family by associating with him."

I looked up at her with horror. I was exposed. My hopes, my wants, my fight had all been close to my vest. Quiet. The most I'd shared was with Riggs—who was safe, unjudging. My mother would soon hear of my Indian sympathizing act. Though I believed in my choice, my deepest sense of myself still wanted my mother to approve. I hated being a disappointment to her. Part of me would always be a little girl, small Emma, wanting the safety of clinging tightly to my mother, who'd protect me from anything scary in the outside world. But as much as I wanted my mother's love, it seemed I endlessly pushed away from her. I was so deeply different. She had no understanding of what Riggs, of what her own daughter, was working for. As her hand pressed to my side to move me forward, I looked back into the darkness and saw Riggs walking towards the church. My worry crept behind him. If my own mother was so angry with me, I feared the treatment he'd encounter.

I begrudgingly took a seat in the row with my family. The cozy sanctuary was decorated with strings of popcorn, paper chains, red ribbons strung into bows. Candlesticks lined the aisles and rested in the windowsills. "Joy to the World's" notes rang out from Uncle Allen's fiddle. I looked back as Riggs appeared in the entryway. Pastor Vogel shook his head at the sight of him. How terrible, the leader of the church disowning his own missionary. Pastor tipped his head toward the back corner, indicating Riggs wasn't to sit in the front as he had in the year past. I could hardly take it. I felt ashamed of my ability to sit anonymously in a row with my family. No one aware of where my heart truly stood. A fire lit inside of me—I wanted to be seen as I am. The woman God had called me to be. No matter what that meant. Send me out. Hate me. Hate me for seeking justice for an innocent man.

I was torn inside. I was still relieved for Tashunke. Justice had been achieved. But watching Riggs be outcast . . . my spirit couldn't settle. A wave of shame washed through me at the thought of being called a traitor. I personally had recorded all the deaths, over five hundred people killed, in the survivor's log. I knew the horrific acts—women, children, infants murdered. Slaughtered with less humanity than we spare the pigs each spring. Would sympathizing excuse these atrocities? I couldn't. But seeking justice. Seeking truth. That alone seemed to be an act of betrayal. Through the entire service my insides twisted. My own mother calling Riggs an embarrassment. I'd been a misfit in this world until I connected with him; my mind felt like a window in the spring, opening after a long hard winter. I couldn't let Riggs go through this alone. I needed to be with him.

Outside the church windows, the dark prairie was beyond us. I wondered where Tashunke was on this Christmas evening . . . pardoned. A free man. What was even left for him to return to? I wondered if he remembered me. Remembered the attack. If he thought it was worth it to save Ida and me. How much could one life mean in this cold world? I looked down the pew. Ida's eyes were fixed ahead diligently on Pastor Vogel. Otto gave me a wink. Catherine played with her doll. Ma and Pa sat near each other; Ma shushed babbling baby Peter. Tashunke's choice to save us that day changed the future for our family, but a heaviness settled in my chest. Thirty-eight to die tomorrow. I had told myself that number was so much better than the 303 originally planned, better than thirty-nine. I was sure Tashunke was important to someone else in this world. I hoped he would go somewhere safe, far from here. Somewhere better than this.

Pastor Vogel announced, "For our closing hymn, we join our voices in singing, "*Stille Nacht*". Please, move to the perimeter of the church, join hands, and unite to celebrate the birth of our Lord and Savior, Jesus Christ." The congregation lifted from their seats and moved about to form a circle around the sanctuary. I stood between Ida and Otto while across from us, Riggs stood awkwardly; Mrs. Kuhn to his right refused to take his hand. My heart seared with a protective anger. She could not treat him as an outcast. Not after all he'd been through. I couldn't stand it. I dropped my brother and sister's hands from my own, and I walked alone across the circled congregation. My heart pounded in my ears. Eyes were upon me. I was uncomfortable with the attention. But not letting Riggs be alone in this moment was more important. I relocated myself to the one break in the ring of held hands. In my right hand, I assertively took Mrs. Kuhn's hand; and with my left, I grasped tightly on to Riggs. I warmed the second I felt his hand in mine, but my knees felt weak in my boldness. I looked at Riggs; I wanted peace for all, peace among us. The very thing I felt God asked us for in this hymn. I took a deep breath, looked up, and prayed for the music to start soon.

My mother's eyes were fixed on me, her face tightly unmoving in anger. If I'd stayed by my family—it would have been a betrayal of Riggs. Of the truth. But standing by him now . . . I'd instead betrayed my family. My stomach tightened with embarrassment as the sound of snickers came from Hanna, Charlotte, and Elsa. Taking Riggs's hand was an act of solidarity. I looked down at my shoes as my heart trembled, but I knew, this was where I wanted to stand. I'd walked away from being a child. Walked away from their approval. And moved towards what I wanted in the world. What I believed in. I was scared, but certain.

The lonely vibrations of the violin introduced "Silent Night".

I treasured this song. I usually loved Christmas. But this year, the magic was lost, my sense of belonging severed. My throat stung with sadness; I couldn't sing along. Instead of hopeful lyrics, I let out a long shaky breath. There was no coming back from what had happened. Or from what would come. Tomorrow was ahead of us, a slithering shadow. The executions. Even with Tashunke's pardon, thirty-eight men would die together. I blinked hard to pinch back tears; Riggs squeezed my hand. Candles flickered, and our dark silhouettes danced on the church walls, as voices celebrated our savior. "Stille Nacht" the German words a reminder that not long ago we lived somewhere far from here. Not long ago, this prairie wasn't ours. I squeezed Riggs hand back; we were alone in this, together.

The song concluded, and the congregation shuffled back to the pews for their coats. I didn't want to let go of Riggs's hand. "Thank you for sharing Tashunke's good news with me," I said, attempting to focus on the good. But I caught Hanna Kuhn's judgmental eyes. The disapproving attention made my skin crawl. "I don't believe folks are particularly fond of our . . ." my mind went blank. I didn't know how to define exactly what Riggs and I were receiving judgmental glances about.

"Determination," Riggs said with a defeated acceptance. He understood. I was so grateful to have someone else who could put words to it. Everything that was confusing. What we believed in. These people gathered in the glow of Christmas had been my whole world. But I felt like I'd stepped outside of them. Outside of belonging.

"They'll say what they may," I said, resigned.

"*You* said something when it actually mattered in this world." Riggs gave me a fatigued smile. "Merry Christmas, Emma." His words gave me pause. I'd said something when it mattered. In the shimmering sanctuary, I looked out the frosted window pane at my side. Snow silently wandered towards earth. . . the prairie still and white. Each perfect snowflake glittered in the darkness beyond us.

Tears stung and made a kaleidoscope of the beauty. *Christmas* was holding onto something of hope beyond understanding, beyond this world. Exactly the hope I needed now.

Riggs buttoned his long coat. I worried if he had a warm place to sleep tonight. As he headed towards the door, he said, "I suppose I'll be seeing you tomorrow."

We would be reunited in hours . . . at the executions.

TWENTY-EIGHT

Emma Heard

Friday, December 26, 1862

Dark clouds hung low in the sky; the unseasonably warm December air was thick with humidity. Thousands were gathered in the streets to watch the hangings; it was the largest gathering I'd ever seen. All us Heard children followed Ma and Pa in the crowd. Angry voices clamored in my ears. My mind couldn't hold all the noise; the agitated group's energy crept along my skin and up the back of my neck. The hangings had turned into holiday entertainment; people had traveled from far and near. Many weren't even from New Ulm or the countryside—most hadn't been in the area for the attack and no one else witnessed the unjust trials. How could people crow so loudly about the fates of these men? They didn't seem to care to contemplate the missed annuity payments. Or the fraud. My thoughts I realized were Indian sympathizing thoughts. I washed with nervousness. What would the crowd do to someone who cared about fairness for the Dakota? I followed right behind Ma, matching my steps in her footprints. She hadn't spoken a word to me since last night. Her cold eyes had said enough. I was a disappointment. I felt uncomfortable, embarrassed of my very being around her. It was as if something deep inside my existence was displeasing to her—I was some kind of wild being, with an obnoxious bark, who refused to be tamed. I stepped quietly into her footprints—trying to match her in the only way it seemed I could.

As my family progressed through the crowd, we passed by Mrs. Duta. I thought back to her story—strangling her dog to save her family. Then I remembered the mousy hair of the Eastlick boys . . . *all* murdered at the hands of Dakota warriors. We needed to find justice for them, some kind of justice. It was so hard to keep my mind straight, my heart straight, to find the "right" answer. The exact "right" amount of justice. Who gets to decide such a thing? If I hadn't seen Tashunke protect Ida in the yard, if his command hadn't saved my own life . . . would his justice, his life, have mattered to me? To anyone? By fighting for him, was I denying the depths of the horror of what was inflicted upon the Eastlick family? We must do something to avenge the innocent lives lost. My heart hopped between the black and white. I craved a simple answer, a simple solution, but my mind was as sloppy as the trampled winter slush under my feet. I needed to shut off the part of me that was preoccupied with the Dakota. I needed to focus on those who died at their hands. Focus on the Survivor's Log. I wouldn't watch what they'd to them; I'd just stare at Ma's boots the rest of the day. Don't look up.

Finally, we made our way through the crowd.

"There it is!" Otto exclaimed. I looked up to see it. The gallows. My brother was proud of his weeks of work, ready for the big event. But my heart trembled at the sight. It was unnerving—the grand platform built to kill. Ominous and looming. I jostled forward, as the crowd seemed to have a mind of its own, cheering raucously, pushing forward, pitching sideways, groaning with excitement. I could barely keep track of Ma's boots in the chaos. I thought the arrangement couldn't get any worse until Pa turned back to me and announced he and I were summoned to the front, to stand alongside General Pope and the other members of the military commission. I was mortified. We were singled out, directly associated with the hangings. I didn't want any of this. Suddenly, anxiety bolted down my legs and up through my chest; I needed to escape the crowd, escape the commission. So many people swarming round. I couldn't see or think straight. And to be right next to the hanging stage? My body quivered in anticipation of the horror of hangings. I couldn't take it.

"Please Pa," I begged. "May I stay back with Ma and Ida? Pope won't even notice my absence."

Before Pa could say a word, my mother responded in snappy disapproval. "Do not bring any more shame to this family. Stay quiet and go where you are told." She was embarrassed by me. I nodded submissively while inside I was still fraught with an urge to run.

Pa took my hand and moved us through the mob. We worked our way toward the square hanging stage. Ten nooses hung from three sides; one side held nine. Thirty-nine nooses prepared, as they'd planned to hang Tashunke until just yesterday. My bones chilled looking at the twists of rope. They were so real and ready. We moved to the very front; the foreboding sight filled me with dread. I looked through the empty loop of a noose and up toward the gray sky. Black crows circled overhead, matching the oval shape of the dangling rope. An eeriness seeped into my veins. The rope's intention: singular and simple.

The spectacle of the gallows seemed to intensify the anticipation of the crowd. A man next to us proclaimed, "I'll find that Injun that escaped yesterday. Make my bounty. More money in my pocket." Foolish man. Tashunke hadn't escaped. I was disgusted by the thought of him profiting from killing another human. An innocent one at that. I doubted it mattered to him. A bounty was placed on all Indians; innocence or guilt didn't matter. The Dakota were banished from the state. Forever. There would never be another attack on the settlers. Never be another hanging like today. I prayed Godspeed to Tashunke. *Get as far away from here as possible.*

Pa and I lined up alongside Sibley and the rest of the commission. We nodded hello to our familiar counterparts, all regrouping for the final outcome of our work together. I could see Riggs on the other side of the structure, by the door to the pen that contained the condemned Dakota.

The well-adorned monster, General Pope, strode in front of his commission. I thought my heart would stop in shock when he turned to me.

Pope's spiteful eyes looked down into mine. "Had to make sure you and your friend," he looked over toward Riggs, "were front and center, to witness the thirty-eight savages we *do* have the pleasure of executing today." He had been informed of Tashunke's pardon . . . and knew Riggs and I were responsible. My body shuddered with fear at his powerful intimidation. I glanced at Pa, his eyes connected with mine—a slight flicker of questioning, then dismay in his eyes. Instinctively, I felt an urge to apologize. But as I opened my mouth to speak, Pa looked away from me. My head dropped in humiliation; my own Pa looking away from me in disgrace. I suddenly questioned everything I'd done. Acting against the commission and betraying my town's wants. Shame poured over me as the noise from the crowd spun inside my ears. I was alone. An embarrassment. Pope speaking to me directly for the first time—to say this. Nausea churned in my stomach, as I looked up to the stage, the nooses were gently waving back and forth in the slight wind. The general was intentionally making me and Riggs watch the hangings. Bringing me to the front. Rubbing our Indian sympathizing faces in the mass execution. My knees trembled, and my boots sunk into the sloppy earth. Pope's power was absolute today—God and devil in one.

The rat-a-tat of rolling military drumbeats signaled the beginning of the execution ceremony. Farmer Krause stood near the base of the scaffold. They'd appointed him, a civilian victim, the honor of cutting the rope and letting out the gallows floor, when that ultimate moment would soon come. The audience cheered as Riggs, looking grave, led the 38 doomed warriors out. The Dakota men walked in a straight line, standing tall and upright. The crowd taunted, spitting, throwing items, screaming insults—"Die animals!" But the native men continued step by step, faces looking ahead. Their confidence in the face of death wrenched my heart. I could barely look at them . . . but I forced myself to own up to the moment; it wouldn't be right to look away from what we'd chosen to do here. My heart turned over, pleading with my brain to remember the murdered settlers. Why had I never seen the warriors who attacked Ida? Where were they? Maybe I could accept this if they were the ones being led out. I watched the long processional of ill-fated men. How weren't these Dakota kicking, struggling, fighting for their life? They appeared earnest and confident. Some were even glancing up ahead in the line, almost looking eager to keep things moving. These men were the men whose names I had written during the trials. Chaska, Cut Nose, Red Otter . . . At the time I'd been busy, hurried, transcribing their names quickly as I could. Now, I saw each man slowly moving toward their final moments, their bare feet so alive. Riggs reached the base of the staircase to the execution platform. Our eyes caught for a brief second. We shared something in our reaction. Pain. Powerlessness. This was bigger than us. The process had swallowed us whole.

My shame turned inward, not because of Pope's words, or my mother's anger. But because of the impossibility of reconciling this heinous act. Tashunke's choice to defend Ida and me in the yard was the noble one. A debt I could never repay. Though Tashunke had his life . . . we'd still taken everything.

Soldiers led the group up the staircase to their assigned rope upon the gallows stage. The Dakota footsteps were light, not making a sound; some men hopped the steps two at a time. The logistics of execution were more than I could bear. I had to blame someone. My mind ran backward. The government. Couldn't they have stopped this all before it began? Where was that annuity payment when we, when *they*, needed it? Otto and Pa defending New Ulm . . . My heart ached thinking of my exhausted father and brother in those long nights. Their bravery protecting their family and their town. Without their determined defense, we wouldn't be alive today. Somehow, I had to be grateful for that. But fate was falling upon us all now.

Courageously, one Dakota warrior broke into song. Soon, a chorus of voices blended together. A united song. The mortal melody intermingled in unforgettable harmony. My eyes were fixed upon them, my ears mesmerized; I'd never heard anything like it. My arms tingled with goosebumps. Their voices were evocative; so powerfully alive. The crowd hushed, seemingly entranced by the scene. The trilling Dakota voices sang over the spectators, as if they were calling out to another realm. The sound was beautiful and despondent as if their voices were summoning a world we couldn't see. The men were powerful; I hoped for a second the winds had changed. There was more to this process. These singing men couldn't possibly be killed. Not all of them. My mind questioned as my heart was spellbound by their voices. But General Pope stomped forward; he would tolerate no more. He waved up his next assignment of soldiers, all holding bags. The condemned wouldn't steal his show.

The soldiers covered each Dakota man's head with a white muslin sack then pulled the loop of rope down, finding a hidden jawline under the muslin. As the ropes were fitted snug, the singing quieted. Their covered faces had seen the last daylight of their lives. An eerie silence fell in the space their voices had been. My heart raced. I looked to Pa; he bore a somber look and seemed to be staring at the sky just above the scaffold. He wasn't looking at the Dakota. Pa couldn't bear to watch their killing, either. I looked back at the gallows. With a confident comradery, the Dakota stretched out their arms, blindly found each other's hands. They were joined, united, in their final moments.

As the last soldier stepped off the stage, Pope's voice belted out through the cold air, "Now!" Three drumbeats sounded with finality. Their fates were sealed. Farmer Krause lifted the ax high above his head. In a swift chop of vengeance, he sliced the rope. The Dakota fearlessly held hands as the floor dropped out underneath them. With a quick thud, 38 nooses caught at once.

NO! I screamed in my mind as the darkness of the sound hit the bottom of my stomach. I averted my eyes at the horror; my breath caught in panicked terror in my chest. It was done. Pope gave one command and there was no undoing it. The wooden gallows creaked and groaned with the weight of the dying men. It was done. I hated myself. Hated that I thought a single pardon was worth celebrating. This horror was irreversible. Nothing could be reconciled. When I lifted my cowardly eyes to the act in front of me, I kept my gaze fixed on the lone unoccupied noose. It swayed back and forth in rhythm with the bodies beside it. Tashunke would have been hanging there. *Go.* I heard his voice again and shuddered in my memory of him. My hands shook. Every land patent I'd copied. Every execution I'd recorded. The permanence of the words was suspended in front of me and the stains were on my hands.

Cheers erupted from the crowd while 38 lifeless Dakota men dangled in haunting silence.

The winter sun had only just set. I laid in my bed. The scar on the side of my head throbbed. It hadn't pained me like this since we had sheltered at the Kuhns' house. *Leaves of Grass* sat opened next to me but I couldn't read. My mind was still stuck on that empty noose. I flinched when I thought of the swaying bodies. Bruno's boots. My physical pain was consuming, and the memories bent the agony tighter inside of me. My stomach couldn't bear the thought of food, of sitting for supper. Ma didn't fight me to make me join them. I supposed she preferred to have me away. Her foolish, naively hopeful daughter. Fighting for one Indian. What could it even have mattered? I felt defeated thinking of all the men who died today. My embarrassing association with an Indian missionary. I'd failed my own mother so deeply. I wrung my quilt in my hands, resentment and shame tightened my twists. Even when I thought of Riggs's embrace. His kiss. My heart felt a stabbing. I must just be a foolish girl to him, as well. At the time, our mission felt so important. But now I was trapped at the bottom of a well. Our shared optimism a faint light so far away. I closed my eyes against the pain, only to see them clawing at Ida's chest. Her torn skirt. The bloodied raw heels. There was so much blood. Her blood. My blood. My stomach turned. I opened my eyes to shut away the memory and the pain increased, and I rolled to my other side. My memory of Ida's voice "No! Nonono. . ." calling out from her nightmares. . . Her agony. This whole mess. Our nightmare.

Somehow, I drifted off to sleep, only to be awakened by a gentle touch on my back. Pa. I sat up. I couldn't remember the last time he came upstairs.

His voice was steady as his eyes looked directly into mine. "I was surprised to see only thirty-eight of the nooses occupied . . . one going unused. But Pope seemed to indicate that you were not as surprised as I?"

I froze. He'd heard Pope confront me. My father knew that I was involved in the final pardon. Tashunke's freedom. I felt enormous guilt—all the hours Pa had allowed me to work in his office. Given me access to knowledge and opportunity. And I'd used it to serve my own purposes. Pa continued to look at me, giving me space to explain myself. I was nervous to tell the truth, but it seemed the only fair explanation.

"He saved us, Pa. That thirty-ninth man *saved* me and Ida the day of the attack." My voice came out timid but truthful. I wanted to cry. I wanted Pa to make it all okay. Accept it. Stand behind me. Don't let them cast me out. I'd done my best. Just as I had every day working with my father. I wanted him to see me . . . see my intention.

Instead, he looked toward the window. It seemed he was processing the information. I ached for him to respond.

Finally, he spoke. "Perhaps there's a rationale for your choice. But I don't accept your dishonor to the town or the military commission."

Logic and obedience prevailed in his view of me. Pa stood up and walked down the stairs without another word. He didn't accept it. Didn't accept me. My head dropped hearing his opinion of my insubordination. Shame filled me again . . . Not from the thought of dishonoring the military commission or the other townspeople. But to dishonor my *father*. I was alone and pulled my quilt to my face, pressing it into my eyes with my shame. Betraying him was the worst thing I could do. I wanted to cry but didn't want to further disappoint him with my pointless tears. I'd made a choice and had to live with the consequences. The bottom of the well deepened impossibly. I was trapped in my own disgrace. Physical pain swirled with my hopelessness. Time seemed to stand still. I couldn't find any way to change what happened. I didn't know how it'd ever get better.

Surprisingly, I heard footsteps coming back up the stairs. Not Otto's heavy quick ones, or Ida's soft even steps. By the time I turned over, Pa was back, sitting on the edge of the bed.

I sat quiet, fearful to make anything worse.

"I suppose I do owe a debt of gratitude to the man that saved my daughters," he said.

I couldn't hold the tears back then. My father's expression of appreciation to Tashunke. I suddenly felt pain lift from my head and my body warmed with overwhelming love. "I'm sorry if I've disappointed you, Pa." I wanted to put into words my reasoning. My hope for peace. For justice. I was trying for the things *he* had taught me about.

Before I could elaborate, Pa said, "This came for you." He passed me an envelope as he stood up from the bedside. It was Miss Knudsen's handwriting. My mouth dropped open in shock. I looked up, even more stunned Pa would give it to me. After I had betrayed him with my testimony letter? He had every reason to hold it back. Scold me. Banish me. But him passing me this felt like something quite the opposite . . . something of respect. He didn't agree with me, but he respected me. In astonishment, I took it. I could barely remember my last correspondence with her in the blurry days after the attacks. Writing Miss Knudsen to let her know I'd missed the teaching deadline. I hadn't even considered she'd respond. I thought I'd just failed her . . . I tore open the envelope and unfolded the single piece of paper.

Dear friend Emma,

I am so glad to hear you have survived the terrible events that unfolded. Do not concern yourself with apologies regarding the missed teaching application. You have been focused on the things that matter most—I hope you feel pride in that.

I would like to inform you of two things. First, you may correspond with me at my new address: Lawrence University Appleton, Wisconsin.

Secondly, I invite you to enroll at Lawrence University. There is fantastic opportunity within the new women's program which I'm currently attending. Your proficient studies in my classroom, work in your father's office, and duties as a court recorder more than qualify you. Perhaps you could study law at the university? Please consider this opportunity.

Your friend and teacher,

Dorothea Knudsen

It was unexpected. I reread the letter. The invitation to attend *university*. I didn't know that was even a possibility in this world. Women at a university? Gathered together. Learning. Light flooded down into the dark place inside of me. The second the idea took hold I felt my future change. Studying law. Back in a classroom. All the joys of the country classroom from my childhood came back to this moment. Precious education. Unbelievable opportunity. A new feeling bubbled up from somewhere within. Hope. An aspiration for myself . . . I looked out the window towards the darkening eastern sky. Looked across the prairie that held my most painful, terrifying memories. And all the precious, miraculous ones. I could hear my family sharing a laugh at the dinner table downstairs. But my eyes were fixed east. The new horizon was calling to me.

TWENTY-NINE

Oenikika

January 10, 1863

Listlessly, I tossed an armful of frozen buffalo chips beside my tipi in a heap. The season was in its depths; this was the Moon When the Wolves Run Together. I was relieved the daylight was short, the long nights allowed me solitary slumber as if my soul itself was in hibernation. Each day at dusk, I prayed. *Show me my husband. Let me speak to my parents. Help me.*

Snow sparkled as it swirled round me in the constant wind, drifts had blown up against my tipi at the edge of camp. The village was quiet as the howl of midwinter buried us. Women had been generous, bringing me portions of food. I offered my medicines in return. In the spring, I would learn more about their ways. Share what I had witnessed in my land. Bring up the memories that lay dormant within me. For now, I kept to myself in my season of grieving. I looked at my pile of buffalo chips; I had enough fuel to keep me warm to survive another night. I glanced up and into the nothingness beyond my tipi. In the dancing bands of snow blowing across the tundra, my eyes spotted a dark figure. A man on foot. My mind must be playing tricks

287

on me, as it did so frequently. I pulled my hood up around the edges of my eyes. The figure grew larger from of the bleak world behind him. I watched carefully. He seemed so real. Not a mirage. My spirit began drumming inside of my chest. What was I sensing?

Behind the man walked a line of horses. Seven horses moving together against the grit of midwinter. The golden flaxen mane of the front horse danced in the wind. Her whinny cut through the emptiness inside of me.

I scurried forward in disbelief. Goosebumps of truth ran down to my fingertips. Could it be? My soul prickled with unbearable hope.

He continued towards me. My heart felt his pull.

Thoughts froze in my mind and my legs began to run through the hard crust of snow, slipping through the top crust into the drifts of softer snow below. I couldn't move fast enough. My entire being buzzed, my body desperate to get to him.

"Husband!" I called into the space between us. He moved with swiftness, reaching out from his cloak. My arms moved through my layers of blankets until I felt his arms grabbing around me. Our skin upon each other. We collapsed together as the snow puffed out around us.

Tashunke.

His warmth.

His steadiness.

I felt his realness with impossible hope. Warm tears of astonishment brimmed in my eyes. My husband.

"My wife." He stared at me intensely. I let him take me in as I held his forearms tightly, steadying myself. I prayed I wouldn't wake up. That he wouldn't disappear. For the first time, I wasn't anxious to be in my dreamworld, I needed to hold on to reality. We sat intertwined as the swirling snow spun around us.

"How . . . how are you *here*?" I asked. How was he alive? How was he real? How had he found me? My heart held a thousand questions.

"I followed the vision of a dream. I continued towards the sunset."
I nodded. Our dreams had spoken to us. Guided us. The Great
Spirit had never left us once.

The horses I'd freed surrounded us. Wicapi bent her head, touching her nose to the top of my hair, breathing me in. I reached my
hand up and rubbed her velvety face.

"Thank you," I whispered to his mare.

She'd brought him back to me. Reunited us. It was the look in
Wicapi's eyes as she stood in the rain that had let me know he was
gone. I'd run after her with all my pain, screaming, terrifying her. The
spirit had guided her too. Protected her. Protected us. A gust of wind
blew, pushing us into one another, spinning our dark hair together.
Tashunke touched my face, running his fingers over the texture of
my scars. Where I'd torn myself open for him. Where the winter,
where my sorrow, had burned my skin. I felt the perfect roughness
of his fingers upon me. My tears fell warm and soothing on my skin,
healing me under his hand. My husband pressed his cheek to mine. I
could feel the jaggedness of where his own scar tore through his face.
I closed my eyes and took him in. Tashunke. The past was visible
upon us both.

We held each other.

"Where is your father? Who from our band is with you?" Tash
asked.

He didn't know. I was alone. No one else from our band was here.
Sharpness caught in my throat at the pain of saying the truth aloud. I
took a deep breath, and finally explained. "I am here alone. My father
died when we rode together trying to summon a war call."

"Highest honor for the chief who dies in battle," he replied
solemnly.

My eyes flooded again with tears, hearing my good husband honor
his chief. I nodded in agreement. But I knew, my father's spirit lived
within me. His wisdom guided me. All of our campfires together, the

stories he told, stories he had me repeat. Little Crow was ensuring his daughter was prepared to carry on the ways of the Dakota. And I was. Tashunke looked to the east, back at his tracks in the snow.

"What happened to my husband?" I asked. "You were missing in battle, and I feared. . ." I had more than feared. I'd thought my husband was dead.

"I was with the horses when they surrounded me. They took me captive. Then held me with Cut Nose, your uncle Chaska, and the other men." He looked at me, as if he were trying to read my face, understand what I knew.

I held his strong hand in mine. I couldn't imagine what horror captivity would be like for him. Where had he been kept? It would have been like my time in the white man's four walls but much worse. Then my mind questioned . . . "You were with Cut Nose? *And* my uncle? The men who surrendered were in the same place as Cut Nose?" I asked, confused. Then I had a thought of optimism. "Are they free as you are?" Perhaps Grandmother, Wenona, Kimimela—everyone who surrendered could journey to safety as Tashunke had.

But Tash averted his gaze. "No. They are not. Riggs tried . . . but it was only my release he secured."

I hardened the walls of my stomach. Braced myself. I would always need to be able to fortify myself in this way when I thought of our past. What had happened to our people in all the moons I journeyed alone? The men of surrender, like Chaska, kept with the men of battle like Cut Nose? That wasn't logical. And my husband . . . somehow freed. I remembered the Indian missionary for the first time in many seasons.

"That missionary freed you?"

My husband's dark eyes darted back and forth looking into the beyond. The unending whiteness of the winter world surrounding us reflected in his gaze.

"He knew my spirit was not of war. Knew I'd guarded the young women when your cousin was attempting cruelty."

"You protected . . ." I began to ask, as my mind went back to those days of war. The chaos. My husband had said war was not in his heart. He guarded white women? I looked at his chest. His necklaces were missing. They must have been taken from him. Suddenly, my heart filled with understanding and my eyes filled with tears of pride. "My husband protected. Just as he wanted to do for his own people long ago."

"And I thought of my wife. No man should bring harm to any woman," he explained. I remembered my comment taking Dina the deer after Cut Nose's foolishness. That moment, the summer sun, our family seemed like a lifetime ago. I looked at him, the impossibility of Tashunke in front of me now. He felt like a stranger and yet the only real thing I knew in this world. I dropped my head, overcome.

"I never forgot the goodness, the healing, eternal in you," he said quietly.

I looked up; his gaze fixed upon me. I'd never forgotten him. Touching him felt like the first piece of home I'd had in many moons, and I too was seen. I was recognized. My soul was known. I felt the steady thump of Tash's heart through his cloak. He was alive. So hopefully alive. I felt my own veins pulsing with life within me. The healing in me. *You carry the heartbeat of the Dakota.*

I explained the calling I felt here. What I'd learned of the tribe I was with, their leader whom had I appealed to for safety. "This tribe's leader, a man named Crazy Horse, is young. He's eager to make his people strong. I—and now you too—can share what we know of our battles with the white man."

Tash nodded his head. I looked towards the village where our own tipi stood tall and familiar. The gift of our past would keep us warm.

"Our home."

We both rose together from the snow. I let out a long breath of disbelief. The strength in me. The strength in him. We'd withstood life and death. My husband was here. Though with a new band, we could return to *our* tipi. Everything I'd hoped for as a girl, traditional life in a camp circle, was still what I wanted as a woman. Tash moved ahead of me. The horses followed him, walking past me—majestic, steady—though the journey long, their spirit unchanged.

I held back a moment. My gaze spun upward to the wonder of the winter sun. My soul felt warm and comforted; my mother was near. I turned into the unrelenting wind. I wouldn't just survive. Wouldn't just continue . . . the Great Spirit had brought me new hope. New resolve. Tashunke and I would carry on tradition. And we would continue the fight for our people. I heard my father's voice speak clearly through my memory *"The buffalo turn and face the storm. They are not afraid."*

In the death of the frigid air, I saw my own breath steaming out in rhythmic determination. *I am Oenikika.* I stood proud through the pain, both my feet strong upon Mother Earth. *And I am the Breath of Life.*

THIRTY

Emma Heard

April 5, 1863

I folded two dresses and placed them with my other items packed inside the small carpetbag. I didn't know what I'd need at university and I wished I could ask Ma for guidance. But she'd been distant these past few months. She hadn't expressed any support of my plan for university. Or any anger. She barely talked to me at all, really. It'd been agonizing to be in her disappointed wake. I'd felt anxious in so many moments and now knew that I didn't realize how, even as I grew, my mother still helped me in many ways. I wished she were by my side now, helping me review my belongings, deciding what to bring on my journey. But I didn't want to upset her by involving her further in my leaving, so I did the best I could to pack on my own. Move into the unknown alone.

My heart trembled as I looked about, folding up our blue quilt for the last time. I tucked my old boots in the back of the wardrobe, alongside tired mittens and a worn towel. From the nightstand, I picked up *Leaves of Grass* and set it below the mittens. Could I actually bear to leave it? The book was a piece of my soul. It looked so out of place among the meaningless items I was leaving behind. Should I bring it? Have it make the long journey with me? But I didn't want to appear foolish, arriving to university a young lady lugging in a heavy carpetbag of unnecessary items. Perhaps Catherine would read Whitman's book one day and remember her older sister who loved it, and her, so much. With a shaky breath, I closed the wardrobe door. I must be practical. I'd leave it for Catherine. I must move on.

The space was so bare. Ida's items were already gone; she'd married Rudolph Richter last month. He was widowed with a small child on a farmstead, so it was a perfect alignment of necessity and hope that Rudolph had asked for Ida's hand in marriage. The war with the Dakota had left holes in families. Ida filled that void for the Richter man and boy; her hardworking nature and generous caretaking tendencies would fill that Richter farm with light. Our lives had dimmed, without her—that I knew, for sure.

I wondered at how empty the entire upstairs; the entire house would feel two weeks from now when Otto left, too. Otto had enlisted in the Union Army. His first assignment was to go west after the escaped Dakota with Colonel Sibley; they were setting out at the end of the month. My heart hurt to imagine Otto back at war. And more than once, it crossed my mind: Tashunke must have fled west . . . would my brother set off on the same trail as the man who saved my life? Would worlds collide again? Unease churned within me whenever I thought of the western horizon. I wished I could hold back my dazzling brother; he was so much larger than life, and it seemed a waste of his cheerful spirit to set him off to war in a drab army uniform. I wished I could keep him safe, tending our field, smiling, joking with Uncle Allen, forever. But we each had found our own path. I couldn't stop his; and he wasn't stopping mine. I lifted the bag—it was surprisingly light. This was all I had, and it would have to do.

The door opened downstairs and Rudolph's deep hello could be heard echoing with Catherine and Peter's footsteps as they ran to meet Rudolph's little boy. Ida's adopted son. She was a mother now and it suited her wonderfully. Ida was still silent at our family gatherings but when visiting their farmhouse earlier this month, I'd seen her whispering in the boy's ear. My heart softened at the sight. Ida's voice finally let out in the world. I wished I were able to stay, watch if, when, how she'd use it more. My heart imagined Ida and I going for a picnic by the river under the willows. We'd take her son along and Ida would quietly speak to him in the safe space between us. I'd get to hear her voice again. It was almost worth staying for . . . but my journey called to me, and my opportunity seemed to be a wind at my back, pushing me forward to my own potential. Hearing my own voice in this world. I looked about the upstairs room for a final goodbye. I didn't know when I'd be back. I told myself it would not go empty long, as Catherine and Peter would make new memories here soon.

I walked down to the sight of my whole family. It was my final moments with them. Ma stood, her arms crossed as I approached, and her eyes bore tears. I couldn't stand to look at her hurt. It was all too much. There was too much I'd disappointed her in. I felt so far from her.

"We saw Riggs coming over the hill," Rudolph announced.

"I suppose it's time to say goodbye then," I said with contrived lightheartedness, for my heart was starting to feel quite heavy.

Riggs was heading back east and, on his way, would be escorting me to Lawrence University. Miss Knudsen said I'd love the library—books and books stacked floor to ceiling. My dream was impossibly magnificent, and it was beginning now. But something had caught in my throat; it tightened with the word *goodbye*. Over the past four months, I'd been anticipating my arrival to university. The coursework would be rigorous, I'd be living in a dormitory—I couldn't quite imagine what that even meant . . . maybe a set up similar to the new Dakota Hotel they're building in New Ulm? Miss Knudsen assured me the other women in the program were "free thinkers," friendly and open-minded. But I wavered with nervousness. All I knew of friendship was Hanna, Elsa, Charlotte, who I'd always been anxiously associated with, and I worried the other women in the program would probably be so well-read. Likely come from Chicago. Not some tiny prairie town, a wide-open farm with overflowing fields and crowded bedrooms. Though I was eager for my next step, I suddenly couldn't quite bear the feeling of leaving my home. My family. I quickly kissed Catherine and Peter on the top of their heads. We all moved towards the door.

As we got to the porch, Riggs rolled up with a small wagon pulled by his faithful chestnut horse. He tipped his hat to our family. I gave him a smile and a nod. It was time for me to leave.

Otto put an arm around me and with a jostling said, "Ahh, you know I love you mighty, smartest sister."

"And I love you, brother," I said. I prayed I would see him again, safe, someday.

"You'll have an adventure story from the east, and I'll have one from the west when we're reunited," he said. I nodded and breathed deep to hold back the tears. A worry lingered in the back of my mind. Otto bringing home an adventure story from the west . . . what would he encounter if he pushed further into Indian Territory? I feared it'd be nothing good. We'd already seen what happened when our boundaries crossed. Looking at the excitement in my brother's eyes—I wondered what look his face would bear when I saw him again.

I walked over to Ida and Rudolph. Rudolph said warmly, "She's told me how she'll miss her best friend. We wish you safe travels."

"She's *told* you as much, has she?" I asked with playful pointedness as my eyes moved to Ida's. She looked back at me, with an affectionate confirmation. My heart knew it. My sister was speaking in their home. I wasn't mad with her for not doing so with me. I was just so sad to miss hearing her. To be so far away from her new life; I wanted to see my sister thriving. But in many events in the past year, one massive and many slight, our mirrors had shifted. We no longer reflected each other. We reflected our own selves. Ida nodded as she moved towards me, holding her little boy in her arms. She wrapped an arm tight around my neck. It felt as if she were squeezing all the love out of me. Leaving her was leaving my childhood. We held onto each other. Nothing said. That would be enough for me. Her future had found her; and I'd found mine.

I stepped back from my lovely sister, and Uncle Allen gave an awkward tip of his hat. "Goodbye, Uncle Allen," I said before I took another breath and turned towards my mother.

Though I could barely look at her, I could see Ma's chin trembled. She gave me a tense hug, and said, "Travel safely."

I nodded and kept my eyes averted. Safe travels? That was all? I was so saddened in our goodbye. I wanted her to hug me, hold me tight as if she couldn't bear for me to go. Say she was *proud* of my opportunity. Help me find a plan for a return visit home as soon as possible. But she didn't say any of that . . . I stepped back in my disappointment and tears of hurt mingled with the sadness of farewells.

My heart ached as I looked at my father. I would miss my time in his office. The roaring fireplace. Working quietly together. Pa gave me a nod, and I thought I saw pride in his eyes. It was everything I'd been longing for. He'd never been to university—was entirely self-taught in law. Was my enrollment in higher education what he dreamed of when he moved his family to America? He'd probably hoped for this opportunity for Otto . . . but I reassured myself. I was doing something special. There was conviction in my heart, same as I had when I knew I had to submit my testimony for Tashunke. The right thing had been growing deep inside of me. Blooming despite the fear, doubt, shame. I might not be the perfectly-pleasing daughter my parents had hoped for. But I think my father still saw something in me he was proud of. A part of me that was him.

We began walking towards the wagon. I passed my bag up to Riggs and took up my skirt in one hand. Pa took my other hand and helped me up to the wagon. I looked back at my family. Ma had already gone inside. Why would she not wait for me? It stung bitterly. The moment of my departure was here. My heart skipped in a painful realization that this was the last time I'd be looking out to my family until . . . until I returned someday. In a year? Or two? Would it be more? My absence would be indefinite.

Pa said to Riggs, "See her there safely, sir. And best of luck in your own journey east."

"I will, Attorney Heard." I looked at Riggs. He was my friend and confidant. I was grateful he was bringing me to Lawrence University. He'd been "relieved" of his missionary duties; he reported the separation was mutual. Riggs would return to the east coast and sort out his own future. There was no one I'd rather make this trip with. I was looking forward to being close to him for the miles to come, though I didn't think I could bear to say goodbye to him. My mind had begun churning the options . . . could he enroll in university, as well? Would he come and visit me? When I thought of my future, it now held too much that my heart wanted. Him. *And* my own education. Could we find a way to achieve them both? Another shared mission?

Riggs raised his eyebrows as he looked at me. "Are you ready to head on to university, Miss Heard?"

"Ready as one can be, I presume," I said back, though my willingness sounded shaky through the grief. As I looked to wave a final goodbye to my family, my mother came running out of the house.

"Emma! Wait!" she yelled as she ran to the wagon. Hearing her voice made everything inside of me stop . . . seeing her run churned up a hope inside of me. I desperately wanted her hug. Her love again. *Please, Ma!* Say you've always loved me even when I've disappointed you. Say you'll always be my mother who cares for me, whether I was a small child in your arms, a court recorder, or a lady heading to university. She stepped up the rung of the wagon wheel. Her eyes looked sincerely into mine, as she reached her arm up, holding something. "You musn't leave your most treasured belonging behind," she said with sincerity as she passed me the worn text, *Leaves of Grass*... my beloved book. I was more surprised than if she'd thrown her arms around me. My heart stopped in my chest at the sight. Her caretaking for me, checking my room, making sure I had all I would need. I filled with relief at her attention. It was all I'd wanted. My heart broke open from all the pain of the past months, all the pain of leaving home—all I wanted was my mother's soft care around me.

"You think it's acceptable to bring along?" I asked, wanting to hear her guidance. Her help to make sense of my step into the unknown.

"I do," she said with kindness in her eyes. Tears spilled out of mine. The book had been beside me for years. Held my most precious secrets. I'd never thought my mother noticed it, cared for me reading it. But she *had* seen me. Maybe she had noticed what mattered to me over all these years. Even when I wasn't the daughter sitting, sewing nicely, in the evenings as she'd wanted. I was still a daughter she'd noticed and loved. And in passing me this book, she gave me her support. Her love. I took it in my hands. It felt wonderful to feel care from her again.

I craved her advice and approval, so greatly. "I've packed my two decent dresses, my pointed boots, the wool socks..." Through tears I anxiously reviewed the contents of my carpetbag.

She nodded, gave me a hug, and said softly into my ear, "I believe you're ready, darling."

I could barely speak, I was so moved by her gesture. Calling me darling. I was still her little girl that she loved. I didn't know what I'd actually do without my mother or father in these next years of my life. "Thank you, Ma," I said as teardrops spilled onto my cheeks.

A quivering laugh of delighted relief escaped my throat as I looked down at my book. I'd taken such pleasure in these pages over the years. It was comforting to hold them in my hands, like taking a piece of home, of my heart, with me. I had everything I needed. And with that, I had true courage to move forward. Ma glanced back at me with softness in her eyes as she stepped down from the wagon. I knew our relationship would never be as easy or straightforward as hers and Ida's. But I knew holding this book, there was a home, a mother, I could come back to someday if I ever needed. I looked to Riggs as I wiped a tear from my eye. "*Now*, I'm as ready as I can be," I said as I patted the soothing hardcover in my lap.

"Git on," he called out as he flicked the reins. I looked to my side and waved to my family. The cart rocked forward, and we were on our way east. Though I couldn't see them anymore, my family stayed with me long after they were out of sight. I trusted the lessons they had taught me, all the love they had shown me, would be with me no matter where I was. Riggs and I rode in comfortable silence. The tears finally dried in my eyes and I let myself take big full breaths of the fresh air. Being near Riggs brought me renewal warmer than the spring day. I appreciated his quiet company. I watched his hands gently holding the reins. . . I seemed just a girl in my memory, when our hands first connected at the harvest dance. After all we'd been through, I wanted him in my future. I hoped he'd discuss it on the ride. But if for some reason he didn't, I may just have to be the one to propose another plan to Riggs, as I had in that empty courtroom.

I breathed in the world around me. The prairie flowers. The gentle winds. The worn wagon wheel trail. I knew they'd been banished but instinctively, I glanced about to check for sight of any Indians. Far as I could see were just stalks of tall grass dancing on the breeze. A lone black crow circled overhead. It seemed we ran them off entirely. I thought back to Pa's office and the tall pile of land patent copies he'd be working on alone this year. The void left by the Natives would soon be filled with settlers. Would it be as if the Dakota had never been here at all? A sound ran down my spine . . . the memory of the Dakota men singing their haunting song before the hanging. I couldn't forget it. Couldn't forget them. As I'd never forget Tashunke telling two girls to escape. He saved me that day. His voice told me to *Go*. And indeed, I was leaving now. Saving myself this time. I left this Minnesota prairie, a changed woman. A Heard woman.

ACKNOWLEDGMENTS

Though this novel is about events in 1862, for me the story starts on Christmas Eve 2005. A bitter wind blew snow over a country road. I was cozy riding in my parents' suburban, making the final turn to my grandparents' home, when my blue eyes spotted something new. Headlights illuminated shapes moving across the darkening horizon. A group of Native American men on horseback. Curious, I asked my parents why people were riding in the cold. My mother explained, "They're Dakota who are marching to show they haven't forgotten what happened here long ago." Since that winter night, I've spent the last 15 years of my life learning what they hadn't forgotten. And just like Emma and Oenikika, I've grappled with the complex history of the place I call home and finally found the courage to use my voice to tell this story. Thank you, Dakota 38+2 Riders.

Additional thanks belong to all those who have helped me turn a seed of a story into a fully grown book . . . The Brown County Museum staff, Lower Sioux Community, Cheyanne St. John, and Deborah Peterson for help during my research. The wonderful crew at Author Accelerator—Laura, Abby, Terri, Whitney, and Sheila. Therese at the Women's Fiction Writers Association. The Spun Yarn—Sarah, Lauren, Angela, Diane. The team at SparkPress—especially, Brooke Warner and Samantha Strom. Emir Orucevic at Pulp Studio for the brilliant cover design. Fauzia Burke and her team at FSB Associates. And a huge thanks to Diane Wilson for her thoughtful review.

To my editors—Jennie Nash and Kathleen Furin. Jennie, thank you for seeing me as a "serious" writer and owning my professional sense of self. You went into the pages with me and truly saw through eyes of each character. Kathleen, you believed in the message that was the core of this novel and, with an eagle-eyed sharpness, guided into the story it could be. Your encouragement to find the true story that's inside stretches beyond these pages.

A random but necessary thank you to the fictional character of Marge Gunderson from the movie *Fargo*. "There's more to life than a little money, you know. Don'tcha know that? And here ya are, and it's a beautiful day." Marge is a strong Minnesotan character that I truly love and am fully inspired by.

My gratitude to the Mound Westonka High School English Department. In particular, Mr. Bray, Ms. Nelson, Mrs. Wallace, and Mr. Bulman. Mr. Bulman, I still remember when you told me "it's okay to break a few rules" in writing. That moment gave me confidence and the freedom to both have fun and to fail in my writing. Without those, I could have never gotten here.

My wonderful friends who were there on the writing journey. Jill Zimmerman, thank you for the cover feedback and your songs on my writing playlist. Maddie Johnson, thank you for saying "do it." Katie Fleming, thank you for an honest and encouraging read of the painful first draft, the ten-mile bike ride spent brainstorming titles, and most of all for listening to my doubts and fears.

Even as a writer, it's difficult to put into words my gratitude to my family. Still, I'll try. Thank you, to my grandmother, Sue, for attending the local historical society events with me and for cutting articles from the newspaper you thought would be helpful for my research. My brothers, Zachary and Andrew, thank you for showing me that there is no journey too long or too difficult for the mind to overcome.

We'll call this my book of 10,000 casts. To my parents, Colin and Wendy, you've supported me at each turn I needed to take on my journey—as a person and as a writer. Mom, when it only existed as a word document on my laptop, you were the founding and sole member of the *Dovetails in Tall Grass* fan club. Thank you for always rooting for me. Dad, thank you for your excruciating evaluation of if I should, or should not, or wait, yes, I should, delete that comma during your edits of the manuscript. Charlotte—thank you for keeping my feet warm as I wrote. Lastly, thank you to my husband, Markus. You encouraged me, "You need to write that story you keep talking about!" and let me have the space to be truly myself—beside you and outside of us. I smile whenever I hear that you've enthusiastically shared about the importance of the events in southern Minnesota during the 1800s at another business dinner.

Finally, a message to my daughter, Philippa. Much of this was written when you were just a hope in my heart. Pippa, I am so happy you and this book are both finally here.

ABOUT THE AUTHOR

© Russell Heeter Photography

Samantha Specks is a clinical social worker who has worked on a child/adolescent psychiatric unit, as a Dialectical Behavioral group therapist with adults and adolescents, and as an outpatient psychotherapist. She currently lives in Texas, but her heart and mind resided in Minnesota, her home state, while working on *Dovetails in Tall Grass*, which is her debut novel. Her happy place is reading a good book or watching a terrible TV show with a cup of tea and her leggings covered in dog hair. Sticking with the theme of strong young women, Samantha and her husband welcomed a baby girl to their family while she was writing this novel.

Names of the Dakota 38 + 2

Dan Little, Chaska dan

Taju-xa, Red Otter

Marpiya te najin, Stands on a Cloud (Cut Nose)

Tipi-hdo-niche, Forbids His Dwelling

Wyata-tonwan, His People

Hinhan-shoon-koyag-mani, Walks Clothed in an Owl's Tail

Maza-bomidu, Iron Blower

Wapa-duta, Scarlet Leaf

Wahena

Sna-mani, Tinkling Walker

Radapinyanke, Rattling Runner

Dowan niye, The Singer

Xunka ska, White Dog

Hepan

Tunkan icha ta mani, Walks With His Grandfather

Ite duta, Scarlet Face

Amdacha, Broken to Pieces

Hepidan

Henry Milord

Baptiste Campbell

Tate kage, Wind Maker

Hapinkpa, Tip of the Horn

Hypolite Auge

Nape shuha, Does Not Flee

Wakan tanka, Great Spirit

Tunkan koyag I najin, Stands Clothed with His Grandfather

Maka te najin, Stands Upon Earth

Pazi kuta mani, Walks Prepared to Shoot
Tate hdo dan, Wind Comes Back
Waxicun na, Little Whiteman
Aichaga, To Grow Upon
Ho tan inku, Voice Heard in Returning
Cetan hunka, The Parent Hawk
Had hin hda, To Make a Rattling Noise
Chanka hdo, Near the Woods
Oyate tonwan, The Coming People
Mehu we mea, He Comes for Me
Wakinyan na, Little Thunder

Wakanozanzan and Shakopee:
These chiefs fled after the war, were eventually captured, tried and convicted in November 1864 and their executions were approved by President Andrew Johnson. They were hanged November 11, 1865.

Characters inspired by actual people:

Little Crow / Taoyateduta
Cut Nose
Chaska
Brown Wing
Breaking Up
Killing Ghost
Runs Against Something When Crawling
Red Otter
Red Iron
Sleepy Eyes
Wabasha
Traveling Hail
Crazy Horse

Indian Missionary Stephen Riggs
Andrew Myrick
Henry Sibley
Isaac Heard (court recorder during military commission)
Major General John Pope
Colonel Olin, Crooks, Grant, and Bailey
Dr. Mayo
Lavina Eastlick & Family

Fictionalized Characters:

Oenikika
Emma Heard

Tashunke
Woman of the Winter Sun
Owl Woman
Aunt Mika
Wenona
Little Rapids
Wolfchaser
Kimimela
Kayawi
Bonko
Dina
Scarlet Woman
Nine Tails

August Heard
Anna Heard
Otto Heard
Catharine Heard
Peter Heard
Uncle Allen
Bruno
Pastor Vogel
Mr. Albrecht
Miss Knudsen

Hermann

Mr. & Mrs. Ulrich

Mr. & Mrs. Kuhn

Hanna

Charlotte

Mr. Ayer & Mrs. Ayers

Lena Lundberg

Theobalds

Farmer Krause, Mrs. Krause

Mrs. Duta

Mrs. Mayo

Gerald and Mrs. Schein, Elsa

SELECTED TITLES FROM SPARKPRESS

SparkPress is an independent boutique publisher delivering high-quality, entertaining, and engaging content that enhances readers' lives, with a special focus on female-driven work. www.gosparkpress.com

The Takeaway Men: A Novel, Meryl Ain $16.95, 978-1-68463-047-9
Twin sisters Bronka and JoJo Lubinski are brought to America from Germany by their Polish refugee parents after World War II—but in "idyllic" America, political, cultural, and family turmoil awaits them. As the girls grow older, they eventually begin to ask questions of and demand the truth from their parents.

Child Bride: A Novel, Jennifer Smith Turner $16.95, 978-1-68463-038-7
The coming-of-age journey of a young girl from the South who joins the African American great migration to the North—and finds her way through challenges and unforeseen obstacles to womanhood.

Watermark: The Broken Bell Series $16.95, 978-1-68463-036-3
When Angel Ferente—a teen with a dysfunctional home life who has been struggling to care for her sisters even as she pursues her goal of attending college on a swimming scholarship—doesn't come home after a party on New Year's Eve, her teammates, her coach's church, and her family search the city for her. The result changes their lives forever.

Seventh Flag: A Novel, Sid Balman, Jr. $16.95, 978-1-68463-014-1
A sweeping work of historical fiction, *Seventh Flag* is a Micheneresque parable that traces the arc of radicalization in modern Western Civilization—reaffirming what it means to be an American in a dangerously divided nation.

Sarah's War, Eugenia Lovett West $16.95, 978-1-943006-92-2
Sarah, a parson's young daughter and dedicated patriot, is sent to live with a rich Loyalist aunt in Philadelphia, where she is plunged into a world of intrigue and spies, her beauty attracts men, and she learns that love comes in many shapes and sizes.